PRAISE FOR *BLOOD RUNS COLD*

'Utterly compelling, ingeniously plotted and
incredibly entertaining, this puts Neil Lancaster
up at the forefront of T⋯⋯ ⋯⋯'
Liz Nugent

'Absolute belter of ⋯
Marion Tod⋯

'A nailbiting, energetic read that will keep you up all night.'
The Sun

'Compelling, emotionally charged, and impossible to put
down… The standout crime read
of the year so far.'
John Barlow

'A masterclass in how to deliver a taut,
pacy thriller hot off the page.'
Imran Mahmood

'Want pulse-pounding, shallowed-breathed, toe-curling
police action? Here you go. Thank me later.'
Helen Fields

'Thrilling, gripping, breathlessly brilliant crime-thriller
that just won't let you go until you know how it
ends. I loved every minute of this thrill ride!'
Miranda Dickinson

'Neil Lancaster is not only a terrific writer,
but also a brilliant storyteller.'
Paul Gitsham

NEIL LANCASTER is the No. 1 digital bestselling author of both the Tom Novak and Max Craigie series. His first Craigie novel, *Dead Man's Grave*, was long-listed for the 2021 McIlvanney Prize for Best Scottish Crime Book of the Year. The second Craigie novel is *The Blood Tide*, which has topped several ebook and audio charts, and was also longlisted for the McIlvanney Prize, and shortlisted for the Dead Good Readers Award. He served as a military policeman and worked for the Metropolitan Police as a detective, investigating serious crimes in the capital and beyond. As a covert policing and surveillance specialist he utilised all manner of techniques to investigate and disrupt major crime and criminals.

He now lives in the Scottish Highlands, writes crime and thriller novels, and works as a broadcaster and commentator on true crime documentaries. He is a key expert on two Sky Crime TV series, *Meet, Marry, Murder* and *Made for Murder,* and will shortly be appearing on a BBC true crime show, *Big Little Crimes.*

🐦 @neillancaster66
ⓕ @NeilLancasterCrime
www.neillancastercrime.co.uk

Also by Neil Lancaster

The Max Craigie Novels
Dead Man's Grave
The Blood Tide
The Night Watch

The Tom Novak Novels
Going Dark
Going Rogue
Going Back

NEIL LANCASTER

BLOOD RUNS COLD

ONE PLACE. MANY STORIES

HQ
An imprint of HarperCollins*Publishers* Ltd
1 London Bridge Street
London SE1 9GF

www.harpercollins.co.uk

HarperCollins*Publishers*
Macken House, 39/40 Mayor Street Upper,
Dublin 1 D01 C9W8, Ireland

This edition 2023

1
First published in Great Britain by
HQ, an imprint of HarperCollins*Publishers* Ltd 2023

Emojis © Shutterstock

ISBN: 9780008551292

This book is produced from independently certified FSC™ paper
to ensure responsible forest management.

For more information visit: www.harpercollins.co.uk/green

This book is set in Sabon

Printed and Bound in the UK using 100% Renewable Electricity at
CPI Group (UK) Ltd, Croydon, CR0 4YY

*Dedicated with thanks to two wonderful teachers
who inspired me to believe that one day I'd be
able to write a book. It took forty years before it
happened, but I never forgot what you said.
To any teachers reading this dedication, just remember
that one well-placed piece of praise, may make a kid
dare to dream. And a book begins with a dream.
So, with that in mind I'm saying a belated, but heartfelt
thank you to Martin Chilvers, and David Yabbacome.
You both made a young man believe that
maybe one day, it could happen.*

Prologue

AFRODITA DUSHKU WAS staring out of the window of the high-speed train as it carved its way through the Scottish countryside. She had no idea how long she'd been in the sleek and modern carriage, which was nothing like the one she'd travelled on during her interminable trip all those months ago. She assumed it was months, but so much had happened that she'd lost track of time, so it could have been a year. One thing she could say, though, was that British trains were far superior to Albanian ones.

The lush, green scenery clearly fed by the driving rain sped by in a blur as the train's velocity pushed droplets horizontally along the windows. She couldn't get used to the colour of the countryside in the UK after the dry, dusty Mediterranean climate of Albania. It was seemingly so cold and wet all the time here.

Soon the landscape became more built up, with housing and factories, as the train began to slow, presumably for a stop. She couldn't understand the announcement that erupted out of the tinny speakers, but she did hear the word 'Falkirk'. The train pulled to a gentle halt at a station and the signs that read *Falkirk* confirmed what the announcer had seemingly said. The doors hissed open and a few passengers got on board, stowed their luggage in the racks and settled in their seats. Very soon the doors were shut again, and the train gathered speed as it passed into what looked like the edges of a town.

One of the recently joined passengers, a youngish-looking man wearing a hoodie and baseball cap, walked along the carriage, a phone in his hand, which he was apparently studying. There was something about him that didn't add up. He had no luggage, and his dark, swarthy complexion just didn't seem to fit with the other passengers. Suddenly, he looked from his phone, straight at her, before immediately averting his eyes again. Afrodita froze, her blood like ice water in her veins. He was wrong. He didn't belong. She stared at the table in front of her, trying not to show that she was trembling.

She pressed her back into the firm, yet somehow yielding upholstery of the comfortable seat, and tried to relax, despite the lump in the base of her spine. The thought of what was causing the lump in her back made a fresh wave of nausea grip her stomach. She shuddered violently, and her head swam.

She reached into her pocket and pulled out the ticket, which she looked at with feigned interest, and then let it fall from her fingers onto the floor. She reached down to pick it up and took the opportunity to glance behind her. There was no sign of the suspicious newcomer. She breathed, just a little, as she sat back up straight.

An elderly lady with short, dark hair and a gentle face nodded at her, a smile in her kind eyes. The woman said something to her in English, the tones of which seemed to indicate concern, but they meant nothing to her. She understood a little English, but it hadn't been a priority for her, and it most definitely hadn't been encouraged by Jetmir.

Afrodita averted her eyes, feeling the hot flush in her face intensify so that it almost burned. Even without the language barrier, she didn't want to speak to anyone. Another wave of nausea overcame her, like a fist wrenching at her stomach. She couldn't afford to be sick, not here, not now. It would draw far too much attention, which was the last thing she needed. Without looking up, she leapt to her feet and staggered off to the toilet cubicle at the end of the carriage. The electronically operated doors opened agonisingly slowly, and she felt that every occupant of the carriage was staring at her; her cheeks flushed even more. The doors closed at a pace that seemed even slower than they had opened. Willing them to shut faster, she felt the urge to vomit rising in her throat.

As soon as the doors hissed shut, she engaged the locking mechanism and retched and coughed into the stainless-steel toilet bowl, although all that came out was a thin, acidic yellow drool. It had been so long since she had eaten that there was nothing in her shrunken belly. She heaved again, trying to limit the noise. Sweat beaded on her forehead, and she shuddered at the icy feeling in her stomach. She panted, trying to regain her composure before she stood up, her head spinning.

She stared at her reflection in the mirror. The blush on her thin face was fading as she returned to her more usual pallor – just like the colour of the wheat bread dough that her mother used to knead in the kitchen of their tiny house in Albania. Her long, dark hair was scraped back into a ponytail, which was greasy, lifeless and badly needed washing, but facilities at the London apartment were sparse, and there was rarely hot water. Her forehead was dotted with acne, and her green eyes were flat – surrounded by dark circles. To her, she looked much older than her twelve years. Not yet a woman, but no longer a child. Her grubby, baggy tracksuit jacket and loose track pants gave no signs of the figure that was hidden beneath. Another benefit of the voluminous garments was that they effectively concealed the flat package that had been tucked by Jetmir into the small of her back and secured with parcel tape that encircled her tiny waist. She hadn't asked what was in the package, as Jetmir wouldn't have told her in any case, and she'd often found it best not to question it.

Her stomach gurgled, a mixture of nausea and hunger. It had been hours since she'd eaten, and yet despite the twenty-pound note in her jacket pocket, she had shaken her head each time the food trolley had passed her seat in the centre of the train. She didn't want to talk to anyone, and she was so scared that she didn't think she could eat without throwing up.

There was a sudden pounding on the door, which caused Afrodita to flinch. 'Tickets,' came a deep, authoritative male voice.

Fear gripped Afrodita, her stomach lurching again, her breath rasping, her face greasy with sweat. She had no choice; she had to leave the bathroom and return to the carriage. She ran the tap and splashed some water on her face, before drying it on a coarse paper towel. She took one last look at herself, inhaled deeply and pressed the button to open the doors again. The progress was painfully slow; she held her breath, only letting it out when she saw the uniformed ticket collector who had walked the train length earlier.

'Ticket?' he said, his face and voice softening as he looked at Afrodita.

She wordlessly held up the ticket that Jetmir had given her, and the guard gave it a cursory glance, before nodding, his eyes registering concern.

'Are you okay?' he said. His voice was kind and Afrodita wondered if he was a father.

She just nodded before heading back to her seat, her stomach spasming as she tried desperately to control her breathing. She felt hot tears begin to well, which she swiped away and glanced at the lady opposite her, who smiled as Afrodita sat.

She'd delivered a few much smaller packages before, but this felt different. Previously she'd taken packs wrapped in clingfilm that she concealed in her underwear and she had only visited smaller towns within a couple of hours of London. This package felt like it was at least a kilogram, and her destination today was much farther away. She'd never even heard of Glasgow, let alone travelled there.

Her instructions, given harshly by Jetmir, rang in her ears: 'Speak to no one. Look at no one. And do nothing to attract any attention. If you lose the package, the debt will be yours, Afrodita, and if not yours then we know where your sister is in Albania. You understand me?' His black eyes glittered as he'd handed her a ticket, a scratched mobile phone and a twenty-pound note at a railway station in London. He had messaged her on the phone on several occasions as the train passed through stations, clearly just to let her know that he was tracking her, presumably with the device. It made her anxiety even worse, knowing that she was being watched and wondering if one of the Mafia Shqiptare, the violent Albanian gang, really was on the train with her as Jetmir had suggested there would be. She looked around the carriage but saw only bored passengers reading, tapping on computers, or staring at phones or tablets, earbuds in their ears. No one showed her any interest, apart from the kind-looking woman opposite, whose gaze she still refused to meet.

'Relax,' she muttered to herself, but she knew it was pointless. Today was different. Today she was doing something that she suspected could get her into big trouble. She'd had no contact with the police in London, invisible as she was. However, if they were anything like cops in Albania, she didn't want to encounter them ever, and particularly not now.

Afrodita took several deep, deep breaths, trying to force the panic away. 'Get hold of yourself,' she said under her breath, reminding herself of Jetmir's earlier words. 'You look so young and innocent, Affi, that no cop or gang-banger will suspect you. Do as we tell you and you'll be fine.' She'd smiled as he'd lightly brushed his fingers against her cheek. He could do this, just a touch from him could make her feel special, despite the other side of his personality being so dark and scathing.

She was so tightly wound up that she flinched and gasped

when the phone in her pocket vibrated. Concern crossed the lady's face, but Afrodita didn't meet her gaze as she picked it out.

Thjesht largohesh nga Falkirk? read the message on the screen.

Po, she replied, her face flushed, the feeling that she was being watched flaring again.

She craned her neck to look behind her and then she saw him. A new face that she hadn't seen in the carriage before. One that had most certainly appeared after they had stopped at Falkirk. He was young and muscular, with a short goatee. He stared down at the phone in his hand, his baseball cap perched on his head. His eyes flicked up and momentarily caught hers before he hurriedly looked down again. Her heart began to pound in her chest. Who was he? She knew that couriers had been robbed before; was he going to rob her?

Her mind felt as if a cog had worked itself loose and her mouth was suddenly bone dry. If she lost this package, then the whole debt would be hers and she'd have to work it off. She couldn't run away – where would she go? She had no money, no papers, she spoke barely any English. She was effectively a prisoner. Worse still, the gang had made it clear that if she did run away then it would be her sister in Albania who would pay the price.

She enabled the selfie camera on her phone and pretended to check her face with it whilst zooming in on the man in the baseball cap. Her stomach almost shrank inside her. He was staring straight at her, there was no doubt about it. His phone was clamped to his ear and his lips were moving, but his dark eyes were fixed directly on her. She felt the panic surge in her like an irrepressible wave.

All semblance of calm deserted Afrodita as she leapt to her feet, desperate to be away from her watcher. She needed to escape, find somewhere to hide, just to be anywhere else. She was going to be robbed – she knew it. She stumbled away, lurching to one side as the train jolted on the rails. She blundered along the carriage, feeling the rising spectre of sheer, unadulterated terror beginning to overwhelm her. She risked a glance backwards and saw the man in the baseball cap rise to his feet, still talking on the phone, but he had more of a sense of urgency in his movements now.

He was coming for her.

Afrodita broke out into a run towards the sliding doors, not caring about all the other passengers turning to watch.

'Stop,' a deep voice came from behind her, but she didn't pause, didn't glance back. The doors opened as she approached and she made her way past the toilet that she had been in just a few minutes ago. The sliding doors in the next carriage came apart, far too slowly for her liking, and she risked a peek over her shoulder again. The man in the baseball cap was closing in on her, his face firm and determined. 'Stop,' he commanded again.

Afrodita turned and entered the carriage, but to her horror her path was blocked. An older man with short grey hair was standing, legs planted firmly, looking directly at her, his face hard.

Afrodita froze, as if suddenly her feet were glued to the floor. She let out an involuntary yelp, before she felt her legs give way, and she fell to the floor, curling up into a ball in the narrow corridor.

'Nr!' she felt herself shout; her eyes screwed shut as she prepared herself for the inevitable beating that would come.

But there was nothing. No one touched her, no one kicked or punched her, there was just silence.

She opened her eyes, only to see the man in the baseball cap squatting next to her, looking concerned whilst holding out a small leather wallet that had an official metal crest on one side and a photograph of the man on the other.

'Police,' he said, his voice soft, a kind smile on his face. He spoke again, but the words meant nothing.

He and the older grey-haired man gently helped her to her feet and they all moved back to the space between the carriages where the toilet was. Panic and confusion were still gripping her, but something in the attitude of her captors made her begin to relax a little.

The man with the baseball cap handed her a mobile phone with a nod, and Afrodita took it and raised it to her ear.

'Hello?' said a woman on the other end, in Albanian.

'Hello,' replied Afrodita, in a small voice, her mind whirring like an out-of-control clockwork toy.

'My name is Samira and I'm an Albanian interpreter who works with the police. What is your name?'

'Afrodita,' she said.

'How old are you?'

'I'm twelve,' she said, so quietly it was barely audible.

'The gentleman who has handed you the phone is called Greg and he is a police officer. He wants me to assure you that they know what is happening to you and that you have been tricked. Afrodita, these officers are here to help you. You're safe now.'

Afrodita's face crumpled, and she wept, tears coursing down her pale, thin face.

1

Three years later

VALERIE SMITH SMILED with affection as Affi sat on the kitchen chair and put on her brand-new trainers, a huge, beaming grin spreading across the girl's face as she admired the Asics once they were securely laced. She was dressed ready for action in running leggings and a lightweight running jacket. Her long, shiny auburn hair was secured with a Day-Glo headband. She stood, admiring the multicoloured trainers. A Jack Russell terrier fussed around her feet, sniffing the new shoes.

'Valerie, they look so amazing. I'll be running at light speed with these bad boys on, as long as wee Jock here doesn't chew them, eh boy?' she said, giggling and tickling the ears of the little dog, who instantly rolled onto his back, demanding continued attention. As she looked up at her foster mother, her green eyes shone with a mix of pleasure and amusement, her skin was clear and bright.

'Aye well, price I paid, I expect a gold medal, my girl, so happy birthday,' said Valerie.

'We can try now; I need to train today. Can you drop me at Fyrish? I want to run up the hill. I need to get stronger,' she said, stretching her arms above her head, unfurling her long, lean frame. She had a natural runner's physique, with long legs, a slim body that carried no excess weight, and most importantly, the heart of a lioness. Affi had entered Valerie's life almost three years ago now, and she and her husband, Reg, had watched her blossom from a terrified twelve-year-old who'd experienced such misery to the bright, clever and talented young woman that she now was.

'What, now? It's your birthday, lady, and Reg will be back soon. Maybe today of all days you can have a day off?'

'Please? I can be there and back in an hour, Valerie. I feel I need to try these mega creps out,' she said, bouncing from foot to foot.

'Creps?' said Valerie, shaking her head.

'Slang for trainers, Grandma.' Affi giggled, a trace of her Albanian heritage evident in her voice, which was quickly being edged out with a soft Highland twang.

'Cheeky wee thing. Come on then, lady. I'll drop you at the car park and you can call me when you're back, and I'll collect you. I'm cooking your favourite tonight.'

'Is it haggis?'

'No, pizza.'

'Thank God for that,' she said, laughing. 'Will Reg be back in time?'

'I hope so. He's out on the hill with some tourists who are going after some fallow bucks.'

'Ew, I don't like venison and I feel bad for the poor wee things. Why do they have to shoot them?'

'They need controlling, and it gives Reg the job he loves. Can you imagine him in an office? He'd be scunnered all the time.'

There was a ping from Affi's phone. She picked it up from the coffee table and looked at the screen, her face splitting into a wide smile.

'Who is it?'

'It's Melodi wishing me happy birthday. She must have found a phone, bless her,' she said, eyes shining at the message from her sister in Albania.

'Oh, that's nice, toot. I've a call with Katie at the solicitors soon. Home Office seem to say that they'll look on the application for her to join us, but they need some more evidence. It's been such a bureaucratic nightmare; we want your sister here with us all.'

'Soon, hopefully. I hate thinking of her in that horrible home.'

'It's not as bad as yours was. Hopefully not too much longer, toot. We're doing everything we can.'

'I know you are, Valerie, and I love you for it, even if you are getting very old.' She flung her arms around her foster mother's neck and hugged her tight.

'Cheeky wee mare. Come on, let's go.'

They left their small cottage just outside the pretty Highland village of Evanton, in Easter Ross, where Affi had been since arriving nearly three years ago having been rescued from the traffickers. Back then she had almost no English, was badly underweight and was almost in a perpetual state of terror. It had taken time and effort, and there had been many ups and downs, but they'd grown into a family, and now Valerie couldn't imagine life without their little firecracker of a foster daughter. The missing piece of the puzzle was twelve-year-old Melodi, still in a children's home in Tirana. They were trying to reunite the siblings, but the paperwork was mind-blowing. Affi was now with them indefinitely on a permanence order with authority to adopt, but the hurdles for adoption were such at her age that they were all happy with the status quo.

Valerie looked at her foster daughter as she buckled herself into the passenger seat and felt an almost overwhelming surge of love for the girl. She'd grown so much from that startled child into a confident fifteen-year-old who was beginning to excel at school, after a few hiccups early on. They'd discovered that she was a talented athlete, particularly in distance running, which had become her passion, at first representing her school, then onwards to the district competitions and very soon heading towards national trials. She'd found a real focus after some difficult times, and it had been transformational. Valerie's heart ached for the poor wee thing, with all the cruelty she'd suffered in her earlier years, there were bound to be good times, and bad times. She just hoped that the bad times were behind her now.

'What?' said Affi, her eyebrows raised but lips turned up at the edges in amusement as she met her foster mother's gaze.

'Pardon?'

'You're staring at me, Valerie. What is it?'

'Just thinking how quickly you're growing, Affi Smith. You're turning into a beautiful young woman, you know. Boys will be chapping my door down soon.' Affi had quickly taken their family name, mostly for security, but she was happy to be known as Affi Smith at school. It made life less complex.

'Don't be ridiculous. No one notices me at school.' She turned away, securing her hair behind her head with a scrunchie.

'Aye, you wait, girl. You can do much better than Lewis McPhail, that's for sure.'

'Oh, Valerie. Lewis is nobody. I only dated him for a tiny while as he had a car,' she said, giggling.

'Well, that's no reason. He's a bad one, that boy. Just like his father.' Valerie pursed her lips, put the Vauxhall into gear and moved off the drive.

'Aye. That's why I dumped him, you know. He's leaving me alone, and he hasn't called or messaged in a while. Anyway, enough about boys, I have a race soon and I want to hit the hill. My power isn't good enough, so let's get to Fyrish.'

*

Twenty minutes later Valerie was steering the little Vauxhall into the car park at the base of Fyrish Hill, which was swathed in woodland. There were only a few cars dotting the car park and no other walkers about. Being early spring the trees were beginning to shake off their winter malaise and a green haze was already overpowering the light brown of the foliage that had been dominant through the harsh cold months. The weak sun was casting late-afternoon shadows through the trees and there was still a chill in the air as Affi opened the car door.

'Will you be warm enough, toot?' said Valerie, shivering as the breeze hit her.

'Valerie, I'm about to run almost two miles up a very steep cnoc that normally takes people two hours to scale. I won't get cold – if anything I'll get far too hot.'

'Aye, but I worry about you. It's awful slippy.'

'But I have spanky new trail runners on. I'll be fine.'

'You have your phone?' said Valerie as Affi stepped out of the car.

'Of course.' She shook the iPhone in front of her and slipped it in a zip pocket. She pulled on her compact CamelBak rucksack and secured it in place, taking the flexible straw out and sucking a mouthful of water from it.

'Well, call me when you're at the top, and I'll make tracks back. I need to pop to the shop, so I won't be going home, okay?'

'Sure.'

'Be careful,' said Valerie to her foster daughter's retreating back as she ran off at her usual breakneck pace towards the footpath that led steeply up to the summit of the cnoc. She shook her head with affection at seeing the tall, lean frame speeding through the trees and out of sight. She was a formidable character, that girl, and any man that took up with her would have his work cut out. She smiled at the prospect. She and Reg had never managed to have kids, but they couldn't have loved Affi more if she had given birth to her. Her heart pounded with emotion as she thought about the last few years they'd shared with that girl. They'd had the full range of emotions with her, from intense, powerful love, to exasperation and occasionally fear. Affi hadn't always made the best decisions, but it was a relief to see that she'd found her passion.

Valerie engaged the gear and steered out of the car park. She needed to get to the shops to get some food in for Affi's birthday tea. She smiled in contented anticipation as she drove off.

2

IT WAS NOTICEABLY colder at the summit of Fyrish as Affi sprinted the last three hundred metres to the monument perched at the very top. As always, she was astonished by the view that stretched for what seemed forever all the way to the Cromarty Firth and the Black Isle that hulked, its black soil stark against the ice-blue sky. Massive oil rigs sat in the firth juxtaposed jarringly against the beauty of the sweeping landscape. She reached for her straw and sucked thirstily at the cold water as her breath began to return to normal. She checked her watch, nodding at the time which was right up there with her best efforts. These hill runs were exhausting, but she really was feeling the benefit in the strength of her legs and, perhaps most importantly, the indefinable attribute of operating in the pain zone. The more you experienced that pain, the more effectively you could perform within those parameters. She was determined that she would make the national squad in the next few years.

She walked up to the monument, transfixed by the folly that sat overlooking the firth. It was as ever mysterious as it was curious. They'd had a school field trip here a while ago, and the local historian, a short, grey-haired woman called Verity, almost fizzed with enthusiasm about the folly, which had been built in 1782 by Sir Hector Munro. He had been an army man in India and once he retired to the Highlands, he wanted to recreate a monument similar to the Gate of Negapatam in Madras. She shook her head at the incongruity of the huge monument, a trio of arches, the central arch slightly higher than the others, with ruined pillars to either side. She remembered that she thought it strange that Sir Hector's justification for building the folly was to provide work for displaced and starving Highlanders after the clearances. She couldn't shake the feeling that it sounded like slave labour to her.

Her breathing now under control, she picked her phone out of her pocket to call Valerie. She frowned seeing the red battery sign indicating that she had very little power left. As always, the old phone dropped its charge quickly in the cold, and it was starting to get chilly as a biting wind whipped from the Cromarty Firth attacked her exposed skin. She shivered, feeling her fingers begin to numb as she scrolled to Valerie's name. She pressed dial, but the phone's screen went immediately blank.

'Shit,' she muttered, pressing the button to power it up again, feeling suddenly exposed on the top of a hill, all alone. She looked around her but could see no one else about. The phone stayed frustratingly blank. She swore again. She'd have to run back down and hope that Valerie would be there soon. The light was beginning to fade as the early-spring sun dipped towards the horizon, taking any warmth in the air along with it.

She turned back towards the monument and caught movement just beyond one of the pillars. Was someone there? She felt a chill shoot up her spine that wasn't caused by the buffeting wind.

'Hello?' she called as she walked towards the far pillar. A lone figure stood there, facing away from her towards the wide-open vista that stretched towards the hulking Munro of Ben Wyvis.

He was a lean and compact figure wearing a lightweight insulated jacket and wool hat. His hands were stuffed into his pockets as he stared out across the dramatic landscape.

'Excuse me, my phone has just died. Can I borrow yours to call for a lift?' she said, feeling a knot of nerves in her stomach.

The figure didn't turn around; he just continued to stare at the scenery. Affi wondered if he was listening to music or something, but a part of her subconscious told her that something was wrong. She suddenly felt very alone and very exposed on the side of this sheer, steep hill.

She opened her mouth to ask again, but then thought better of it. She'd just run back down the hill; surely Valerie would be back soon.

She began to turn but froze when a cackle came from the figure. It was a low, throaty sound, somehow familiar to her.

Run, she thought, but it felt like she was stuck, her feet held by the soft ground.

The figure turned, a smile across his slim, unlined face.

Horror hit her like an express train. The face, once so handsome, was punctuated with cruel, dark eyes, a half-mocking smile and stained teeth; it was unfathomable in the shadow cast by the tall stone column of the monument.

'Hello, Affi.' His voice was deeper and harsher than she remembered, mocking, his mouth split in a wide smile that in no way touched his eyes.

Affi let out a scream, terror gripping her like she'd been shocked by a faulty plug, and then she ran. She ran as if her life depended on it, the fear coursing through her veins.

3

AFFI DIDN'T STOP. And she didn't look back until she was at least three hundred metres from the monument. Glancing over her shoulder, she could see that the figure hadn't moved an inch, still rooted to the spot, staring out towards Ben Wyvis. She carried on running as fast as her legs would carry her, thankful for her new grippy trainers and intimate knowledge of the slippery and craggy footpaths.

She didn't stop again. She sprinted as hard as the terrain allowed her, her head feeling like it was full of static electricity, her thoughts jumbled.

How? Here and now on the top of a cnoc in the Scottish Highlands. Now more than ever she wanted to be home, in her bedroom with the dog at her feet and her family downstairs.

She slowed her pace as the terrain levelled off and she entered the woodblock that led to the car park. She looked behind her again, but there was no one to be seen. She gradually came to a walk, and stopped for a moment, breathing heavily, checking over her shoulder, but there was still nothing. She pulled out her phone again, pressing the power button. Her heart leapt as it briefly sparked to life but then it died almost immediately. She hissed with frustration. 'Shit, shit, shit.'

As she entered the car park, she saw a large Volvo SUV parked, with a middle-aged woman wearing a baseball cap by the open tailgate. She was fussing a Labrador, whose tail thrashed as she tickled his ears. She looked over towards Affi and smiled, her face lined and soft with bright eyes.

'Are you okay, hen?' she said, her face suddenly registering concern at the sight of the shocked teenager. Her accent was a mix of Glasgow-laced Scottish with something else that Affi couldn't put her finger on.

'Can I borrow your phone, please? I need to call my mum, someone is trying to hurt me.' Affi felt the words tumble out of her.

'Oh my goodness, hen. Are you okay? You look like you've seen a ghost.'

'I just need to call my mum,' Affi said, the tears prickling in her eyes, feeling cold against her hot, flushed skin as they trickled down.

'Of course, come and sit down and I'll fetch my phone,' she replied, closing the tailgate of the Volvo and going to the rear passenger door and opening it wide.

Affi felt a wave of relief course through her as the lady handed her an iPhone. She woke the screen. A code request flashed up.

'Needs to be unlocked,' said Affi.

'Ach, of course, I'm useless with technology, hen. My husband says I'm a disaster, which is why I have an old bloody phone. Hold up, let me fetch my glasses, and take a seat, hen. You look terrible. I think I have a flask with some tea, here.'

Grateful, Affi sat in the scratched and worn leather of the Volvo, her breath harsh in her throat after the running. 'Please hurry, I must call my mum,' she said.

'Aye, I have it now. Wouldn't you like me to run you home, hen?' she said, offering the phone.

'No, thank you. I just want to call Mum,' said Affi, accepting the phone, her hands trembling.

'Are you sure? I'm heading off now, so it's nae bother, hen.'

'I'll be fine, thank you.' She looked down at the phone and pressed her fingers to the screen. It was blank, dark and inert.

Affi looked up, just as she felt a sharp jab in her thigh. Terror gripped her as the woman, her previously kind eyes now hard and cruel, stood back; a syringe glinted in a shaft of sunlight. She had a phone to her ear.

'I have her' was the last thing Affi remembered hearing, as the world shifted on its axis and everything went black.

4

DS MAX CRAIGIE and DC Janie Calder faced each other in his cramped garage, both lathered in a sheen of sweat. Max held up the boxing pads high and barked at Janie.

'Right, come on, you're lazy. Go again, jab-jab, cross, jab, uppercut, and finish with a straight, yes?'

'You're a shite, DS Craigie. I have no idea why I put myself through this with you. All I did was offer you a lift to work,' said Janie as she launched into the combination of punches, the gloves smacking into the leather of the pads that Max moved with tremendous speed, the jabs, crosses and uppercuts landing.

'Stop moaning. Harder and faster this time, punch through the pad, imagine the pad is DI Fraser's face, and move your head and feet. I could lay you out any time, you're so bloody static,' Max continued to bark at his friend and colleague, who had arrived early to collect him before work. It had become a twice-a-week routine that they work out in his garage gym before work, improving each other's techniques in their chosen sports. Max was a boxer, Janie practised mixed martial arts, and both had come a long way with each session.

Janie grunted as she lay into the pads, shifting her body weight, her head constantly moving as she smacked at the pads, her face grimacing with effort.

'Better, much better. Water break,' said Max, throwing Janie a plastic water bottle, which she drank from thirstily.

'Bloody sadist, you are, Craigie,' she said between gulps, smiling widely with the adrenaline of the exertion. 'My turn tomorrow – your kicks are shite still, and your grappling is garbage.'

'Ned's sport, Janie. Kicking, wrestling and shite, not pure boxing.'

'Aye, right, because boxing has no connection with criminals, right? Wasn't Tam Hardie a boxer?' she countered.

'MMA, as well, which is why I battered him.' Max turned to throw his pads on the bench. Suddenly and with lightning speed Janie grabbed hold of Max as his back was turned, her forearm digging into his windpipe and locking into place by gripping against her other arm, her free hand forcing his head forward and securing the lock. Max tried to struggle, but she tightened the rear naked choke. Max felt his oxygen supply cut off, and the blood suffusing in his ears. He tapped her forearm twice in surrender and she released him, with a snort of laughter.

'Bloody cheat,' said Max, rubbing at his neck.

'Sorry, what were you saying about wrestling?'

'Aye, well, it's still a ned's sport. You just got lucky. One more second and I was gonna batter you.'

Their banter was interrupted by Max's phone buzzing on the weights bench.

'Predictably it's Ross. He must be listening to you imagining punching his face,' said Max, picking up the phone.

'Your idea.'

'Ross?' said Max.

'Are you two twats gracing us with your fucking presence this bastarding morning? I have work, lots of work to give you, and something else has just come in,' he blasted in his rough Highland accent. Ross was full of bluff, bluster and foul language, but it was mostly a façade.

'Aye, Janie and I are just finishing a workout at home. I thought we weren't in until midday?'

'I've no desire to hear what you two bloody weirdos are up to, and you're a married man, as well, Craigie. I know I said twelve, but something's come up. Get your arses in here double quick.' The phone clicked in Max's ear.

'Whilst I couldn't hear that, it sounded typically Ross levels of bluntness,' said Janie, wiping her face on a towel.

'He wants us in double quick. Something's going on.'

'Aye, well, I need a shower first.'

'I need a bloody coffee more,' said Max as he raised his water bottle to take a long draught. 'Katie will be making a pot right now. Come on.'

They walked out of the garage, feeling the bite of the morning chill. It had been misty when they had gone into Max's makeshift gym, but the rising sun had quickly burned it off, and it was shaping up to be a beautiful early-spring day.

'View just gets lovelier, Max,' said Janie, looking into the distance from the front of Max's small, semi-detached farm cottage. The uninterrupted vista down to the Firth of Forth was dramatic and stunning, and the sun's pale rays danced on the surface of the expanse of water.

'Perfect, isn't it?' said Max.

An eruption of barking came from the side of the house and three dogs trotted around the corner to greet Max and Janie. It was Nutmeg, Max's little shaggy blonde cockapoo, and his neighbour's two dogs: the larger, similarly coloured Tess, who tried to remain serene, her tail wafting; and Murphy, an old, shambolic, happy dog, who was an unidentifiable mix of breeds.

'Morning, Max. It's a grand day,' said the short, stout figure of John, his elderly neighbour, who appeared soon after the dogs.

'Morning, John. It sure is,' Max replied, smiling.

'Come on, you two, in the house and leave Max alone,' he barked at his two dogs. They sheepishly loped off, disappearing into the house, tails wagging.

With Nutmeg on their heels, Max and Janie walked into the house, thoughts of showers and coffee uppermost in their minds.

'You two are disgustingly sweaty. If I wasn't so relaxed and trusting of my husband, I'd be worried about what you'd been up to. Morning, Janie,' said Katie, a big smile stretching across her face as she sat at the breakfast bar, a pot of coffee and a pile of buttered toast on a plate in front of her.

'Morning, Katie. You're completely safe. I wouldn't touch Craigie with a barge pole,' she said, laughing.

'Neither would I right now. Look at the sweaty state of you, Craigie. Coffee and toast here, help yourself,' she said, screwing her nose as Max kissed her on the cheek.

'Life saver,' said Janie, pouring out two cups and reaching for a slice.

'Melissa okay?' said Katie.

'Aye, she's grand.'

'You must both come for dinner soon. It's been far too long, particularly with you two and your inability to not work stupid bloody hours,' Katie said, standing up and brushing toast crumbs from her business suit.

'It's not our fault. Ross Fraser is a slave driver, and it sounds like something has come up. He's just called full of bluster and foul language.'

'Well, that's hardly unusual, is it? Sounds like standard Ross Fraser. How's his health kick going?'

'Badly. He's back on the biscuits, big time. Mrs Fraser is not happy at all, and he's constantly moaning about her.'

'He's like a cartoon character, your boss is. He'd be impossible if it wasn't for the fact that he's actually quite nice underneath the disguise.'

'Well, it's a very good disguise, as the last few weeks he's been particularly irritable,' said Janie.

'Right, enough of this, I have work to go to. What are you two up to?'

'Quick shower, then in. Something's brewing. You have much on?' said Max, taking a long pull on his coffee, his mouth bulging with toast.

'Yeah, a bit of a worry, do you remember me telling you about Affi Smith?'

'Errm, possibly?' said Max, his voice indicating that he didn't remember.

'He definitely doesn't remember, Katie. He never listens to a bloody word I say either,' said Janie, chuckling.

Katie smiled. 'He has a brain like a sieve, Janie. You must remember her, a lovely Albanian girl who was trafficked over and was running drugs for a mafia gang. With Valerie and Reg, Reg is the ghillie who was going to take you on the hill, remember?'

'Yes, of course. I was looking forward to some venison.'

'Well, she's been doing brilliantly, despite the Immigration service being a pain in the arse. I had a meeting with her and her foster family about her application for indefinite leave, and about the possibility of Affi's twelve-year-old sister joining her from her children's home in Albania. Well, she's gone missing. Went for a run and disappeared. It's so worrying; they're the nicest people. She's on a permanence order with Highland Council, and they have authority to adopt.'

'That sounds concerning. What have the local cops done?'

'Not much from what I can see. Valerie and Reg are going out of their minds with worry, and it sounds like the local cops haven't taken it as seriously as they might.'

'How long has she been missing?'

'Two and a half days, now,' said Katie, her brow furrowed.

'That doesn't sound good. Surely it was categorised as high risk,' said Janie.

'I don't know, but she had some ups and downs with boys

and a bit of school-skipping up until about six months ago, but since then, she's really settled and has discovered athletics. She's destined for national squads. It just doesn't make sense, but it seems to me that the local cops are just treating her as a regular absconder.'

'Is she?'

'Like I say, not for a good while. She'd really turned a corner.' Katie pursed her lips, which Max recognised as a sign of worry.

'Want me to ask about?'

'Would you, babe?'

'Sure. What's her full name?'

'Afrodita Dushku, although she's known as Affi Smith; she's taken the foster family's name, mostly for security reasons. Her location and identity should have been completely confidential. She's just turned fifteen and she's a lovely kid.'

'Okay, I'll have a little poke about and we'll see what we can come up with, as long as Ross isn't sending us to Benbecula or somewhere, which you can never be sure of.'

'Thanks, babe. Right, I'm off. Don't work too hard.' Katie smiled, and left the kitchen.

Max watched his wife's slim form as she walked out of sight towards her car.

'Punching above your weight there, Craigie,' Janie said.

'Takes one to know one, Calder,' Max riposted.

'All going good?'

'Aye, touch wood, things are going great. Right, we need to get weaving – big bathroom is all yours, I'm in the en suite.'

'Oh, to have more than one bathroom, you've no idea.'

'Well, you will live in the expensive bit of Edinburgh, Calder.'

'Where it all happens. Right, ten minutes and I'm good to go and see what tier of foul-mouthed abuse our erstwhile leader has in store for us.'

5

MAX PUSHED OPEN the door at their office at Tulliallan Police College just fifteen minutes from Max's cottage in Culross. A curling, laminated A4 sign was Blu-tacked to the door that proclaimed, POLICING STANDARDS REASSURANCE. The office was dusty, old and tiny. DI Ross Fraser and Norma Kirk looked up from their computers; Norma smiled widely, Ross did not. Ross didn't smile a great deal, and this morning he looked even less likely to than usual.

'You two lazy buggers took your bloody time. I'm here with Norma carrying this team whilst you two were farting around bashing each other in the head boxing or doing bloody Brazilian judo jitsu, or fucking origami shite,' said Ross, staring at his computer screen, his face red and his tie askew.

'Ross, we came straight here,' said Janie, sitting down on a swivel chair, the fabric of which was held in place by gaffer tape.

'Not bloody fast enough. I need my people to react like coiled springs, quivering with tension ready to do my bloody bidding, not pissing about battering each other in your sado-masochistic garage.'

'We *are* reacting. You only called us half an hour ago. We're here, in case you hadn't noticed. Tea?' said Janie to Max.

Max let out a throaty chuckle, nodding to Janie's offer. 'So, what's so urgent?'

'What?' said Ross, staring at a biscuit that he had just dunked into a steaming cup of tea. The biscuit wobbled, but he managed to cram it into his mouth before it fell. He chewed contentedly.

'You called us in for an urgent job. Like, the call under an hour ago. Please tell me you haven't forgotten already?'

'Oh, forget it. It was urgent, then I looked into it and it's a pile of shit and batted it off back to that fud of a bag man in the chief's office. He wanted us to look at some snidey expenses claims on a central crime unit but I told the pencil-pushing, shiny-arsed bastard to take a running jump into a big cold loch. If he thinks we're here to get him the next rank by shitting on some cop claiming a bit extra mileage he's got another think coming.' He dunked his digestive again, but this time it broke off, splatting in a wet mess on a file. 'Oh, bollocking fuck,' he blasted.

'Isn't he a superintendent?'

'Aye, and your point is?'

'You've never had much respect for the rank structure, have you, Ross?' said Max, chuckling.

'Like fuck I have and he's an absolute bloody melt. Thinks he controls access to the boss. He forgets that I know where the bodies are bloody buried.'

'So, what are we doing?'

'I don't know. Amuse yourselves in whatever foul and depraved way you see fit. I've a budget meeting with some faceless bureau-crat imminently who's scunnered at how much money we're costing, and I have to justify your frankly shocking overtime claims.'

'So, you called us here on a double urgent job that in fact isn't important at all. I broke speed limits getting here. I hope you're going to write the tickets off,' said Janie.

'Bollocks' was all that Ross said, turning his attention back to his computer screen indicating that the good-natured banter was at an end.

It was always the way. DI Ross Fraser was a skilled, experienced and dedicated police officer, but for reasons best known to himself he camouflaged this with a bluff, crass and sometimes confrontational exterior. Despite appearances, they were all good friends and had an excellent working relationship.

Janie tapped at her computer keyboard. 'What was the Albanian misper's name?' she said, before sipping at her tea.

'Afrodita Dushku aka Smith,' said Norma from behind her array of high-definition monitor screens.

'How on earth did you know that?' said Janie.

'Max messaged me half an hour ago. I've sent you summaries of the misper report, and the details of her trafficking. It's not nice at all – poor wee thing has had a terrible time of it.' Norma was an intelligence analyst who had moved from the National Crime Agency when their small team had been created. The name was something of a misnomer, being as deathly dull as it was. In fact, they had been formed at the insistence of Chief Constable Chris Macdonald to investigate and act against corruption within law enforcement and beyond, that other teams, for whatever reason, could not. They had already chalked up several big successes since their inception and yet had managed to remain essentially covert. They had free rein to investigate corruption wherever it might be having a negative impact on law enforcement, irrespective of how, where or when it occurred.

'What's this?' said Ross, with only scant interest as he typed, two fingered, his tongue half out of his mouth in concentration.

'Katie wants me to check on a misper she's not happy about.'

'Since when did we work for your missus?' he said, his face softening at the mention of Katie's name.

'Her firm has been representing a foster kid and trafficking victim, trying to get her immigration status regularised, and reunite her with her wee sister who's still in a children's home in Albania.'

'Why isn't she happy?'

'Seems the locals aren't pulling out all the stops.'

'Is that all? Misper inquiries are often low priority.'

'It's totally out of character and in addition she was rescued by some cops a few years ago from a really nasty Albanian drug gang. Her identity and location would have been heavily protected, so if it's been leaked, it could be argued that maybe a little peek from us wouldn't be wholly out of order.'

Ross paused and stroked his misshaven chin, and his eyes flicked up to the ceiling as he thought. 'Well, we've nothing much for you to do at this particular minute, so why not give it a quick "thematic review".' He waggled his fingers as if quotation marks. 'Thematic review' being code for a scoping exercise into the background of the case. Often policing departments didn't like outside interferences, but one of the advantages of the team reporting directly to the chief was that they got access whenever they needed it.

Ross sat back in his chair and stretched, yawning widely. 'I like your missus, fuck knows why she's with you, so have a look and let me know if I need to have a word in the chief's lug-hole. Right, I'm off to defend why you bunch of money-grabbing bastards have decimated my overtime budget, which incidentally I don't see a bloody penny of,' said Ross, standing up and pulling his jacket on.

'Fine. Are we okay to take a run up there?'

'Well, it's hardly just around the corner; it's about three hours each way. Have a dig through the intel and run some ideas up flagpoles or whatever bollocks people call it nowadays. If it looks necessary, then let me know and get up there first thing. Your tardiness has meant it's too late today unless it's urgent, and the last thing I need is a twelve-hour claim each for fannying about in the Highlands.'

'Fair enough,' said Max.

'Ross,' said Norma just as he turned to leave.

'What?'

'Biscuit stain.'

'Eh?'

'Dunked biscuit stain on your tie,' she said, pointing at a pale brown sticky mark on his blue tie.

'Ah shite and fannybaws,' he hissed, smearing the area with his sausage-like fingers.

Norma giggled but reached into her drawer and came up with a tasteful, plain blue tie, which she threw to Ross.

'You're a star, Norma, but why do you have a tie in your desk, or shouldn't I ask?'

'For this reason. It's one of my old man's many cast-offs. Now off you go or you'll be late, and the finance manager is a grumpy bugger,' said Norma.

Ross pulled his stained tie from round his neck and left the office, knotting the new one on as he barged through the door.

'Top work. That'll put him in a good mood,' said Max. 'What can you tell us about Afrodita?'

'Well, she was trafficked over by an Albanian gang as a twelve-year-old having been living on the streets of Tirana. You know the drill: promises of work, a home and a wonderful life. Soon after, an NCA anti-trafficking operation was following a member of the Hellbanianz drug gang when they saw him with Afrodita at King's Cross Station in London. She was heading to Glasgow, so they stayed with their target, a dealer called Jetmir Xhilaj, and got a couple of surveillance officers to intercept her in Scotland. They pulled her in just outside Falkirk, and found she had a kilo of high purity coke strapped to her waist.'

'Shit, that's horrible. I've not heard much about Hellbanianz, sounds a bit amateurish,' said Janie.

'Yes and no. They've really been gaining traction in East London and were coming across our radar a fair bit when I was there. They do a lot of drill rap tracks on YouTube; you must have seen them. All very highly produced, lots of flash cars, fast women and gold jewellery as they rap about guns and drugs. Bad people and not to be underestimated, despite the brash shite,' said Max.

'Definitely not. They seem to be the ground-level commercial operation that supports the Mafia Shqiptare, who are the wholesalers. They've totally cornered the large-scale market for cocaine as they deal directly with the cartels. Their coke's high purity and far cheaper than when the likes of Tam Hardie was bringing it in,' said Norma, staring intently at her screen. 'So, serious people. Poor Afrodita was begging on the streets of Tirana when she was brought across Europe to the UK with the promise of work as a model, usual shite. When she gets here, she's working on a cannabis farm for a while and then they got her county lining drugs. Small batches at first, and then a kilo when she was intercepted.' Norma looked up from her screen and adjusted her spectacles.

'Jesus, poor kid. So, what about going missing?' said Janie.

'Her birthday, of all days. She went for a run up Fyrish, which isn't far from Inverness. She's a competitive athlete, destined for the national squad apparently. She lives in Evanton, and her foster parent, Valerie Smith, dropped her at the car park with the arrangement that she'd call when she got to the top. She never called, and she never returned.'

'I know Fyrish well. It's a cnoc with a massive great folly on the top. Close to where I grew up. What have the locals done?' said Max.

'Well, seems like a decent first response. Obviously first thought was that she may have fallen, so they sent the Search and Rescue helicopter up from Inverness airport, and put the mountain rescue teams on the hill, but there was no trace. It's like she disappeared into thin air. They even searched the hill with thermal imaging, but nothing.' Norma shrugged.

'How about phones?' said Max.

Norma clicked her mouse as she switched between screens. 'They live-traced it, but it had gone off the network an hour after Valerie dropped her off. It briefly sparked back on a short while later, but went off immediately.'

'Which cell sites?' asked Max.

'Well, when it first left the network, it was hitting a cell mast west of the hill, presumably because she was at the summit. The next activation hit a mast at Invergordon to the east.'

'Does that suggest that she tried to switch the phone on at the base of the hill?' said Max.

'That would be my interpretation of it,' said Norma, looking up from the screen.

'That's a concern. What has the inquiry team surmised?' said Max.

'Well, there had been some issues with a boyfriend a while ago. A slightly scrotey older boy had been sniffing about her, and she went out with him a few times, but the parents didn't approve. All seemed to stop six months ago, although he didn't take it well, apparently. She'd been a bit rebellious for a while, and had gone missing a few times, but had always returned after a day or so. Apparently, she replaced boys with athletics, and had gone from moody teenager to dedicated athlete,' said Norma.

'Well, it seems a bit strange. Any contact with anyone from Albania?'

'Her sister is in one of the better kids' homes in Tirana, and they're in contact via messages, and they Skype regularly, but her location has been kept secret in case the gang try to get her back, same with her taking the Smith surname. She was very much Jetmir Xhilaj's girl.' Norma settled her glasses on her nose, and yawned.

'Anything on him?' said Janie.

'He lost his surveillance team on the day Afrodita was rescued, and was never seen again. Totally dropped out of sight and was thought to have left the country, although we have no confirmation of that. He's not dropped any new rap tracks on YouTube, anyway. Maybe he's fallen foul of the Mafia; they don't take failure well, and the loss of a kilo of product, as well as a trafficked girl, will be viewed very dimly,' Norma said, a trace of a grimace on her face.

'That's true. "Besa", or honour, is big with the Albanian gangs, and losing product and a trafficked girl will have gone down like a cup of cold sick,' said Max.

'Thanks for that simile,' said Janie, putting her mug down. 'Please tell me she wasn't put to work in the brothels?' Her face registered distaste at the very thought of it.

'From what I can see, no, although the records on the databases I can access are scant. She was deemed as a trafficking victim via the National Referral Mechanism at Sheffield, so she got temporary leave to remain in the UK, despite being an illegal entrant. Poor thing. Seems she was really turning a corner, and now this.'

Max frowned, looking at the report on Norma's screen, which had a photograph of Afrodita attached. She was slim and very pretty with fine features, splodged with freckles. She had shiny, long brown hair; her eyes were a vivid green, and shone with intelligence. A big smile showed white teeth that were only slightly marred by braces. Something shifted in Max's gut. A sense of unease which he had learned to trust.

Max then turned to the photograph of Jetmir Xhilaj, who scowled at Max from the screen. He had a heavy brow, deep, dark eyes and his face radiated arrogance and petulance simultaneously. The photo was clearly a screen-grab captured from a YouTube video. His right hand was extended, his ring-laden fingers mimicking a pistol pointing directly at the camera. Max looked from Jetmir back to Afrodita, and then back again.

'Norma, can you check if he's back in the country?'

'Already have. No sign on border targeting database, but that means little if he came in on a boat, or with a snide passport. You want me to run all the usual checks to see if he's back?'

'Yeah, I'm not sure I like any bit of this case. It all feels wrong. How well known was her address?'

'It should have been locked down tight, with only the FLO and maybe the National Referral Mechanism at Sheffield knowing, and she was on all government databases under Smith, so she should have been right off the radar.'

'How about the Home Office? If they were trying to regularise her stay, then there must have been somewhere to send the paperwork to?'

'Maybe. Not sure I can do those checks.'

'What have the locals done about her phone?'

'They did the live-trace on an urgent basis on the night she went missing, but nothing else.'

'What, no billing, history of cell sites, in and out call data?' said Max, incredulously.

'Not that I can see.'

'Let's go worst-case scenario. She's been abducted. Now, that could be for several reasons, but the most likely is the trafficking gang, which means that someone must have leaked where she is. That could be social services, Immigration, cops, NCA, and you know what that makes this?'

'I've a nasty feeling about what you're going to say,' said Janie.

'Yep. It makes it our remit. Norma, can you look into any other trafficking victims who have disappeared in suspicious circumstances?'

'On it. Any location or date parameters?' she said, scribbling on her pad.

'Wherever you see fit, but I'd go nationally and keep it broad; we can always filter things down a bit later.'

'Shall I prepare for a "thematic review" of the missing person inquiry to assure stakeholder confidence?' said Janie, fingers waggling in quotation marks.

'Yeah, whatever BS we need. We'll set off first thing then. Let's use the time left today productively by putting feelers out there. I'll contact central Covert Human Intelligence Source units and see if any of the informants are talking about anything, and I'll also call the Met modern slavery unit; they have a really good picture of the trafficking gangs. Janie, can you get into the vice teams and see if they have any clues?'

'On it.'

'Okay, we'll work up the best intel picture we can on the Albanian gangs and trafficking networks. Let's come up with some theories soon. We'll head north early tomorrow and see Afrodita's foster parents and generally poke about, okay?'

Janie stood by Max's desk and looked at the picture of the smiling Afrodita. 'She's a pretty wee thing. What time shall I pick you up?'

'Six?'

'Fine.'

'Not moaning?' said Max, grinning.

'No. I want to find this wee girl. I'm worried, and if some bastard has given her location away, I want to find them.'

6

MAX HAD SLEPT well, so he felt fresh when Janie pulled up outside the farmhouse just before six. He had been untroubled by dreams for some time now, probably the result of a settled period at work and at home. Katie had barely stirred as he kissed her goodbye, and Nutmeg pretended to be asleep, her eyes following him around the room as he dressed, her tail twitching imperceptibly. She had clearly not fancied a walk this morning, as the rain and blustery wind bashed against the window.

'Nice weather,' said Janie as Max jumped in the car, pulling the hood down from his jacket as he fastened his seatbelt.

'Typically Scottish, aye. You okay?'

'Fine and dandy, ready?'

'Hit it,' said Max in an approximation of The Blues Brothers.

Janie, as usual, drove – her concentration palpable as the wipers struggled to keep up with the deluge of driving rain as she negotiated the roads from Culross heading north. Max was under no illusions as to who was the better driver of the two of them, and Janie was a nervous passenger and a terrible backseat driver. The car was, as per normal, immaculate. The plastics shone, the carpets were just vacuumed and there was even a new air freshener dangling from the indicator stalk in the big Volvo. Janie was tidy to an almost obsessive degree and couldn't countenance embarking on a journey in a dirty car.

They were on the A9 north of Perth when Ross called.

'Max, Norma tells me you're on some wild bloody goose chase. Fancy telling me why, bearing in mind I'm supposed to be the bloody boss?' His voice boomed out of the car's speakers.

'Ross, we spoke about this yesterday. It was your idea that we go north today, rather than yesterday, to preserve your overtime budget.'

'Aye, as well as may be, but you could have sent me a message at least.'

'I did. I sent you one on the WhatsApp group at four o'clock yesterday.'

'I've no idea how to use the stupid fucking thing. Whatever happened to a bloody phone call, eh? Anyway, what's the deal with it, she still missing?'

'Aye, she is. I've just a bad feeling about it. I don't like that she's a trafficking victim having been almost three years with foster carers and somehow, she disappears off the face of the earth. Also, Katie is convinced that it isn't right, either, and you know that she's not one to overreact.'

'This is very true, whereas you're a right panicky bastard, no idea why she married you. Look, I get it, the circumstances are concerning, and if we do have someone in social services, Home Office or another agency leaking the locations of trafficking victims, we need to be over it. I'm calling Inverness CID now to say that the chief is dip-sampling misper inquiries to ensure corporate accountability, or some such shite like that. DI Dan Calman is the SIO for it. I don't know him, do either of you?'

'I certainly don't,' said Max.

'Me neither,' said Janie.

'Okay, well, tread carefully. I don't want to ruffle any feathers, and I know what you can be like when you wade in with your size ten clod-hoppers. What you gonna do?'

'I'll speak to the team, then maybe have a look at the locus. I've not been for a while. Have you ever been up Fyrish?'

'Max, do I look like Edmund fucking Hillary? I spent my youth in the pubs of Dingwall, not pissing about on a Munro.'

'It's not a Munro – it's a cnoc.'

'Oh, get tae fuck, you smug numpty. Okay, crack on and see what you can come up with. Let me know if I need to escalate.'

'Will do. I may see if I can speak to the foster family. Katie has a really good relationship with them, so hopefully they'll be receptive.'

'I think you'll be right. They haven't even appointed a bloody family liaison officer. They have six other mispers from care right now, and a murder which broke last night as well as an industrial accident at a building site, so they're stretched to breaking point. Try not to offend anyone, and just make yourself helpful. Last thing I need is angry detectives from Inverness moaning at me.'

'You can rely on me, Ross.' Max winked at Janie.

'Aye, right,' said Ross, with as much sarcasm as was possible to put into those two words. He hung up.

'He sounds in a positively good mood,' said Max.

'Aye, almost cheery. Maybe Mrs Fraser is being nice to him.'

Max laughed and dialled.

'Hey, babe. Any news?' Katie's warm Yorkshire-accented voice came out of the speakers.

'On our way up north now. Can you call the foster parents and see if we can go and see them?'

'Sure, but what do you think has happened?'

'I'm not sure yet. We're going to see the inquiry team, and go and see the family. I want to make sure that nothing's been missed.'

'Thanks for this, Max. I'm really worried about her. Valerie and Reg are going out of their minds. They took her in and treated her as their own, and they're even trying to get the sister over. That's some commitment, Max. They're lovely people, be nice to them, yeah? And maybe don't let Ross meet them.'

'It's just me and Janie. Ross is out of harm's way. We'll be there in an hour.'

'Hi, Katie,' said Janie.

'Hi, Janie.'

'I'll call you as soon as I have anything,' said Max, and he hung up.

*

Max and Janie walked into the open-plan CID office at Burnett Road Police Station, which was almost empty. A harassed-looking plainclothes officer was surrounded by evidence bags, his face displaying a mix of panic and worry as he stared at a property register.

Max cleared his throat, and the cop, a young guy with a shock of scruffy red hair, looked up.

'Help you?' he said, his eyes flicking down at his register.

'DS Craigie and DC Calder. Is DI Calman about?'

'Aye, he should be somewhere. He was up with the super,' he said in a broad singsong accent that Max guessed came from one of the islands, probably Orkney.

'Thanks. Where is everyone? Like the *Mary Celeste* in here,' said Max.

'It's all gone crazy. We've a murder on the go, an industrial accident, a shite load of other crap. It's bloody crazy, pal, and I've lost a bloody bit of property. DI will go bloody mad.'

'You know anything about the Albanian misper from Fyrish?' asked Janie.

'Not a great deal. It was a big deal at the time. They got the coastguard helicopter up with the thermal camera on the hill, had dogs out and the local mountain rescue, but no trace of her anywhere. I think she's one of the regular mispers from care, so they feel she's awa' with a boyfriend, ya ken?'

'Aye, right enough. Will the boss be back?'

'I bloody hope so. He has to sign this register off before I take it to court,' he said, rifling through the bags.

On cue a middle-aged man entered the room wearing a smart, well-fitting suit. He had neat grey hair and a trimmed, tidy beard. He looked over at Max and Janie.

'You the guys up from Tulliallan?'

'Aye, DS Craigie and DC Calder,' said Max, extending a hand.

'Dan Calman. I'm the DI here. Your boss is an interesting character, right? His language is choice to say the least.'

'You could say that,' said Max, smiling easily.

'You're doing some kind of review on one of our mispers, right?'

'Aye, that's right. The Albanian girl from a few days ago, Afrodita Dushku, aka Smith.'

'You're welcome to look at whatever you like, pal. We're decimated for staff, and we're getting bugger all support. I have precisely seven high-risk mispers, plus a breaking murder, and all manner of other shite so I've no bloody staff at all. You want to see the decision logs and the like?' He rubbed his hand through his hair and yawned, his pale face drawn and lined. It looked like long hours had been the order of the day.

'That'd be grand, boss. You mind if we go and nose about ourselves? We could lend a bit of a hand at the same time.'

'Be my guest. We're utterly screwed here, and to be frank I'm shitting myself. We've put her case to the back of the queue. No sightings of her on Fyrish and it's been properly searched. Helicopters, mountain rescue teams with dogs and local volunteers. She's not on that hill, that's for sure. She was a frequent absconder, so the feeling is that she'll turn up. I'd love to do more, but I have literally no one left, and even this incompetent bugger over here is losing bloody property that we need to sort before court.' His eyes flashed towards the hapless DC who was frantically searching through the assorted bags of property, a look of panic developing on his ruddy face.

'We'll stay out of the way, I promise.'

'Aye, well, when you report back to the chief, tell him I can't do bloody anything with no staff. The log's on my desk in the glass office over there, the rest is on the misper database, help yourselves. We threw the kitchen sink at it when she went missing, worried she'd fallen down a bloody hole, but we now think she's most likely just winding her foster carers up and are all hoping to God that she turns up along with the other bloody six.'

'Thanks, boss.'

'Right, if you'll excuse me, I need to crack on. Macca, where's this missing bloody production?' He moved away to the officer, who was brick red in the face and jittery as he continued to rifle through numerous bags of evidence.

Max and Janie walked into the tidy, glass-walled office, where there were several piles of documents all topped with pre-formatted decision logs that senior investigating officers use to record all the decisions made in a major inquiry.

'I feel sorry for the poor DI. All those high-risk jobs on at the same time. He must be feeling it, and it shows why so little's been done for Afrodita.' Max picked up the decision log and flicked through the pages. He found exactly what he had expected. A decent initial response whilst she was missing on the hill followed by the standard checks since then. Basic phone intelligence, screening of her friends, a cursory search of her bedroom. Max couldn't find the heart to be critical, such were the demands on what was effectively a small team with resources being as stretched as they were.

'Not a lot, is it?' said Janie.

'Agreed. Let's go and see the parents. I still think there's more to this than meets the eye, and we're not going to learn anything here,' said Max.

'How far is Evanton?'

'Half an hour or so.'

'Can we get a coffee en route?'

'The parents may make us a coffee,' said Max.

'Do you trust a coffee at a house you've never been to before? Powdered instant stuff?' said Janie with a look of distaste.

'Good point, well made. There's a nice wee coffee place on the way.' Max didn't drink alcohol anymore, but he loved good coffee.

Janie picked up a photocopied picture of Afrodita and stared at it, taking in the cheeky smile and youthful features. 'I don't like this job, Max. Something about it is making me nervous and that poor wee thing is out there somewhere.'

'I agree. Let's go.'

7

AFRODITA SHIVERED AS she lay on her side, eyes closed, trying to stem the rising panic that was threatening to overwhelm her. She pulled the moth-eaten, frayed and coarse blanket around her, hoping to conserve what little warmth that her slight frame could generate.

The putrid room was dark and depressing, with just a single bulb suspended from the pendant in the middle of the ceiling. The place hadn't been illuminated since she'd arrived, however long that had been. She was losing track of time. She could have been here a day, three days or maybe a week. One thing was sure, the gnawing hunger in her belly told her that she'd been here a while. The hollow feeling rekindled thoughts of her past begging on the streets of Tirana. That sense of panic when you realised that you had not eaten and that you may not eat again. The memories of warmth, comfort and love that she'd experienced in the last few years were fading fast, and frankly it terrified her. More than anything, she wanted to be at home, in her bedroom with Jock at her feet. She felt hot tears begin to seep from her eyes; she made no effort to stem them, instead she just let them trickle.

The carpet she lay on was stained, worn and tacky, and smelled of must. The windows were filthy and obscured by what looked like metal shutters outside the glass that had been securely bolted into place. She'd seen shutters like this on the estate in East London she'd stayed on after being trafficked over, and she'd been told that they were there to stop intruders getting in. What little light there was in the room filtered in through the tiny holes in the shutters. The only facilities they'd left her with were a bucket, which was serving as a makeshift toilet that she'd been forced to use a few times, and a two-litre bottle of mineral water, which she'd drank from only when her body demanded it. She'd eaten nothing.

She was still dressed in her running gear, but her trainers had been removed and were not in the room with her. Although she hadn't been tied or shackled in any way, the stout door and secure windows had made any chance of escape impossible.

She squeezed her eyes tightly shut trying to picture the face of the man on the top of the hill that had startled her. That face that she'd hoped never to see again. The man whom she'd once viewed as her saviour from her filthy existence in Albania had turned into something else. His eyes were clouded and dark, and his teeth, once white and even, were stained and dirty. He no longer looked cool and glamorous; he looked nasty and grimy.

Her head ached terribly and she felt nauseous and thirsty. She began to shake violently. And not just because of the chill in the barren, horrible room – utter terror sat in her stomach and chest as if she'd swallowed lead weights.

She remembered nothing at all since asking to borrow the woman's phone in the car park at Fyrish. The first memory after that was of being roughly shoved into the room that she now occupied, the door slamming shut followed by the rattle of keys. She'd seen no one since then, and there hadn't been a single sound. The place was as quiet as a grave. She'd tried screaming and shouting until her voice had grown hoarse, but there had been nothing. No one had come. There was no traffic noise at all; in fact the only sounds she could faintly hear was the dawn chorus from the birds as the sun rose. She was in the countryside; she was sure of it.

The UPVC windows were shut tight, and locked, and however hard she pounded they didn't move a millimetre. She soon gave up and accepted that she was not getting out of this room. Even if she could get through the double glazing, there would be no chance of breaching the external shutters, which she knew were designed to keep squatters out and as such were tightly bolted in place.

A sudden crash from outside the door made Afrodita flinch, and she sat up, eyes wide and staring, her heart pounding in her chest.

Footsteps were audible outside the room, and she felt herself almost shrink inside her running clothing, her breath coming in gasps that quickened as she heard a jangling of keys and a sliding of bolts at the door. She shuffled backwards into a corner of the room, drew her knees up to her chest and encircled them with her arms, pulling the musty blanket around her bony shoulders. Fresh tears began to well in her eyes. 'Please, please let me go,' she said in a hoarse whisper, feeling the dread in her stomach and bile rising in her throat.

The door was pushed inwards, and a dark figure appeared along with a blindingly bright torch beam piercing the shadows. She couldn't make out any features, such was the strength of the torch, which she now realised was a head torch that made the figure resemble an alien. Heavy footsteps approached her, a hand extending forwards, clutching something. Instinctively, she rolled up into a ball, falling to her side in a foetal shape, and she screwed her eyes tightly, waiting for the first blow to arrive.

'Please, don't hurt me. Please, please, please,' she whispered, her voice laced with terror, as she rolled even tighter, to protect herself from whatever came next. A reflexive action of muscle memory of all those beatings she'd endured in the children's home, years ago.

'Shh,' the dark shape said. Afrodita dared not open her eyes.

The impact was light, as an object was thrown at her, followed by a lighter one. She flinched, but then realised that there was no pain.

There were more footsteps, and then a crash as the door was slammed shut, and the keys rattled once again, followed by more footsteps fading away.

Afrodita opened her eyes and scanned the room.

Empty again. She exhaled, a mix of relief that was blighted by the realisation that she was alone again in her prison cell. She recalled memories of being locked away in a dank room in Albania. As well as the beatings, ridicule and deprivation of food, isolation had been one of the favoured punishments in the children's homes. Desolation settled on Afrodita like a thick cloud.

As her night vision began to return, she knew that something had changed. Two items lay on the carpet just in front of her: a packaged sandwich and a packet of crisps.

8

VALERIE AND REG Smith lived in a neat, compact cottage on the outskirts of Evanton, an attractive Highland village with a small parade of shops.

'Nice wee place, this,' said Janie as they sat outside in the Volvo.

'It is. There's a lovely walk with a deep gorge just up the road here. They filmed a bit of one of the Harry Potter movies there.'

'Really? Oh, man, I'd like to see that. Which film?'

'Sorry, that's the limit of my knowledge.'

'Not a Potter fan, then?'

'Well, not generally. I take it you are?'

'I was obsessed as a kid. When I was at boarding school, I used to wish I went to Hogwarts, rather than the actual public school I went to. No magic, no dragons, no Quidditch, just bullies, shite food and an uncomfortable bed.'

'What house did you imagine yourself in?'

'I didn't,' said Janie, suddenly looking away from Max.

Max chuckled. 'That's a massive porky. You definitely had yourself allocated to a house. I bet you're a Ravenclaw.'

'You seem to know more than you should.'

'Maybe I have watched a couple.'

Janie sighed. 'Hufflepuff, if you must know. They value justice, so it's relevant.'

'Such a geek,' said Max, laughing.

'That's enough, sergeant, let's go and see these poor parents.' Janie opened the door to indicate that the conversation was over.

They walked up the path, the lawns to either side of which were immaculate, with well-tended flower and vegetable beds, and lots of mature shrubs, all with the early-spring haze of emerging leaves.

'Nice place,' said Max as he rapped on the rustic door. There was an explosion of high-pitched barks from inside.

'Nice enough to make me wish that I had a garden, but herbs on my tenement windowsill is as far as I'll get for a while.'

The door was opened by a stocky middle-aged man, with short greying hair and a clear, ruddy complexion that spoke of his outdoor life. He wore smart tweed slacks, a check shirt and looked every inch the ghillie. His eyes were shrouded and cloudy, and his face was lined with obvious worry. A tiny brown-and-white Jack Russell terrier flew out of the house in mock-outrage, barking in apparent fury but his thrashing tail telling a different story altogether.

'Stop it, Jock. Help you?' he said in a rich Highland accent. The dog stopped barking instantly, and rolled on his back, tail still twitching.

'Mr Smith?' said Max.

'Aye, but please call me Reg. Are you Max?' he said, his eyes brightening.

'That's me, and this is Janie.' Max proffered his warrant card.

'Come in, come in. Your lovely wife said you were going to call in. Thank you for coming, and excuse the daft wee doggy. He likes to think he's big and tough, but he's really a big jessie,' he said, stepping to one side and opening the door wide. The dog bounded to his feet and ran into the house. 'Is there any news?'

'Unfortunately, nothing right now, Mr Smith.'

'Reg, please. Come through to the kitchen, kettle's just boiled,' he said.

They followed Reg into the hall towards the back of the house. Max's attention was drawn to a colour photograph of a group of muddy, camouflage-clad soldiers, clutching rifles and holding a Union flag; each wore a red beret that bore the badge of the parachute regiment.

'Falklands?' said Max, pointing at the photograph.

'Aye. I was the youngest in our platoon. Just eighteen. Have you served?' said Reg.

'Aye. Black Watch.'

'See any action?'

'Afghanistan and Iraq,' was all that Max said.

Reg just nodded, but something passed between them. A mutual respect.

They carried on through to a large, open-plan kitchen with new units and appliances. A rich smell of coffee was redolent in the air, and a woman sat on a stool at the breakfast bar, a mug in front of her. She faced them as they entered the room; her eyes were red and heavy and her soft, kind face was pale and lined.

'Max?'

'Aye, and this is Janie. I take it that Katie told you we were going to pop in?'

'She phoned me a wee while ago. I take it nothing new?'

'No, not at the moment, but the boss of the team at Inverness is happy for a fresh set of eyes on the case.'

'Please sit down, both of you. Well, I'm grateful you're here, Max. She's a wonder, that wife of yours. She's just so kind and she's been a tower of strength to us.'

'She is, that's true,' Max said, smiling as he and Janie sat on kitchen stools.

Jock settled by Janie's feet and whined softly. She reached down and stroked the dog's ears. 'Cute dog,' said Janie, smiling.

'Aye, he's a wee darling, and he's only just turned two. He's missing Affi awful bad, she dotes on him. He's very much her doggy. He always sleeps every night tucked up next to her, so he's a little lost now that she's not here,' said Reg.

'Can I make some coffee?' said Valerie.

'Thanks, but I think we're good. Literally just had one,' said Max.

'So, what do you think you can do that the other cops haven't? They searched the hill thoroughly, which was impressive, but I'm not so sure they've done much else. The local mountain rescue has been on the hill loads with plenty of volunteers, and we're all going out again later. Reg knows the hill like the back of his hand. Local cops seemed to focus on the fact that she'd went missing a few times in the past,' said Valerie.

'I've read something about that, but Katie did tell me how much she's settled since getting into athletics,' said Max.

'Well, we'd had lots of problems with her when she hit her teen years, as you'd expect with her background. Usual stuff, smoking, staying out and poor choice of boys. Then suddenly, she discovered athletics and out of the blue she turned herself around. Aye, she's obsessed. She can't get enough of it, and her coach has been wonderful with her; literally nothing is too much for him,' said Valerie.

'Has he been spoken to?'

'Not by us, but I guess he knows. You know how word gets about.'

'How about boyfriends?'

'There was a boy, Lewis McPhail, who lives in the village. We didn't like him a lot, he was a bad influence, but Affi was smitten for a while probably because he's a few years older, and he had a car. We didn't approve, and we told her so, which caused a big argument. Thankfully she ditched him once she discovered athletics and he discovered other girls, but I don't think he took it very well. He was stalking her and all sorts, you know. Constant phone calls, messages, Instagram and stuff. We got the local cop to have a word with him, and he stopped. I think he has some other poor wee thing on the go, now. Leastways, he seems to have a different lassie in his car every time I see him.'

'What was the local cop's name?' asked Janie.

'I can't recall. Italian-sounding name. From Dingwall, he was. Nice chap, and I think he put the fear of God into Lewis.'

'How long ago was this?'

'Six months or so, maybe less.'

Janie scribbled into her notebook.

'Have you had any issues with anyone from Afrodita's old life?' asked Max.

'No. Nothing, but then her presence with us isn't well known. We don't let on that she was trafficked, and the gang were all in London. She's still in touch with her sister, with Skype and messages. Katie probably told you that we're trying to reunite them, but it's just so much paperwork.'

'What type of phone did she have?' said Janie.

'IPhone, second-hand one we bought for her birthday last year.'

'Was she on the phone a lot?'

'Och, all the time, but just on social media with her pals. We get no mobile signal here at all, but kids don't seem to use phones for phoning, do they?'

'Very true. Any other devices?'

'She has an iPad and a school Chromebook in her room.'

'Do you have parental controls on anything?' asked Janie.

'No. We were keen for her to feel she was trusted. We did have it on for a while, but when she started behaving well, we rewarded her. We trust her.'

'Do you know the password for her phone? If we can enable location services, we may get an accurate GPS if it gets switched on again.'

'Sorry, no, we don't, sorry. She'd been so good that we felt she needed her privacy. She's had such a tough life.'

'Are the phone and the iPad linked with the same Apple ID?' asked Janie.

'I don't know.' Valerie's voice cracked, and her eyes began to moisten.

'Sorry to ask so many questions, Valerie. We just want to learn as much as we can. It gives us the best opportunity to find Affi,' said Max.

The tears spilled out of her eyes like a dam bursting. Reg slid an arm around his wife's shoulders, and she buried her face in his sweater, her shoulders heaving in sorrow.

'We'll do everything we can, I promise,' said Max.

Reg nodded, his own eyes full of tears.

'Can we go and see Afrodita's room?' said Janie.

'Aye, help yourself. Cops from Inverness hardly even looked at it. Top of the stairs, first room you come to.' He hugged Valerie tight as Max and Janie stood and left the kitchen. They climbed the stairs and were met by a painted door with a printed sign declaring it to be *Affi's room*.

They entered into what was a typical teenager's space. Posters adorned almost every inch of the wall. Various teen bands competed for space with horses, athletes and what seemed like a hundred photographs of Jock the terrier.

A single bed was covered with a pastel pink duvet and a fluffy pink blanket.

'Fairly typical teen room, eh?' said Janie.

'Aye.'

'I never had a room like this. I was in a boarding school room, and when I was at my aunt's, I wasn't allowed posters and stuff. I even had old-fashioned sheets and blankets and a counterpane.'

'What the hell's a counterpane?' said Max, his brow furrowed as he looked at Janie.

'It's what my posh and unpleasant aunt used to call a bedspread, no idea why.'

'Is that why you're so odd and fastidious?'

'I prefer the terms organised and methodical, sergeant.'

'What are we looking for? Diary?'

'Diary? Get with the programme, Grandpa.' Janie walked over to the dresser and picked up an iPad in a pink case, which she flipped open. The screen woke up to a wallpaper that was a photograph of Jock with a ball in his mouth, his eyes alive with mischief. Janie pressed the home button, and the black unlock screen appeared asking for a six-digit passcode.

'Any ideas?'

'Mine's always been six nines. Or maybe six ones.'

'That's a bit predictable, but maybe worth a try.' Janie tapped on the keys trying both '111111' and '999999', but the screen wobbled, staying black and locked.

'Her date of birth?' Janie said, looking at her notebook and tapping at the screen once again. It just wobbled.

'How many goes do we get?' said Max.

'I think we're safe. It locks for a minute if we try too many times. We've a few guesses left.'

Max looked around the room, his eyes finding a calendar tacked to the wall. It was the ring-bound type, with a photograph of Jock on one half, the month and days below. Max flipped a few of the calendar pages. Each one had a different picture of Jock on it. Some with Afrodita, but most of the dog, playing with a ball, paddling in a burn or asleep on the carpet.

Max let the pages fall back against the wall and looked at the calendar again; he smiled at the entry written in blue ink with a doodle of something approximating a birthday cake.

He turned to Janie, took the iPad from her hand and pressed six digits into the keypad. The screen woke up as it unlocked.

'Jock's date of birth. That's his fourth birthday,' he grinned.

'Oh God, you're gonna be so bloody unbearably smug about this, aren't you?'

'You can't teach it, constable. Razor instinct.'

'Aye, that and she wrote it on her bloody calendar. Right, what first?'

'I don't really do much social media, but don't youngsters do Instagram?'

'I don't do that much, either.'

'Is that because you're a little odd and have few friends?' said Max.

Janie glared at Max before answering. 'Insta, or maybe Snapchat. She has an Instagram account here.'

Janie pressed an icon and a page opened showing a profile picture of Affi with Jock; her username was 'Affi-Smudge'. The screen was full of photographs, again mostly of Jock, but more recently there were several of athletic events. The latest post was a selfie of Affi in running gear, her tongue poking out mischievously: *birthday run up Fyrish to test new creps*. There were lots of hearts and comments below wishing her a happy birthday. They both stared at the iPad, scrolling down.

'She looks like a fun kid,' said Janie, passing the device to Max and walking over to the side of the bed where a simple laptop lay on the floor. 'I guess this is the school Chromebook?' she said, opening it and sitting on the bed.

Max said nothing, just continued to scroll along the feed and taking in the pictures, noting a slight change in type of posts as he went back about six months. There were a few shots of Affi with a skinny youth, wearing a baggy tracksuit, a Burberry cap and a sneer on his face. In one he was leaning against the bonnet of a Citroën Saxo that had a dodgy body kit on it, and far lower profile tyres than the manufacturer could have intended. He was even throwing a gang sign with his fingers, which were all bedecked with sovereign rings. The gold chain that hung from his wrist was as gaudy as the one around his neck.

'Lewis McPhail looks a bit of a scrote to me. Check him out.

Thinks he's in the Evanton mafia.' Max turned the iPad to face Janie.

'Jeeze, would you look at the state of him. Who does he think he is, Tupac?'

'Tupac?'

'Tupac Shakur? Rapper with Death Row Records, got shot dead years ago. Some of his early stuff is seminal.'

'It was prog rock last time you were listening to weird stuff.'

'I have eclectic tastes.'

'Odd is more accurate, I'd say.'

'Whatever, Grandpa. Have you checked direct messages?'

'Not yet, but I will.'

Max tapped into the inbox, his eyes locking on a message sent just a few hours before Affi had disappeared. He clicked on it and read.

'Janie?'

'What?'

'We may need to go and have a chat with wee Tupac McPhail. Maybe give the locals a call first, get them on notice if we have to shout for transport.'

Janie looked at her phone. 'Not even a bit of signal here. Why do we need to go and see him?'

Max didn't answer, just flipped the iPad and moved it closer to Janie.

You're a stuck-up Albanian bitch, and you're gonna get merked.

'That's not nice. What does "merked" mean?' said Janie.

'Usually heard amongst street gangs in London, not so much in a pleasant Highland village.'

'And?' said Janie, her brow furrowed.

'Murdered.'

9

AFRODITA'S MOOD HAD darkened along with the fading light as time passed in the grim space she was still locked in. She'd seen no one since the sandwich and crisps had been thrown at her, however long ago that was. Time had become meaningless, and every passing minute felt like an hour.

So, when she heard noises on the other side of the door, her heart lurched with a mix of fear and hope as the rattling of keys and sliding of bolts were followed by a shaft of light from a single bulb outside the room.

A shadow appeared at the door, a bright, white light from a head torch flooding the room as it strode in, full of purpose and bristling with aggression. Rather than approach her, it stepped to one side to allow a second figure to enter, also shrouded behind the light.

Wordlessly, the head torch moved and raised its hands to the ceiling and fiddled with the light flex that had been dangling inert in the centre of it. The figure at the door flicked a switch and suddenly the room was bathed in a soft yellow.

After hours or days with almost no light, the assault on her eyes was brutal and immediate. She raised her hands to her face and bowed her head, partly to shield herself from the glare and partly because of the fear which had made her stomach churn. Her skin prickled in the intense, almost cloying silence and she could feel herself being studied.

'Look at me.' A command. Not a request. It came from a female voice in sharply accented Glaswegian with a trace of Albanian.

Afrodita let out a small yelp, her face feeling flushed as tears formed in her eyes. A cold, hard dread began to overwhelm her as she lost control of her breathing, panic overtaking her.

'Look at me now, Afrodita,' said the voice, matter-of-fact and laced with venom.

Afrodita just sat there, her back to the wall, eyes shut, hands clasped over them. 'Please, let me go. I'll say nothing to anyone. I just want to go home,' she sobbed, tears spilling out from between her fingers.

Strong hands grabbed her wrists, and she was pulled up to her feet, her blood rushing as it suddenly gave way to the force of gravity. Her head spun, and a bolt of pain gripped her stomach. She cried out, 'Please, please, please' – her voice cracked as her vocal cords were so constricted.

'Open your eyes, girl.' The voice was harsh and full of unkindness and malevolence.

Afrodita pushed her head down, chin against her chest, but she didn't resist the vicelike hold on her forearms. 'No, please, no, please, just let me . . .' she began, but the words died in her throat at the sound of a male voice. A familiar voice.

'Affi, open your eyes.' A softer tone, deeper and resonant of Albania.

Peering up through her brows, as she used to when begging on the streets of Tirana, Afrodita searched for the person who had given the command.

Jetmir Xhilaj looked down at her, a half-smile on his face. A face that her childish mind once thought of as impossibly handsome, was now sallow and greasy, the skin mottled with spots, and the previously mischievous eyes were muddy. A sour smell of body odour wafted, and she wrinkled her nose.

'That's better,' he said, smiling, showing stained and decaying teeth. She'd seen that smile many times in her dreams, along with the eyes, black and capable of intense charm, or frightening malice. Now here he was in this putrid room, looking at her with a mixture of triumph and amusement, with an expression somewhere between a smirk and a leer of desire. Affi shuddered.

She looked from Jetmir to the woman, whom she immediately recognised. It was the woman who had pretended to be her saviour in the car park at Fyrish just a few days ago.

'You're going to be working for me, Afrodita Dushku. You're very beautiful, my clients will pay well for you, and you still belong to us.' Her accent was a strange mix, the guttural Glasgow coupled with the cadence of her home country. She was middle-aged, stout and matronly, with short, bobbed dark hair. She reminded Afrodita of the manager of the children's home that she'd escaped from all those years ago. She looked solid and cruel. It was her eyes. They were deeply set, unpleasant, and yet, somehow managed to convey nothing. She nodded at Jetmir and turned to leave the room.

Afrodita opened her mouth to speak, but she realised that she had nothing to say. All she could manage was a husky 'please'.

The slap that came from the woman was sudden, vicious and as fast as a bolt of lightning as her hand cracked across Afrodita's face. Pain flared in her cheek, as her head rocked to one side with the force of the blow. Afrodita tried to scream, but the slap had knocked the wind out of her.

'Shut up, girl. You speak when you're fucking spoken to. One more word and I'll do much worse than a tap like that. You treat me with respect, yes. From now on you call me Sheff, do you understand me?' the woman said, using the Albanian word for 'boss'.

Afrodita sucked air into her panicked lungs, her hot cheek throbbing. Tears cascaded from her eyes, but she managed to calm herself. Memories of the almost constant beatings at the orphanage flared. The quickest way to more beatings was to cry, wail or protest. Afrodita shut her mouth and looked at the stained carpet. The inbuilt conditioning of the institutions was instinctive. To survive, the best response was complete and utter capitulation.

'I say, do you understand me?' the woman said.

'Yes,' said Afrodita, in barely a whisper.

The blow was immediate and hard, an open-handed slap across the back of her head that stung like hell. 'Yes, what? You forget your manners already, child?'

'Sorry, sorry. I mean yes, Sheff,' said Afrodita, lowering and covering her head.

'Look at me, child,' said Sheff.

Afrodita raised her head and looked at Sheff, feeling the tears streaming down her face.

Sheff stared at her with those dark eyes. 'Do as you are asked, and you'll be well treated. You'll have food and nice clothes, and I'll only send you to good clients. If you defy me, I'll send you back to Albania and you can work in the brothels there, which I'm sure you can imagine won't be as pleasant. Someone who looks as you do, my dear, will command a high price from the clients. If you behave, I'll make sure you have everything you need. You're now one of us again, back amongst your own kind. You didn't belong in the Highlands.'

Afrodita didn't meet her gaze. That was something else she'd learned in the orphanage. Eye contact could be taken as insolence, and that always resulted in a beating.

'Get her ready. She needs to clean up, and then get her some nice clothes, Jetmir. She's now our property, so she needs to look good. Try not to lose her again.'

'Yes, Sheff,' said Jetmir, leering at Affi. That same expression that had made her so uncomfortable.

'Not for you, Jetmir, for clients,' barked Sheff, harshly.

Jetmir just nodded and lowered his eyes.

Sheff then shook her head as she glanced at Afrodita before turning and striding out of the room.

'Please. I want to go home,' said Afrodita, looking up at Jetmir, who stared at her with a half-smile.

He reached over and brushed her cheek with the back of his hand, ignoring her flinch as his icy knuckles touched her flesh. 'You've grown up so much, Affi. You were just a spotty kid when you deserted me. Now you're a beautiful woman.' He smiled, but no trace of it reached his eyes, his breath was fetid, and she felt bile begin to rise in her throat. 'I was punished harshly by the Shqiptare for losing you. You owe me a large debt, which you need to pay back and that starts now. Come on, we're leaving, but know this, Affi. If you try to escape again things will not only be bad for you, but for little Melodi. How long will she survive in a Tirana brothel, Affi?'

Her insides froze at the mention of sweet little Melodi's name. She opened her mouth to speak, but closed it, and just nodded.

'Never forget who you are. A worthless little Tirana street kid. Cross me again, and the consequences will be bad. You cost me almost thirty thousand pounds, so you're mine until that debt is paid.'

10

'HARDLY LOOKS LIKE a gang-banger's crib, does it?' said Max as they stood outside a modern semi-detached property on a newish estate. The garden was well-tended, and there was a Honda Jazz on the drive alongside the Citroën Saxo that they'd seen in the Instagram feed. It was electric blue, had skirts and spoilers, and an after-market exhaust gaped like a tunnel.

The peaceful scene was only offset by the distant thump of music from within the premises.

'The car couldn't be more ned, could it? He's even painted the brake callipers red,' said Max, sniggering.

'Less Biggie Smalls, more Ali G, right?'

'Looks like Tupac McPhail lives with his parents in a pleasant semi in Evanton. A nice wee Highland village rather than straight outta Compton, eh? Shall we?'

'Let's. Fancy hanging back, just in case young Ali G feels like running?'

'That's the worst ever hip-hop reference, you know. Vanilla Ice was a joke of a rapper.'

'If you say so. I prefer Radiohead,' said Max as he opened the garden gate and made his way down the path.

'Predictable for a man of your age. I'll keep an eye on the back of the house,' said Janie, going down the drive and towards the path that seemed to lead to the back garden.

Max rapped at the door and then stood back, looking up at

the upstairs window. There was no movement, and the music was faint enough that Max suspected that it was being played at the rear of the house.

Within a minute the door was opened by a small, compact woman in her sixties.

'Help you?' she said, brushing floury fingers on her apron, a wide smile on her ruddy face.

Max produced his warrant card. 'DS Craigie. Is Lewis in?'

Her face hardened. 'What's the wee shite been doing now?'

'Just need a word, that's all. Is he in?'

'Aye, he is, as you can no doubt hear from that dreadful racket from his room. You want to come in?'

'That'd be great, thanks, Mrs McPhail.'

Max was just about to step over the threshold when he heard a shout from the back of the house. 'Max, he's running,' yelled Janie.

Max sprinted off and down the alleyway that led to the back garden. When he rounded the garage, he was met by the sight of Janie, calm and collected, with Lewis McPhail pinned down, face in the lawn, dressed in his boxer shorts and a vest top. He was screaming as she wrenched his arm behind his back.

'You okay?' said Max.

'Aye. Daft nugget jumped out of the window and legged it, but he's not so fast. He thought he could fight his way out of an arm bar. Keep still, ya dafty. I think he threw his phone, by the way. Over there by the hedge,' said Janie, nodding to the privet bush at the side of the garden.

Max walked to the shrub and immediately spotted a smartphone facedown on the grass. He stooped and picked it up before returning to the struggling Lewis. 'Pal, I'd keep still if I were you. She's really good at this shit and you'll just get hurt.'

'Get this bitch off me,' he said, his face contorted in pain, screaming like a banshee as Janie tightened her grip on his arm.

'Being abusive to a police officer who does cage fighting for a hobby is a bad idea, pal. Just relax,' said Max, feeling a smile spreading across his face.

'Get her fucking off, or I swear down—' He let out another scream. 'Okay, okay, okay,' he yelled.

Janie looked up from the ground, her face totally relaxed and wearing an amused smile. She eased her grip on the young man and within a few moments he was standing looking at his mud-streaked bare feet.

'Why you feds hassling man, fam? I'm getting bare pissed, and I swear down that man is gonna call his lawyer, ya get me?' he said, his Highland accent shot through with an affected accent that Max had last heard when dealing with gang members in London.

'What did he say?' said Janie, frowning.

'He's asking why we're bothering him and begs to inform us that he's getting rather annoyed and he's promising to seek legal advice,' translated Max.

'Shut up, man. You makin' me vex, either lock me up or call my brief,' he blurted out, eyes flashing and rolling side to side.

'Why is he talking like that?' said Janie.

'Watching too many diss-rap grime videos on YouTube. Come on, bro, we're going inside, although I think your mum is probably cross with you. I need your PIN code for the phone.'

'No way, you wasteman,' he said as his mother appeared in the garden, her face red and contorted.

'Just what the hell is going on here?' Her voice was shot through with anger.

'Mum, these dick heads are giving me beef . . .' he began to say, but he was stopped in his tracks as she strode across the lawn and unleashed a wild slap that connected with the back of his head with a sound like a pistol shot.

'You keep a civil tongue in your head, young man!' she said, her voice as sharp as glass shards.

'Ow!' he yelped.

'Mrs McPhail, please?' said Max, struggling to contain the laughter that was bubbling in his throat.

'Sorry, officer. You'd better come inside. What's he been doing?'

'We're investigating the disappearance of Affi, and we believe he sent her a message a couple of days ago. We need to speak to him about it.'

'What, the lassie who's missing?'

'Aye.'

'His phone code's all the nines. He thinks I don't know it, but I'm not stupid.'

'Mum, that's bare invasion of my fucking human rights,' he said, his voice an octave higher than it had been, his eyes wide with a mix of indignation and alarm.

Her hand flashed through the air again and cuffed him around the back of the head once more. 'Shut your stupid mouth, you daft fud,' she said, drawing herself up to her fullest height in her slippers.

'I'm sorry, Ma,' he said, head bowed, his petulance beginning to magically subside.

'Right. Inside. Lewis McPhail, you're going to tell these officers everything that you know about this. Do you understand me?'

'Aye, Mum,' he said, voice low and his eyes downcast to his muddy feet.

'You're gonna have to come with us, Lewis, once we've searched your bedroom,' said Max.

'Search? What for?' he said, eyes wide, his head snapping upwards, the colour draining from his face.

'Evidence of the offence. So, if you know anything, and I mean anything, about where Affi is . . .' Max left the sentence hanging.

'What if there's other things in my room?' said Lewis, a tremble in his voice.

'Lewis, what are you talking about?' said Mrs McPhail.

'I don't want no wasteman bloody feds in my room,' he said, the belligerence returning, as he squared his narrow shoulders.

'Well, young man. It's my house, and I say that they can search. Anything to help, and if you're hiding anything from me, I swear you're out, Lewis McPhail.'

Lewis opened his mouth to argue, but then shut it again, his shoulders sagging.

'Och, the shame of it. Polis coming to my house and taking my boy away, and in front of the neighbours, as well. Officers, you can search his room as much as you like.' She nodded, her jaw set tight.

*

Max stood looking at Lewis McPhail sitting on the bed in his small room, his face still wearing a trace of a frown but his shoulders hunched. The room reminded Max of every teenager's bedroom he had been in. There was a Ross County FC poster on the wall and several others of various bands, none of which Max recognised.

'What's he been doing then?' asked Mrs McPhail, looking at Max and Janie in turn.

'Could murder a cup of tea, Mrs McPhail,' said Max.

She pointed a stubby finger at her son. 'I'll want to know everything. Everything, you hear. You better tell these officers bloody everything, or so help me God, you'll be out on your ear, and where else are you gonna stay, eh? In town in the hostel with all the jakeys? If you know anything about that poor wee toot, you tell them now.' She nodded and headed off to the kitchen.

'Aye, Mum,' said Lewis at her retreating back.

A thick silence enveloped the room and Max sat on a hard chair and stared at Lewis, his eyebrows raised.

'What?' said Lewis, looking from side to side, his eyes wide.

'You know what,' said Max.

'I don't know shit, man.'

Janie cleared her throat and held up a small wooden box from which she produced a self-seal baggie.

'Oh dear, Lewis. What do we have here?' she said, with a tut and a slow shake of the head.

The young man's face fell at the sight of the baggie, which was full of a light green herb. Janie sniffed at it, and wrinkled her nose. 'Cannabis. Smells like skunk.'

'It's not mine,' he said, what colour that had been in his sallow cheeks draining away.

'Well, *that* makes it worse. Are you selling? There are at least ten baggies the same in here. This isn't good, supplying could get you properly locked up, Lewis.'

'Ach, it's just a wee bit of ganja, man. Just for my bredrin,' he said, affecting defiance, but the quiver in his voice telling another story.

'Lewis, just bloody stop with the petulant hard man thing, eh? We don't give a shit about the weed, but Afrodita is missing. She's been gone long enough for everyone to be worried, so if you know anything, I mean *anything*, you need to tell us now, or I'm dragging you out of here in your shorts and locking you up. What's your mum going to think of that, eh?'

'I don't know anything. I haven't seen Affi for ages, since she dumped me.'

'Why'd she dump you?'

'I dunno. She got into running, innit, with that bloody running club and suddenly I wasn't good enough for her.'

'Bit young for you, anyway, eh?' said Janie.

'Just four years. My mum's four years younger than my dad.'

'And?'

Lewis opened his mouth to retort, but something seemed to stop him.

Max said nothing. Just stared at the younger man, his face expressionless. A classic interview technique. Leave an uncomfortable silence. People are social creatures; they don't like uncomfortable silences. The wall clock ticked, and in the cloying quiet it was almost deafening. Janie was looking through his bedside drawers, which seemed to be filled with socks and pants.

Max opened his mouth as if to talk, but then closed it again, and sat back in the chair and crossed his legs.

Predictably, Lewis broke first.

'I . . . I've nothing to do with her going missing, I promise. I stopped after the local fed came.'

'I never said you did.'

'Then why're you here? I don't appreciate feds coming to my door. I've a rep, you feel me?' he said, sitting up in his chair, his narrow shoulders squared, his yo-yoing bravado making a resurgence.

Janie cleared her throat, and Lewis turned to face her. She was holding up an iPad with a pink cover, her eyebrow raised. 'I'll give you ten seconds, Lewis, and then we're taking you in right now. We can hold you for twenty-four hours whilst we sort this out, and then charge you for the weed. Or you can level with us now and we can have you interviewed and out in a couple of hours.'

'I don't know any—'

'That's five seconds,' said Janie.

'But—'

'Eight.'

'Honestly—'

'Time's up. Stand up, you're coming with us.' Janie pulled a pair of handcuffs from her jacket pocket and before Lewis could even protest, he had been efficiently handcuffed.

'Right, let's go,' said Max, standing just as Mrs McPhail came into the room clutching two mugs. 'No time for tea, I'm afraid. Lewis has agreed to come with us to help us out. He'll be back later. Isn't that right, Lewis?'

'Aye, that's right.'

'Let's go.'

11

LEWIS MCPHAIL STARED at the desk in the interview room, then at Max and Janie and looked down again, but they could tell. He'd quickly admitted to possessing the cannabis but they knew that there was more to come.

'We don't care about the weed, Lewis. We'll hand that over to the CID here, but we want to know what you know about Afrodita, and we don't have time to fanny about,' said Janie.

'Okay, okay. I'll tell you everything, but I have no clue where she is.'

'Go on then. We're listening,' said Max.

'Look, I was cut up when she dumped me, so I was following her around a bit, but then Luigi the local fed came and had a word, so I stopped. That's it.'

'Tell me about the message you sent her the other day on Instagram,' said Max.

'I was steaming pished when I sent that. I was looking at her Insta feed and saw the pictures of her doing her running, all happy, like. So, I got a bit crazy and sent that message, but it meant nothing, man. I'm sorry, I'd never have hurt her, I loved her.' He looked down at his feet.

'Is that the only one?'

'Aye, I promise.'

'Well, look here, Lewis. We're going to take your phone and put it into a bit of software and we'll be able to tell exactly what you've been doing. Everything. Every website, all your GPS data, all your photos, all your messages, everything you've done. The whole lot, pal. Understand?'

'Look. I didn't do anything, but I was cut up when she ditched me, you get me?'

'Why don't you enlighten us?' said Janie.

Lewis paused, his eyes moving from side to side, his face slick with a sheen of sweat. 'I just sent her some messages when I was pissed, I promise. I don't know anything about her going missing.'

Max looked at Janie, who just shrugged. He turned back to the now pathetic Lewis McPhail, his face pale and crumpled.

'I think you're too much of a nugget to do this, Lewis, *but* if we find even a suggestion that you've done anything you shouldn't have, we'll be back, and we won't be as understanding as we've been today. I'll have you charged and on remand in Inverness jail, you feel me, bro?' said Max in an approximation of Lewis's faux accent.

'Is that it, then?' said Lewis.

'No, Lewis. That's not it. Cannabis is still a criminal matter, and you were stalking Afrodita.'

Lewis said nothing and lowered his head.

'But all that can wait. We'll get you out of here, but don't think for one second we'll not be back if we find anything else.'

'Aye. I understand.' He scratched his scalp vigorously. 'One thing?' said Lewis. 'I hope you find her, she's a nice wee girl. Too bloody good for me, that's for sure.'

'Interview terminated,' said Max, adding in the date and time and getting Lewis to sign the seals for the DVDs that had been used to record the interview. Within a few minutes he was processed by the custody sergeant and had been shown out of the police station.

'How do I get home?'

'Call your mum, although I think your chances are limited,' said Janie.

'Can't you give me a lift?'

'Let me think about that.' Janie paused for a full thirty seconds. 'No. Bye, Lewis. The walk will do you good.' Janie waggled her fingers in a wave.

Max smiled as the hunched-shouldered figure slouched off. 'You're harsh.'

'Wee bloody ned, he is.'

'Do you believe him?'

'Aye, you?'

'As much as I could believe an Ali G–impersonating loser like that. I don't see him doing anything to Affi.' Max shrugged.

DI Calman appeared at the door, a cigarette in his mouth and lighter in his hand. 'Any good?' he asked through pursed lips as he applied the flame.

'He sent her a stupid message, has stalked her and had fifty quid worth of weed, but I don't think he had anything to do with her disappearance. He's too much of a bampot.'

'How long's he bailed for?'

'A week.'

'Does he have a phone to interrogate?'

'He does, but we can take that on if you like? We have some specialist kit available.'

'That'd be great. There's a bloody huge backlog on phone forensics, so it'd be a massive help, particularly if you share the results with us.' He yawned, exhaustion written across his face.

'Of course, we will, boss,' said Max, smiling.

'Okay, we'll deal with him for it all, thanks for your help, but I wish we had something else to go on.'

'Our phone specialist is a real ninja at it, so we'll soon know if Lewis was lying, and maybe we can do some more work around Afrodita's phone.'

'Keep me informed, yeah?' he said, tossing the cigarette and grinding it under his shoe.

'No problem. One thing, boss, do you know a cop at Dingwall called Luigi?'

'Aye, Luigi Ricci, one of the community officers. Don't know much about him; he's been up here less than a year. He transferred from Glasgow, why?'

'He dealt with the ned ex-boyfriend when he was hassling her. Just wondering whether it's worth speaking to him,' said Max.

'Probably not if reputations are correct.'

'Not great?'

'Lazy bugger by all accounts. Often hard to find him. Right, I gotta go. I have a MIT team arriving soon to take over the murder, thank Christ.' He nodded and went back inside the station.

'What's next?' said Janie.

'I have an idea, and I know just the man to help. Seen Barney recently?'

'Isn't he out and about in his van?'

'Let's see.' Max pulled out his phone and dialled.

'Ayup, Max lad. What gives?' Barney was ex security services who worked freelance for the team as a 'technical attack consultant', but could turn his hand to anything related to surveillance, or communications interception.

Max explained the situation with Lewis McPhail's phone. 'What can we do with it? I think there's a possibility that whoever has taken Afrodita could have been using her phone to track her, bearing in mind that she was taken away from a cnoc in the Highlands.'

'Well, I can download his phone easy enough. What sort of phone does yon lass have?'

'An iPhone. We have the number and account details.'

'Password?'

'Unknown.'

'I'll probably need that to access her GPS, but you never know, I may be able to find a workaround.'

'Okay, we'll start making our way to you. Are you far away?'

'Nah. You never know, mate. I know a few shortcuts; you don't spend the amount of time I have fiddling with phones to not know a few little tricks. Send me all the info you have and I'll start digging about, and get the phone to me asap.'

'Janie's sending it now. Where are you?' Max nodded at Janie, who pulled her own phone out and began tapping and swiping.

'Plockton.'

'What you doing there?'

'Well, you lot have been keeping me so busy that I've been staying in me camper van rather than toing and froing to Leeds. As there was nowt on, I decided to take a trip out west. Plockton's lovely, palm trees and everything; well, it did until they fell down a while ago. Weather's been champion.'

'I know it well. Stay there and we'll head down. Do you have your kit with you for a phone download?'

'Of course, always prepared, me,' said Barney, his Yorkshire accent warm and rounded.

'Are you staying there tonight?'

'Aye, it's dead quiet and I've a nice spot on the harbourside, and I've had a couple of beers, so I guess I'm not driving anywhere with the Scottish drink-drive limits.'

'See you in a couple of hours,' said Max, hanging up.

Janie looked at her watch. 'We're going now, then?'

'No time like the present, right? It's almost four now, there by six and then let Barney do his thing. Not in a rush to go anywhere, are you?'

'As if. I want to find this girl.'

'Cool. Let's go to see our geriatric ex-spy.'

12

AFRODITA GAZED AT the large, red-stoned tenement building in an untidy street somewhere in Glasgow. They were sitting outside in the Volvo, Jetmir at the wheel, Sheff next to Afrodita in the rear. Both had smoked almost constantly during the three-hour journey south along the A9 and the air was thick with an acrid stench, which had given her a pulsating headache. Jetmir's persistent body odour really didn't help either and served as a reminder to Affi just how far she'd progressed, and how far Jetmir, the man she once idolised and feared, had fallen. She looked at the back of his head, the hair lifeless and greasy.

'What are you staring at?' he said, his eyes on her via the mirror.

Affi's stomach lurched, and she cast her eyes down to her lap. She knew she mustn't anger him – that would only end up in a beating.

The journey had meant little to Afrodita, and she didn't take in any of the route beyond signs welcoming them to Glasgow. Her heart sank at the realisation of what the building represented, and what was likely to be happening within. She was only too aware of what some of the older trafficked girls were required to do once set up in buildings like these. She knew what a brothel was, and the thought of it caused a wave of nausea to sweep over her. She breathed the fetid air in an effort to clear the cloying sensation. She had fooled around with a few boys, Lewis included, but she was still a virgin. She felt her face flush and hot tears seep from her eyes as the realisation began to bite.

She was going to be forced to sleep with men, men who would pay Sheff to sleep with her. She shuddered at the thought.

The tears flowed even more, and she swallowed what felt like a golf ball. She had to hold herself together, for Melodi's sake.

'This will be your home from now on, Affi. Remember what we said. No doubt you'd be able to escape should you wish to do so, but that won't do you any good. We found you once, and we'll find you again, and of course . . . Your sister Melodi . . .' Sheff left the sentence hanging but raised her phone so that Afrodita could see the screen. Her heart lurched as she saw the tiny, slight form of dear, sweet Melodi sitting on a step outside the drab children's home.

Afrodita almost felt her heart tear in two at the sight of her beloved sister. She had grown so much, but at the same time was almost waif-like, and her face was just so pale that she felt the tears well in her eyes again. 'Please, not Melodi,' she said in a hoarse whisper.

'Don't cry, zemra, she'll be safe, and she'll be left alone in Tirana as long as you do as you're told. Do you understand?' said Sheff, her voice syrupy and full of unpleasant sympathy. Her use of the term of endearment, zemra, Albanian for 'heart', was full of implied malice. Her meaning was clear. It was a threat.

The silence in the car was almost turgid and overpowering. Not Melodi. She'd do anything to protect poor, sweet Melodi.

'I said, do you understand?' Sheff repeated, with steel in her voice.

'Yes,' Afrodita whispered.

'Then come inside. There's food ready and you need to shower. You stink, and you start working in two days. You too, Jetmir. She has an excuse to stink, you don't.' It was telling as to the relationship between Sheff and Jetmir that he didn't react to this slur.

They got out of the car and walked up the weed-cracked path

that led to the door of the tenement. Sheff unlocked it and they all filed into a dingy communal area. She unlocked another door and Afrodita found herself in a tidy, warm flat. She breathed in a heady scent that was tinged with cigarette smoke and the faint aroma of fried onions. Her stomach growled, and despite the gnawing fear that she was trying to contain, she was suddenly aware that apart from a sandwich, she hadn't eaten for what felt like days. The muscle memory of her desire to survive that had been born from those years on the streets in Tirana rose to the fore. She'd get through this. She had to.

'This is your room,' said Sheff, opening a chipped, painted door.

The room was clean and smelled of paint and air freshener. Looking on the windowsill, she saw a glass bottle with several reeds sunk into some pale liquid, like one she had in her bedroom at home. The floral scent was overpowering and yet curiously comforting.

There was a double bed in the centre of the room, and a lava lamp boiled and churned on a bedside table. A newish towel was spread across the cheap-looking white duvet cover. A string of fairy lights had been tacked to the wall, and a large print of a shapely, naked woman adorned the opposite wall. There was what looked like a newly assembled wardrobe in the corner, with mirrors affixed to the doors. The windows were covered by louvred wooden shutters, and it seemed like there was no obvious way to open them. A large, full-length mirror was fixed to the wall opposite the bed, with a TV on a wall bracket next to it. Whilst the sight of the place made Afrodita feel sick, she was simultaneously pleased that it was clean, warm and dry. Memories swirled of sleeping in doorways in Tirana, always at risk from thieves and predatory men. Terrible as her current situation was, it was still better than that dreadful time in Albania.

'You can't see it, Affi, but there is a camera in here. We see everything that you do, okay? For your protection, and ours.

Most clients will be nice, but just in case . . .' She left the sentence hanging.

Afrodita said nothing. She just looked around the room, realisation arriving like a truck that this was real. This was happening.

She was going to be forced to be a prostitute.

'You like?' said Jetmir.

Afrodita couldn't find the words to answer; it felt like she was watching herself from above, wanting to scream out loud and run. To get out and go to the police. She trusted Scottish police, they helped her before, but the image of Melodi loomed and pushed the urge away.

'I'll show you the bathroom. You need to be clean, to clean your teeth, to trim and paint your nails,' said Sheff, her bright-red lips parting, showing her large teeth, asymmetric and crowded. The smile was unpleasant in its insincerity and her eyes were blank and flat. 'You're a beautiful young girl, my darling. The clients will pay big money to spend time with you, so you need to look your best. If you work well and make them happy, I'll pay you good money, feed you nice food and give you lovely clothes. But if you make them unhappy, you will suffer. It's an easy choice, no?'

Afrodita felt her face begin to flush again, resolve gripping her insides. Her time in Albania had left her with many scars, but it had also left her with an overwhelming desire to survive. And, now, an almost overpowering urge to keep Melodi safe.

'Yes. An easy choice.'

13

'THERE'S OUR AGEING ex-spook,' said Janie as they pulled into the long, narrow car park by the harbour in Plockton, a small village in Wester Ross known for its microclimate and the fact that it was the only place in the Highlands that could grow palm trees – until a storm had recently blown them down.

A blue VW California camper van was parked close to the wall that separated the tarmac from the empty, muddy and rocky beach. The tide was far out, and the vista was interrupted by only a few scabby-looking boats listing in the sand, rusting chains hanging from their bows. The evening sun was weak and milky, casting long shadows across the almost deserted car park. The distant sea sparkled as rays of light danced on the surface. The hills across the harbour were clothed in evergreen, vivid and stark against the cobalt sky. It was stunningly peaceful. Barney was sitting on a folding chair next to his van and a smoking barbeque; he was dressed in an ancient green fleece and baggy zebra shorts. Incongruously, he was wearing wellington boots. He raised a hand without looking back as Max parked nearby.

'Now then,' he said, flipping a burger on the compact grill, the roll-up between his lips wobbling as he spoke. The air was redolent with the savoury smell of the frying patty. He turned and smiled, his blue eyes twinkling. A bottle of beer was tucked into the armrest of his chair. He gave off a sense of utter contentment.

'Nice spot. You look relaxed,' said Max.

'I am. I was even more relaxed before you buggers made me think of work. Got the lad's phone?'

Max handed him Lewis McPhail's phone. Barney turned it over in his hands and went to the side door of the van and pulled out a battered laptop bedecked with Leeds United stickers. He plugged the phone into a cable which he attached to the computer. 'PIN?' he asked.

Max told him.

Barney nodded, and busied himself with the phone and laptop for a few moments before setting them down on the seat in the van. 'It'll take a minute or two. I'll do a full extraction including deleted messages, emails and browsing. Fancy a burger?'

'Aye, I'm starving,' said Max.

'Me too,' said Janie.

Barney reached into a cool box by his chair and pulled out a pack of burgers. He separated two and threw them on the grill, which crackled and spat as the flames danced.

'Staying here long?' asked Max.

'No idea. Depends on what I find on this phone, I imagine.' He turned to Max, his eyes creasing with a mischievous smile.

There was a muffled 'ping' from the van. 'And on cue, download complete,' said Barney, standing up and picking up his laptop, which he disconnected from the phone. He tapped at the keys. 'Just extracting data into an Excel for messages and Es. Hold up. I'll just throw a couple of keywords at it, and look at recent time parameters.' He began to whistle tunelessly, his brow furrowed in intense concentration.

'Interesting,' he said.

'What?'

'He has a Samsung, so why was he accessing an Apple account? What was her email address again?'

Janie read it out from her phone.

'The little beggar,' said Barney.

'Barney, please. Just spit it out,' said Max.

'He was hacking her account. He logged into it after she went missing. Hold up. Yep, the little shite had hacked her phone many times. Her password was JockTheJack, capital J, capital T, capital J. If I access her iPhone account it'll give me GPS data. Give me a second, and keep an eye on the burgers.' Barney continued to tap at the computer, his tongue wedged into the corner of his mouth, his eyes narrowed.

'What about two-factor authentications?' said Janie.

'Please, it's me you're talking to, love. 2FA, my arse. Won't take long.' Barney shook his head and smiled.

Janie shrugged, took a pair of tongs and flipped all the burgers whilst Barney tapped away.

'Her GPS data shows her going up Fyrish until the phone goes off the network totally under an hour later. It then comes back on right by the car park at the foot of the hill about thirty minutes later just for a moment.'

'So, she definitely got off the hill. That's useful. What else?'

'Well, your pal Lewis McPhail didn't even try and disguise his ISP with a VPN, the bloody amateur. He was at his parents' place and used their Wi-Fi.'

'He's only twenty.'

'Aye, well. Wouldn't have done him any good, anyway. He accessed it a few times some months ago, and then after the young lass went missing. Just the once, mind.' He paused to take a swig from his can of lager his eyes narrowed in concentration.

'Is that it?'

'Nope. Not even a bit. Someone else accessed it,' he said.

'What?'

'Aye. It was accessed from an account in Dingwall.'

'And?'

'Hold up, just accessing ISP records.'

'How can you do that from here?' said Janie, incredulously.

'Never you mind, love. You'll need to parallel prove this from official records, but it was definitely accessed.'

'From where?'

'It was accessed from a computer at Dingwall Police Station.'

'What?' said Max, his eyes wide.

'Aye, that's what I thought.'

'Well, maybe that possibly makes sense. I mean they were looking for her. Maybe someone worked out her password, or similar,' said Janie.

'I doubt it,' said Barney.

'Why?'

'I'm not sure how they bypassed two-factor authentications, but it was accessed two hours before she went missing.'

14

'SHIT,' SAID MAX. 'Someone had unrestricted access to her GPS; they would know exactly where she was at any time.'

'Aye, that's about the size of it. They could follow her on a map easily, but how would they know where she was headed if they wanted to get ahead of her?' said Barney.

'Social media's curse, Barney. They didn't need to find out as she'd already announced to all her followers that she was headed up Fyrish,' said Janie.

'And somehow, they knew who she was, where she lived and where she had come from. That's inside information. Anything else obvious from the Evanton massive's phone downloaded, yet?' said Max.

'Just checking,' said Barney, taking another swig from his beer can.

'Search for Luigi in the messages,' said Max.

Janie raised her eyebrows; she didn't need to ask what Max's reasoning was.

'A minute, them burgers are ready, by the way. Buns in the cooler,' said Barney, tapping at the keys.

Max opened the cooler lid and pulled out three burger buns. Within seconds there were three burgers loaded with sauce on a single paper plate as Barney worked.

'Aye, got it here. Luigi is in McPhail's contact list.' Barney sat back and grabbed a burger, taking a big bite. 'Hungry work this.'

'Why would a local dealer have a local cop's number in his phone? I'm assuming it's a personal phone, as well. They don't issue mobiles to uniform cops; they use their airwaves for job use.'

'Informant?'

'I doubt it. He doesn't sound the type of cop, and they use specialist CHIS units. I'd say Luigi is a dodgy bastard. We probably need to get Ross on board with this. I reckon we have enough to move on him, or at least put a surveillance team behind him. Janie, can you message Norma and get her building a profile, in case we need to move fast.'

'It's still circumstantial, though. Will it even satisfy a surveillance authority application?'

Max paused, thinking it over. All they had was the fact that a community cop had direct contact with a suspect. Using a personal phone wasn't usual, but it also wasn't unheard of.

'I'd say it's more than circumstantial,' said Barney, through a mouthful of burger.

'Why?'

'Three months ago, Lewis sent a message to a contact listed as "Luigi-Fed". It was in his deleted messages, but I've retrieved it.'

'What'd it say?' said Max, feeling his skin start to prickle.

'JockTheJack, capital J, capital T, capital J.'

Max pulled his phone from his pocket and dialled.

'About bloody time. Where the hell are you two?'

'Ross, we have an issue.'

'Now how did I fucking know you were going to say that? Why don't you ever call me to tell me something nice. What type of issue?'

'Bent cop issues.'

'Where are you?'

'Plockton.'

'Are you with that senile old duffer?'

'Aye.'

'Give it to me then,' said Ross with a deep sigh.

Max told him everything.

'So, looks like we have a Dingwall cop hacking a kidnap victim's phone shortly before she goes missing. We need to get moving on this and I need to brief the boss.' Ross's voice, so usually full of bumptious sarcasm, was serious.

'Shall we head south?'

'No, not yet. Let's see what develops first. You may be better placed there.'

'Maybe. Can we get Norma to do some digging on PC Luigi Ricci at Dingwall? I think Afrodita is out there, somewhere, and we need to find her. That cop is the key to it, leastways, he's the best lead we have.'

'I'm on it,' said Norma, clearly listening in.

'Okay, you two hold fire there, do whatever shite you need, work up what you can with grandpa spook, and we'll touch base later once we know what's what with our dodgy cop, yeah. Maybe book yourselves into hotels, does Barney need one?'

'No, he's in his van.'

'He's a weird bugger. Why's he staying in a stupid rust-bucket of a van with a bloody chemical potty and no telly? Hasn't he got a bloody house?'

'He likes the simple life.'

'Aye, well, simple creature, simple life.'

'What's next then?' said Max.

'Norma is working up a profile for PC Ricci now then we'll make a decision, but we already know that he was ex central Glasgow but got transferred under a cloud, something to do with being found in a brothel,' said Ross, a self-satisfied tone replacing his normal machine-gun-like patter.

'How do you know that already?' said Max, puzzled.

'Because of my inspired and instinctive leadership. I'm a world-class detective, you know,' said Ross.

'Janie messaged me a while ago, after someone mentioned his name; she said it didn't sound right,' said Norma, her voice tinny.

'Craigie, will you get bloody hold of your subordinates, eh? You clearly have no idea what's going on.' Ross's serious voice was replaced with the more usual sardonic tone.

'Right, if you can pause the abuse for a while, I'll go and source us a hotel.'

'Stay by the phone, Max. We may need to move fast,' said Ross, hanging up.

15

PC LUIGI RICCI was sitting in a garage forecourt just outside Evanton sipping a coffee he had purchased after refuelling the small liveried hatchback. It had been a long shift, full of tedious weariness, with residents complaining about dog shit on the pavement, noisy neighbours and errant kids. It was just so bloody boring.

The burner phone he always kept in his kit bag buzzed. With what had been happening recently, he had kept it permanently switched on. He frowned as he looked at the number, which he didn't recognise.

'Yeah?'

'Luigi, it's Lewis.'

'Why are you calling me? I gave you my number for one fucking reason, son, and it wasn't for you to call me for a blether.'

'Aye, I know, man. I'm sorry. I've just been bloody nicked though. Two cops from the central belt just took me in.'

'Who were they?' He felt his stomach tighten but kept his voice even.

'Just two cops, one called Max Craigie, the other was called Janie, I think.'

'What does this have to do with me?'

'It was about Affi going missing.'

'What? What the fuck did it have to do with you?' He felt a sudden jab of nausea at the mention of the girl.

'They found a message I sent to her a while ago on Insta.'

'So? She was your girlfriend.' He felt his face flushing even more and it felt like his guts were being squeezed.

'I only sent it a wee while back. I was pished and got mad.'

'What did you send?'

'I called her an Albanian bitch.'

'You bloody idiot. What did they do?'

'They took me to Burnett Road and interviewed me.'

'Please tell me you said nothing.'

The pause told him everything.

'What did you bloody say?'

'I just said I knew nothing, but sent her a nasty message when steaming. They also found my weed supply.'

Luigi exhaled. That wasn't too bad. He didn't care a bit if that stupid bastard got himself in a bother. 'So how does this affect me?'

'They took my phone. They said they were going to download it.'

'Yeah, but that won't help them, will it? You ditched the phone, after you sent me her password, right?'

There was another pause on the phone.

'Lewis, tell me you ditched that phone after you sent me that bloody message.'

'It was a new iPhone, cost me a fortune . . .' His voice trailed off, the nervousness detectable.

'You idiot, you fucking idiot. I *told* you to ditch the phone, after you were stupid enough to send me a bloody text with that password.'

'Sorry . . .'

'Don't bloody sorry me, you nugget. First, you're daft enough to send me a text rather than tell me in person, and then, even worse, you draw attention to yourself by sending her a bloody message. Have you hacked her since then?'

'Just the once. After she went missing. I was worried, man.'

His head swirled as he tried to organise his thoughts. 'Oh man, this is bad. This is very bloody bad. You have no idea who you're dealing with here, Lewis. It's not the bloody cops you need to worry about, it's the fucking Albanians. They'll slice you up, you stupid bastard. Whose phone are you calling from?'

'My mum's.'

'Your *mum's*? Stay out of the way, Lewis. In fact, I'd get the fuck out of town, if I was you. If the Albanians think you're a liability, then they'll come for you. In fact, screw that, *I'll* come for you. Now fuck off.' He hung up, his heart beating like a drum in his chest. He rubbed his hands through his thinning, dark hair. This was bad. This was very bad. He leaned back in his patrol car, his hands trembling as he tucked his phone into his pocket. He cursed himself for being so bloody stupid and weak, and for what? A free shag with a young Albanian hooker in Glasgow a couple of years ago?

His career was already dead. Cast out to the bloody backwater of Dingwall as a community officer, far from his previous job on a proactive crime team in Glasgow.

How could he have been so stupid. 'Shit, shit, shit,' he muttered to himself as his mind raced. They had the stupid bastard's phone, which meant they'd soon know that they'd been in contact with each other; he was glad he'd used a burner phone. Lewis assured him that he'd deleted the message, but you never knew what the capabilities were of some of these central teams. That poor girl was probably in a brothel somewhere, so it was just a matter of time before she was found. He had no choice. He had to warn them. They had to get rid of her, either out of the country, or . . . He didn't want to think about the alternative.

He dialled a number from memory.

'Yes?' answered an accented female voice.

'It's Luigi.'

'Louie, darling, what can I do for you, and why you not visit me anymore? I have some girls you'll like.' She giggled.

'It's about the girl. Cops are on this case, they'll be closing in on you soon. They'll probably soon know I used her phone to track her and tell you where she'd be. I can't get dragged in for this. You need to let her go, then maybe it'll be okay.'

There was a long pause on the other end of the line.

'You worry too much, Lou-Lou. It'll all be fine. She's very beautiful, you should come see her. I let you have one for free with her, baby.' Her voice was simpering and gooey.

'But it's gonna get really bloody heavy. Central squads are looking for her. They have her ex-boyfriend's phone; that means they might find out she was hacked. The net will close. I know how these things work. If they find her, we're all screwed, you know that.'

'Louie, she wouldn't say anything even if cops had her in a room all to themselves. We know where her only living relative is in Albania. We have photographs of her and we'll make sure she knows that one word from her will be very bad for her little sister. Albanian brothels aren't as nice as one of mine, you know.' She giggled, and it was a singularly unpleasant sound.

'Why not just let her go?'

The same long pause. When she spoke next her voice was flatter and harder. 'Louie, she belongs to me, now. She owes us a lot of money, and she's going nowhere. You do what you must do to keep police off the case. If police come to my door looking for Affi, I may just show them the photos I have, Lou-Lou. Remember those photos, baby? You have such odd urges and desires. What would your wife and kids think, eh? Or your employer when we load them onto every social media platform, eh? "Cop snorts cocaine from young prostitute's breasts." That'll be on the front page of every newspaper, no?'

Luigi opened his mouth to argue, but then thought again. He

knew enough about the woman to know that it wouldn't help. She was a malicious witch who enjoyed a sense of power like this. He took a deep breath to steady himself.

'Okay, okay. I'll put up some smoke screens, maybe some diversions.'

'Good boy, good boy. Now come and see me soon. You can try out Affi, she's very beautiful.' And with that, she was gone.

Luigi sat there, his mind feeling like it had been shocked with electricity. Slowly he began to regain control of his thoughts. He had a sudden jolt of realisation. He had no choice; he'd have to make the call that he promised he'd never make.

He dialled another number from memory.

'Why are you calling me on an open fucking line?' The voice was sharp and accusatory.

'Sorry, I forgot. I'll ditch the SIM after the call, we're good.'

'You idiot. Fresh SIM and use WhatsApp. You know that.'

'It's a fresh SIM, never been used,' he lied, ignoring the calls he'd just made and received. It didn't pay to annoy this particular individual.

'Okay, make it quick.'

Luigi breathed deeply. 'We have a big problem.'

16

AFRODITA WAS SITTING on the bed in her room, an unfinished sandwich lay on a plate next to her alongside a bottle of mineral water that she had drunk from. She had no appetite, but her mouth was permanently dry, like sandpaper.

She'd just been left in the room on her own, the TV in the corner switched on, although she hardly looked at it, her thoughts being full of Melodi and her foster family. Tears welled in her eyes as she imagined her little sister in that putrid home in Tirana. She shivered, pulling on the thick, towelling robe that Sheff had made her wear. There were no clothes in the room at all, and Afrodita thought that was probably to dissuade her from leaving.

The door handle rattled, causing her to flinch a little as Jetmir walked in, some clothes and a pair of shoes in his hands. 'Put these on,' he said, tossing them onto the bed.

'Where are we going?' she said, her voice trembling.

'It's photo time.'

Afrodita looked at the garments. A short plaid skirt, long knee socks, a white shirt, and a maroon-and-blue tie, not too dissimilar to the one she wore for school. Shoes were a pair of Converse sneakers.

'Jetmir, please, I don't want to,' she began, but stopped with a cry as he strode towards her, his face screwed up in anger.

'I don't want to fucking hear it. Get the fucking clothes on now.' He grabbed her arm and squeezed hard, his nails digging into her flesh, his face close to hers. His body odour had been replaced by a less sour, musty scent, but his breath smelled strongly of tobacco and vodka and his eyes were glazed and red. He looked frankly pathetic. What she'd remembered from her time with him all those years ago had gone. He was no longer the well-dressed rapper; he was just a skinny, grimy fool.

'Jetmir, get off me,' she said sharply, her eyes narrow, but he just squeezed tighter, and she cried out at the intense pain as he pinched hard at the flesh on her arm.

Jetmir pushed his face closer to hers and hissed, 'It's only because Sheff wants your face unmarked that I'm not slapping you now, you bitch. Now get dressed, and put some lipstick on. Bright red, like the slut you are. You have five minutes.' He pushed her back onto the bed and stormed out of the room.

Tears pricked at her eyes, but she wiped them away, realising that she had no choice if she was to make sure that Melodi was safe.

She shrugged off her robe, noting how thin her normally lean frame was looking already. She'd barely eaten anything since she'd been grabbed, and her head spun as she stood looking at herself. This was no good, she suddenly decided. If she was to get out of this shit situation, she'd need to keep her strength up. She quickly dressed in the clothes, noting with distaste how short the skirt was, and how tight the shirt was as she buttoned it up. She applied some vivid red lipstick and flicked a little mascara on her already thick lashes. When she was done, she picked up the sandwich and took a large bite. Peanut butter, she realised, but she barely tasted it. She normally loved peanut butter, but it tasted rank and bitter. Still, she forced herself to swallow it down.

She was still chewing as she laced her sneakers when Jetmir returned to the room, a camera in his hand. She stood as he entered, her stomach feeling like it was being gripped by a large fist.

He stopped as if rooted to the spot, transfixed by the sight of her as he looked her up and down, a grin spreading across his thick lips.

Afrodita shuddered involuntarily at his gaze, which would more correctly be called a leer.

'Affi, you look so pretty,' he slurred, moving towards her. His smile was wide, but his eyes were flat. She felt herself shiver again, her face flushing as he approached her, the camera held loosely in his hand. She instinctively backed away, but stopped when her legs connected with the wooden frame of the double bed. Something inside her forced her to remain standing, almost in defiance.

Jetmir came so close that she could feel his breath and the smell of vodka was stronger than ever. He raised his hand and touched her cheek, gently, moving his fingers up to stroke her hair, which was still tied back in a ponytail.

'You've grown so much, Affi, no longer the child I brought here, are you?' He leaned forward, and she knew at that moment he was going to kiss her. Her mind whirled. What should she do? She wanted to kick him, punch him, force her nails into his eyes and fucking gouge them out, but the image of Melodi stopped her, and she just stood stock still, like a shop mannequin, rooted to the spot. His head came a little closer, the rank smell of his breath jolting her.

'Get the fuck away from me,' she hissed, with real venom in her voice.

Jetmir just stood there, inches away from her, his rancid breath in her face. The air in the room was turgid and thick, and the only sound was the faint murmur from the TV flickering in the corner. 'Oh, Affi, you've got spiky as you've got older, I like that,' he said, his lips pulling back in a wolfish grin, exposing his stained and decaying teeth.

'Jetmir,' came a sharp voice from the open door. Afrodita turned and saw Sheff standing there, hands on hips, together with a brute of a man who stared straight past Jetmir to Afrodita, an unpleasant look on his face. He wore a suit that he was almost bursting out of, he was so huge. His face was heavy, his brow low over piggy eyes. He looked dangerous and nasty as he leered at Afrodita.

Jetmir flinched, just a touch, and backed away, the smile disappearing from his face.

'W . . . we're about to take photos,' he stammered.

'I can see. You don't interfere with the merchandise, Jetmir. Ever. You know this. Now take the photographs and then take her out to the postbox for a verification shot. I'm uploading her onto the website today, and we start with clients tomorrow.' Sheff stood there, feet planted firmly on the floor, hands on hips. She was a formidable woman, and she scared Afrodita witless. She knew that she had no choice, none whatsoever, but to cooperate.

'Okay, sorry,' said Jetmir, a look on his face like an errant child.

'Who's this beautiful creature?' said the large man in gravelly Albanian, his eyes shining as he licked his lips.

'My new girl. Not for you yet, Enver. She's just getting settled in, and I think you'd be too much for her.' She giggled, placing a hand on his arm.

'Shame, she's very beautiful.'

'I have a nice girl at my West End place for you, darling. Affi is our prize asset, but is off limits for a little while.'

'Don't worry, I can wait.' He shrugged his massive shoulders, staring intently at Afrodita.

Afrodita cast her eyes to the shiny laminate floor and nodded, her shoulders sagging; she knew she was all out of options.

'Now make sexy photos, Affi. You'll be so popular, I'll be able to send you only the nicest of men, not big brutes like Enver here.' She smiled widely, but it was a deeply unpleasant expression. Sheff nodded as if satisfied, turned on her heel and headed towards the door.

Enver looked crestfallen, before his face hardened again. 'Time for payment, Toka. The boss is impatient, and West End brothel is now due. How long until this place is earning money?'

'Come to the office and we'll discuss it there. I have a nice bottle of raki in the fridge, darling.'

'Raki? I'd rather have whisky,' said Enver, screwing up his face.

'Whisky it is then, come on.' She took the man's massive arm and led him away.

'Let's go to postbox,' said Jetmir, who had now regained his bravado after his scolding from Sheff, although it had definitely taken a knock. He looked a little downcast, and it was obvious that he was terrified of Sheff. Afrodita wondered if this could be used to her advantage. No way was she going to let the disgusting creature near her, if she could avoid it.

'Why do we need to go to the postbox?' said Afrodita, furrowing her brow.

'Verification shot for internet. Come on, it's only a hundred metres away. Put this on.' He threw her a three-quarter-length wool coat, which she slipped on. They left the house and set off along the uneven pavement on the street of tenement buildings. She looked around but could see no road signs, or clues as to her exact location. It was disconcerting to have absolutely no idea where she was. Even though she was in a city, with people, shops, phone boxes and cafés, it felt like she was in an alien environment.

The light was beginning to fade as they walked down the street at a brisk pace. The thought occurred to Afrodita that she could just run. She was fit, and she was fast. There's no way that Jetmir, with his smoking and drinking habit, would catch her. She looked behind her and saw that the street was empty. It would be so easy. Just do it, run like she was in a race. She glanced around again, her head swivelling left and right.

Jetmir looked at her, his eyes narrowing. 'Just in case you're thinking of running, Affi . . .' He held up his phone as they walked: a photograph filled the large screen, pin sharp and vivid.

Afrodita stopped dead in the street, eyes glued to the screen. Melodi was sitting on a pavement next to a young girl of a similar age. They were both smiling and were in front of a drab, grey building with a sign outside that Afrodita couldn't read. She still spoke Albanian well, but had never mastered reading it. She knew, though, that it was the children's home that Melodi lived in.

'You bastard,' she said, eyes blazing as she looked directly at Jetmir, who just smirked.

'Don't do anything stupid, Affi. Just don't. Come on, let's keep going. The light's fading and we have to get this done.'

Afrodita squared her shoulders and wordlessly followed in Jetmir's footsteps, feeling her insides begin to boil in a mix of terror and rage. How had this happened? What had she and Melodi done to deserve this?

'Here, hold this,' said Jetmir, handing her a newspaper as they arrived at a red postbox at the end of the road.

'Why?'

'Affi, will you just do as you're told? Open your coat and show your outfit, look sexy and hold the newspaper up in front of you. Can you manage that without moaning?' he said, his face flushing.

'I just wanted to know.'

'It's because the website has to prove you're a real person, in a real area with today's date. That's it, now fucking pose. Pout your lips and look sexy. You better get used to this, or so help me God, you'll regret it. The people in charge wouldn't hesitate to have someone throw acid in your little sister's face, so do as you're fucking told.' He spat the words out with real venom, his face flushed and his eyes dark.

Terror and horror gripped Afrodita, but she did as she was told. She opened the coat and posed, a foot pointed out, her free hand lifting the hem of her skirt showing the expanse of slim thigh. She pouted her lips, just like she used to for her Instagram posts, before she discovered athletics. This seemed to calm Jetmir, who raised his camera and began snapping.

'That's better, super-sexy girl. If Sheff wasn't such a bitch we'd have fun together, Affi,' he said, laughing.

'Is that it?' said Afrodita, her voice hard as she stared defiantly at Jetmir.

'Yeah, that's it. Come on, back home for more photos. On the bed this time, maybe show a little more, no?'

Afrodita said nothing. She handed the newspaper back to Jetmir and folded her coat back around her, covering her terrible clothes, a mixture of shame and fear making her skin prickle.

One day, she'd make Jetmir pay. He'd pay for everything, but not now, and not here. An image of her sister swam into her mind and her resolve returned.

She had to survive. To keep on living, and one day her chance would come. And when it did come, they'd regret taking her.

They'd regret the day they ever met Afrodita Dushku.

17

'SO, WHAT DO you know?' said Max without preamble, answering Norma's call as he sat in the passenger seat of the Volvo. Janie was steering through the dark, narrow Highland roads on their way back to Evanton. They couldn't decide the best place to locate themselves, but it seemed logical to be as close to where Affi had disappeared from, and close to Dingwall, even though they hadn't hatched a plan, yet.

'Well, our friend Luigi Ricci is a bit of a one, I must say,' said Norma, her voice distorted through the car's speakers.

'Meaning?' said Max.

'As we thought. He was working on a proactive squad in Glasgow targeting street vice and low-level drug dealing. A raid on a pop-up brothel in Glasgow went down whilst he was on leave, and he was caught, as they say, in flagrante delicto by his own squad. They'd mostly been working on managing the tolerance zones, where the sex workers are basically allowed to operate, but they would also work against the pop-up brothels that had been appearing and hit them with closure notices. He was lucky; there was little obvious evidence of it being a brothel, no madam, no piles of contraceptives and the like. Just him and a girl, who was unknown as a sex worker, so he managed to talk his way out of it.'

'How?' said Janie.

'Not clear. He claimed that he'd just met her in a bar, and she'd brought him to the joint. No one was prosecuted, insufficient evidence, but he was carpeted and kicked off the squad. He found himself transferred to the Highlands and Islands and wound up at Dingwall working as a local community officer that covered Evanton. That's what was on the file, anyway.' Norma paused, and it was clear that there was more.

'I'm sensing there's something else,' said Max.

'The intelligence was that a new high-class brothel was being set up in Glasgow by an Albanian madam backed by an Albanian OCG. It was a nice house in a decent bit of the south side of Glasgow and had been refurbed to a high standard, so the feeling was they were setting up a proper high-end joint. Again, post incident intel was that Albanians had set the place up with a madam, but they busted it before she really got going. It seems that the new MO is to set up much higher-end brothels, with decent surroundings, attractive girls with prices to match.'

'Who was the madam?' said Janie.

'Albanian lady. Toka Kurti. I've emailed some bits over to you. She's no convictions for running brothels, although there's plenty of intelligence that she has done so. Seems to be very much a Teflon brothel keeper, which is worrying.'

'I heard of her when I was on vice a few years ago. Albanians were really taking over vice in the central belt and her name was mentioned. Never had anything solid on her, though, but if she had a tame cop, that's probably why,' said Janie as she manoeuvred the big car along the dark, twisting road.

'Anything else?' said Max.

'Ross put the feelers out and as always, rumours abound. Ricci was widely unpopular and considered by most of his team members, particularly the women, to be a creep who would get far too close to the working girls, so . . .'

'Rather than discipline him, they transferred him,' said Max.

'That's about the size of it. Typical police mismanagement of unsavoury types.'

'Where's Ross?' asked Max.

'He went to see the chief, who isn't at all happy. Seems we're getting far too good at our jobs, but he wants action.'

'I can imagine. Any ideas on timelines?'

'No time to waste. Tentative plan is to get hold of Ricci when he logs on at Dingwall nick tomorrow. We have force IT setting up a mirror on his work computer. I think the feeling is right now that we don't have enough. All we suspect is that he had Afrodita's password texted to him by Lewis McPhail, and that phone number isn't registered to him, so could be a burner, so we're stuffed if he doesn't have it on him,' said Norma, the tapping of keys audible over the line.

'How about billing on the phone, anything to support that?'

'I'm still waiting on it. It's high priority, as we have a missing teenager, but still not here. I've sent off for his phone that's registered with the police, and the number of the suspected burner that was in Lewis's phone. Also asked for bank account details and a monitoring order to see what the bugger's up to.'

'Nice work, as always. We also must assume that Lewis has called him to warn him. So, we can be sure that he'll be clearing evidence, if it's there. Also, we can't necessarily prove that it was him sat in front of the computer terminal when Affi's iPhone account was hacked. Was he stupid enough to use his own login?' asked Max.

'Force IT services are working on that. It's not that simple, particularly as Barney got the intel from, shall we say, unconventional sources?'

'Aye, I can see the issue. Maybe we need to rattle his cage, somehow?'

'Maybe, but anyway, Ross and I are heading up there imminently. I've booked hotels for all of us in Inverness.'

'Where?'

'Travelodge.'

'Classy. How long will you be?'

'Leaving now, so three or four hours. Ross has just messaged me to say he's waiting. I better go, you know his attitude to waiting more than thirty seconds. I've emailed you the research profile for Toka Kurti and what I have for Ricci, but bear in mind I'm still waiting for data, so it's incomplete,' said Norma.

'Will do. Okay, see you later.' Max hung up.

'She's an intelligence research ninja, is our Norma,' said Janie.

'She's that, all right. The document is in my inbox already. I'll have a scan,' said Max, opening the file on his phone.

'Shall I head to the hotel?' said Janie.

Max paused as he studied the detailed research document, his eyes settling on the photograph of PC Luigi Ricci, noting his dark eyes, thinning hair and heavy stubble. He looked at the address underneath and the details of the vehicles registered to the address. Max made an instant decision. 'No, let's head to Ricci's address to scope it out. Nice to get a feel for it, and Ross and Norma won't be up for a few hours.' Max programmed the address into the Volvo's sat nav and a voice announced that the route was being calculated before it flashed up on the map on the control panel.

'It's got easier being a navigator in a cop car, hasn't it? Just have to leave it to the sat nav. I miss the days of map books,' said Janie.

'Surely you're too young to remember map books,' said Max as he looked at the intelligence profile.

'I'm not that young, Max, and there's something about map books that are comforting, don't you think?'

'You're a right weirdo, Janie. I thought your generation were all about tech, social media and smartphones. And yet you love real books, vinyl records and peculiar, old music.'

'I have taste.'

'Weird-arse taste.'

Janie glanced at Max and scowled. 'His address is only ten minutes away in Dingwall which is convenient,' she said, quickly changing the subject.

'Very. Okay, he lives there with his wife and two kids, decent-sized mortgage, and they own two cars, a Ford Fiesta and an Audi RS 4. Let's go and see if they're there. We don't have the phones to tell us whether he's home or not, but the cars will be a good indicator. He was on an early shift today and starts at ten tomorrow, so he should be home.'

'What do you think of the plan to get him at work? I'm not so sure.'

'Me neither, but we're so short on evidence that it's hard to come up with a workable strategy. I think I'd rather bash his door in at 4 a.m., but we can discuss this when the others get up here.'

'We also still don't have much evidence, do we? If Luigi denies everything and has ditched his burner and didn't use his own login on the computer, what do we have?' said Janie.

'We have his association with Lewis McPhail. He'd have to explain why he sent that text.'

'Doesn't take us very far, does it? Okay, he sent her password, which may cause him a problem discipline-reg-wise, but it wouldn't satisfy a criminal court, would it?'

'I guess not, but we have more than we had, and I reckon we have to make our own luck here.'

'I've heard that before. It always ends badly,' said Janie.

*

PC Luigi Ricci's house was a nice-looking yet anonymous white-washed bungalow, in a long, wide street full of similar properties. From Max and Janie's vantage in the Volvo, tucked into a side street thirty metres from the property, the curtains were all drawn tight, but shafts of light peeked around the edges. Two cars sat on the gated block-paved drive: a dark Fiesta and a sleek Audi with a personalised plate whose numbers and letters spelled 'Luigi' if you squinted and tilted your head. The small lawn to the side of the cars was well trimmed, and hanging floral baskets swayed in the slight breeze to either side of the part-glazed front door. A cat swaggered from underneath the Audi towards the side alley that seemingly led to the back of the house. A sudden burst of harsh, white light was cast onto the drive, startling the cat which immediately disappeared.

'Security conscious, is our Luigi,' said Max.

'Aye, I saw. Motion sensor lights, a flashing alarm box, and I'm pretty sure there's a camera over the door. Won't be fun for a tech attack.'

'I'm sure our geriatric ex-spy wouldn't have too much trouble. Although the Peeping Tom neighbours may be a problem.' Max pointed at the house immediately next door, where light spilled from the curtained windows as a dark form looked out, presumably because of the security light activation.

'Is the Audi an RS 4? The wheels look wide enough,' said Janie.

Max looked down at his phone. 'Aye. Is that a fast one?'

'You know nothing about cars, do you?'

'Not a great deal. Ask me anything about motorbikes, though.'

'Yes. Very fast. 4.2 litre V8. Big, expensive car for a uniform PC to own. That's at least thirty grand worth of car, there.'

Max said nothing, just looked down at his phone again for a full minute before speaking. 'Lots of finance outstanding on it, according to Norma's document.'

'Is there anything we can achieve here?' asked Janie.

Instead of answering, Max lifted his phone to his ear.

'Max, how's it going?' said Norma.

'You on your way?'

'Aye, almost at Perth, what's up?'

'Is the phone data back?'

'Just now pinged up on my phone. What do you need?'

'Where's Luigi's phone?'

'Which one?'

'Both.'

'Personal phone last hit a cell site in Dingwall. Burner that received the text from McPhail is switched off and has been since it was sent, he's likely got a new SIM in it, I guess,' said Norma. Max could hear Ross chuntering in the background.

'What's he saying?'

'He says we get him tomorrow. No need to go in now and we need to get our heads together first.'

'Fine, any bank monitoring back?'

'Not yet, unsurprisingly.'

'Fair enough. We'll see you at the hotel.' Max hung up.

'Is that us, then?'

'Aye, let's get to the hotel. I'm hungry again, and I could murder a cranberry juice.'

Janie engaged the gear of the Volvo and eased back into the main street. As they passed the bungalow, there was a movement at the curtains: a small, pale face appeared at the window, peering out. A boy, aged about ten, looked both ways up and down the street, before a youngish woman with a kind face and short hair stood at the window. She put her arm around the boy's shoulders and guided him away from the glass, allowing the curtain to fall back into place.

'Shame,' said Max.

'Why?'

'I suspect their lives are going to get turned upside down tomorrow, when they discover whom they're living with. Nasty side of our job, right? We nick bent coppers, and we celebrate our successes, but we sometimes neglect the forgotten victims.'

'Aye. The victims aren't where you always first think they are, right?'

Max and Janie looked at each other, eyes meeting. Max nodded, his face quietly determined.

'I fancy a steak,' said Janie.

18

ALBAN HOXHAJ WAS sitting in the back of his Range Rover Sport as it sedately cruised through the West End of Glasgow. He had a large cigar clamped between his teeth that was filling the enclosed space with a choking fug. His driver, a huge man called Enver, wrinkled his nose and cranked the window down a notch as he negotiated the heavy traffic.

Hoxhaj's fat and meaty face was flushed red with anger as he listened to the Italian-accented voice on the other end of the phone he held to his ear. He ran his hand over his dark, slicked-back hair, his palm coming away a little sticky from the product he covered it in to hold it in place. He pulled the cigar away from his mouth and exhaled, the thick blue smoke wisping from his nostrils and between his teeth, one of which glittered gold in the half-light of the car.

'I don't care how or when, Luca, but the package needs to be here by the end of the week. I have customers waiting, and they have customers waiting, and their customers have customers, you understand me?' His voice was deep, dark and thick.

'Alban, what can I do? We must wait until our man is on duty at the port. We can't run the risk if he's not there. You never know who will screen the truck,' said Luca, a slim and resourceful Italian who was arranging the latest consignment that was now overdue. Serious money had been invested by the family and they needed to make sure the container that was full of cheap plastic toys landed. It wasn't the toys they wanted but the hundred kilograms of cocaine that was secured in the tightly boxed packages.

'When's he on duty then?' said Hoxhaj, puffing at his cigar again, his eyes bulging as he sucked.

'Saturday, all day. Can we delay until then?'

'Do I have a choice?'

'Not really.'

'Okay, Saturday then. Call me on this number as soon as you have confirmation as I need to warn Gezim to prepare for the arrival.'

'Saturday. I guarantee it,' said Luca, his normally jolly voice a little tense.

'Luca. Make it happen and don't mess up. We're paying this man a fortune for free passage through the port, and if he makes us wait a moment more, I'll be somewhat disappointed. Now I have to go.' Hoxhaj hung up.

Despite the angry and somewhat pugnacious tone, he was pleased. This was a very large consignment coming in via a new method, and if it all worked out, which he was sure it would, it would be a lucrative and safe new route into the UK. He smiled and took a long pull on his Cohiba, letting the fragrant blue smoke wisp from his nostrils before exhaling. He remembered the day, over twenty years ago, when he had made the journey across Europe from Albania after the Kosovan conflict. Injured with a shrapnel wound, he'd managed to get away from the marauding Serbs and make his way to Dover. Once there, he simply claimed to be a deposed Kosovar Albanian, rather than his actual native Albanian nationality, and they let him in. Almost no questions asked. The UK had been good for Alban Hoxhaj, and he soon made inroads into the criminal underworld simply by becoming the most ruthless criminal that anyone had encountered. Others used henchmen to mete out the violence needed to run their empires, whereas Alban Hoxhaj preferred the personal touch.

To leave the work to underlings struck him as cowardly, and he was never shy of getting his hands dirty. It gave him a certain cachet that the others lacked. The word soon got out that if you crossed 'Kirugu', then retribution would be personally delivered with maximum pain. The Turks, Jamaicans, Russians and Brits couldn't compete with the ruthless, and sometimes illogical, application of extreme violence that he and his fellow Albanians were willing to use. They were weak, but then they hadn't had the experiences of dealing with the bastard Serbs, like he had as a young man. It wasn't just for effect that he had soon become known as Kirugu, Albanian for 'The Surgeon'. Removal of fingers, ears, lips or eyelids with a scalpel was his speciality. He chuckled at the thought, drawing on his cigar again. He'd soon realised the value of fear when running a business.

A tone erupted from his other phone on the white leather seat next to him. He picked it up and looked at the notification. A message had been left on an Albanian community internet forum. Hoxhaj frowned; this was the signal. It meant that contact was being requested by the asset and that the request was urgent.

'Pull over,' he said to Enver, who nodded and drove into a parking bay alongside some industrial bins outside a small parade of shops. The street was bustling with late evening diners from the trendy West End bars and eateries, and the roads were still busy. 'Wait outside,' Hoxhaj commanded the driver, who nodded again and got out of the car, slamming the door shut behind him. Enver was a good man, if a little taciturn, and Hoxhaj trusted him. Enver's sense of besa matched his own, and that was as important as his massive stature and willingness to die to protect his boss.

Hoxhaj reached into a small leather bag on the thickly carpeted floor of the car and pulled out a brand-new mobile phone, still in its box. Quickly and efficiently, he opened the back of the cheap, basic phone, slotted in a new SIM card and quickly downloaded

WhatsApp. He could have used the encrypted phone he'd just been speaking to Luca on, but to communicate with this individual they had a set method which had served them well, so far. The message was from an asset; in fact, it was from *the* asset. He looked at the telephone number that had been left on the private message on the forum and dialled via WhatsApp. He smiled knowing that with the end-to-end encryption there was no way they could be listened in on.

'Yes?' The asset's voice was flat, level and almost unaccented.

'You requested contact.'

'Yes. Are you alone?'

'Yes.'

'New phone and SIM?'

'Yes.'

'Do you know Toka Kurti?' the voice asked.

'Yes.'

'Does she work for you?'

'Well, she pays tax to me, but I am not personally involved in her businesses, day to day.'

'Then we have a problem that requires urgent attention.'

'I'm listening,' said Hoxhaj, his voice firm enough to show he felt no intimidation. The asset was valuable, but he was under no illusions as to who was in charge.

'She has a particular girl, Afrodita Dushku. She was taken from somewhere up north recently by Toka and some fool called Jetmir Xhilaj, who trafficked her over here a few years ago.' The asset pronounced the name 'Exhilaj', rather than the more accurate 'Zilaj'. Hoxhaj shook his head at the stupid fool who couldn't even pronounce Albanian names correctly.

'And why is this my problem?' he said, his mind swimming with the memory of Jetmir and the lost courier girl with a kilo of product. The same Jetmir he'd banished back to Albania as a punishment, but he felt no compunction to reveal this to the asset.

'Because they didn't do it cleanly and she's far too hot to handle. The Chief Constable himself has ordered a review, and a couple of cops are up from the central belt. It's only a matter of time before they find her, and then we're all in trouble. They may be able to link her via her ex-boyfriend to a stupid cop who was one of Toka's customers in Glasgow. She's been blackmailing him.'

'Toka's good at blackmail, as you know only too well, eh? I bet you're glad that I took care of that with her.' Hoxhaj laughed.

'Look, we need to sort this.'

'Okay, what do you need?' said Hoxhaj, feeling his face flush at the thought of this activity without his authority.

'They need to let her go, urgently. If she's released, they'll stop looking and we can start limiting the bloody damage. So far, this is a low-level missing person, so if she returns quickly, this goes away. Otherwise, several people run the risk of exposure, and it will put your operation under the spotlight. Just get Toka to release the girl, urgently.'

'What will the girl know?'

'She knows Jetmir as he trafficked her over. Just get him out of the way back to Albania and Toka can look after herself.'

'Why don't we just solve this permanently?'

'Jesus, Alban. If you're talking about killing a fifteen-year-old trafficking victim then no.'

Hoxhaj felt his hackles rise. 'No blasphemy. You know how I feel about cursing and blasphemy,' he said, his voice as hard as steel. Despite his occupation and status, one thing Hoxhaj couldn't stand was bad language, or even worse, using the Lord's name in vain. His people knew this, but some of the fools he was forced to deal with clearly didn't.

There was a pause on the line, then the caller spoke. 'I'm sorry, but the cops will never, ever leave it alone if she's killed. She's a big success story, rescued from traffickers and now settled with a good family. She's about to represent Scotland at junior athletics.

The press would go mad. I don't think she'll say anything in any case, as Toka apparently has control of her little sister in Albania. Once she's returned, this inquiry will shrink back to one man and his dog, and the Inverness cops are so stretched they'll just give up. I can maybe muddy the waters enough for this to go away, but she needs releasing, now.'

Hoxhaj sighed; this really was scrutiny they didn't want. 'I'll make a call.'

'Good, even if Toka does get arrested, it's not like that's much of a problem for you, is it?'

'No. She'll say nothing.'

'Good. Message me when it's done. Usual procedures.' The phone went dead.

Hoxhaj unpopped the back of the phone and pulled out the SIM card. He bent the chip in half, opened the car door and ditched it in the gutter. He tossed the phone into one of the large industrial bins adjacent to the car before slamming the door shut again. He took a long, slow draw on his cigar, deep in thought as he inhaled the fragrant smoke. He shook his head. 'Stupid Toka,' he muttered to himself, before calling Enver back to the car.

19

'IS THIS THE best bloody hotel we could get? A man of my status deserves better,' said Ross, looking at the reception area of the hotel, which was typically corporate and safely bland. Max and Janie were sitting at the bar, Janie nursing a bottle of beer, and Max a glass of cranberry juice.

'It's fine. Stop bloody moaning,' said Norma. 'Drink?'

'First bloody sensible thing you've said all day. I'll have a pint of heavy. Let's sit down, my bloody feet are killing me,' he said, heading to a table in the far corner of the deserted bar.

Soon they were all sitting at a table with food orders placed with the taciturn barman. The menu was limited, so everyone ordered fish and chips.

'Any updates?' said Max.

'Nothing on the intel front, but we have irons in the fire, and by we, I mean Norma, who has been very busy calling in favours. I have the word out on the downlow to locate Toka the prozzy-boss, but so far, no trace of her.'

'Is she getting arrested? Surely it's too early for that,' said Max, sipping his juice.

'Nah, just want to know where she is, but she's an elusive bugger. So, what do you know?'

Max updated them on Luigi Ricci's home address visit.

'So, not a place for an easy sneaky beaky approach?' said Ross, taking a swig of his beer.

'No. Not impossible. We couldn't do it quickly, but there may be an option.'

'Go on?'

'We nick him early, once his kids have gone to school; that may give us some tactical options, and the house to ourselves, if the chief will authorise. We nick him, get him in and keep him in a cell for a few hours whilst we interview him, and then let him go. Hopefully he'll be indiscreet around the house and we'll get a firm lead. There's more to this than a horny cop playing about with prostitutes.'

'How can you be sure about that? Maybe Ricci was just doing a favour for Toka in locating Afrodita and passing on her movements.'

Max shrugged. 'Doesn't feel right. There's something bigger behind this. Why go to the trouble of getting Afrodita back? She's just one girl, and it's not like there's a shortage of them out there, is it?'

'I guess,' said Ross.

'I think I agree with Max,' said Norma, who was staring at her laptop on the table.

'Why? He normally talks utter shit. Why do you agree with him now?'

'Because of the others,' she said, looking up from the screen, her face solemn.

'What others? Will you stop being fucking obtuse, you daft mare,' Ross spat before taking another sip of his pint.

'I put feelers out with the NCA, the Met, the National Referral teams and others. I'm getting some results back and there are concerning similarities with other missing trafficking victims. Hold on, I'm just scanning the document, which has literally just arrived in raw form.' Her brow furrowed, her eyes widening behind her glasses as they swivelled from left to right.

'Similarities? What kind of similarities?' said Ross, puffing his cheeks out.

'A pal of mine at the NCA whom I totally trust thinks that nationally there are a number of juvenile victims of trafficking who have just vanished. All in similar circumstances, all a similar age. One or two have been found; others haven't and are believed to be across Europe, possibly working in the sex trade.'

'What, all Albanian?' said Ross.

'Yep.'

'Any similarities in circumstances?'

'What, other than being Albanian trafficking victims?'

'Obviously.'

'Still being analysed, but one thing sticks out.'

'Come on, woman. Spit it out, I'm a busy man who's away from his beloved family. What?'

'They were all going through applications to the Home Office for leave to remain.'

'What, all of them?'

'Aye.'

'I thought they all got leave to remain once they were designated as trafficking victims by the NRM.'

'I had a bloke from Immigration intelligence called Steve Vipond call me to tell me about some worrying links that he has been discussing with a pal of mine. He was going to come in to do a bit of intel sharing, but then we had to rush out. He's coming in when we get back, he seems smart. Apparently, they all get status, but it needs to be ratified to get permanent leave to remain and still needs a completely new application to the Home Office.' Norma looked up from her notepad.

'Well, surely that's no surprise, then?'

'Well, yes and no.'

'Meaning?'

'Another pal of mine is a computer whizz. She's amazing at

uncovering links to crimes by feeding them into a program they use, and she's come up with a significant imbalance when she looked at the raw data supplied by Steve Vipond. She sampled a total of a hundred and fifty trafficking victims, both male and female, who had been approved by the NRM. Women tend to be trafficked for sexual exploitation, men for modern slavery. She then looked at the long-term missing person stats and compared them. One thing was significant, when it was factored in as to who returned after going missing, the entire group had an average of fifty per cent undergoing applications to remain permanently in the UK.' Norma paused to sip her wine.

'And?'

'The group that went long-term missing, a total of twenty-one over the past eight years, have something in common. One, they were all undergoing applications to remain in the UK.' She paused again and swirled her wine.

'Fucking hell,' muttered Ross, his eyebrows raised.

'Two, they were all young girls around fifteen.'

There was a long, dense silence around the table as it sank in. They had an almost identical group of Albanian girls, of a similar age, all undergoing applications to the Home Office. And they were all missing.

Ross was the one to break the silence. 'When are you meeting this Dougie Vipond?'

'Steve Vipond, I think Norma said. Dougie is in the band Deacon Blue,' said Janie.

'Whatever, Poindexter.' Ross scowled at Janie. 'When?'

'As soon as I'm back in the office. He's only at Gartcosh.'

'Right, we're pulling that Ricci in. We'll let the kids get to school, then we're bringing him in, tomorrow morning. There's no time to waste. Where's Barney?'

'Probably snoring in his camper van in Plockton.'

'Get hold of him and get him here early tomorrow. We've

sneaky shit to plan. I'll call the chief, he'll need to authorise stuff. I should be able to get past Sofia, his PA, who is actually very nice, unlike his dickhead of a staff officer, who thinks he's the sole arbiter of who talks to him. We're doing this tomorrow, guys. Get some rest. It'll be a long day.'

20

TOKA KURTI SAT in her newly decorated office in the brothel and looked at the pictures on her laptop that she had just loaded onto the adult services website that she always used, and gave a satisfied nod. Afrodita looked stunning, and Toka was sure that even with the eye-watering prices she was going to charge, she would be besieged by clients wanting to sample the schoolgirl-like Afrodita, or Electra, as she was called on the website. She began to list all the services that Electra would offer, and it was going to be everything other than sex without a condom. She always insisted her girls were protected, not for any reasons of kindness, but a girl with a dose of the clap was no use to anyone. She was sure that Afrodita wouldn't like it at all, especially some of the more extreme services, but she'd get used to it. She had no choice, especially with her little sister in Tirana. One of Toka's associates had easily tracked her down and taken the photos, and that's all she needed. That would be all the control required.

She finished the profile, and then noted down the unique reference number in a brown leather-bound notebook with a silver propelling pencil that she had pulled out of the slot at the side. Her handwriting was tiny but neat, and the reference number was added to a long list of similar ones. The book was only just over palm sized, and the leather was scratched and worn. Once satisfied, she retracted the lead from the pencil and slotted it back into place. Rather than leave the notebook on the side, she stood and went to a small picture hung on the wall behind her desk. It bore a stylised portrait of Enver Hoxha, the former Prime Minister of Albania who ruled with an iron fist in the late 1940s to the early 1950s. Toka really didn't care about the leader who was still widely revered by some, but she always smiled when she hid her notebook in a hollow in the back of the print. It felt a little like a 'fuck you' to authority, of which she was no respecter.

Her buzzing phone drew her attention. She didn't recognise the number, and surely it was too early for any clients. She answered, 'Hello?'

'Toka, you know who this is, yes?'

Toka's heart lurched and the hair on the nape of her neck prickled. The voice was deep and dark and sounded as if it was full of gravel. She shivered.

Alban Hoxhaj was not to be underestimated and certainly to be treated with serious respect. He was the head of a family crime organisation that was controlling vast swathes of cocaine importation and distribution. He wanted a piece of everything, and that would doubtless include Afrodita and the other girls who were being prepared.

'Alban, how are you, my angel? I didn't recognise your telephone number,' she said, hoping that the tremble she was feeling wasn't audible in her voice.

'I changed it. You have a young girl in your establishment, Afrodita Dushku.' His voice remained even; it wasn't a question. Not by a long way. It was a statement of fact that was unarguable.

She paused for a heartbeat. If she denied it then she'd only anger him, and that was always a bad idea. He'd take it as a mark of disrespect, and to a man like Alban Hoxhaj, besa was everything.

'Yes, Alban, she's being prepared now for work. I was planning to tell you about—'

Hoxhaj cut her off dead. 'I'm not interested, Toka. Not at all. You're to let her go, do you understand?' Again, it was a statement of fact, not a question and certainly not a request. His voice had a bored quality that made the hairs on her arms rise.

'Alban, darling, she's only just arrived, and I've spent much time and money. Of course I always intended to make sure that you received your share.'

His response cut straight through her, his voice changing from bored to stern as if a switch had been flicked. 'Perhaps you didn't hear me, woman. You let her go, and you let her go now, or the consequences for you and that stupid fool Jetmir will be severe. I don't care how you do it, blindfold her, take her somewhere remote and let her go unharmed. What you do other than that is of no consequence to me, but you've caused me and my operation some difficulties by taking this girl. She is to be released without delay and by the way, the only answer I need to hear from you now is "Yes, Alban", am I clear?'

She opened her mouth to argue, then paused, there was nothing to gain by angering Hoxhaj. She could easily let her go with the threat against her sister in Albania. Toka was sure that she'd say nothing. There were plenty of other fifteen-year-old sluts that Jetmir could bring to her, even if they wouldn't be as lucrative as Afrodita.

'Toka?' Hoxhaj's voice was flat and emotionless.

'Of course, Alban. I'm so sorry. I had no idea she was off limits. Of course if I'd known . . .'

'She goes now. Like as soon as you hang up with me. Tell that cretin to get rid of her, unharmed. Not a mark on her, am I clear?'

'Perfectly clear.'

'Will she speak to the police?'

'No.'

'You're sure?'

'Yes. We have her sister under control in Tirana. She knows this and will never tell.'

'Good. We need to talk about your tax situation. I think I'm being a little generous to you, particularly if you bring trouble to my door like this, eh?'

'I'm sorry, darling. Of course, I'll arrange immediately.'

'Call me on this number when it's done.'

'I'm sorry, Alban, darling, but that fool Jetmir is at fault.'

The three short beeps in Toka's ear told her that the gang boss had gone. Her stomach churned as she sat looking at the handset, knowing that she had no choice. She knew only too well what happened to those who displeased Alban Hoxhaj. She stood and pulled out her notebook from behind the portrait again and using the small eraser at the top of the pencil erased the number for Hoxhaj, listed as 'Kiru', and copied the new one from her phone screen in its place. The frequency with which people in her world changed phone numbers meant that one needed a good system for remaining up to date. She herself would often ditch phones, so the old-fashioned 'little black book' system was efficient and reliable. She replaced the pencil and tucked the book away again behind Hoxha's scowling face, straightening the picture on the wall.

She picked up her phone and dialled.

'Yes?'

'What have you bloody done, Luigi?' she said, her voice hard and flinty.

'What? Toka, I've no idea what you're talking about. What's happened?'

'Alban Hoxhaj has just called me. You know who he is right?'

There was a long pause before Luigi spoke, the word almost a whisper. 'Yes.'

'Of course, you do, everyone knows Kirugu. I have to let the bloody girl go. Who did you call?'

'No one, I promise. I've been putting up some smoke screens, dummy intelligence reports and the like. What's he said?' The cop's voice was jittery and she could feel the tension down the line.

'You need to get here. Get here immediately. We need to talk this over and come up with a strategy, but not over the phone. When can you come?'

'Toka, I can't. I'm still working.'

'Tomorrow, then.'

'I don't know, Toka . . .'

'I don't care. Get yourself down here, soon, or I promise you, you'll regret it. Remember, I can finish you any time I like. Call me tomorrow to tell me when you're coming.' She hung up, her cheeks burning with anger. That stupid cop must have said something to someone, there was no other explanation, but he was just a low-level nothing. Who could he know that would lead this to the head of the most feared Albanian crime family? She stood, pacing the floor, thinking over her options. Realising that she effectively had none, she dialled another number.

'What?' said Jetmir.

'Where are you?'

'Almost back. I've just been buying more towels and sheets like you told me to,' he said.

'Okay, as soon as you're back, we're getting rid of Affi.'

'What? What do you mean?' His voice crackled in the speaker.

'She has to go, unharmed.'

'Toka, I don't understand. It was so much work to bring her back to us, why?'

'Because of Alban Hoxhaj.'

There was a pause before he said, 'Alban? Why does he care?'

'I don't know, Jetmir. I didn't ask him because he sounded very pissed off. You can ask him if you like, but I wouldn't advise it. Your reputation is on the floor as it is. I knew it was trouble bringing her back, just so you could try and get some kudos after losing her. You're a bloody fool, Jetmir. This is your doing.'

'But Toka—'

'I'm not interested, Jetmir. Not at all. You've caused me enough problems with Kirugu by taking this girl, so you need to make it right. As soon as you're back, drive her away from here. When you're there, give her phone back to her and give her some money, maybe enough for a train home. I'm going to speak to her now and warn her of the consequences of telling the police about us. We still have her sister under control, so we can be sure she won't say anything.'

His sigh was audible. 'After all that trouble getting her to us. She'd have earned us a fortune.'

'Well, it isn't going to happen. Get back here immediately.' She hung up, slumped back in her chair and stared at the ceiling, letting out a low hiss before vigorously shaking her head. It really didn't matter a great deal. Much of it was massaging Jetmir's ego to recapture the bitch, which had been a stupid idea. He also seemed still to have the hots for her, the stupid bastard, and after the trouble she'd caused him by escaping. She almost leapt to her feet. Toka knew that she had limitations, but indecision was not one of them. She went to the cupboard in the office and pulled out Afrodita's running gear that she'd been wearing when they'd taken her from Fyrish.

She then strode down the corridor and pushed open the door to her room. Afrodita was sprawled on the bed wearing her bathrobe watching TV. She turned to Toka, her eyes wide with alarm.

Toka threw the clothes on the bed. 'You're leaving. Get dressed.'

'What?' said Afrodita, sitting up as fast as if she'd been electrocuted.

'Get dressed. Jetmir is going to drive you to town. He'll give you some money for a train, so use it for the next train to Inverness, and take the time to think over what you're going to say to your family, okay?'

'I don't understand, Sheff,' she said, her eyes brimming with tears that sparkled in the half-light.

'You don't need to. You don't need to know why, or how. All

138

you need to know is this one thing, Affi.' Toka paused before sitting on the bed next to the girl, fixing her with her hardest and darkest of stares whilst letting a smile spread across her face. 'Hear this, and remember it well. We are letting you go, because we have no choice, but if you say one word about any of this,' she waved her hand around the room, 'then I will call my associates in Tirana. You've seen the photos, yes?'

Afrodita nodded, the tears spilling down her cheeks.

'One word. Just one word, Affi, and she'll be taken by my people in Tirana. She'll be taken, and she'll be put into a brothel in Albania. You know how bad that would be, yes?'

Afrodita just nodded again.

'She'll be worked to death in the most putrid brothel that can be found, and when she's all used up, they'll slit her throat and throw her in Farka Lake. Am I making myself clear?'

Afrodita's face was as pale as alabaster and shining with tears, but she nodded, vigorously.

'Make up a story, tell them you ran away because you were depressed, whatever you like. Just don't mention me or Jetmir, and definitely not this place. Now put your clothes on. Jetmir will be here soon.' Toka stood and stomped out of the room, slamming the door behind her.

21

MAX STARED AT his iPad that displayed a live feed of the front of PC Luigi Ricci's bungalow. The video was pin sharp and being relayed from a small camera hidden in Barney's VW camper van parked in the same street that Max and Janie had watched the house from just a few hours ago. They were now parked in another side street a little farther away, now that the camera in the empty van was in place.

Max checked his watch; it was almost eight thirty. The curtains had been pulled back at about eight o'clock by Luigi's wife, yawning in her dressing gown as she looked out at the street, which was slick with rain, the early morning sun glinting on the sodden tarmac.

The front door opened and an attractive blonde, petite woman appeared, fishing for keys in her handbag and shutting the door behind her. Two small faces popped up at the window and began waving to her as she unlocked the Fiesta and sent a wave back, followed by a blown kiss.

The car started and she reversed off the drive and drove away.

'That's the missus off to work,' said Max into the handset.

'Received,' said Ross.

'A perfect picture. Tell Barney he's done a good job, as usual,' said Max.

'He's grumbling about police use of his camper van and wants to know where to send the invoice for its rental.'

'What did you tell him?'

'I politely advised him to jam it where the sun don't shine.'

Max laughed. 'Is he there?'

'No, he's gone with Norma to Burnett Road custody centre to prepare for our arrival. Are you all set there?' asked Ross.

'Yep. Just waiting for him to appear. Are you all set?' said Max.

'Aye, just waiting for you to give the word that Luigi's in cuffs, and then we'll swoop like the elite troops we are,' said Ross.

'Who's with you?'

'Two of DI Calman's most trusted detectives. The calls went in from above to ensure cooperation. They seem decent to me.'

'I hope you're being polite, Ross?'

'Of course, as if I could be anything else.'

'So, no swearing or offensive behaviour. Subtlety is the name of the game.'

'I resent that remark. I can be rather subtle when the mood takes me.'

'I'd say that you're as subtle as a hundredweight of prunes, Ross.'

'That's a shite analogy, ya fud.'

Max was about to retort when the door opened again. Two children, a boy and a girl, both under ten, appeared at the entrance, in royal blue sweatshirts, followed by a stocky man with dark, thinning hair, who was pulling a jacket on. Max looked across at the photograph of a uniformed PC Luigi Ricci on a sheet of A4.

'Right, that's him out of the house, with the kids. The car's being unlocked and they're all getting in. Christ, he doesn't look overly chirpy,' said Max, taking in the man's stubbly lined face and dark-circled eyes.

'School run?' said Ross.

'Aye, both kids in uniform. Hold up whilst I check the tracker.' Max opened the map application on the iPad and saw the flashing blue icon in the centre. 'Yep, good to go, we'll let him do the school run. He's in his trackies, with no bag, so he'll be back before he heads to work for his shift at ten.'

'Right, are you just going to hang on there?'

'Aye, he'll not be long. We'll intercept him as he gets out of his car.'

'Received. I'll join you once he's back. Let me know.'

'Will do. Stand by for updates.'

Max tucked the radio into the door pocket and yawned. They'd been up early and met Barney, who had set up his camper van as a makeshift short-term observation point, grumbling in his broad Yorkshire accent about 'tekkin bloody liberties, you buggers are'. He'd been his usual efficient self and within a few minutes they had a perfect-quality video feed of the house, and a small tracking device planted on the underside of Luigi's Audi, ready for any follows. They hadn't had time to brief a surveillance team, as they were already deployed elsewhere, so they'd improvised by using technological means, which were probably favourable in any case. Following a cop, particularly one with cause to be looking over his shoulder, could be difficult to the point of impossible.

'Is Luigi surveillance trained?' asked Max.

'I don't think so, leastways it wasn't on his file,' said Janie.

'Well, at the very least, he worked on street-level proactive teams, so we have to assume he'll be aware of techniques. We need to be careful.'

'Aren't we always?'

'As long as Ross isn't about, aye,' said Max, chuckling.'

'Aye. How far to the school?'

'Ten minutes, no more.'

Max sat back in the soft leather of the Volvo that was parked in a supermarket car park just two minutes away from Luigi's address. 'Let's move up as close as we can. I want to pull straight onto the drive as soon as he gets back. The moment he gets out of the car we'll nab him, yeah?'

'Let's do this,' said Janie, starting the car and moving off. They were soon in a side street not thirty seconds away from the bungalow.

There was a flash of movement and Luigi's Audi swung onto the drive.

'Bingo, let's go,' said Max, nodding at Janie.

Janie turned left into the road and drove briskly towards the house.

'Straight onto the drive, Janie. Don't give him an escape opportunity.' Max's face was set firm, his eyes hard, his jaw as tight as his stomach with the familiar adrenaline he always felt before a significant arrest.

Janie didn't hesitate, just drove smoothly along the road and swung onto the drive, pulling to a halt, bumper to bumper with the Audi. Luigi swung around to face them as he was getting out of the car, his mouth agape, and eyes wide with alarm.

Max had his warrant card in his hand as he exited the car, holding it in front of him. 'Luigi?'

'Aye, who's asking?' he said. The hard delivery of the sentence was at odds with the shock and fear written across his face.

'I'm DS Craigie. This is DC Calder. I'm investigating the disappearance of Afrodita Dushku, known as Affi Smith. I think you know something about this, Luigi.'

The colour drained from his face and he reached to open the car door to steady himself. Janie approached and snapped the handcuffs in place. He didn't resist when she removed the car keys from his hands.

'We're also going to search your house and your car. Is there anything at all in there that we'll find which you want to tell us about now?' said Max.

'I don't know what you're talking about,' he said.

'You need to tell us, Luigi. Seriously, pal. You need to tell us everything, now.'

'I don't know anything.' He looked down at his grubby trainers, a solitary tear ran down his cheek, and his whole body was quaking.

'Look at me, Luigi.' The police officer looked up, his face pale, his eyes brimming with tears. 'Tell me, why are you so scared?'

'I don't know anything,' he said and lowered his eyes to his trainers again.

'Right, in the car. We're going to Burnett Road.' Max opened the rear door of the Volvo and Janie guided Luigi into the backseat and slammed the door shut.

Max reached through the open window to the front of the car, picked up the radio and raised it to his mouth.

'We have him, move in.'

'Received. Moving in now,' said Ross.

'We all set then?' said Janie.

'Aye, I think so. Let's get him to Burnett Road. There's a custody officer for this joker ready to go.'

Max's phone buzzed in his pocket. He looked at the screen and saw that it was Katie. He frowned as he'd only spoken to her an hour ago.

'Katie, everything okay?' he said as he answered the call.

'Max, I've just had some incredible news,' she said, her voice was thick with emotion.

'What?'

'Affi has just pitched up at Inverness rail station. Valerie is on her way to fetch her now.'

22

'**WHAT?' SAID MAX,** reaching for the car's roof to steady himself.

'Just that. I don't know all the details other than Affi's home. She's exhausted, and no one's sure how she got back,' said Katie.

'What's she saying?'

'Nothing.'

'What, nothing at all?'

'Apparently not, well, not yet, anyway. She's clammed up and is refusing to say anything at all. They say she seems terrified. Can you go and see her, maybe get to the bottom of it?'

'I will. I need to take someone to Burnett Road, but then we'll go. Listen, babe, I have to go.'

'I know, but isn't it brilliant?'

'Of course. I'll speak to you later.' Max hung up and quickly called Ross.

'What? You must know what I'm in the middle of, eh?' Ross blurted.

Max could hear raised voices in the background. 'Everything okay?'

'Aye, all in hand. Settle down, you dafty,' he said, his voice rough amid the commotion.

'Well, listen, very quickly, don't make this obvious to anyone listening. But Affi has just appeared. She's on her way home out of the blue. Katie just called me.'

'What?'

'Exactly. Look, I need to run, but we'll talk at the nick. How long will you be?'

'Forty-five minutes or so?'

'Okay, we're ahead of you. See you then.' Max hung up and beckoned Janie over. 'Affi's back, out of the blue,' he whispered into her ear.

Janie said nothing, clearly aware of who was sitting in the back of the car. 'Does this change anything?'

'Well, not immediately. We have to continue with the plan, but we need to go and speak to her before we interview this clown.'

'Agreed. Jesus, what a bloody turn-up. What's she saying?'

'Nothing. Let's get going. We carry on with the plan, okay? And not a word about this to anyone else, yeah?'

Max dialled again.

'Now then, lad, what's occurring?' said Barney.

'We have our man. Are you ready?'

'Always ready, Maxie boy. Everything's in place.'

23

LUIGI RICCI'S CHEEKS burned hot with a mixture of shame and embarrassment as he sat on the bench in the custody suite at Burnett Road Police Station, on the outskirts of Inverness. It was a clinically clean, modern space that he'd been in repeatedly during work hours when booking in prisoners, so it was something of a shock to find himself going through the same process. He answered all the custody officer's questions monosyllabically, his eyes cast to the floor as he did, squirming inside at the fact that he'd worked with the very custody officer several times in the past, and now here she was booking him into a cell. He fought hard to stop the tears from flowing as he answered questions about his health, his mental health, whether he was, or had ever been, suicidal. It was excruciating.

He looked with not a little concern at the cop who had arrested him. DS Craigie seemed astute and it was killing him that he had no idea what evidence they could have beyond the fact that that idiot McPhail had sent him that fucking message. Well, that and the fact that his history was a little chequered, to say the least. He wondered whether Toka had been arrested and had grassed, but he just couldn't see how they would have linked this to her, and the Albanians were bloody ruthless with grasses. They'd slice her up as quickly as they'd slice him up. None of it made sense, and the more he thought about it, the more confused he became.

The door crashing open, followed by swearing and curses,

made him raise his head, and his heart lurched when he saw Lewis McPhail being dragged in by a smartly dressed detective he recognised from the CID and a large, overweight man in a shabby suit and a warrant card on a lanyard around his neck. McPhail was full of his usual fake gangster bullshit.

'Get ya fucking hands off, man. I swear down, if I see you motherfuckers on road I'll fuck you up,' he spat, his face contorting with rage at the overweight man, who pushed his face closer to McPhail's, and muttered through gritted teeth, 'Try that shit with me again and I'll rip your fucking head off and shit down your neck, do you bastard understand me?'

'Come on, settle down, Lewis. You'll upset DI Fraser and then I'll have to put up with him all day,' said DS Craigie, with a big smile stretching across his face.

'Ah fuck off, Craigie,' said DI Fraser, returning his smile.

This interaction seemed to take some of the fight out of McPhail, who just glowered like a spoilt child.

Oh man, thought Luigi. This was bad. This was very bloody bad. He couldn't trust that idiot not to say anything, so they'd know about the messages, and the password. He breathed deeply, trying to calm his churning guts. *They've got nothing, Luigi. They've got nothing*, he repeated almost like a mantra.

McPhail was pushed onto the bench next to Luigi, still muttering indignantly. He turned towards Luigi, a puzzled look crossing his face. He raised his eyebrows at Luigi and opened his mouth to say something, but stopped when Luigi shook his head, almost imperceptibly, his eyes flashing a warning. Thankfully he seemed to catch on and closed his mouth again.

McPhail looked at the custody officer. 'So when's my brief getting here? He's gonna be vex you've dragged man in here again,' he said, his voice full of insolence.

'Hold on, I haven't even booked you in yet, and I have no idea why you're even here.' She turned to Luigi and nodded. 'Okay,

Luigi, come and sign for your property here.' She pointed to the screen that was behind a Perspex shield on the desk. Luigi stood up, his stomach churning, looked at the list of property and nodded at the custody officer.

'Sign on the electronic pad,' she said, and Luigi obliged with a small stylus attached to the signature block on the desk.

'We've called the duty solicitor, who'll be along shortly. You need to go and take a seat in a cell for a while, so go with the custody support officer, please. Cell fourteen.' The custody officer nodded to a lean, short man with steel-grey hair who wore a dark blue polo shirt with *Police Custody Support Officer* embroidered on the chest.

'I'll come and see you once your solicitor arrives,' said Craigie, extending his arm.

Luigi moved off, fully aware where cell fourteen was. He'd even escorted prisoners to that very cell. The mix of fear and shame almost threatened to overwhelm him, but he knew that he had to hold it together. *Just stay calm, and keep your mouth shut. They have nothing.*

The cell was as he remembered it. Small, square and with a low sleeping platform, on which was a rubberised blue mattress, a pillow made of the same material and a rough, blue blanket. A stainless-steel toilet pan was in the corner of the room.

'This is your pad, pal,' said his escort.

Luigi just nodded, determined to maintain his silence until the solicitor arrived.

The door slammed so loudly that it shook his insides and then there was nothing. Just so quiet, when normally the cell block reverberated with oaths, shouting and banging on the doors. Luigi knew that at this time of the morning all the detainees would have been transferred to the new court that had recently been completed and was now grandly named the Justice Centre. His insides boiled at the prospect of being charged and sent there, but he repeated the same mantra. *They've got nothing. They've got nothing. They've got nothing.*

24

THE PCSO RETURNED to the custody suite, where Lewis McPhail was being booked in by a young DC who had arrived with Ross. The gaoler approached Max and Ross, who were quietly talking in a corner.

'All done?' asked Max, holding up a bunch of keys which the gaoler accepted.

'Reet as rain, mate. We're good to go,' said Barney, unfastening the top buttons of his brand-new polo.

'Uniform suits you, pal,' sniggered Ross.

'Bugger off. Is Luigi's house empty?'

'Yes. His wife has gone to work and kids are at school. How long will you need?'

'Ten minutes only. Are you coming?' said Barney.

'Aye, but I need to go and see Afrodita first,' said Max.

'Want me to come?' asked Ross.

'Jesus, no. This requires a sensitive approach with a difficult teenager. You'll scare the shit out of her. Stay here and do some quality liaising,' said Max, shaking his head in disbelief.

Ross opened his mouth as if to argue, but stopped and simply shrugged. 'Fair point, well made, but until we have proof that she wasn't bloody kidnapped, we proceed as if she was, yeah?'

Max nodded.

'I'll go and get breakfast, then. Is Janie okay?'

'Aye, she found an empty office, ready to rock and roll.'

'Ace. Now you two piss off and do your sneaky treach-ery whilst I go and get a square sausage and tattie scone breakfast.'

25

'SIT THERE PLEASE, Max. Affi will be down in just a moment,' said Valerie, indicating a vacant armchair as she handed him a steaming mug of tea. Her face had transformed from heavy, lined and full of sorrow, to bright eyed and alive.

'How is she?'

'Exhausted and broken. I'm just so conflicted, Max. I'm over-joyed that she's back, but just terrified to learn what happened to her,' she said, sipping her tea and sitting on an overstuffed floral sofa opposite Max.

'What's she said so far?'

'Nothing. Not a sausage. She just said she'd needed some time away, but she was still in the same running gear, which has clearly been washed, but she won't elaborate. It doesn't make any sense. I'm awful scared that something terrible has happened and she can't bear to tell us. Poor wee toot.'

The door opened, and Reg appeared, rolling his eyes at his wife and giving a little shake of the head. Affi followed her foster father in. Her face was pale, thin, and she had big circles around her eyes, which were also red and bloodshot. Her hair, however, was glossy and shiny, and she looked clean.

'Affi, sweetheart, this is Max. He's the cop who was trying to find you, and he's also Katie's husband. He wants to ask a few questions, is that okay?'

Affi went straight to Valerie and sat, snuggling into her, with her long, slim legs tucked under her chin, and her arms encircling them, defensively. She was wearing running tights and a tight-fitting top, and had short white socks on, which Max noted were clean.

'Hi, Affi. Listen, before I say anything, you're not in trouble, okay? You understand that?'

Affi nodded, her eyes downcast as she picked at a bobble that had formed on her sleeve.

'We just want to know where you've been. Can you tell me that?' asked Max, his voice low and soft.

She was silent for a moment, before she spoke in a tiny, almost indecipherable whisper. 'I just went away for a bit. You know, I needed some time.'

'Where did you go?'

'Glasgow,' she said, not lifting her eyes.

'Where did you sleep?'

'In shop doorways, just rough, you know.' Her voice trembled, and Max saw tears carving paths down her face. Valerie tightened her grip on the girl, who leaned her head into her shoulder.

'Are they the clothes you went away in?'

She nodded.

'But they're clean, Affi. They've been washed. What really happened? You can tell me. You know I'm on your side, yeah? I promise we can help with anything that's happened.'

She just shook her head, without looking at Max.

'Would you like to talk to Katie? You trust Katie, right?'

She shook her head, again.

'Did someone take you?'

'No,' she whispered, and closed her eyes tight.

'Please let us help you, Affi. There are people who can make it better for you, and we can protect you from whoever has done anything to you, do you believe me?'

'I believe you can protect me,' she said, her eyes suddenly lifting and looking behind Max.

Max turned and noticed a framed photograph on the mantel-piece of a young Affi with an even younger-looking girl, their arms around each other, both with gap-toothed smiles and wearing rag-like clothes.

Realisation hit Max like a truck. The sister.

'Affi, we can help. I promise, whatever the problem is can be dealt with. We do this all the time.'

Affi took a deep, shuddering breath, and her shoulders began to heave and shake as she wept, softly at first, before she dissolved into harsh, racking sobs. Valerie smothered her with her arms, drawing her into her, whispering in her ears, softly. 'It's okay, toot, I'm here. You're home.'

'Maybe that's enough for now, eh?' said Reg, his own eyes damp with tears.

Max nodded as Valerie stood with Affi still buried into her, sobbing, and they both left the room. Soon there were footsteps on the stairs.

'What the hell's happened to her, Max?' said Reg.

'I don't know, but she's terrified. Look, Reg, we're going to keep going on the basis that she'd been taken, and then for some reason either escaped, or let go. I'm guessing that it's the latter. I'd also say that she's worried about her sister. The way she looked at her photo was ominous.'

'You think she's at risk?'

'I don't know, but I'll put some feelers out with Interpol. Maybe put them on alert.'

'That's good. Why did they let her go, though? I can't get my head around that.' Reg shook his head, his face full of worry.

'I'm not certain, but maybe she became too hot to handle.'

'What do you mean?' said Reg, his brow furrowed in puzzle-ment.

'Whoever took her has been told to release her, I'd say. What I don't know is why, or by whom, but I intend to find out.'

'You need to find them, Max. Because if they come back for her, I'll kill the bastards myself.' His eyes blazed with suffused rage, and all at once Max saw the battle-hardened paratrooper who had stormed Argentine troops in the South Atlantic all those years ago.

26

LUIGI WAS SITTING on his bed in the cell, staring at a bit of graffiti on the wall opposite. 'ACAB' seemed strangely appropriate to him at this moment. The air in the cell was fetid, thick and stuffy.

There was a sudden commotion in the corridor outside his cell that began with a squeaking of boots on the polished hard floor, then shouting.

'Get the fuck off me, you Babylon bastards,' came Lewis McPhail's familiar voice, as identifiably Highland as anyone's but with a hint of gang-banger. 'I swear down, man will fuck you bastards up, and my lawyer will give you beef, you feel me,' he shouted, his voice laced with anger but carrying no authority. The escorting officers didn't seem fazed in the slightest.

'In your cell, ya daft fanny,' came a local accent, deep and full of authority, before Luigi heard the distinctive sound of a cell door being slammed directly opposite.

'Fucking bastards,' shouted McPhail, but the fight was clearly dissipating as rapidly as it had escalated.

There was a rattle at Luigi's door, and the small wicket was lowered as the face of one of the custody staff appeared. Luigi recognised him from previous visits to the custody block. He was a huge, meaty ex-cop who'd retired and then come back to work in the cells as a pension topper-upper. He was always smiling and was well liked by all, as nothing ever seemed to faze him.

'You okay, Luigi?'

'Not gonna lie, I've been better, Billy.'

'Aye well, let it play out, pal. Want some food?'

'I'm good, thanks.'

'How about a tea?'

'Aye, that'd be good.'

'Back in a minute. I'll leave the wicket open, stuffy as anything in here. Don't get your head stuck in it.' He chuckled as he disappeared, his boots squeaking on the floor.

'Luigi?' came McPhail's hoarse whisper from the cell opposite.

Luigi paused and took the opportunity to glance through the wicket up the long corridor. He knew that he wasn't in a CCTV cell, as they were in one of the other corridors and reserved for vulnerable prisoners. There was CCTV in the corridors, but on occasions when he'd had to view it, he knew that the audio was absolute garbage, particularly with all the background noises of a busy custody suite. A whisper wouldn't be heard, he was sure of it, even if they bothered to check the CCTV, which no one ever did unless there were complaints of violence. He'd have to take the chance. If that idiot McPhail spoke in interview, it was all over.

'Luigi?' came the call again, louder this time.

'Shh. Fuck's sake, man, keep your voice down. Why are you in here?' His voice was nothing more than a whisper.

'The phone message I sent you. You know, Affi's password.'

'Shut up, you idiot. What else did they say?'

'Just that they knew all about it, and that they had loads of evidence against me and you. What's going on and what did you do with the password? What should I bloody say, man? I'm shitting myself here.' McPhail's voice rose an octave.

A flash of fear swept over Luigi. He could end up in huge trouble over this if McPhail told the cops why. He looked up the corridor, he could hear Billy's booming voice joking with someone in the main suite. He had to take this chance. His mind was whirring like a clock, searching for the right things to say. He might only have a few seconds.

'Say nothing, Lewis. Not one fucking word, okay?' he whispered.

'But I phoned you from my mam's phone the other day,' he whined.

'That was to a burner. Nothing to link it to me and that's hidden away. So, you say fuck all, am I clear?'

'Ah man, I don't want to get involved in this, man. I could end up in the shit.'

'You'll be in far worse shit if you grass, trust me. It's not me you have to worry about. You've no idea how bad these Albanians are. This isn't just a brothel keeper and her under-age prostitutes, it's who she works for you need to worry about. Now fucking listen, as they will be back in a second. You say nothing when you're interviewed, literally not one bloody word. You sit in the corner, and you don't even open your mouth. They'll let you go, as they won't have enough evidence, and when you do get out, google "Kirugu" and see who you're fucking dealing with. If I hear you're cooperating with the police, and I will hear about it, the first phone call I make will be to tell Toka that you know too much, and that you're going to start blabbing. The first call she'll make will be to her boss, Kirugu, and then you're finished. He'll slice you up, you stupid bastard.'

There was silence from McPhail's cell. Total and utter silence which somehow drowned out the yells, catcalls and shouting from the rest of the cell area.

'Am I making myself clear?' said Luigi, just as the squeaking of boots on the floor became audible again.

'Aye' was all that McPhail said, his voice nothing more than a soft rasp.

Billy appeared at the cell wicket, his big, round face split into a large smile showing uneven, nicotine-stained teeth.

'Here's your tea, pal. I'd best shut the wicket. Sarge goes bloody crabbit if it gets left open.' He nodded and slid the small hatch up with a metallic *clank*.

27

MAX, JANIE, ROSS, Norma and Barney all sat in an empty office at Burnett Road Police Station, Styrofoam cups of something resembling tea, or maybe coffee, in front of them on a chipped desk. Norma had her laptop open, her glasses askew on her nose as she studied the screen.

They all looked at each other as they listened to the crackled and distorted voices of Luigi Ricci and Lewis McPhail coming out of the speaker on the desk connected wirelessly to Barney's iPad, a triumphant look on his face.

'Okay, you smug git, it worked. Now don't expect any fucking plaudits, because they aren't coming,' said Ross, sipping his tea.

'Who the hell is Kirugu?' said Janie after a long silence.

'I'll need to do some more digging, but I think it's Alban Hoxhaj,' said Norma.

'I think I've heard of that name before. He's a bad 'un, right?' said Ross.

'That's an understatement. "Kirugu" is Albanian for "the surgeon".' Norma looked up, a slight frown on her face.

'I'm taking it he's nothing to do with hospitals.' Max raised an eyebrow questioningly.

'No. He's the head of the Shqiptare in Northern England and all over Scotland. Since the Hardies were dismantled he took over Scotland with frightening speed and terrible violence, and now controls all the cocaine distribution and has interests all over the country.'

'Including prostitution?' said Janie.

'As far as I can tell, he taxes the sex trade operatives where he can, and his organisation won't let any Albanians run brothels without his kickbacks. Any other brothels get established not under his control soon get closed with extreme prejudice. Such is the fear, that a handful of madams are running almost all the brothels in Scotland and beyond.'

'You haven't told us why he's known as The Surgeon,' said Ross.

'Do I need to spell it out?'

'Aye, you do.' Ross's face was deadly serious.

'Hoxhaj came to the UK as a refugee from Kosovo and claimed asylum in 2000. Said he was a Kosovar Albanian fleeing persecution, usual drill. He's suspected of being one of thousands of Albanians who got in by pretending to be Kosovan. Soon after, he got into crime and got the name The Surgeon, owing to his ability to remove pieces of his victims' bodies with a scalpel. He's been mostly active in London, but it's got a little warm and crowded there, so he seems to have decided to successfully fill the vacuum left by Hardie. He's not nice at all, guys.'

There was a long, turgid pause in the room as they all looked at each other, the realisation hitting that there was a great deal more to this than had first been apparent.

'Is this shite supposed to be tea or coffee, by the way?' said Ross, grimacing as he sipped from his cup.

'Coff-tea we used to call it in the army, Ross, you know that. Can't tell the difference. I'll give credit where it's due, Barney. Where are the mics hidden?' said Max.

'In the cell call button. Piece of piss, I told you it'd work,' said Barney, taking the roll-up from behind his ear and sniffing it, wistfully.

'See, smug bugger. I still say the CCTV would have got it. Load of fuss and admin for nothing,' said Ross.

'It wouldn't and I reckon Luigi knew that, hence the stage whispers. It's an old shite system with crap quality mics. The background noise and any sounds under a thousand hertz are always useless on custody systems and we would have missed the important bits. We have solid evidence now,' said Barney, trying to keep the grin off his face.

Ross just shook his head. 'See impossibly bloody smug, but Grandad here is right. We have solid, admissible evidence that Luigi is corrupt as fuck and in league with the Albanians. It's all there. We can charge him today, with attempting to defeat the ends of justice if we want to. How'd you get on at his house, Barney?'

'I had to be quick, and we're limited because of the caveats attached to the authority to deploy at his house, so cameras covering his front door, back door and audio in his car only.'

'Covering where, exactly?' said Max.

'Well, back one's sited in a tree so all the back garden covered and two cameras on the front door. It'll at least give his movements in and out. We'll know if he's in and he won't be able to leave without our knowledge.'

'Why the limitations on deploying inside? Surely he's bound to talk about it in the house?' said Norma.

'Surveillance commissioner didn't like the collateral intrusion on the rest of the family. It's apparently not cricket to bug a bent cop's house where we can hear his wife and kids, as well. Fair enough when you think about it. We even have to stop listening if he travels in the car with the family,' said Ross.

'Understandable. It's not their fault he's a wrong 'un. Anything at the search?' Norma added, looking up and sipping her tea with a grimace.

'Not much. Place was so full of clutter it was unbelievable. Got his personal phone, but no trace of the burner. To be fair, we had very little time. I don't think he'd be that daft anyway, to keep anything really incriminating.'

'Have we looked at his phone, yet?' said Ross.

'I have it and am scanning now, using limited keywords. Nothing obvious on it, but GPS puts him at Dingwall Police Station at the time Afrodita's iPhone account was hacked, so it could be him, but force IT are still struggling to tell us which terminal or which login accessed it. They're bloody useless, to be frank.'

'So, where's the burner, then? He must have one, as we know he's used one in the past to receive the password text from McPhail,' said Janie.

'Hidden, I guess. Without a PolSA team at his address we'd not find it if he'd concealed it properly, and we just didn't have the time,' said Max.

'Was he asked about it in interview?' said Barney.

'Aye. Said nothing.'

'What, nothing at all?'

'Neither did. Literally not one word from either of them,' said Janie.

There was a long pause before Ross spoke again. 'So, opinions. Charge now? Conspiracy with Lewis, based on the recorded conversations and the password text. It's a little thin, particularly as Afrodita isn't speaking to us at the moment.'

'I don't think so. I think we let them both go. It'll offer an opportunity to really get to what's behind this. All we have so far are two numpties – there's so much more to learn. If we charge them, that's it. We're no farther forward, are we?' said Max.

'Carry on,' said Ross.

'We're keeping his phone, for examination, right? That means as soon as he's out he's going to have to contact the Albanians. We have his burner number, unless he's changed it, which is possible. I'm betting that he goes straight to wherever the burner is and makes a call. If he makes it in the car, we'll hear it, and if he moves, we still have a tracker on his car. He'll lead us to the bad guys. This is much, much bigger than him. He's just somehow got himself in a bad situation he can't get out of. I'm betting that the Albanians have a hold over him because of his sexual proclivities, which they exploited to get to Afrodita.'

'Observations?' said Ross, looking around at each member of the team.

'It's a risk. The burner number Lewis texted hasn't been in use since it was sent. I'd say it's been ditched,' said Norma.

'Agreed. Norma, can you get a cross-network check done on the handset IMEI or IMSI number. He may have just changed SIM cards but retained the handset, so that would tell us if he's still using it, and if so, what number is being used now. I take it authorities are in place?' Max looked at Ross.

'It'll need a new application for all the network providers, but I have a direct line that bypasses that shit-for-brains in the chief's office. We can apply for urgent authorities for the data, so should be quick. Can we leave the applications with you, Norma?'

'Yeah, sure. Not like I have anything else to do, is it?' she said, frowning and shaking her head.

'I'll help, Norma,' said Janie.

'Aye. Teamwork. There's no I in team, is there?' said Norma, scowling at Ross.

'There is a "ME" in it if you look carefully enough,' said Ross, chuckling.

'Any luck with Interpol and the sister?' said Max.

'Enquiry has been submitted via the international office, on an urgent basis, but you know how these things go,' said Janie.

'We can't forget about that. Whilst this is still ongoing there could be a risk to her,' said Ross.

'I know the guy at Gartcosh who sends the enquiries overseas and he says there's a good liaison in Albania, so hopefully it'll get to the top of the pile.' Janie scribbled in her notebook.

'Okay, then let's get this moving, no time to waste. Both solicitors are waiting and are starting to look a little scunnered as to how long we're taking,' said Max.

'Like I give a flying fuck about a scunnered solicitor,' said Ross. 'I'll get the authorities in place, now. Give it an hour, then let them both go on bail. We ignore that moron McPhail, but stick to Luigi like shite to a blanket, okay? Game on.'

28

BOTH LUIGI AND McPhail had been released on bail at the same time, and had left the station without saying a word to each other. McPhail's mother was waiting for him in reception and hurried him away with a withering glare at Luigi, who stood outside the station for a moment, leaning on a railing. Within a few minutes a cab had pulled up and he'd climbed in. Max and Janie had watched this from their car and had kept a good distance from the cab as it headed to the Kessock Bridge. Within twenty minutes the cab was going towards the police officer's home that Max and Janie had been at several hours ago.

'Don't follow anymore. We know where he's going and the live feed's working fine. The biggest risk of compromise is always when the subject gets home,' said Max, looking at the tablet computer on his lap. Barney's cameras were working fine, with two trained on the front door and one camera focused on the back of the house. The pictures were pin sharp and gave a good view of both front and back aspects of the property.

'Shall we plot up where we were this morning?' said Janie, yawning.

'Aye, fancy a coffee first? Garage over there has a machine.'

'First sensible thing you've said all day, sarge,' she said.

'Janie?'

'Aye?'

'Never call me sarge again,' said Max, smiling but not looking up from the screen.

'Right you are, sergeant,' she said, driving onto the garage forecourt and pulling into one of the parking bays.

They both sat there for a few moments, eyes glued to the screen. Within a few moments the cab pulled up outside the house, the door opened and Luigi got out, stretching his back muscles as he did. He checked over both shoulders, and looked up and down the road.

'See what I mean? He's eyes all over right now.'

They watched Luigi's shoulders slump as he began to make his way towards the front door.

Light erupted from the door as it began to open. His wife stood at the entrance, wearing tracksuit trousers and a hoodie. Max zoomed in, and her face, full of hurt, filled the screen. She opened the door wide and stepped to the side allowing Luigi to enter the house. There was no warmth, no hug and no contact between the husband and wife as the door closed tight.

'I'd call that a frosty welcome, what do you think?' said Janie.

'Arctic would be more accurate, I'd say. Latte?'

'Why not.'

Max smiled as he unbuckled his seatbelt and got out. 'Keep an eye on the feed.'

'Ooh, you spoil me, DS Craigie.'

Within five minutes Max had returned clutching two cups, one of which he handed to Janie, who popped the lid and sniffed.

'Good enough?' said Max.

'Do I have a choice?'

'Not really. It's almost six and things close earlier up here, certainly compared to your bustling Edinburgh vibe.'

'These backwaters are bloody weird and make me nervous,' said Janie, sipping her coffee.

The sky was beginning to darken, and Max watched the screen as the lights came on in the house on the ground floor.

'Are the kids home?' said Janie.

'I scanned through the feed, and I didn't see them come back. I think his wife is from this area, so maybe there are grandparents nearby. I should ask Norma to look into that. It may become important. Maybe Mrs Ricci wants a strong word with her husband and didn't want to be stifled by ankle-biters.'

'You really do have a way with words, Max,' said Janie, shaking her head.

A flash of movement caught Max's eyes as a burst of light erupted on the portion of the screen that was displaying the feed from the rear garden.

'Standby,' said Max.

'Where's he going?' said Janie as Luigi appeared from the back of the house. He crossed the lawn and disappeared inside a small garden shed. A weak glow was visible at the window and there was movement within the shed.

'What's he doing?'

'Searching for something. Did you look in the shed earlier?' asked Janie.

'Just cursory, like we did the whole place. It was a right old shite-hole in there. It would have taken bloody hours to do it properly. He really could do with the team from *Britain's Biggest Hoarders* to sort his life out. Half the house was like that.'

'Clatty bugger, eh?'

Max nodded, not taking his eyes from the feed.

'What's he bloody doing?' said Janie, moving her face closer to the screen.

Luigi had turned back towards the house, looking at a small item in his hand which suddenly lit up.

'A bloody phone. It's his burner. He'd hidden it in the shed, shit. We should have got PolSa in there,' said Janie, her face hard.

'I'm not so sure. This may work out better for us,' said Max.

'How? If we'd got that bloody phone, we'd have got the message McPhail sent him. It would have been brilliant evidence.'

'This could get us more. If we get the number then we have a live phone for him. Offers up all sorts of possibilities. If we'd found it, he'd have had to get a new one from somewhere, or used call boxes, and you know what a ball ache that can be. If that's the same handset, we should get the number.'

'Wouldn't he know this?'

'Maybe not. He was on a street offences proactive unit. No real need for intelligence searches at that level. He was targeting street-level crime and vice. I doubt he has experience with cross-network handset searches.' Max pulled out his phone and dialled.

'Max?' Norma's voice was typically chirpy.

'Any luck on the cross-network checks for Luigi's handset?'

'Applications are in, on a high priority with pressure being applied, so imminently, I hope. The old number is still dead and has been since the text from McPhail.'

'Right. He's just retrieved a handset from his shed which he's just sparked up. If it's the same handset we should get a number. Stay on it.'

'All over it like a cheap suit,' said Norma, the sound of tapping keys audible down the phone.

Max ended the call. 'Is he dialling?' he asked Janie.

'Doesn't seem to be. My guess is he doesn't want to at home. I imagine his stock is pretty low with Mrs Ricci.'

Luigi stared at the handset for a moment longer before cramming it into his pocket. He stood, vigorously scratching his scalp, his eyes casting upwards to the darkening sky. He closed his eyes. The stress coming off him was almost palpable on the screen. Suddenly he dropped his hands down to his waist, opened his eyes and pulled the handset from his pocket. It seemed that he was about to dial, but then the figure of his wife appeared in the garden. Her body language was tight, her head straight as she stared directly at her husband, and she didn't look happy as her jaw moved up and down, clearly speaking, or shouting at him, her face hard and her brow furrowed. Luigi dropped his hands to his sides again and lowered his head, seemingly not arguing back. Although his face wasn't visible, his body language was one of capitulation. His wife strode across the lawn, just a few steps, then she let forth a slap that connected squarely with her husband's cheek.

'Ouch, domestic alert,' said Janie, looking at Max, concern on her face.

Luigi just stood there meekly and offered no resistance as his wife delivered three more slaps, each with diminishing force, her expression changing from anger to sorrow before she stopped altogether, her face crumpled and the harsh light reflecting off her wet cheeks. She turned on her heel and walked slowly back to the house.

Luigi stayed there, shoulders hunched for a few moments, his phone in his hand. He lifted the handset and looked at it before walking back across the lawn and entering the house, pocketing the phone as he did. The door shut, and the lights in the kitchen were extinguished. Within a few moments the security lights went out, and the garden was plunged into darkness.

'Blimey, that looked intense,' said Janie.

'What's next? Will he stay there?'

'I can't see it, can you?'

'Not really. He needed that phone, because he needs to speak to whoever he passed the information to about Affi. He has to warn them, he has no choice, and it doesn't seem like he's going to be welcome at home, does it?'

Janie nodded. 'This case is weird, Max. Really bloody weird. Affi goes missing after Luigi hacks her phone, but then she's let go, with no real explanation, but she's saying nothing and is clearly terrified of someone. I'm bloody confused, are you?'

'Aye, you could say that, but we *do* know one thing, right?'

'Meaning?'

'This goes way farther than just one poor wee trafficking victim, right? So, where are the rest of them? All those other girls in almost exactly the same situations. Who's leaking this stuff? It's not only one perverted cop, is it?'

Janie looked at Max, her brow furrowed. 'No way it has to be much bigger than that.'

'We have a powerful, dangerous Albanian gang boss seemingly calling the shots. That's really bloody concerning,' said Max, yawning.

'So, why did they release Affi? Was she too hot to handle? Hoxhaj must have ordered it, that's clear.'

'The question is, who's giving him the information? Who has enough clout to know all this stuff, and to be able to tell Hoxhaj to let Affi go?'

'Shit, is anyone in Scottish law enforcement not corrupt?' Janie shook her head.

'You do wonder, right? But then we're looking for it, aren't we? We're actively looking for signs of corruption, which is better than just ignoring it. I think we can make things better in Scotland by looking for bent cops and those that profit from corrupting the cops. After all, if we don't look, we won't find. That's my feeling, anyway,' said Max.

'Speaking of looking, standby, standby. Front door now,' said Janie, nodding at the screen.

The front door opened, and Luigi appeared wearing a thick hoodie, a rucksack on his shoulder. His eyes were downcast as he fished in his pocket and produced his keys, the indicators on the Audi blipping as he unlocked the car.

'Kicked out of the house?'

'Looks likely, let's hope the probe in the car is working because I'm betting he's going to make the call that he was about to make before Mrs Ricci slapped him in the mush.'

The speakers on the iPad burst to life as Luigi settled himself in the car, his breath audible in short, sharp gasps. He groaned, and the sound was full of despair. The door thumped shut and there was silence for a full minute, punctuated only by Luigi's hoarse breathing.

'What's he doing?' said Max, eyes glued to the small screen. Luigi was just an unidentifiable blob in the windscreen; sitting back against the dark leather seats he was almost invisible.

'Working up the courage to make the call?' said Janie, posing it as a question rather than a statement.

The light from the handset was all the confirmation they needed that she was correct. The probe in the car was sensitive, and the dialling tones were as sharp as if he was sat in the car with them.

'Fuck, fuck, fuck, fuck,' said Luigi in a hoarse whisper.

'Jesus, Barney's good, right? He's whispering and it's clear as a bell,' said Janie.

'It's in the rear-view mirror, so perfectly positioned. Yeah, he's good.'

The faint sound of ringing was audible for almost thirty seconds before Luigi spoke. 'It's me.'

A tinny noise was indecipherable as the person on the line spoke.

'Aye, I got bloody nicked. What the hell's going on, Toka?' he said, his voice gummy and thick.

'What? She's been let go? Why didn't you bloody tell me? I've just been interviewed for ages by some bloody cops from the central belt. Some corruption squad. What have you done to her?'

There was a pause, the rapid nature of the tinny sound indicated fast speech from whomever Luigi was speaking to.

'Oh man, no. Please no. Cops will be all over her. She'll talk to them, you know that.'

Another pause and more tinny chatter.

'How can you be so sure?'

The tinny noise was longer and seemed more insistent.

'Aye, well, that's something then . . . No, I said nothing, and they bailed me for a week, but I'm suspended with no access to anything anymore. They've also bailed that bloody idiot ex-boyfriend of hers, Lewis. I told him in no uncertain terms what would happen to him if he grassed.'

The mechanical noise sounded like a small insect.

'Aye, we need to talk, sort this out and come up with a plan to keep the cops away. Surely Kirugu can pull some bloody strings? I'm not going down for this, Toka. It was a stupid bloody idea to take her off the hill. It's not like you don't have enough girls to use, is it?'

Another pause.

'Jetmir is a bloody idiot. Why this particular girl? . . . Okay, where are you? . . . Southside, yeah, I know it . . . Not like I have much bloody choice; the missus has just bloody slung me out. I'm leaving now.'

There was a long pause, broken only by the deep, forlorn sigh from Luigi. There was a rustling sound which was followed by a sudden blast of music from the speakers and the engine burst into life. The headlights pierced the darkness and the car moved off.

'Here we go. Is the tracker working okay?' he asked.

'Perfectly,' said Janie, handing the iPad over to Max and starting the Volvo.

'You ready?' said Max, buckling his seatbelt.

'Like a coiled spring, sarge,' said Janie, also slotting her seatbelt into place.

'Okay, loose follow only. He'll be careful, and we can just let the tracker do its job. Stay out of his line of sight, but I think we're heading to Glasgow.'

'Southside?'

'Absolutely.' Max picked up his phone and dialled.

'Tell me something useful, Max. I'm stuck with Norma, who is doing my fucking head in by being smug as an inland revenue inspector who's just discovered a big hole in a yuppie's tax return, because she's got a new number for Luigi,' said Ross, his voice booming out of the speakers.

'He's moving. Kicked out of his house by the look of it. He's just phoned Toka and is heading to meet her somewhere on Southside. We heard half the phone call.'

'Excellent. We'll start moving and meet you down there.'

'He's not happy at all, sounds under serious pressure. He mentioned Kirugu, but he's on his way. We get them together, then this job is good to go. We can nick them both at the same time, which may persuade Affi to talk to us. That could bring the whole bloody lot of them down, right?'

'One step at a time, man. We're at Burnett Road, as Norma needed one of their terminals for her quest to be as annoyingly clever as possible. The cross-network check on Luigi's handset number just came back. He's used several SIMs in it, and a new one went live on the network a moment ago. Live trace has been authorised and we're just waiting for the first update. Hopefully that'll give her something to work on with a new number for Toka and we can cover it from all angles.'

'Jeez, I hope so.'

'Right, we're leaving now. Norma can work on the way down, if the bloody reception in the Cairngorms lets us, but as soon as we know where he's landed, we can plan an arrest strategy.'

'Absolutely. Let's get this job moving.' Max ended the call.

Max looked at the map on the tablet, noting the blue pulsing dot as the Audi moved along the road.

He turned and looked at Janie, and grinned. 'Let's roll, all the way to Glasgow. We're bringing these bastards down.'

29

'**WHO WAS THAT?**' said Jetmir as Toka tossed her phone on the bed, shaking her head.

'That idiot cop, Luigi. He's on his way down now. We need to make it clear to him the consequences of talking, and we have to come up with a plan to distance ourselves from Afrodita. I was mad to let you talk me into going after her, Jetmir.'

'She would have been a real gold mine.'

'Gold mine? You stupid boy, you were just thinking with your bloody cock after you found her on Instagram and saw how pretty she'd become. She's still a bloody liability, that girl. You need to make sure she knows the consequences of speaking.' Toka's voice was as sharp and scathing as a razor blade.

'She knows already, Sheff.'

'Does she? How long before the little slut gets confident and talks? She's your responsibility, so if she speaks to the cops it's your problem, not mine. So you need to make sure she stays quiet. Or would you rather I told Kirugu? He would certainly have a different, and more permanent, solution than you, eh?' she spat, her face full of disdain.

Jetmir's eyes widened. 'She won't speak, and she'd have made money for us . . .' His voice tailed off, and he sat down, sighing heavily, and held his face in his hands.

Toka turned to face him, eyes blazing. 'You pathetic wretch. You've brought this on us. Kirugu is now pissed at us, and no way am I taking the fall for this. It was your idea, you can own it. You can't even keep yourself clean anymore. What made you think that girl would fall for you, eh?'

'I wanted to prove myself. I lost her years ago, and once I found her, I wanted to get her back. Show I was worthy.' His voice was low and shaky, his shoulders hunched as he rubbed his temples.

'Well, what's done is done, Jetmir. We move onwards. We have plenty of girls at other houses, so we can be up and running here by tomorrow and we need to be. I'm paying rent here, you know, and Southside needs this place. The street whores are skanky, and there's nothing for customers who want a clean place and a clean girl. Nothing is for free, and that goes for you too, Jetmir. We have two girls moving here tomorrow, both good ones, so you'll need to be here for security, okay?'

'Fine. Is Kirugu cool?'

'Right now, he's not happy. But he will be once we start paying him his tax on this place, but he's still very pissed at you.'

'Me? Why me?' Jetmir's eyes were wide.

'You failed. You lost a kilo of his product, and lost a girl. You then recapture her without his authority.'

'Toka, you were there to—'

'I don't care, Jetmir,' Toka interrupted, her voice sharp. 'You need to be careful, eh? You need to work very hard for me, and I need at least two more girls if I'm having to move two here from the West End, so you need to get back to Tirana and find them and get them over here. You want me to tell Kirugu you're being a liability? How long do you think you'd last? Bearing in mind he already thinks you're unreliable, and frankly as much of an idiot as I know you are.'

Jetmir's face drained of colour and he opened his mouth to remonstrate, but then clearly changed his mind. 'Sorry, Sheff,' he muttered.

'That's better. Now there's some paint in my office. Start

clearing the back bedroom and get on with it. There's a girl going in there tomorrow, and the room needs to be ready. I want this place to start making money by tomorrow, you understand me?'

'Yes.'

'Get on with it.'

Jetmir turned without a further word and left the room.

Toka sighed deeply, frustrated about the waste of time and resources she'd spent getting that stupid girl Affi and the trouble it caused with Hoxhaj. She'd had to call in a favour with that idiot Luigi, which she hated doing, and it had been a real risk grabbing her in the car park. Added to that, lost days where she wasn't closely supervising her brothels meant a significant loss in income. She almost growled at the thought. The whole purpose of working as hard as she did was to keep saving. She almost had enough to finish the stunning house, on the beautiful peninsular of Lin on the shore of Lake Ohrid. She was planning to one day return and retire from this shit life running brothels for a violent, unpredictable gangster like Alban Hoxhaj. She wanted out, and to live the simple life by the lake.

30

AFFI SAT IN her bedroom, taking no notice of the small TV flickering in the corner. Her fingers tickled Jock's ears as he lay next to her on the bed, snoring deeply and occasionally twitching as he did, most likely dreaming of chasing rabbits, as it was his favourite pastime.

There was a light tap on the door, and Valerie's face peered in, a gentle smile on her lovely face. 'You okay, pet?' she said, for what seemed like the thirtieth time that evening.

Affi's heart softened at the sight of her foster mum. She was a kind lady who had given so much, so she couldn't bear to be sharp with her as she'd been on the last few visits. 'I'm feeling a wee bit better,' she said, smiling, and hoping it showed as genuine, rather than revealing the boiling turmoil she was actually feeling.

'Och, that's wonderful, pet. Are you maybe ready to talk to me about what happened? Problem shared and all that?' She raised her thick eyebrows.

'Maybe tomorrow. I'm really tired and maybe some sleep will help me.'

'What happened, toot? I just want to help.' Valerie sat hesitantly on the bed and reached her hand out to Affi's.

Affi pulled hers away, almost as if she'd been electrocuted, and then immediately felt bad seeing the look of hurt that spread across her foster mum's face.

'Affi, I'm sorr—'

'Maybe some cocoa?' said Affi, interrupting and trying to smile, but sensing that it wouldn't reach her eyes. She was desperate for Valerie to leave her alone and in peace. She loved her foster parents dearly, but right now she wanted to be on her own. She hadn't heard from Melodi since she'd been released by Jetmir, and she was trying to stop the panic from overwhelming her. All her messages to Melodi had gone unanswered, which wasn't in itself unusual, as internet was sporadic at best in that region of Tirana.

'Aye, cocoa,' said Valerie, smiling and standing. 'Cocoa always makes things better, pet. Spray cream and marshmallows?'

'Yes, please,' said Affi, turning to the TV just as she heard the familiar 'ping' from her iPad. It was on the bed next to her and half under the lean form of Jock, who was still snoring.

'Back in a mo, and maybe then we can have a wee chat, eh?' said Valerie, disappearing out of the door.

Her heart thumping, Affi picked up her iPad, shifting Jock to one side to free the tablet. She saw that there was an Instagram notification. With an icy hand gripping her stomach she looked at the message request that was from a blank-faced icon and the name Safe-Space, written in Albanian. Whilst she couldn't read Albanian, she recognised the name as being Melodi's children's home. With trembling hands, Affi accepted the message.

A photograph of her sister playing on a cracked pavement, a skipping rope in her hands and the big smile on her face lurid in its intensity on the high-definition screen. But it wasn't the picture of her happy, beautiful sister that made her blood turn to ice in her veins. A bulky man was standing directly behind her, leaning against the wall, slouching in ripped jeans and a leather jacket. His face was obscured with a yellow grotesquely grinning emoji, but his hands were crossed in front of his chest, thumbs hooking against each other and the splayed fingers resembling the wings on the Albanian flag, like Reg would sometimes do when making shadow shapes of birds. Affi took in a sharp breath that was almost painful in her dry throat.

The hand signal of the Albanian Shqiptare just three feet away from dear, sweet Melodi.

31

'OKAY, STANDBY, STANDBY. Looks like he's stopped. Southside close to Queen's Park. We're moving up now.' Max spoke into the radio mic that was hidden in the light in the roof of the car which was linked to the car's radio. Holding the iPad, he looked at the pulsing blue dot on the map, indicating where the Audi was parked, just two streets across.

The journey south had been unremarkable, with Luigi driving at a sedate pace down the A9 and taking the most direct route to the south of Glasgow. He never seemed to practise any anti-surveillance, such as sudden stops, back doubles or circum-navigation of roundabouts. He just drove steadily, within the speed limits, and they followed from a distance using the tracker secreted on the underside of the car, never getting within line of sight of the big Audi.

Norma's voice came out of the speakers, the smile evident even over the airwaves. 'Update from phone intelligence, he's been using the phone. He's messaged a number he's called or messaged several times in the past on previous SIMs. Unregistered pre-pay phone, but open-source intelligence links it to several Glasgow-based prostitutes advertising on an adult services website. I'm digging into it now, and checks on the number have been requested fast time.' Norma sounded particularly pleased with herself, which was reasonable, thought Max.

'Brilliant work, Norma. In awe as always.'

'Ah, don't fucking say that, Max. Her head is the size of a fucking hoose already, for just poncing about on a computer whilst I did all the bloody driving,' came Ross's voice, crackling through the speakers.

'Do we have a timescale?' said Max, chuckling.

'No, but hopefully pretty quick,' said Norma.

'Not quick enough. We need an address, now. He's clearly visiting Toka and we need to catch them together to sew this bloody thing up.'

'What do you suggest?' said Ross.

'I need eyes on him. Put him to an address and we can bash the doors in first thing; there could be victims in there right now.' Max turned to Janie. 'Drop me at the bottom of the road where the Audi's parked.'

'You sure? He's met you and you want a walk past?'

'Aye, come on, let's get moving.'

Janie nodded, engaged the automatic gears and pulled off.

'We need to put him to an address now. If this is a brand-new brothel, then intelligence won't take us there. They could have under-age girls working in there now, Janie. We can't let that happen.' Max reached round, dragged a rucksack into the front seat and pulled out a stained and dishevelled cap, together with a pair of glasses. He fit the cap low on his head and slotted the spectacles onto his nose. He delved back into the rucksack and took out a battered and stained windcheater jacket, the type that runners wear in inclement weather.

'That jacket looks bogging, Max. You'll look like a bloody jakey,' said Janie.

'Aye, that's the point. Let me out here,' said Max, already reaching for the door handle of the car as Janie slowed at the end of the road where the tracker continued to pulse.

'Okay, the car's about forty metres up on the left. Stay out of sight,' said Janie.

'Not about being out of sight, pal. It's about not being noticed. I just have to fit the street scene. Meet me at the top of the road,' said Max, jamming in an earpiece and smiling as he got out and slammed the door shut.

Max zipped the grubby and ripped jacket up to his neck as he turned right into the street. He stooped and picked up a discarded, empty can of lager that was rolling on the pavement in the stiff breeze. Max saw the Audi parked by a skip outside a tenement building on the opposite side of the road. He could clearly see the outline of Luigi still sitting in the car, his face illuminated by the glow of a phone screen.

'Approaching the Audi. Any phone update?' whispered Max into the covert mic clipped on the inside of his shirt.

'Messages going back and forth,' came Norma's voice.

Max slowed his pace and began to sway and wobble as he walked up the cracked pavement that was strewn with broken glass, his feet crunching as he wobbled, pausing every few steps to rest against the walls that separated the tenements from the street. Max began to mutter to himself, his voice slurred in the perfect impression of someone who had consumed far too much beer. He held up the can of strong lager to his mouth, being careful to keep it well away from touching his lips.

The distance closed between him and the Audi, which was sitting, dark and inert, at the side of the road. Max didn't hesitate, and he didn't even think about hiding, skulking or ducking into doorways. If anything was going to raise suspicion, or attract attention, it was out-of-the-ordinary behaviour. A scruffy, apparently drunk man, at this late hour in the middle of Glasgow, wouldn't attract any attention whatsoever. It would be normal.

So, Max didn't panic when the car's interior light came on and the door opened. About fifty feet ahead of him, Luigi Ricci got out and glanced back, towards Max, who paused to apparently stare at the can with disproportionate interest whilst swaying and muttering like a drunk who had discovered he had finished his last beer.

'Ah, fuggit, ya fucking basa,' slurred Max, dropping the tin onto the ground, where it clattered, the noise shattering the late-night peace of the quiet street.

Luigi looked again, but just shook his head and slammed the car door shut before crossing the road towards the tenement opposite. Without a backwards glance he strode to the front door and pressed the bell.

'Oh, Danny boy!' sang Max, his voice raucous and overtly Glaswegian as he continued his wobbly journey along the dark side street, watching Luigi in his peripheral vision.

A shaft of light erupted from the tenement door, and a stolid-looking woman appeared and opened the door wide. Max immediately recognised her as Toka Kurti from Norma's intelligence profile picture. She stepped to one side, her face stern, and Luigi entered, his head low like an errant schoolboy attending the headmaster's office.

Max staggered along the cracked pavement until the door shut tight and both figures disappeared. He straightened a little and picked up his pace. 'That's Ricci confirmed into number twenty-eight, let inside by Toka Kurti.'

'Received. I'll pick you up at the far end from where I dropped you,' said Janie.

'No, meet me where I got out. I'm just going to walk by and check out the door,' whispered Max. He crossed the road, still weaving and wobbling, his head down low, muttering. This could be their only opportunity to check out the physical security on the door, which would be important for the tactical plan when considering method of entry. He turned back on himself and lurched along the pavement making no attempt to be silent, or to skulk. Hiding in plain sight.

The door to the brothel was newly painted jet black, glossy

and stout in the sodium streetlights, the numbers were stark stainless-steel. Max noted the new, high-quality locks and the brand-new bell push, almost certainly connected to a camera.

Ross's voice sparked up over the airwaves. 'Received here too. I've been onto the chief. He wants a full briefing and set of options ready to go tomorrow. He's authorised the cameras to be put in, updated the surveillance commissioners, and he has resources being put on standby ready to deploy to support us when we raid it.'

'We need to keep this tight, though. You know how leaky the force is.'

'I know. I'm not giving out specifics, just getting resources on standby to support the operation, OSU, Immigration, interpreters and the like. We may need to go in at a second's notice.'

'We could go in now,' said Max, picking up his pace towards the Volvo as it pulled to a halt at the top of the road.

'I agree with you, but oddly for him, the chief wants impact and full risk assessments. His view is that we don't know who, or what's, inside. Trafficking for sexual exploitation is a major force priority, and he wants to be bulletproof. We'll get a camera on the front door so we know who's in. Barney's on his way now, moaning like the old git he is. We have the evidence of association between Ricci and Toka now. We go in tomorrow, with all the proper support.'

'I'm not sure about this, Ross. We should go in now. We can whistle up some support from local teams and deal with what we find. Why is the chief suddenly being so bloody hesitant?' said Max, getting into the car and slamming the door shut.

'Well, we have little choice. I guess we can't just smash our way into a brothel like this, right now. I don't want to put the call out for help locally, as fuck knows who's listening. Toka had one Southside cop on the payroll – she could have more, eh?'

'Aye, I guess, but I'd still go in now, if it was my shout.'

'Me too, but last time I looked, the Chief Constable of Police Scotland outranks us by a fair old bit, eh?'

'Fair enough. What now?'

'Back to the office. We need to get our heads together. Chief wants an in-person update first thing, and then it'll be a multi-agency briefing after that. Once the brothel gets up and running in the morning, we'll strike.'

'What if Ricci buggers off overnight?'

'Aye, that's possible, but unlikely and it doesn't even matter, does it? You watched him go in and meet Toka with your own eyes. Why come here if he's not going to stay? You two thought it looked like he was out on his ear at home?'

'Seemed that way.'

'Matters not, anyway. Once we get hold of their phones, that'll prove the whole bloody lot. Right, to the office, now.'

'That sounded a bit Batman. "To the batcave, Robin."' Max winked at Janie.

'You're such a dickhead, Craigie,' Ross quipped.

'You sure?' said Max, raising his eyebrows at Janie.

'Aye, I fucking am, and you can take the superwhatchamacallit tone out of your voice.'

'Supercilious?'

'That's the one. Right, arses back here, and stop talking shite.'

'Okay. See you at Tulliallan.'

'He's sounding irascible,' said Janie.

Max just shrugged, unable to shift the uncomfortable feeling in his stomach.

'You're not happy, are you?'

'Not entirely. I can't quite understand why we aren't bashing the door in now. I'm worried about any girls that may be in there. I think that's what's worrying me, anyway.' Max yawned.

'It's been a long day. We could all do with some sleep.'

'Maybe, come on. Let's head to Tulliallan. It sounds like this is going to morph into a big job with every man and his dog involved.'

'Ugh, I hate jobs like that.'

'Aye, me too, but I get Ross's point. We have no evidence that that place is running as a brothel, and little evidence that Toka has done much wrong. We can get the evidence with cameras of the comings and goings, maybe send in an undercover client and we're good to go. It's still painfully thin. We need more than just Ricci and that moron McPhail, pal. We want the whole bloody lot of them. Let's go.' Max nodded and fastened his seatbelt.

'I hope you're right, Max. I really don't want any more harm to come to any vulnerable victims, do you?'

Max's jaw was tight. 'Let's go.'

Janie put the car in gear, and they drove off in silence.

32

TOKA STARED WITH disdain at the pathetic form who sat slumped in the faux leather armchair in the corner of her office.

'I've nothing left now, Toka. My wife has kicked me out, and I'm almost certainly finished in the police. I just don't know what to do next,' he said, his voice cracking and tears brimming in his dark eyes.

'Louie, darling,' she said, summoning up the false concern she could turn on when speaking to clients whose wives 'didn't understand them'. She forced a smile onto her face, confident in the fact that Luigi was so wrapped up in his own malaise that he wouldn't get the blatant sarcasm.

'I mean, I've just been a bloody idiot.'

'Poor Louie,' she said, looking at a text from one of the girls who ran her West End brothel. At least two girls were being sent here early tomorrow. That was good. Competition was stiff in the West End, but the only working girls close by were streetwalkers turning tricks in doorways for fifteen pounds a pop. The two girls who were coming in the morning were far classier, for the time being, at least.

'I can't believe I did it to the kids,' he whined.

Pathetic little wretch, she thought, wondering how she could get rid of him. Trouble with Luigi was that he knew a little too much about her operation. She'd let him get a bit too close to her when he was on the street offences team. He was less use to her now that he was working in Dingwall. *Stupid bastard*, she thought, stifling a yawn.

'Can I stay here for a few nights, Toka? Just until my wife calms down a wee bit,' he said, almost mewling like a sad cat.

A pussy, anyway, she thought, a smile crossing her face. Toka had to work hard to keep the sneer at bay. Typical of all these stupid, weak-willed men, led by their cocks into situations they couldn't control. If he wasn't a serving cop, she'd have thrown him out, there and then, but Toka was smart and realised that a cop in her debt was always likely to be valuable, even if he was based over a hundred miles away. He had access to all sorts of databases that could be of use, and he still had contacts.

'Louie, darling. Of course, you can. I'm always here for you, my angel, you know this. Stay tonight, and then go make up with your lovely wife, Kimberley? I want to say Kimberley, no?'

She enjoyed seeing Luigi flinch at the mention of his wife's name. She knew that he would be wondering if he'd ever mentioned it before. She decided to press. 'And of course, you must miss poor wee Luigi Junior and Georgia, too,' she said, her smile was as much a threat as any overt words of warning could ever be. She had the idiot exactly where she wanted him. Typical man, just so easy to manipulate. Her smile grew at the wide-eyed expression on the cop's face.

'How do you know my kids—'

The door buzzer interrupted his question and Toka looked at the sharp image on the monitor that was operated by the bell push Jetmir had installed. Her heart jumped a little when she saw the huge form of Enver, Alban Hoxhaj's driver and minder. Her eyes widened. What could he possibly want? He had sometimes dropped by the brothels, either to collect tax, or more often when he was feeling horny for a free session with one of the girls. Her eyes flicked to her little black book on the desk, silent and full of secrets.

'Enver darling. I have no girls here today,' she said, her voice deep and sultry as she moved seamlessly into madam mode.

'I have to collect for Mr Hoxhaj,' he said, his cold, dark eyes staring at the camera.

'But, Enver. I have no money. We're not operating here, yet.'

'I can't go back without money, or Mr Hoxhaj will be displeased. You want this?' he said, his eyes unmoving and eerie, like a shark's. The emphasis he placed on the word 'displeased' was significant. That single word was far more ominous than could be defined in a dictionary. 'Displeased', when uttered by Alban Hoxhaj, was a word which should be interpreted as 'furious', and nobody wanted a furious Kirugu bearing a grudge, certainly not Toka. She had several thousand pounds in the small safe in the corner of the room; maybe a small payment would keep Alban happy until they got up and running.

She turned to Luigi. 'Go and wait in the back bedroom, lock the door and don't come out until I tell you to do so.'

'Toka, who's that?' he said.

'No one for you to concern yourself with. Go now. If he finds you in there, just say you're a client waiting for a girl who's coming later from West, okay?'

'But—'

'Go now, Luigi!' she said, her voice as sharp as a shard of glass and her deep-set eyes flashing with alarm.

Luigi's eyes widened, but he meekly stood, head bowed and shoulders hunched, and left the room without another word.

Quickly she picked up her book and tucked it back behind the portrait, and closed her eyes in a silent prayer. She hated it when Enver came. He was a perverted brute and she couldn't be sure he wouldn't want her to have sex with him. He'd expected it in the past when there were no girls, and he was so heavy and really didn't smell good. Despite her advancing years, Toka knew she was still a handsome woman, and there was a good chance that Enver would want a piece of her if he was feeling horny, which he nearly always was.

She pressed the microphone. 'Okay, come in, darling,' she said, her stomach heavy as she pushed the button that operated the door lock. She cursed under her breath; she wasn't even operating yet, hadn't properly earned for a couple of days and now was most likely going to have to hand over several thousand pounds because of that idiot Jetmir.

She made an immediate decision. Jetmir was finished. Luigi still had his uses, but Jetmir was just deadweight and to be frank, a bloody liability. She was getting rid of him. A smile stretched across her lips as she applied thick red lipstick in anticipation of Enver coming into the room.

Jetmir would regret the problems he caused her. In fact, he'd regret the day he was fucking born.

She stood and checked her hair in the mirror, nodding at her reflection. She still looked good and a little flirting with Enver always worked. He didn't say much, but he was still a man and was as susceptible to her feminine wiles as any. She unfastened the top two buttons of her blouse, exposing her voluminous cleavage, as she walked towards the front door so she could meet Enver in her normal effusive and welcoming hostess manner.

As she moved along the tiled corridor, the door to the vestibule opened, and the stern-faced Enver appeared, square and intimidating, his heavy brow and square jaw bathed in the weak light. He nodded at her and then stood to one side, deferentially.

Alban Hoxhaj stepped out from the huge man's shadow, his oiled, slicked-back hair shining in the overhead light.

Toka's heart lurched and a cold fist gripped her insides, but she managed to widen her smile. 'Alban, darling. To what do I owe this unexpected pleasure?'

'Toka, my love, it's time to pay your taxes,' he said, a grin that dripped with insincerity stretching across his face and his gold front tooth glinting.

33

MAX, JANIE, ROSS and Norma were sitting in their poky office in the deepest recesses of Tulliallan Castle, sleepily clutching mugs of coffee and stifling yawns. Janie sat glued to a live feed of the front door of the brothel that Max had watched Luigi Ricci go into just a few hours earlier.

The door burst open and a bright-eyed Barney strode into the office, his face wide with a toothy smile. As always, the smell of cigarette smoke accompanied him into the room.

'Ayup, I take it feed's working alreet?' he said, his Yorkshire brogue broad and rich.

'Crystal clear, Barney. How close did you get?' said Janie.

'Fifty yards away, and camera's hidden in a Coke can on the dash and zoomed in tight, no bugger will see it. In my bloody van again, though. Ross, I'm gonna invoice you for the hire of it. It's not free to tax and insure, you know.'

'Aye, sure thing, file it in here,' said Ross, holding up a battered wastepaper bin.

'Cheeky bugger.'

'Anyway, how come it took you almost four hours to get here? The feed's been live for ages,' said Ross, yawning.

'I just had a kip in't van before I whistled up an Uber to get back here. Nay good reason for me to spend brass on a hotel when I've a perfectly good bed in it, is there?'

'You're a right weird bugger and a typically tight-arsed

Yorkshireman. When did you last sleep in your house?' said Ross.

'Not for a while, which is your bloody fault, always getting me out on chuffin' jobs. It's never worth me going bloody home.' He walked up to the coffee machine and poured himself a mug of thick, dark coffee, which he sniffed with relish. 'Owt happening?' he added between sips and nodding at the screen.

'Nope. Not a sausage, but by the time you got the feed in place we hadn't had the door covered for a couple of hours. Luigi's car is still there, so we can safely assume both he and Toka are inside.'

'Phones are switched off,' said Norma, chewing on a pastry.

'Is that a worry?' said Janie.

'I don't know. Should it be?'

'Are they being careful?'

'Maybe, but neither has left the premises,' said Janie, inspecting a biscuit with relish, before stuffing it in her mouth and chewing.

'Where did you get that bloody biscuit? There's none in the tin last time I looked,' said Ross.

'No,' said Janie.

'No what?'

'No, you can't have one. You've been falling off the diet wagon, and if I supply you with a Hobnob, which incidentally is delicious, you'll get in trouble with Mrs F when you go home covered in crumbs.'

'Bloody bastarding liberty, constables denying the DI a bloody biscuit when his blood sugar's dropping. I'm expected to brief the boss, and I'll be doing so whilst risking a diabetic coma or something because you won't give me a bastard Hobnob.'

'For your own good, sir,' said Janie, stifling a giggle.

'Get fucked,' Ross said, his face reddening, and he turned an angry gaze back to his computer screen.

The team had all come straight back to the office after Luigi had gone into the brothel in Glasgow. They'd all grabbed a few hours' sleep in the transit accommodation normally reserved for recruits under training and were back in the office ready to plan further. It would have been simpler to take them both out last night, but the reality was they didn't have half the evidence they needed yet, and they all knew that. If Afrodita maintained her story that she hadn't been abducted, then they had nothing at all and they'd have to be bailed. If that happened, Toka was bound to flee.

This was so much more than a lone trafficking victim being abducted and released without explanation.

They also knew that it was bigger than a brothel keeper wanting her girl back, and Toka and Luigi were a vital lead. They were a start point, and every proactive policing operation required a start point.

'What's the chief's position on this?' asked Max.

'You can ask him yourself. Mr Macdonald wants to see us straight away,' said Ross, looking at his screen.

'What, all of us?' said Norma.

'No, just me and Max. You guys crack on with the intel, and keep an eye on the live feed and tracker. We'll go and sweet talk the boss. Chances are we'll need some resources if we're to bash this place up properly, particularly if there are vulnerable wee girls, or illegal immigrants in there. No use if Max goes charging in there in his size tens, is there? This kind of job requires subtlety, eh?' said Ross.

'Cheeky bastard,' muttered Max.

'A fair point, I'd say. Come on, boss is waiting for us now.'

*

Chief Constable Chris Macdonald's office was a large, open-plan affair in the prime bit of real estate at Tulliallan Castle, far from the bowels where Ross and Max's team was located.

Unfortunately, at this point they couldn't gain access to the office as Chief Superintendent Barry Carlisle was barring their entry, his desk cleverly positioned in front of the chief's door. He had been in place for a few years now, becoming increasingly irascible and protective of his boss's time, and was known to be nakedly ambitious, searching for the next rank. Sitting at the desk next to him was Sofia McLennan, a slim and immaculately attired woman in her thirties who was the chief's PA. She did all the actual work that Carlisle didn't want to, the supposed role of the staff officer being far above a personal assistant. She was smiling with obvious enjoyment at the terse exchange currently underway between Carlisle and Ross. This was typical of Sofia. Carlisle was somewhat bumptious and officious, whereas Sofia was warm and welcoming with an ever-present smile on her face.

'He told me to come straight down,' said Ross.

'Well, I wasn't told,' said Carlisle, puffing out his cheeks, his eyes not meeting Ross's or Max's as he looked at his sleek Apple laptop. He wore a sharp business suit that couldn't quite hide his somewhat 'gone to seed' physique. His wavy hair was thick and speckled with grey, and he wore round wire-frame glasses.

'Literally ten minutes ago, Barry. He instant-messaged me.'

'What, the Chief Constable instant-messaged you?'

'Aye, did I not say it right first time, Baz?'

Carlisle shook his head, just slightly, as his fingers flashed across his keyboard. He sat there staring at the screen in total, cloying silence. The only sound was the loud ticking of a wall clock. After a tense few seconds, Carlisle stood. 'Well, I'm going in to ask him personally.'

'Nice one, Bazza,' said Ross, taking a seat with a grimace, as Carlisle disappeared into the chief's office.

'Ross, you're so naughty, eh. Winding Barry up like this,' said Sofia with a chuckle. Her accent was a mix of Scottish tinged with something else that could have been Eastern European, or even German, but no one had ever asked her.

'Ach, he's a bit of a flapper is our Bazza, Sofia. Anyway, how are you?' Ross said, his face softening.

'I'm good, Ross. You guys have been working so many hours, you must never see Mrs Fraser?' She cocked her head to one side, her face full of genuine concern.

'Aye, as she constantly, regularly and incessantly reminds me, hen.'

Barry stormed back out of the chief's office, his face dark and his narrow shoulders squared defiantly. 'Okay, he'll see you now, but next time I want more notice, and preferably an agenda.'

'You got it, Bazza,' said Ross, standing up, grimacing again.

'And Ross,' said Carlisle, just as Ross was moving towards the door.

'Aye?' He turned and fixed Carlisle with a crooked smile.

'I know I'm an informal type, but I *am* a detective chief super-intendent. You really ought to call me "sir", or at least "boss",' he said, his voice gently chiding, like a teacher reprimanding a naughty child.

'Whatever you say, guvnor,' he said in a poor impression of a broad cockney accent that owed more to Dick Van Dyke than anyone born within the sound of Bow Bells.

Carlisle opened his mouth as if to protest but closed it quickly, clearly realising that this wasn't a battle to engage in. Instead, he just shook his head, once more.

'I'll show you in. You want coffee?' said Sofia, trying to hide the smile that was stretching across her face as she opened the office door.

'Aye, that'd be grand, Sofia. Thanks,' said Ross.

'Max?' she said.

'I'm good, thanks,' said Max as Sofia led them into the office.

'Are you upsetting my staff officer, Ross?' said Chief Constable Chris Macdonald, who was sitting behind his desk, resplendent in his full police uniform.

'As if,' said Ross.

'Leave Barry alone. He's a good man, if a little prissy.' Macdonald tried to hide the smile that was threatening to overwhelm his face.

'Aye, something beginning with P, anyway.'

Macdonald snorted with amusement. 'Coffee?'

'Already sorted, Mr Mac. I'll bring it straight in. You want one?'

'Thanks, Sofia. I'd love a cup.'

Sofia nodded and left the room.

'So, gents, update me. I've only really had half a story, so far,' said Macdonald.

Ross gave him the whole story, briefly, clearly and concisely.

Macdonald sat, his fingers steepled in front of him, his face set in a mask of concentration.

There was a soft knock at the door, and Sofia entered with a tray on which there were two steaming mugs. She handed one to Ross and deposited the other at Macdonald's elbow on a Police Scotland coaster. She smiled again and left the office, her footsteps almost silent.

'Hmm' was all he said when Sofia had left the room.

'Just hmm?' said Ross, his eyebrows raised.

'It's all a little thin, wouldn't you say?'

'It certainly presents as thin, but we can't get away from the facts. The statistics on female Albanian trafficking victims don't really lie, boss.'

'Yeah, I get that, and I don't like the sound of PC Ricci and his dealings with the sex trade, but there's so much in this, we really need a multiagency approach, which is why I didn't want you busting the place last night. We potentially have multiple trafficking victims, and inside information coming from outside organisations, don't we?'

'We do. Being honest, boss. If we're going to try to get to the bottom of this, we need close cooperation with social services, Immigration, the National Referral team for trafficking and possibly some of the trafficking charities. We're only a small team, and we just couldn't handle multiple victims.'

'Did I hear that Norma has a contact at Immigration wanting to information share?'

'Aye, some bloke called Steve Vipond.'

'Vipond like the bloke from Deacon Blue?' said Macdonald.

'God, not you too. Aye, like the bloke from Blue Deacon.'

Macdonald snorted in amusement. 'So why not hand the whole thing over? Serious and Organised Crime could take it on and work with those organisations, couldn't they?'

'They could, I guess, but . . .' Max paused.

'But?'

'There's no way that whoever's behind this could manage it without significant help from people inside the cops, the NCA, social services or Immigration. I just can't see it. Locations and identities of trafficking victims, once they're approved by the NRM, are closely guarded. How have they all gone missing?'

'So, what do you suggest, Max?'

'We keep primacy and just request assistance when we need it from key stakeholders to support individual operations. Starting with the brothel on Southside, which we need to get to quickly.'

'Okay, so prioritise that, then. What will you need?'

'At least one immigration officer, a representative from social services, an Albanian interpreter, representatives from the NCAIU child abuse teams and a medical professional. We go through the door and arrest Toka, Jetmir and Luigi, and the backup team can deal with the trafficking victims. We may need them to deploy to other brothels, once we start digging. Intel is that Toka runs several venues, so it could be quite onerous,' said Max.

Macdonald nodded, slowly. 'Hopefully they're all on standby already. We need to move fast but I want some distancing from you two, so I'll get the request to come from someone from Serious and Organised, as that'd be more normal. Hold on.'

He picked up his phone and pressed a button. 'Barry, pop in a minute, will you?'

Within a second Barry Carlisle appeared.

'Barry, who do we have on standby after last night's request?'

'Well, I put Miles Wakefield at Serious Crime on notice. He has representatives from NCAIU, Immigration, trafficking teams, social services and at least one medical professional ready to brief as soon as we give the word.'

'Okay, I'm giving the word. Let's get it sorted.'

Carlisle looked a little stunned. 'When for?'

'Immediately. Like right now. There's an operation happening in the next couple of hours and we need the support urgently, and with the highest priority. Whatever they have on, they need to delay to facilitate this. Understand?'

'They'll likely want more information,' Carlisle said.

'Well, they'll get it as soon as it's operationally appropriate.'

'Who's lead on this?'

'Ross for the moment, but it may fall to Miles's team, depending on what happens.'

'Okay, sir. Anything else?'

'Is Inspector Joe Lyle of the Operational Support Unit on standby? You'll need method of entry, right, Ross?'

'Aye, possibly. I know Joe well – he'll be happy to help as he's done work with us before. We'll also need his officers to secure the back of the premises.'

'He's waiting for a call. Do we have a location?' said Carlisle.

'Meeting will be here in the conference room.'

'No, I meant location of the operation,' said Carlisle.

'Scotland. Cut along, Barry. Priority one, okay?' Macdonald turned away from his staff officer indicating that his presence was no longer required. 'He's a decent sort, is Baz. A little officious and overly ambitious, but he means well, and he's very efficient,' said Macdonald when Carlisle had left.

Ross just sniggered.

'Okay, I'll leave you to plan. Meeting hopefully within two hours. Will you liaise directly with Miles Wakefield?' said Macdonald.

'Aye, he's a good guy, is Miles. He'll know the score.'

'Well, keep me informed. I won't come to the meeting. Let's lower the obvious profile of it, but I'm not happy, Ross. I'm getting bloody sick of fighting fires caused by corruption. I'm not going to rest until this is stopped. Clear?' He stood up, indicating that the meeting was over.

'Clear,' said Max and Ross simultaneously.

34

THE ASSET PUT the phone down, unable to believe how fast things were moving. Something big was brewing, and it was clearly something that could badly affect several people. This was exposure that they just couldn't risk.

The timing was bad, particularly with the girl being released by that idiot Toka. Had the girl spoken? Surely not, with the hold that Toka had over the girl's sister in Albania. It didn't make sense.

However, a sudden, covert operation ordered by the Chief Constable of Police Scotland was a worry. What did they know?

The mention of Ross Fraser and Max Craigie was a real concern too, being as they were in some type of small, secret anticorruption unit that nobody seemed to know anything about. However, rumours always flew in law enforcement. The asset had heard of their involvement in bringing down a whole corrupt cell of NCA and customs agents, although the headlines seemed to give all the credit to Serious and Organised Crime.

The asset sighed, guts churning with nerves. There was no choice. A call would have to be made. If they arrested the wrong person, or came across the wrong piece of intelligence, then it could open doors that would be hard to close. The asset knew that they were protected. Such care had been taken, but now was not a time to take chances.

The asset picked up their burner phone and posted to the usual message board.

Need to speak now.

Almost immediately a message pinged back with a telephone number. The asset dialled.

'Yes?' The gruff voice of Alban Hoxhaj was deep and gravelly.

'Something's happening. The Chief Constable is doing something relating to prostitution and trafficking. We just got notified about it from his office.'

'When?'

'Imminent. A DI and a DS connected to some kind of covert anticorruption unit are pulling resources from all over: social services, Immigration, Albanian interpreters. It must be to do with brothels – nothing else makes sense. Are you exposed on this?'

'No. No issues at all for me or my organisation. Who are these officers?'

'I don't know a lot about them. Just whispers that they're anticorruption and that they've already brought down several bent cops, and other law-enforcement officers. Apparently, they have access to every kind of resource. I even heard they've used Special Forces.'

'What are their names?'

'I'm told they're DI Ross Fraser and DS Max Craigie. I don't know them well at all.'

'Find out more. It could present a problem.'

'I will. What about Toka Kurti?'

'She won't be a problem.'

'What about the brothels she runs, though?'

'Nothing to worry about, my friend. It's good you warn me. It's why you get paid so handsomely.'

'I'm worried about Toka. She knows everything and everyone. Jesus, the amount of important people who have visited her brothels.'

'Oh, my friend, have you been playing with Toka's boys and girls, eh?' He guffawed, and it sounded full of phlegm. 'I told you. She'll say nothing. Toka has never said anything after all these years in UK, and she never will. She knows me too well, my friend, so relax.'

'How about the girl, Afrodita?'

'Has she said anything?'

'I don't know. There's almost no detail coming from the chief's office.'

'Should we do something about the girl? Safest option is to make her disappear, you know?'

'Jesus, Alban. We can't be killing a fifteen-year-old; the ramifications would be way too big. The press would go mad and the chief will throw every resource at it. It would be devastating.'

There was a long pause on the line, and the asset could almost hear the waves of displeasure coming from Hoxhaj. When he spoke, his voice was low and softer than normal. 'My friend, if you take the Lord's name in vain again, the consequences for you will be severe, am I clear?'

The asset's heart began to pound and sweat began to prickle. 'Apologies. It's just the stress of all of this.'

'You should know by now how important my faith is to me, so remember.'

'I will. I promise.'

Hoxhaj chuckled before continuing. 'Maybe it won't be necessary, but I won't have my operation risked for a stupid Tirana street kid. If I have to, I'll have her dealt with. Do we know her address?'

A cold shiver travelled up and down the asset's spine. 'It won't come to that. Look, just do whatever it is you have to do and make sure that whatever this raid is about, it comes to nothing. If this blows out, they'll probably just let it fizzle out.'

'I'll make sure we are not exposed; I appreciate your call, my friend. You earn your retainer, that much is true.'

The line went dead.

The asset sat back and exhaled, stomach churning with a gnawing, gripping sensation.

Dealing with Hoxhaj was lucrative, but terrifying. You just knew that however valuable you were to him, it would take only one mistake, one miscalculation or one key piece of missing information and that would be it.

Someone willing to kill an innocent fifteen-year-old victim of crime wouldn't hesitate to put a bullet into the asset. Or worse, to live up to his nickname, The Surgeon.

The asset shuddered at the thought.

35

NORMA WAS ENGROSSED in a large and complex chart on her central monitor, her glasses perched on her nose as she added a new address, and linked it together using lines with the nominals. The lines never crossed, and the chart, which to her looked neat and formulaic, was a maze of differing icons denoting premises, individuals, phone numbers and vehicles. To a casual observer it would have been meaningless, but to a trained analyst, it was a map of everything they knew about Hoxhaj, Kurti, Ricci and everyone else connected to the inquiry. She sat back in her chair, satisfied. It was clear that they were on the right track, they just needed the last few pieces of the jigsaw, but essentially, she understood what was happening.

She was adding the address of the brothel into a new subject box when there was a tap at the door of the office. A tall, lean man, dressed in a long, dark coat over an open-necked shirt, entered the room. He had light sandy hair and an ID badge on a lanyard.

'Norma?' he said, in a central belt accent.

'Aye?'

'Steve Vipond, from Immigration intelligence at Gartcosh. You should be expecting me.'

'Ah right, yeah. Come in, Steve. Glad to meet you,' she said, extending her hand as she stood.

'I was told to bring these?' he said, extending his hand which was clutching a box of Tunnock's teacakes.

'Oh wow, you can stay. Did Stella say I was a fan?' Norma said, her grin widening at the sight of her favourite treats.

'She did. I also have an absolute ton of data on trafficking victims, and status approvals.'

'I love data, so damn yes. Tea or coffee?'

'Tea would be great,' he said, smiling warmly.

'Okay, take a seat.'

'Quiet here. Just you?'

'Aye, they're all out on a job,' said Norma, switching on the kettle and dropping bags into two mugs.

'Anything to do with what I have here?'

'Connected, aye.'

'Care to say more? Or would you have to kill me afterwards?'

'Very possibly.' Norma laughed.

'Thought so. Cops are always secretive.'

'I'm not a cop, I'm an analyst, but I can be pretty secretive.'

'Well, I'm not here to get intel. I'm here to share. I have it all here on a disc, which I'll leave with you. I didn't want to send it on normal email. It's all in Excel, with hyperlinks and links to raw data, so should be easy to sift, but I think we may have misled you with the numbers a little.'

'How so?' said Norma, handing a steaming mug over to Steve, who accepted it and followed Norma to her desk. He sat in the unoccupied chair to the side.

'I think the numbers have been underestimated. Blimey, that's a complex chart. I'm i2 trained myself, and I've never come up with anything like that.' He sipped his tea and screwed up his face. 'Any sugar?'

'Sorry, I should have asked, how many?'

'Nae bother, two spoons, I have a sweet tooth.'

Norma took his mug from him and moved to the fridge where all the makings sat. She spooned sugar into the mug and returned, handing it to Vipond, who sipped and nodded appreciatively.

'So, underestimated numbers?'

'Well, I think you were told that the total of long-term missing girls was twenty-one in number, all of which were undergoing applications to the Home Office.'

'Aye, as I recall.'

'Well, we realised that we hadn't included unaccompanied minors from Albania, of which we get a lot. Until recently they used to exploit the Lille loophole, where they'd board a Eurostar train, buy a ticket for Lille, and just stay on the train until they got to London. Then they'd claim asylum.'

'I remember something about the Lille loophole, go on.'

'Well, when we adjusted for this, the number of missing persons from foster homes etc. rose.'

'By how much?'

'It rose to close to a hundred.'

'What?' said Norma, mouth agape.

'Aye. It's a lot, I know.'

'It's five times worse than we realised.'

'Aye.'

'I'd better call this in. This raises the stakes more than ever.' Norma picked up her phone and dialled. 'Ross. We have a problem. This is bigger than we thought. Much bigger.'

36

'WHAT?' SAID MAX, after Ross whispered what he'd just learned from Norma over the phone.

'Aye. Potentially well over a fucking hundred mispers. A bastard hundred, Max.'

'Does it change anything?'

'Not now, we still have to do what we're about to do. Come on, let's get on with this.'

The briefing room at Tulliallan was busy and buzzing with people, all of whom were helping themselves to the coffee and pastries set on a table at the back of the room.

Ross and Max sat at a desk at the front of the room before a large rolled-down screen, on which was projected the Police Scotland crest on a background of blue.

'Okay, folks, can we get started?' said Ross from behind an open laptop.

The room's occupants quickly settled and a hush descended.

'Thanks for coming at short notice, ladies and gents. This is a fast time operation against a suspected brothel which is connected to another ongoing covert inquiry. Can we have a quick round robin so we all know who's here?' said Ross, looking at a tall and skinny uniformed Immigration officer, whose shoulders bore a rank crest.

'Chief Immigration Officer Mick Phelps.'

Ross nodded at a grey-haired uniformed police inspector, who sat next to CIO Phelps. 'Inspector Joe Lyle, OSU.'

'Maggie Smith, children's services, social services, Glasgow City Council,' said a petite young woman with a shy smile.

A solid-looking and widely smiling middle-aged woman spoke next. 'Agnes Shehu, Albanian interpreter.'

'DS Leo Gray, National Child Abuse Investigation Unit,' said a smartly dressed, dark-haired officer.

'Thanks, all. Okay, the purpose of our presence today is that we are going to raid a suspected brothel in Glasgow Southside as soon as we finish here. We have solid intelligence that individuals within are connected to an abduction of a young trafficking victim. Now that victim has been found alive and well, but we believe there could be other juvenile victims within that property possibly being exploited. This is an arrest operation and an intelligence-gathering opportunity, but much of the details are remaining covert at this moment, clear so far?' Ross looked around the room.

'What I can give you is the subjects of the arrest operation, but this must remain covert. I can't stress how important that is. Am I clear?' Ross paused, and the silence in the room was heavy. He pressed a key on the laptop and photographs in lurid colour appeared on the screen. They showed Toka Kurti, Jetmir Xhilaj and PC Luigi Ricci, whose picture was clearly taken from his warrant card. There was an audible intake of breath at the sight of a serving cop in uniform.

'Jesus, a serving cop?' said Joe Lyle.

'Aye, unfortunately. We have good evidence that he is at the target premises and that he was involved in the abduction of the victim by Xhilaj and Kurti. So, we can now all see why we're taking this as seriously as we are, yes?'

The nods were more vigorous, and the room was energised at

the realisation that this was a corruption inquiry centred around a serving cop. This would be big news.

'Right, we'll deploy from here. Myself and my team will attend to the actual property along with the OSU. We'll secure entry and once through the door we can assess what's next. The rest of you will stand by at the local cop shop and we'll call you forward as and when required. All clear?'

The door to the briefing room opened, and Chief Constable Macdonald entered, accompanied by Chief Superintendent Carlisle. The cops all made to stand.

'Don't get up, guys. I just wanted to come in and personally thank you for your help at such short notice for this operation. I know you all have horribly busy schedules, but this goes to the centre of law enforcement in Scotland. Corrupt cops in the pockets of Albanian gangs are corrosive to everything we stand for.' He pointed up at the screen that still bore the photographs of Kurti, Xhilaj and Ricci. 'These people are at the heart of an evil trade in young and vulnerable women, and they need to be stopped, and stopped today.'

He looked around the room and somehow managed to catch the eye of every person who was looking at him.

'Thanks again, guys. Over to you, Ross.' He nodded, and left the room with Carlisle.

'Okay, let's saddle up and hit the road, folks. All radios on channel seventy-seven, and let's be safe.'

37

Sceptre: Cops are going now to an address in Southside – briefing has just happened. They know everything about Toka, Jetmir and Luigi. You need to get them out of there.

Kiru: Luigi?

Sceptre: The cop.

Kiru: Why is this my problem? He knows nothing of me.

Sceptre: It could be a problem.

Kiru: How long?

Sceptre: Now. They're on their way.

. . .

Sceptre: They know too much, get them out of there. You have just minutes.

. . .

Sceptre: Are you there?

Kiru: You worry too much.

38

MAX, JANIE AND Ross sat in the Volvo just around the corner from the brothel.

'Are we all ready?' said Ross.

'Aye, as we'll ever be. Where are the backups?' said Janie.

'We have an interpreter, social worker, Immigration officer and NCAIU officers all holding at Aikenhead Road ready for us to call them in. We only want those that are essential to go through the door, if we're to remain as covert as we can. Some of Miles Wakefield's team are with them, in case it all goes bandy,' said Ross.

'Door-boshing team are here,' said Janie, looking in the rear-view mirror at a liveried van, filled with uniformed cops, pulling up behind the Volvo.

'Madness if you ask me. Why don't we just chap the bloody door?'

'Well, they may not answer. It has strong locks and a camera. You'd hurt your shoulder if you tried to bash a thick door like that in.'

'True enough, state of my bloody shoulders, I'd struggle to bash down a door in a Japanese tea hoose,' Ross said with a rueful smile.

Max sniggered.

'Aye, you'll not be laughing when you're my age, Craigie,' he said. 'Shall we?'

'Aye, let's do this,' said Max.

Ross picked up his airwave radio and said, 'Joe, we're game on. Send three of your guys to the back, and the rest to the front with the big red key.'

'Received,' came the immediate response.

Steadily, and without rushing, Janie engaged the gears on the Volvo and they sedately moved off towards the tenement, the van close behind. Ross began to whistle tunelessly during the two-minute journey, a sense of calm anticipation enveloping the car as it moved onto the cobbled street.

'Anything on the feed, Barney?' said Ross into his radio.

'Nowt. Quiet as a brothel wi' no hookers, pal,' said Barney in reply.

'I'm glad you stayed behind, you negative old get,' said Ross.

Max looked over his shoulder and saw the van pull over and three uniformed cops get out and go down the passageway towards the rear of the tall, red-stoned tenement. Janie drove smoothly until she pulled up almost directly outside the premises, but not so close as to be caught by the camera.

'Ready?' said Ross, once again.

'Cooking on gas, boss,' said Janie, unbuckling her seatbelt and adjusting her body armour, which they were all wearing.

'Shall we, then?' said Ross, fidgeting with his own armour.

'As we used to say in the Met, "Strike, strike, strike."'

'Aye, a wee bit more sedate, though. I'm tired and could do without lots of fucking shouting. Let's go.'

They all got out of the Volvo and walking up to the tenement door, they were joined by Joe and two other officers, one clutching a heavy, bright-red enforcer door ram, the so-called big red key. Another officer held a hydraulic breaching tool, also painted bright red. Joe nodded at the two cops, both wearing public order helmets with visors down to protect them from splintering wood or shattering glass. The cop with the breaching tool jammed the steel teeth in the gap in the door that had been widened by Joe leaning in against it. All slow, steady and silent. No one spoke, and no instructions were necessary. Method of entry was part of the OSU's remit, and their calm, efficient movements reflected this.

'The camera bell,' said Max.

'Eh?' said Ross.

'It's gone,' said Max, pointing at the screw holes in the freshly painted door frame.

'Can't do much about it, can we?'

'Ready?' said Joe, looking at Ross.

'Aye, go for it.'

The cop with the breaching tool pumped the hand pumps together, immediately exerting four tonnes of hydraulic pressure, forcing the teeth apart and separating the door from its frame.

Joe nodded at the other cop, who quickly swung the enforcer back, his face contorted with determination as he brought it crashing against the central lock with tremendous force. All that kinetic energy against the frame had only one result. The heavy black door sprung inwards with a sharp crack, hitting the wall with a loud bang.

'Police!' bellowed Max as he took off into the flat, powering into the hallway, closely followed by Janie, and the others rushing to clear all the rooms. The sound of smashing glass came from the back of the house as the rear cover team breached the back door, 'Police!' being yelled by gruff, aggressive voices. Overwhelming force, lots of shouting to disorientate the targets and reassure the innocents.

'Kitchen clear,' came a voice.

'Living room clear,' came another.

'Bedroom one clear,' shouted one more.

Max came to the door of what had been identified as the bathroom from the building plan that Norma had secured from the local authority. Sounds of chaos reverberated around the floor and the radio chatter in his ear suddenly went frantic, but Max tuned it out, ready for whatever was in that room, sensing something terrible was behind that door.

He reached for the handle and twisted it, but it was locked. 'Police, open up!'

No response. 'Open up,' Max repeated. He stepped back, braced himself against the wall and kicked out with his boot, banging the centre of the door, which splintered inwards, just about a foot before rebounding back at him. He caught sight of a Timberland boot on the other side of the door. 'Someone in here,' he yelled. Janie appeared at his side.

'Open the bloody door!' shouted Max, shoving in against it again, but it stopped dead, once more. Max looked down and saw the sand-coloured boot in the gap.

It was soaked in dark, congealed blood.

'Shit, someone's hurt.' He pushed at the door, which felt like a tonne weight was behind it, until he had enough room to poke his head through the gap and look in.

Max's insides turned to ice as he saw a scene of unimaginable horror on the other side. A thick, putrid and fetid odour filled his nostrils. The soft breeze coming from the partially open frosted-glass window only served to waft the smell into Max's face. Nausea gripped him like a vice.

The stench of death.

39

-KOMUNITETI SHQIPTAR NË Glasgow-

Sceptre: What the hell have you done?
Kiru: What had to be done. ☺
Sceptre: Call me as soon as you can.
Kiru: Later.

*******************Message deleted**************

40

'MAX?' JANIE SAID, her voice soft with concern.

Max said nothing. He just looked inside the poky bathroom that had once featured white and pristine tiles, linoleum and enamel, but was now like an abattoir. Three mangled bodies lay on the floor in a congealed puddle of blackening blood, all on their backs, all staring upwards at the ceiling. A neat, round hole was central in each forehead, and the walls behind them were decorated with splattered blood, grey flecks and white shards, of what Max could only assume were fragments of skulls.

So much blood – So. Much. Fucking. Blood.

It glistened in the harsh light of the modern bathroom. The metallic, coppery smell filled Max's nostrils as he took in the pale, alabaster faces of Toka Kurti, Jetmir Xhilaj and Police Constable Luigi Ricci.

Max had seen much death in his career. He'd seen countless bodies, some perfect, some decomposed, some shot, some stabbed, but nothing could be worse than the scene that was before him in that once clinical, small bathroom.

Toka's face was frozen in a grotesque mask, her teeth uneven and broken and fully exposed, because clearly her lips had been sliced off with a sharp instrument. The lack of blood suggested that this had been done after her heart had stopped pumping, and therefore, after death, or 'postmortem' as a pathologist might say. Her mouth was a ragged black, gory frame for her crooked and crowded teeth.

Jetmir was on his side, his floppy hair thickly matted with blood. His ear had been neatly sliced off and stuffed between his lips. Again, the lack of blood at the site was indicative that this too had been inflicted after he'd been shot.

Max's breath was coming in short staccato gasps as he forced himself to look at PC Luigi Ricci, his instinct already telling him what he was going to find. The small, round hole in his head was neat, with scorch marks, indicating that the barrel of the firearm had been close to his head when the trigger was pulled. A cavity where his right eye had been gaped like a borehole in snow; the eyeball had clearly been gouged out, again the absence of blood on his face was telling.

The room began to swim, and bile rose in Max's throat. He backed out of the room, hardly seeing Janie's face, pale and wan, her eyes wide. 'Max?' she said, a tremor in her voice.

'They're all dead. Call it in. Call everyone in. MIT teams, CSI, the fucking lot. We need to withdraw.' Max set off towards the front door, his stomach churning and face burning at what he'd seen. He felt the bile rising again, and he upped his pace, his thoughts colliding in his head, as if a component in a complex machine had failed.

It was a scene of brutal, unimaginable carnage, and its message was clear to Max, even in his shocked state. Ear, eye, mouth.

It was a warning. No, even worse. It was a declaration.

The three wise monkeys. Hear no evil, see no evil, speak no evil.

41

MAX SAT ON the bonnet of the Volvo, breathing steadily and evenly. Square breathing as taught by his counsellor, which had been the only thing he had found useful from their sessions together a few years ago.

He closed his eyes, trying to banish the sights he had just witnessed. He breathed out, steadily and calmly. Then in slowly, to the count of four. Then held for four before exhaling for four and then holding for four. He went through this routine, four times, eyes shut, trying to empty his mind, to chase away the creeping dread. To stop it overwhelming him.

As always, memories of Afghanistan began to surface, the sight of his friend dying on the harsh, desiccated desert floor, the light fading from his eyes. 'Not now, not here,' he whispered to himself.

As he went through the familiar routine, he felt some calmness return. *Focus, Max*, he thought. *Fucking focus, you've a job to do*. He took his time to exhale once more before opening his eyes. Janie stood in front of him, her eyes soft and full of concern. She'd witnessed this before and knew that she had to let Max find his way back. She stepped closer and lay her hand on his shoulder, and gripped. Max looked up, and their eyes met, reassurance and understanding shone from hers. Max allowed a small smile to disturb the straight, bloodless line of his pursed lips as Janie's touch relaxed him. They'd shared so much over the past couple of years that her touch almost seemed to spread warmth into his body, and his tensed muscles began to ease.

'I'm okay, now.' He nodded, even managing to summon up a bigger smile, although no part of it reached his eyes, and his mind was still spinning.

Ross emerged from the house, his normally ruddy face at least two shades paler than when he had entered.

'A-Anyone called it in?' he said, his voice shot through with the mildest of tremors, before properly looking at them. Janie's hand was still on Max's shoulder. 'What are you two fucking weirdos up to?' he said, his face confused.

The insensitive blast from their bumptious senior officer reassured rather than rankled. Sensitivity from Ross would have caused far more consternation. 'Nothing,' said Janie, a slight chuckle in her voice, as she removed her hand.

'Thank fuck for that. Don't need you two going all weird and sensitive on me. We've evil scumbags to find, and I need mean and nasty cops fully focused on bringing them in. Fucking awful situation though this is, we need to get our heads back in gear, and bloody sharpish. Am I clear, folks?' Ross's eyes took on a steely, determined look. They had to focus and get fired up and ready to go. There was work to be done.

'Absolutely crystal, Ross,' said Janie.

'Aye, fucking right,' added Max.

'Anyway, to go back to my original point that was interrupted by watching a frankly nauseating moment of tenderness between you two, have you called it in?'

'Aye, I just shouted. Control room are on it, getting on call MIT, CSI and anyone else they can think of. It's a bloody house of horrors in there.'

'Damned right it is. You okay, Max? Look like you've seen a bastarding ghost,' said Ross.

'I'm fine. Just needed some air.'

'Aye, stank like shite in there. Dead a while I'd say by how the gore is congealed, and the bodies are as cold as one of Mrs Fraser's most withering stares. How the hell did we miss whatever happened?'

'There was at least a two- to three-hour window between us seeing Luigi in there and Barney putting his van in position with the camera. It must have been within that timeframe, unless they gained access by the bathroom window,' said Janie, scribbling in her notebook and looking at her phone.

'That won't go down well. Any idea which MIT will take it?' said Ross.

'Well, detective super is Miles Wakefield, but I guess it'll be whichever team is in the frame for the next one. This is gonna be big, though, as in all over the bloody press. A Cat A triple murder including a serving cop.'

'Who's on call?'

'DCI Marina Leslie,' said Janie.

'Ah bollocks, she's a fucking nightmare. We're gonna get slaughtered for this,' said Ross, massaging his temples.

'Why?'

'She doesn't like me. She thinks I'm uncouth and rude. In fact, she *complained* about me for being allegedly uncouth and rude.' Ross flushed.

'That's not unreasonable, to be fair,' said Max.

'Don't you bleeding start. She misinterpreted a bit of passionate discourse from me for abuse.'

'What level of swearing was it? DEFCON 1?'

'DEFCON 5, more like,' said Ross, shaking his head.

'One is worse than 5, you know,' said Janie.

'Well, that makes no sense at all. I'm gonna catch some bastarding serious flak, I just know it, so we need to get ahead of it. This is a death following police contact for Ricci, so PIRC will be all over it, and you know what they think of us after the last job,' said Ross.

'Why? All we did is what happens on every surveillance job. Follow the subject to wherever he's going and then stand down. We weren't on a twenty-four seven follow on a homicidal maniac, were we? All we did was follow a dodgy cop to a brothel, which whilst unsavoury it's hardly the great train robbery. Minor corruption at best, and now we have our three targets about to get zipped into body bags. It's a bloody miracle we got a camera on at all in the timeframe available,' said Max.

'You think DCI "oh so fucking perfect" Leslie will see it that way? All she'll see is three stiffs that we had been watching, and we'll be told fuck all. We'll be kept well away from it, and the MIT will close ranks, whilst we take all the shit from PIRC and every other twat. We'll be trying to do what we do with our hands tied behind our backs.'

'We should have gone in last night. They were still alive when we bloody left,' said Max.

'Aye well, spilt milk and all that. No point thinking about that,' said Ross, shrugging.

'Why was the chief so bloody adamant we wait?'

'You know why. And what the fuck are you insinuating?'

'Nothing. Just nothing.' Max shook his head.

There was a long pause as the three colleagues looked at each other, only punctuated by a buzzing. 'Control room,' Janie said before answering and stepping away.

Max continued, 'Well, it's not for us to investigate the murders, is it? We'll leave that to the MIT and we go after bent cops, and the only bent cop we know about is now dead with his eye gouged out.'

'Aye. We need to have a quick shufti in the house again, you know. At least we'll see what's there, and there may be a clue or two. You know, give us a head start to go after whoever fucking leaked this raid, which some bugger clearly did.'

'Are you sure about this?' said Max, a frown forming on his

face. This wasn't standard operating procedure. In fact, it was way off SOPs.

'Aye, damn straight. DCI Leslie is a control freak, and if you even push back mildly, she goes fucking doolally and makes formal complaints. Last one took bloody ages to sort out.'

'Going back into a murder scene having just left is kind of frowned upon, Ross?' said Janie.

'We've only just left it, and maybe we didn't search for any outstanding suspects, or further victims properly, did we? In fact, maybe I just heard a little noise from within?' Ross, said, eyes glinting.

'Erm, Ross. OSU, just over there?' said Max, pointing to the small clutch of uniformed officers all standing together, pale faces nodding as Joe spoke to them, his voice steady and impassive.

Ross nodded and addressed the team leader, 'Joe, get your guys back to the nick. We'll debrief there once SIO has been, yeah?'

Joe Lyle looked at Ross with a mildly suspicious frown, before nodding. 'You happy to run scene logs until the MIT get here?'

'Aye, we'll be shouting the locals up. They'll manage the scene, and we can get back for a proper debrief and to get statements done. Your guys could all use a cuppa. That was pretty grim, Joe.'

Joe's face softened. 'Thanks, Ross, see you back at the factory,' he said before ushering his team back to their van.

'Control room just confirmed. DCI Leslie and her team are preparing to leave and will be making their way from Gartcosh, ETA thirty minutes. Duty inspector is on his way as well, here in twenty minutes, and we have two uniform units coming,' said Janie.

'Who's the duty officer?'

'Inspector Gordon Campbell,' said Janie, her forehead creased in a frown.

'Ah bollocks. Can today get any worse? Cordon bloody Gordon. He'll be a pain in the arse, as he always is. Let's get in fast. We need something to work with, people.'

Max and Janie just nodded, the need to act fast chasing away the shock of the terrible sight they'd witnessed in that house.

'Okay, here's what we do. A quick poke round, photograph anything of interest, and we write it up as a double check to ensure life extinct and making sure there are no other victims, or suspects. Once we're done, we come out, get a log and scene tape going and look all efficient. Once we've scrutinised the images and saved them for intel purposes, we'll share with the MIT team, so we are squeaky clean and just wanted to be totally transparent, or some such bullshit like that.'

Janie looked at Max, a touch of puzzlement in her body language. 'Are we sure about this?'

'Aye. I know Marina, she'll tell us absolutely nothing and will take the greatest pleasure in doing so. We need a lead, and it could be in that hellhole.'

Janie sighed and looked at Max, who just shrugged. 'Come on then. I suggest we run a film from the moment we walk through the door, yeah?'

'Let's go,' said Ross.

42

ALBAN HOXHAJ STEPPED out of the battered BMW which had swept into the scrapyard on the outskirts of Glasgow. A short, squat and tough-looking man dressed in oil-stained overalls pulled the large, solid ply gates closed and shot a bolt across. He approached Hoxhaj and nodded, smiling deferentially, showing stained teeth.

The yard was cluttered with shells of cars, piles of seats, tyres, springs and rusting panels from a thousand corpses of cars of years gone by. The compacted earth was spotted with oily puddles.

'Alban,' he said, his head slightly lowered, as he wiped his hands on an oily rag before extending his right.

'I don't think so, Mac. I don't think it would be wise,' he said as he removed a pair of blue nitrile gloves and stuffed them into a carrier bag held by the hulking form of Enver, who had appeared at his shoulder. Enver then removed his own gloves, which he dropped into the bag.

After leaving the brothel, Enver had driven them to an empty property owned by an associate. They'd parked the car in the attached garage and then just sat watching TV for a few hours. Hoxhaj was a professional, so he knew that getting them and the car off the street for a few hours was a sensible precaution before they attended to the necessary administration of sterilising themselves, and ensuring that there would be no forensic evidence for the cops to find. They had no idea if anything had been reported to the authorities, but rather than making a run for it and risking ANPR cameras, CCTV or vigilant local cops picking them up, staying out of sight until they could be sure that nothing had been reported was good tradecraft. Hoxhaj had avoided ever being arrested or prosecuted because he was so careful.

The flat had been prepared for them, with plastic sheets laid on the floor and the two armchairs to prevent any evidence being transferred onto the carpet or furniture. They'd stuffed all the plastic into a bag and taken it away when they'd left hours later, leaving no trace of their presence. Once he was satisfied that there was no police activity, they'd moved and driven to the scrapyard.

'Nae bother, man. We're ready over there. I'll take care of the car in a moment. It'll be like a fucking Oxo cube in twenty minutes, and there's a fire roaring over there for your breeks and jacket.'

'Only you here today?'

'Aye, as you wanted. Gave my boys the afternoon off.'

Hoxhaj nodded, his face flat and unfathomable. 'You have showers ready?'

'Aye, it's no' the Ritz, man, but there's hot water, soap, new nailbrushes and disinfectant there,' he said, pointing to a small, shabby portacabin the other side of the yard.

Hoxhaj turned to Enver. 'Get the bag,' he said and walked towards the coal brazier that was smoking in the middle of the yard, already unzipping his fleece and shrugging it from his shoulders.

Enver went to the rear of the BMW and opened the boot, removing a black bin bag and carrying it to the fire, where Hoxhaj was removing his plain black trainers and black jeans. Those items followed the fleece onto the raging furnace, the smoke blackening as the man-made fibres caught, spitting, burning and melting as they were consumed by the white-hot coals. From the black bag, Enver pulled out the plastic sheeting that had covered the carpet and furniture in the flat. This he threw onto the fire, and it immediately caught and began to melt, giving off thick, acrid smoke.

Enver began to remove his clothing, which joined his boss's on the brazier. They both stood there, unable to stop staring at the burning mass of fabric, plastic and rubber as the dark smoke spiralled up into the Glasgow sky.

'Shower,' barked Hoxhaj.

They disappeared into the portacabin, both returning after a few minutes in clean, plain grey tracksuits and plastic sliders, their faces pink and scrubbed and hair still damp.

Mac came alongside the pair. 'Anything else I can get you?'

'Yes. A hammer,' said Hoxhaj as he threw other items of clothing onto the fire.

Mac nodded and disappeared into the scabby-looking office in another portacabin before returning with a heavy lump hammer, which he handed over to Hoxhaj, who in turn handed it to Enver with a nod.

The taciturn Enver produced two mobile phones from his bag. Squatting down, he grabbed a brick that was securing a tarpaulin over a big pile of parts and placed the phones on the brick. He raised the hammer and began to reduce the two phones to their component parts by repeatedly smashing them. Soon there was just a pile of broken glass, electrical circuit boards and shattered plastic. Enver sifted through the debris and picked out the SIM cards, which he bent in half and pounded with the hammer. He then scooped it all up and deposited the lot onto the fire, with a satisfied grin.

'Shall I get on?' said Mac.

Hoxhaj just nodded, not taking his eyes from the fire.

Mac turned away and crossed the yard, getting behind the controls of a beaten-up crane. The engine barked into life, and within a few moments, giant metal claws grabbed the roof of the battered BMW and dropped it into a bright-red crusher.

Alban watched with interest as the walls of the crusher began to squeal and screech, the sounds of tortured metal being crushed inwards, until the big car was soon nothing more than a rectangle of compacted metal, wiring, shattered glass and rubber. A few more twists and turns of the crane controls and the crushed BMW was deposited on the back of an unhitched, waiting trailer. With incredible speed and efficiency, the crane loaded three more cubed and destroyed cars onto the back of the trailer, leaving the wrecked BMW at the bottom of several tonnes of scrap metal whilst the two Albanians just watched.

The machinery fell silent, and Mac crossed over the yard and joined the Albanian gangsters again. 'All done. I'll get straight off to the recyclers in Newcastle. They'll reduce it to shredded metal and rubber by later today. A whole team of CSIs wouldn't be able to even find the fucker amongst all the other shite.'

'Good work, Mac. I owe you a favour,' said Hoxhaj, nodding.

'Any time, pal. Any time.'

'Phone,' barked Hoxhaj, and Enver passed over a small handset.

Hoxhaj dialled, his face impassive as he stared into the burning coals.

'Yes?' answered the asset.

'It's me.'

'Is this a clean line?'

'Of course.'

'Please tell me you've not left a trail?' The voice was panic stricken.

'Of course not, what do you take me for?'

'This is really bad. I mean really fucking bad. Why the theatrics?'

'No swearing. I don't like foul language, you know this.'

'Sorry, I'm just stressed.'

'Reputation, my friend. Toka was a liability. She knows who you are for one thing, because of your taste in women.' He sniggered.

'I can see that, but Jetmir and the cop?'

'Jetmir was a fool, but he was causing problems. You were too close to the cop. He knew too much. Imagine he had been arrested and decided to cooperate? As you share a taste in women, that would have been dangerous to you, and inconvenient for me. You are still useful, which is why you're still drawing breath, so be thankful for that. Am I clear?'

There was a pause at the other end of the line before the asset replied. 'Perfectly.' The voice was tight and croaky. Hoxhaj smiled to himself, and winked at Enver. This was the most enjoyable bit. More enjoyable than the money, the women, the cars. The power over other people. The power to take three lives in the fashion that he had just done was the ultimate thrill, and he felt it course through his veins. It was intoxicating.

'What's happening now?'

'DI Fraser and his team found the bodies when they went to arrest Toka and Ricci today, but a new team is coming to take over the murder inquiries. DCI Marina Leslie is the SIO and she's very competent. I've heard it's like a bloody slaughter house in there. Jesus, I just hope you weren't seen and have alibis in place.'

'No blasphemy, either. You don't take the Lord's name in vain; you know this.'

The asset sighed deeply, but just muttered, 'Sorry.'

'Nothing will be found.'

'How about phones?'

'No problem.'

'Good. Look, I have to go. I'm expected at a briefing about this right now, and I can't be late,' said the asset, his voice tight and strained.

'Keep me informed,' said Hoxhaj.

The asset rang off.

Hoxhaj opened the handset and took out the SIM card, which he bent in half and tossed on the fire. He passed the handset over to Enver, who quickly reduced it to a small pile of plastic shards that soon found themselves disintegrating on the brazier.

'Once it's out and cooled, dispense of the ash where it won't be found,' said Hoxhaj, turning to Mac.

'Right you have it, chief,' said Mac, a smile spreading across his face.

Enver walked up to the gates, opened them and peered out. He nodded at Hoxhaj.

They walked out onto the nearly deserted street in the industrial estate. An anonymous Ford pulled up almost immediately and both men got in.

'Take me home,' he said to the stern-faced driver.

43

THE BROTHEL WAS clean to an almost clinical level, apart from the bathroom which currently still resembled a slaughterhouse.

Max, Janie and Ross moved systematically through each room, Janie filming every step of the way. The three bedrooms had been clearly staged to be ready to accommodate prostitutes, but they were so clean and untouched that it was inconceivable that any activity had taken place on the cheap, but immaculate beds. The large mirrors, chintzy décor and bowls of condoms all told their own story.

'Not that I know much about it, you understand, but it looks to me like no hooker ever got shagged in one of these rooms. Paint's barely dry,' said Ross.

'Eloquent and correct, Ross. Typical MO for someone trying to set up a high-class joint,' said Janie as she swept her phone across the room.

The kitchen was functional and basic, but again, immaculately clean with only the most basic of cutlery and utensils.

The back room contained a small office, comprising a desk with a newish laptop, printer and a large stack of flyers all ready to be distributed. A slightly askew picture of a stern-faced man adorned the wall.

'Anyone seen a phone, yet?' said Max.

'No,' said Janie.

'They could be in the pockets of the stiffs in the bathroom,' said Ross.

'I put money on it that they're not,' said Max, pointing to the charger cable that was on the desk next to a bunch of keys.

'I bet you're right, which I never like to admit. I'd say whoever sliced those poor bastards up didn't want us getting our hands on them. They got killed because they knew too much.'

'Isn't Alban Hoxhaj's name The Surgeon?' said Janie.

A thick silence enveloped the room as they all looked at each other, realisation dawning as to what they were dealing with.

Ross lightly touched the trackpad and the laptop sprang to life. The screen was displaying a web page titled 'TK Adult services', with a photograph of an impossibly young woman wearing a school uniform.

'Looks like she was getting things up and running. This is classic. Get new girls photographed, upload them onto the adult service websites and then get the punters coming to you. No street walking, or flyers in phone boxes anymore,' said Janie, herself an ex–vice squad officer.

'Phone boxes are rare as tits on a fish, and all stink of pish, anyway,' said Ross.

'Beautifully phrased, Ross,' said Max with a chuckle.

'Who's the scunnered-looking gadgie on the wall?' said Ross, pointing at the portrait hanging behind the desk.

'Enver Hoxha, leader of Albania after the communist revolution in 1941, as I recall. Statues of him all over the place in Albania,' said Janie.

Max and Ross both stared at Janie, who coloured slightly.

'Shite, do you think you're getting the best value out of your history degree by dicking about in the Polis?' said Ross, shaking his head.

Janie smiled and said, 'It's a strange thing for her to have up there, though. Hoxha was a brutal dictator who almost ruined

Albania. Many of the difficulties in the country can still be traced back to his policies.'

'Maybe she was being ironic?' said Max.

'She was a bloody brothel keeper, not a satirist.' Janie went to the portrait and pulled it from the wall with her gloved hand. A small, black leather-bound book fell to the floor.

'Well, hello there,' said Max, stooping to pick up the pocket-sized book and beginning to leaf through the pages.

'What is it?'

'I'd say it's Toka Kurti's little black book. Shitloads of phone numbers, email addresses, bank account numbers and the like. All handwritten in pencil. Even have expenses and takings in here. All sorts of stuff. This is a lot of work to investigate.'

'Aye, but that's down to the MIT, though. We can't remove evidence from the scene, can we?' said Janie.

'No, but nothing stopping us photographing it. Get on it, Janie. Every page. We can work through it later with Norma. I'm betting there's a big fat lead in that book. It was hidden, and I reckon she was the type to not trust mobile phones, particularly as criminals change their numbers as often as they change their socks,' said Max.

'You sure about this?'

'Aye, definitely. We leave it here, explain to the MIT where it was hidden, and we just have the option to look through it,' said Ross, taking the book from Max and flipping through it.

'Surely the MIT will share it with us?'

'I'm sure they will but DCI Leslie won't be rushing to do so. She'll have their analyst going through it first, and then she'll procrastinate, I can tell you that for a fact. She doesn't like me at all, so it could be ages, and by that time the leads will be stone bloody cold. Do it.' Ross handed the book to Janie, who took it wordlessly and turned the pages, photographing each one as she did.

'Anything else for us to do here?' said Max.

'I don't think so, unless you want to go in there and search the bodies?'

'I don't,' said Max firmly.

'No, me neither. It would probably be a step too far. We've enough to be getting on with just from the book. There's no doubt in my mind that Toka would have known the person who killed her, that's for sure, so there will be something in that book. We just have to find it.'

Max nodded. 'And let's not forget the other big elephant in the room, Ross.'

'Meaning?'

'Why do previously decent people in positions of power end up getting corrupted?'

'No riddles, Max, for fuck's sake, just spit it out.'

'Either because of money or just as often because of sexual indiscretions. Toka ran high-class brothels, which means one thing.'

'High-class clients,' said Janie as she continued snapping away with her phone.

'Bingo. Toka was killed because she knew too much, and the answer is in that book. How much longer, Janie?'

'Last page now,' she replied, closing the leather cover and setting the book down next to the laptop.

'Right, let's get out of here.'

44

DCI MARINA LESLIE was not what Max had been expecting. She was small and petite, wearing a sharply cut business suit and carrying a floral canvas bag. She smiled widely and seemingly genuinely as she stepped out of the anonymous saloon.

'Ross, long time no see,' she said. A well-dressed man got out of the driver's seat and nodded at Ross. 'Do you know DS Matt Hanrahan?' she said, nodding at the driver.

'Can't say I do, pleased to meet you, pal.' Ross's smile was a little more forced, but he managed to turn the corners of his mouth up a touch.

'Been a while since we worked together,' said Leslie, pulling a preformatted log from her bag.

'Indeed, a couple of years at least. You copping this job?'

'Well, we're in the frame for it, so I imagine so. I've just finished an eight-week trial, so we're raring to go. I've had a briefing, a triple homicide Cat A is a hell of a way to get back on the horse. Can you brief me quickly? Once done, you guys can go back to the incident room and get statements done whilst scene processing begins. CSI teams should be here soon.'

Ross briefed her succinctly, mentioning the laptop and the notebook.

'So, let me get this straight, you went back into the scene?'

'Aye, well, once Max found the three bodies in the bathroom, we all needed a moment, but we were acutely aware that there were areas we hadn't searched and didn't want to miss some-one injured, or possibly a hiding suspect, so we did a sweep which we videoed as we did it. We'll share all imagery with you, of course.'

'Ross, this is a little irregular,' she said, sharply.

'Boss, I have to say that we went in thinking we were raiding a brothel, whereas what we actually found were three mutilated corpses in the bathroom. We needed a moment to gather our thoughts, which I don't think was unreasonable.'

DCI Leslie looked at Ross, her eyes narrowed. The silence was long and uncomfortable. Ross just returned her stare, his face blank and impassive.

DCI Leslie broke first. 'Fair enough, I guess. I'll need a full briefing on the intelligence that sits behind your investigation, but that can wait. Processing the scene is the priority, but don't go too far. We need to speak at length. I don't need to tell you that this murder is going to be front-page news, do I?'

'Of course not.'

'The scrutiny will be huge, so I'll need a comprehensive report from you. I hope that's clear.'

'I'll get on it as soon as I get back,' said Ross.

DCI Leslie stood there, her face unreadable almost seeming to stare into Ross's soul.

Two liveried cars arrived, blue lights strobing, and a uniformed inspector got out of the lead car, pulling his cap onto his head.

'Oh, bloody hell, not Cordon Gordon,' said DCI Leslie.

Ross smiled, breaking the impasse. 'Ah, you've met Gordon.'

'On more than one occasion,' she said, shaking her head.

'Enjoy, he's very thorough,' said Ross.

DCI Leslie's smile seemed genuinely warm. 'Thanks a bunch, Ross. Look, make sure your people are okay. That must have been a right old shock to be confronted with.'

'They'll be fine.'

'Well, just make sure, eh? Right, I'd better get suited up and have a look at this scene,' said Leslie, heading back to the car.

'Right, I think we should bugger off, pronto,' said Ross, nodding at Max and Janie.

'Are we going to the incident room?' said Janie as they headed to their car.

'Are we bollocks. We're going back to Tulliallan. We need to see the chief urgently, and I want Norma straight onto the black book.'

'But what about DCI Leslie? She'll be expecting us at the incident room.'

'Aye well, she's gonna be disappointed.' Ross pulled his phone out of his pocket and dialled. 'Barry, I need to see the chief, urgently. We're heading from the murder scene now . . . No, it can't wait. I don't care if he's in a meeting with the chief financial officer. This is fucking important; there are three fucking corpses in a house we were watching, and some bastard leaked what we were doing. We'll be there in forty minutes.' Ross hung up, muttering to himself.

'Upsetting Barry again?'

'Aye, fuck him. We need to see the boss, now. Someone knew what we were planning, and leaked it, and that person got those three poor bastards in there killed.'

DCI Leslie appeared, dressed in a forensic suit and wearing blue nitrile gloves. 'You guys going back to the incident room?'

'Not yet. Need to see the chief at Tulliallan first. He wants a personal update before we do anything else,' said Ross.

'Really, isn't that a little unusual?'

'Not for us, Marina. I'm in the unusual position of reporting directly to him, so I can hardly say no, can I?'

'Fine. I'm going to take a look at the scene with my CSM, and then I'll see you there. Once I've seen it for myself, there's not much I can do whilst the CSIs begin. My DS is getting house to house underway, and I have a DI planning CCTV strategy, so I can get away for an hour or two, and I think the Chief Constable needs all his options laying out for him, both reactive and proactive, agreed?'

Ross opened his mouth to argue, but as he looked at the expression on DCI Leslie's face, he closed it again.

'If we're going to solve this horrible crime, we need to be on the same page, Ross. I'm now SIO on a triple murder. I'm not going to be excluded, that's for sure. Now I know we've had our differences in the past, but my one hundred per cent focus is to solve this case, as I'm sure yours is.'

'Aye, fair enough. See you at Tulliallan soon.'

45

THE ATMOSPHERE IN the chief's office was febrile, to say the least, as Ross, Max and Janie sat opposite the chief, who had his phone clamped to his ear, clearly trying to bat off press interest.

Sofia soundlessly entered the room, a tray of mugs in her hands that instantly filled the place with a rich coffee aroma. She smiled as she proffered the tray and the mugs were taken, before exiting.

DCI Marina Leslie sat next to Ross, arms folded, a stern expression on her face, an open notebook on her lap.

Macdonald shook his head slightly as he hung up, a wry smile crossing his face. 'Press are like bloodhounds, and clearly, we're leaking already. So, where are we then? And before we start, I want no recriminations, accusations or blame games. Plenty of time for that. For now I just want to get to the bottom of where we are, and what our priorities are, and where I need to direct our resources, clear?' He looked from Ross to DCI Leslie in turn.

'Crystal,' said Ross.

'As a bell,' said DCI Leslie.

'Okay, Marina, is the scene processing going okay?'

'Fine, sir. It's going to be a long job, that's for sure. CSM is having to get in extra resources, and just being able to get to the bodies without destroying evidence is going to be a challenge in itself.'

'Any obvious conclusions apparent?'

'Early view is that all three were killed in the bathroom with a single head shot each; no evidence of any blood elsewhere in the apartment. Each was then mutilated, postmortem, and it would appear that the suspect left via a bathroom window.'

'Yes, I heard about the mutilation. Any significance?'

'Eye, ear and mouth. Old Chinese proverb, I believe,' said Leslie, her face impassive.

'Jesus, this will send the press mad. A warning?' said Macdonald.

'It would seem so, sir,' said Leslie.

'Ross, I want to make perfectly clear that I'm attributing no blame to you or your team. It was my decision to delay the raid, for reasons I explained in detail, so I take full responsibility for that. It was amazing to get as far as you did, but was there any sign that this was a possibility?' said Macdonald.

'None whatsoever. We had Ricci under a decent level of control but there was no intelligence that this attack was imminent, or even likely. We had linked Toka Kurti to Alban Hoxhaj and there had been the recording of Ricci warning McPhail to remain silent in interview, which of course they both did. One thing is clear, though,' Ross paused and looked to DCI Leslie.

'Go on.'

'There's someone on the inside feeding Hoxhaj. There must be, unless you believe in huge coincidences. We also have the massive coincidence of the disproportionate amount of trafficking victims going missing in almost identical situations, a number which has just jumped from twenty-one to over a hundred when we factor in unaccompanied minors. I don't like that, at all. It seems to me that the abduction of Afrodita Dushku and how it was leading us to Toka Kurti was a step too far for someone.'

'So, am I right in thinking your theory is that the abduction of Afrodita and your progress in linking it to Toka Kurti and Jetmir Xhilaj prompted Hoxhaj to have them both killed?'

'Essentially, yes.'

'And Ricci, just a coincidence that he was there?'

'More than that, I'd say. He obviously helped Toka to recapture Afrodita, which I think we can demonstrate evidentially, but I think it's more than that.'

'How?'

'As I understand it, Hoxhaj has no role in running brothels. He just allows them to operate and takes a cut of the profits, so how would he know about the abduction of Afrodita? Once we got busy on it, purely because of Max's wife's job, things got too warm. But how did Hoxhaj get to know about this?'

'From Ricci?'

'No chance. He was just a bit of a pervert who liked prostitutes, and as such Kurti had him dangling on a string. There's no evidence that he knew Hoxhaj personally; we heard the conversations in the cells.'

'I've not heard them,' said Leslie.

'I'll have all the data sent to you straight after this meeting. What I suggest, sir, is that Marina cracks on with the reactive homicide investigation. The intelligence is that Hoxhaj is behind this, even if we don't have evidence of that yet.'

'And you, Ross? What will you do?'

'What we're paid to do. We go after bent cops. We had one in our sights, unfortunately he's no longer with us, but there's another one. At least another one, of that I'm confident.'

'How can you be sure?'

'As always, phones. Ricci's phone data is coming back in after cross-network searches identified all the numbers that have been used in it. He tried to be careful by switching SIM cards, but he clearly hadn't considered that we can use the handset to identify other numbers.'

'Really? That was slack,' said Leslie.

'Well, he was on a street crime unit, so maybe not his area of expertise.'

'Well, at least it's a lead.'

'Ricci used the phone to speak with Kurti prior to the kidnapping on Fyrish, after which he switched to a new SIM which then gets a call a few days later from Lewis McPhail's mother's phone just after we let him go from Burnett Road for the threatening Instagram message to Afrodita. I imagine we can be sure it was Lewis making the call. Following that, Ricci immediately made another call to Kurti on the same number as before which lasted a couple of minutes. Kurti's cell sited in Southside, and it's completely plausible she was at the brothel when she received that call. My feeling is that Ricci was telling her to release Afrodita.'

'Okay, I think I'm following, but how can you be sure of that?' said Macdonald.

'There's more. Straight after that call, he dialled another phone ending 419, clearly a burner. It seems the cell-site location is interesting, to say the least.'

'Why?'

'It's only on periodically, but one occasion it was cell sited very close to Gartcosh.' There was a pause as the impact of this sank in. Gartcosh, the Police Scotland crime campus. Full to the brim of specialist cops, NCA, Immigration, Procurator Fiscal and other law enforcement organisations.

'Where else has it been sited?' asked Macdonald, his face dark.

'It hit a cell mast just a mile from where we're currently sitting.'

'Shit.'

'Indeed. So, logic dictates that whoever it is, he or she has cause to work from both sites,' said Max.

'That doesn't narrow it down much, does it? I mean, that includes me. In fact, it includes everyone in this room,' said Macdonald.

'True, but it does suggest that it's someone in a position connected to Serious Crime investigation. What's also interesting is the fact that straight after the calls received from Ricci, the phone accesses the internet via 4G, it would appear, using a VPN,' said Max.

'A messaging service, maybe? Telegram or similar?' said Leslie.

'Possibly, but I'm betting that whoever our bent cop is, he was straight onto Hoxhaj. Our working theory is that Ricci calls Kurti and gets short shrift from her and goes over her head to someone with more clout to deliver the message that Afrodita is getting too hot to handle. Who do we think would have the clout to make Kurti release a valuable commodity such as Afrodita?'

'Hoxhaj. So, our unknown bent cop has the ability to talk direct to a leader of the Albanian Mafia. Jesus,' said Macdonald.

'Can we not narrow that down with phone intelligence to identify a number for Hoxhaj, if that's who is being called?' said Leslie.

'Unfortunately not. There were no calls made after the one from Ricci, so we can't prove how, or even if, our anoncop contacted Hoxhaj. He could have used a different phone, or dialled through WhatsApp or similar, which we then can't identify without access to the handsets used.'

'Shit, this is bad. This is bad. Someone with access to the highest levels of intelligence systems has the influence to reach out to an Albanian gang boss and get a kidnapped trafficking victim released. This isn't low-level corruption; this is a cop in the pocket of the country's most dangerous criminals.' Macdonald hung his head and massaged his temples and paused, his eyes closed for a full ten seconds that felt more like an hour. His eyes snapped open, full of determination. 'No more. This stops, guys. Marina, you continue with the murder inquiry, as you would expect to do. All the usual enquiries you'd do, but I expect full cooperation between you and Ross, understood?' He looked at both detectives in turn.

'Yes, sir,' said Leslie.

'Straight up, boss,' said Ross.

'Ross, get your team working this up, and come up with a plan to identify this bent bastard and bring him in. Whatever resources or authorities you need, you get. Am I understood?'

'Perfectly, but we all need a few hours; none of us have been home, or had any sleep, and my missus is getting a little scunnered at me, as usual,' said Ross, stifling a yawn.

'Understandable. Marina, you keep on pushing with the scene, house to house, CCTV, and the like. Ross, get your people home for a few hours, and then get back on it. Find the evidence, whatever it takes, we're bringing this bastard down.'

46

ROSS, MAX AND Janie went back to the office where Barney and Norma sat around, yawning and staring disconsolately into coffee cups.

'What gives?' said Barney as Ross stumbled over a loose floorboard, cursing.

'We're on. Usual terms of reference. DCI Leslie is running the reactive murder inquiry, and we're going to try to find whoever it is who's been leaking intelligence to Alban Hoxhaj. Great work on the phones, by the way, Norma. I was even able to make it clear that there was a link, even if we don't exactly know how or who,' said Ross.

'I'm still on it. Charts are looking good.' Norma straightened her glasses and pointed at a large chart on the wall. Small avatars, cars, phones and addresses were displayed, all linked together by arrows, lines and graphs. As always, Ross couldn't make head or tail of it.

'You know how I am with these things, Norma. What are we missing?'

'A name.' She shrugged.

'What, just a name?'

'Aye. We can clearly demonstrate how McPhail, Ricci, Kurti and Jetmir are linked and we can show some links are pointing towards Alban Hoxhaj, but without the missing link of whoever has the unattributed mobile phone with the number ending 419, we don't know enough to arrest Hoxhaj. He has plausible deniability, as they say.'

'So, we find who has 419, we bring the whole thing down?'

'I'd say so,' said Max.

'Any suggestions?' said Ross.

'Aye, I've an idea.' said Barney, sipping from a chipped Leeds United mug.

'Go on, Grandpa,' said Ross.

'Looking at data, we think that somehow, Bent Bobby is communicating with Hoxhaj, but only on totally clean SIM cards, or by using web-based apps or browser-based tech, right?'

'I'm not the most tech savvy, but I think so, yes,' said Ross.

'Do we have a reliable address for Hoxhaj?'

'We do. He lives in very swish-looking duplex apartments converted from old townhouses in the Finnieston area. Costs him over five grand a month,' said Norma.

'Any other properties?'

'Not in Scotland. He has a big place in Maida Vale in London, but all the intel is that Glasgow is where he is almost all the time.'

'Anything on the security of the place?' said Barney.

'I haven't deep dived into it yet, but the historic estate agency material I've managed to grab suggests yes, as you'd probably expect with that price bracket,' said Norma, squinting at her large screen.

'Are there any other properties for sale or rent in the block?'

'Hold up, I'll just search.'

'Barney, what the fuck are you suggesting?' said Ross.

'We need to get into the Wi-Fi of the place. If I can get within a reasonable distance, I may be able to hack into the network. It's normally piss easy with the right kit. All I'd need is a sniffer and a decent bit of computer power to dig out the packet data. Once I do that, I run it through software, and I can see everything the bugger does, every website he visits, the lot. May give us a lead.'

'Are you sure you're not just looking for a posh apartment for a few nights?' said Janie.

'Nay, lass, older properties with big thick walls are a right bugger. We need to get inside if we're to pick it up.'

'Couldn't you just use your van?' asked Ross.

'It's a bit overexposed, isn't it?'

'Probably,' said Ross, shrugging.

'There's an Airbnb advertising right in the block, a much smaller studio apartment. It looks to me like all the effort went on the bigger places upstairs, and the studio is an afterthought,' said Norma, smiling widely.

'Available?'

'Yep.'

'Jesus, that's a stroke of luck. What are the chances?' said Ross.

'We're due a bit of luck, aren't we? However, in that part of Glasgow, close to the museum and the botanic gardens it's a good place for a pied-à-terre and will be probably a good moneymaker for someone,' said Janie.

'How much?' said Ross.

'Two hundred a night, give or take,' said Norma.

'Think that'll be close enough?' said Ross.

'Is it in the same building, and with communal access?'

'I'd say so. Looking at local authority records, it was developed a couple of years ago and completely refitted, but I think it shares access, and the studio is only one floor down from the duplex. Looks like the developers were maximising profit by squeezing the studio apartment in a corner that would have remained dead space.'

'If it shares a staircase, I'd say we're golden. Does the duplex have a fire escape?'

'Aye, iron staircase from a fire door at the rear.'

'Ah, well, the only way to tell is for me to get in there and test. I have some kit that'll boost my ability to hook into it. Just depends on how tight it's locked down.'

'Think you can do it?' asked Ross.

''Course I can, man. I'm a pro,' said Barney, twiddling his roll-up that he'd just assembled expertly in one hand.

'Right, get it booked, Norma. Best give it three nights to be safe. It'll piss off the finance manager, but I have zero fucks to give about that. Barney, when do you need it by?'

'Reet now. Gives me a chance to get the kit sorted, and get set up. It'll take a while to hack into the Wi-Fi, and get the packet data in and analysed, but I reckon I can do it.'

'You just want a night out of your van, you cussed old bugger.'

'Ouch, I'm offended,' said Barney, his rough, calloused hand covering his heart.

'Okay, so here's the plan. Our freeloading ex-spy can get into the studio and set up and get busy with his sneakiness. Whilst he's doing that, we can all piss off home for a bit. Back in the morning, okay?'

'Does Barney need backup at the studio?' said Janie.

'Do you want to spend the night in a bijou studio apartment with a nicotine-addicted old codger who smells of pish and biscuits?' asked Ross.

'Probably not.'

'Quit mithering. I'll be fine. I used to do shit like this against the IRA and Al Qaeda, so staying the night in a pleasant apartment in Glasgow is no bother. Bugger off, you lot, and I'll be back here in the morning.'

'Okay, once you're in there, stay in there. Last thing we need is you coming face to face with Alban Hoxhaj,' said Ross.

'My head will be firmly down, Ross. I'll just need to identify the correct Wi-Fi router, which shouldn't be too much of a bother. Norma, can you look into owners of the duplex and see if you can identify who supplies the broadband to the address and IP number?'

'I'm on it,' said Norma.

'All authorities are in place, Norma. Well, take it that they will be; I'm calling in on the boss before I leave,' said Ross.

'Does that include the surveillance authorities, in case an opportunity to bug or get a camera in arises?' said Barney.

'It will do, but don't go doing anything daft. I know what a reckless sod you are. I know you're closer to the grave than the rest of us, but I could do without the paperwork of you being brutally murdered.'

'You're all heart, mate,' said Barney with a wide grin.

'Aye, it's all done, and Norma has a single point of contact with communications intel department, so once you have that in place, you go as well, Norma. If the stars align it could be a long day tomorrow. We need a lead. Once we have that we can do our favourite thing.'

'What's that?' said Norma.

'Chuck a big fuck-off rock in the pond and watch the ripples.'

47

-KOMUNITETI SHQIPTAR NË Glasgow-

Sceptre: You need to be careful. Something's going on.
Kiru: What?
Sceptre: I don't know, but Fraser and Craigie are planning
    something. Just take all precautions, okay.
Kiru: I always do. Keep me informed.

********************Message deleted**************

48

IT WAS DARK when Barney parked his van around the corner from Hoxhaj's property, which was a beautiful old mansion of a townhouse that had been subdivided into apartments recently. He hoisted his heavy sports bag over his shoulder and whistled tunelessly as he walked the short distance to the building.

As he approached the heavy communal front door, he noted the sleek Range Rover that Norma's research had suggested the gangster was using, even if it was registered to a property company in London that bore all the hallmarks of being a money laundering front.

The building was solid and handsome and reeked of Edwardian Britain, but once he'd secured the key from a combination lock-box, he realised that this was no simple renovation. The original features of the property had been retained, and there was a long, sweeping staircase, with a polished walnut handrail that snaked around the stairs up towards where Hoxhaj's property was occupying the entire top floor of the building. Elaborate plasterwork decorated the cornicing and a large, modern chandelier dominated the space. An expensive-looking leather sofa was positioned in front of a huge canvas that was a riot of vivid and contrasting colours. A mahogany coffee table sat just in front of the sofa and had a small bowl full of mints in the centre. The floor was composed of deep-red, polished quarry tiles that shone in the subtle lighting.

Barney let out a low whistle, wondering just what the grand old place must have looked like when it was a single residence, probably with maids, cooks and gardeners. His eyes were inevitably drawn to the discreet surveillance cameras in the vestibule, all four of them covering the door, stairwell and external frontage of the building. He noted the subtle sign *SecureForce Solutions* underneath the cameras. They were ultra-sleek and modern, so he was certain that they'd be web-based. He made a mental note to investigate that when he got settled in the apartment.

He looked up the sweeping staircase and noted another camera above pointing down towards him. He shook his head just a touch and then headed towards the studio flat's door, which was painted in the same sleek black paint as the front door. The key slid in smoothly, and the solid door opened noiselessly on well-oiled hinges as Barney stepped into the studio. He dumped his heavy bag down on the softly carpeted floor, and stretched his lower back with a grunt, wondering if he was getting a little old for this.

It was essentially one large room, with a double bed in the centre, in front of which a large, flat-screen TV dominated the wall. There was a small galley kitchen that was equally well appointed, and a well-fitted, modern shower room, and that was it, but the place reeked of money, and of no expense being spared. He ran his hand along the duvet, noting the smooth, crisp feel of expensive linen, and he smiled. A good night's kip in a proper bed after too long sleeping in the camper van was just what he needed. That and a decent shower and a good, hot meal that he'd get ordered in.

Barney went to the large sash window that looked out onto the back of the property, where low-level lighting in a surprisingly small garden was angled to illuminate tall, ivy-covered walls that enclosed the space. He noted the wrought-iron fire escape just to the right of the window. He tried to open the window, but it was locked in a way that it would open only a few inches on a tilt. He moved his face close to the glass and saw the fire escape stretching up towards the top of the building. He frowned as he pulled his head back in and closed the window, wondering how the lack of an escape worked with fire regulations. It was always possible that a premium was being paid by one of the other properties for exclusive garden access.

'First things first,' he muttered to himself. He unzipped his holdall and withdrew a four-pack of Tetley's Yorkshire bitter, cracked the top on one and took a long pull on the cold beer. Sitting on the bed, he took out his phone and went to a fast-food app, and within thirty seconds he'd ordered a large pizza. Sipping from his beer again, he crossed into the kitchen and put the three remaining tins into the fridge and returned to his bag to get out his laptop. Opening it up, he searched for available Wi-Fi networks and found three: one marked 'Studio', another 'Garden flat' and a third 'Duplex'. The Duplex signal was weak, just two bars as opposed to the five bars for Studio. He chuckled; this was going to be too easy.

Barney picked up his phone again and dialled.

'Barney dude, what gives, my good man?' a drawling, nasal voice answered.

'Clive, mate. Can I ask a favour?'

'Of course, anything for you buddy.'

'I'm at an address in Glasgow that has web-based security cameras. I need to be able to access them and to interrogate the historical imagery. They're controlled by SecureForce Solutions. I just need access for a while for a job I'm on. Priority one, yeah?'

'I can look into it; we can access most systems if we need to. Is it a Box job?' said Clive, referring to the nickname for MI5.

'No, cops. I'm freelancing for them – proper big job, mate. Wouldn't ask if it wasn't necessary,' said Barney, swigging from his beer again.

'I know, man. I know, I owe you, and you taught me everything I know, so I'll get on it, but only use for the minimum amount of time, yeah?'

'Of course. I'll message you the address and router details and whatever I can access here. I just want to get access to the cameras, you know, safety's sake and all that.'

'Okay, Barney. Be careful, buddy, yeah?'

'You know me, Clive. I've a beer on the go, and I'm about to have a smoke, so I'm relaxed.' Barney chuckled.

'You don't change. I'll message you in a minute.' The phone went dead.

Barney quickly composed a text message with all the details and sent it off to Clive. They'd worked together for several years when Barney was a field technical officer at MI5, and he had mentored Clive, teaching him everything he knew. Clive was a typical techie geek, but he was supersmart and had soon eclipsed Barney's knowledge, if not always his practical nous. He was now working as an IT security expert in the private sector but was also still appropriately vetted, and often provided his skills to the security services and other government agencies.

Barney pulled out a small black box, extended a couple of small antennae and plugged it into his laptop. He clicked on the icon that appeared on his screen. Once it had detected the available networks, Barney selected the one marked 'Duplex' and then 'run' on the application box.

A dialogue box flashed up. *Analysing.* Barney ignored that and clicked on the properties of the network noting the manufacturer details for the router. He quickly opened a document from a folder on the home screen, searched for the manufacturer name and copied a series of numbers and letters, upper and lower case. He then waited, watching the status bar on the screen as the sniffer connected with the network.

Password?

Barney pasted the default password into the box, holding his breath. It wasn't all lost if the default password had been changed, but it would be much easier if it wasn't.

Login successful. Downloading packet data. Estimated time: 15 minutes.

Barney smiled and shook his head. It was simple to change passwords on routers, but the reality was no one ever did.

His phone buzzed next to him on the bed. Just a web address, a username and a password comprising a series of letters, numbers and symbols. Barney opened a web browser and entered the address. A web page flashed up on the screen: *SecureForce. Surveillance solutions*. Barney entered the username and password and hit the return key, and held his breath again.

A new web page opened showing five screens in gallery format: one a live feed of the outside of the block, two of the lobby, one of the stairs and one of the landing outside the duplex, giving a clear view of the door to the top-floor apartment. He was in.

He clicked on the time function and began to wind the footage back. It was motion activated so it was simple to go back, firstly to observe himself entering the lobby and moving into the studio. He then went back just over ninety minutes prior to his arrival to the next activation.

He watched with interest as the compact, stocky form of Alban Hoxhaj arrived, along with another man. A massive, hulking brute dressed in a suit he was almost bursting out of. They quickly ascended the stairs, and within a few moments they had both entered the duplex.

Barney clicked to another folder on his desktop, marked 'DP-Hunter'. He clicked on the icon and soon, had synched it with the downloading packet data from the duplex Wi-Fi system. DP-Hunter was a specialist bit of software that Barney had secured from a hacker he'd become good friends with when he was with Box. The hacker was a genius at downloading data from

Wi-Fi networks in order to capture browsing history, user names and passwords.

Estimated time: 5 minutes, read the status bar.

A sudden buzz came from the door and made Barney start just a little. He went to the small monitor near the door and saw a man clutching a pizza box. Barney pressed the intercom. 'Yes?'

'Pizza,' said the man.

'Hold on.' Barney opened the studio door and stepped out into the lobby. He swung the front door wide, and the man, who was small and wiry, and looked like he was in a hurry, handed over a grease-stained box.

'Here you go, pal,' he said in an accent that was a combination of the Middle East and Glasgow.

'Thanks, mate,' said Barney, accepting the box. The man nodded, turned on his heel and jogged down the path towards a waiting car. Barney turned and almost jumped out of his skin. The suited man he'd seen Hoxhaj enter the building with was right behind him, massive and intimidating, scowling at Barney, his heavy brow low over hooded, piggy eyes.

49

THE SILENCE IN the lobby was overpowering. The giant radiated menace as he stood there, surveying Barney, his face locked in a contemptuous snarl.

Barney smiled widely, cool as a cucumber. 'Ayup, mate. Pizza time and I'm that 'ungry I could eat a scabby donkey,' he said, showing not even a trace of nervousness.

The giant's face morphed from a scowl to a confused frown at Barney's strong accent and he nodded, his dark eyes glittering as he stepped to the side and pressed the door release.

'Enjoy your pizza,' he said in a deep and thickly accented voice as he strode outside.

Barney watched as the massive form headed down the path and the indicators flashed on the Range Rover. As the man got in the car and drove off, Barney exhaled, a smile stretching over his face as he walked back into the studio and shut the door behind him, engaging the deadbolt.

He returned to the bed and sat, putting the delicious-smelling pizza down beside him and looked at the screen.

Packet extraction complete. Barney smiled and reached for his phone and dialled again.

'I hope you're not smoking in that horribly expensive bedsit,' said Ross.

'As if. Objective achieved, and as a bonus I've hacked into the CCTV network at the building.'

'Nicely done, pal, despite a lack of authorisation.'

'Is that gonna be a problem?'

'Nah, I'll speak to the chief. He's still in the office burning the midnight oil like me. He's let his overly protective superintendent bugger off, but the lovely Sofia told me he's free for a chat, so I'll pop in and see him on my way out of the office, which is going to be very soon.'

'Will he be able to retrospectively authorise?'

'Yes, although he'll probably want to flag to surveillance commissioners, as you've hacked a secure CCTV network. He's got a direct line to them at the moment because it's all kicking off with corruption being at the forefront of every bugger's mind. What can you do with the data from your download thing? Is it any use?'

'I'm going to sift it now, filter for social media, messaging services and any suspicious browsing. I assume that his phone will default to Wi-Fi when he goes into the house, so it may give us a lead.'

'None of that made any fucking sense to me, but I'll take your word for it that it's a good thing. In fact, this is a real bonus, despite your usual disregard for getting shit authorised. Is he in?'

'He is. Arrived with a massive brute of a bloke, who looks like a minder. Went in a little while before I got in here. I just bumped into him in the lobby; he's just buggered off in the Range Rover.'

'Jesus, did he see you?'

'Well, I was getting me pizza off the delivery man, so I'm gonna say yes.'

'Fuck's sake, Barney. That's far too close.'

'I was just getting pizza. What's more normal than that?'

Ross exhaled, the exasperation obvious. 'I guess. So, what now?'

'Well, I reckon he's down for the night, as his driver's just gone, so I'll keep an eye on the place and see what I can do with the data. Once I can analyse it all, I'll come up with a suggestion. It may be that a well-placed bit of information that reaches the right ears may prompt contact between your bent bobby and Hoxhaj and I'll be ready to intercept. We're in with a chance.'

'Good work, Barney. Now get some rest, and don't get pished. We've a load of work to do tomorrow, but stay out of the way of these bastards. If they twig you're connected to the cops, there's no telling what they'll do. I found out today that he's not known as The Surgeon for nothing.'

'Ach, stop fussin', man. You're not me mam. See you tomorrow.' Barney rang off. He looked at the feed on the screen as he opened his pizza box, selected a big, greasy slice and bit down with relish.

50

Sceptre: Where are you, something is happening.

Kiru: Home. What is happening?

Sceptre: Not sure, but police have you under surveillance.
   I think there's someone in your building. Something is being
   planned.

Kiru: Where?

Sceptre: I don't know.

Kiru: Find out and get back to me urgently. I'm getting out of
   here and going to the safe house.

Sceptre: I'll see if I can find out more, but you've made it
   difficult now. Cops are throwing the kitchen sink at it . . .
   three dead bodies have made them desperate. You should
   consider leaving the country.

Kiru: You worry too much. Keep me informed.

******************Message deleted**************

51

ALBAN HOXHAJ GROWLED as he looked again at the messages from the asset. Damned pigs in his building. He wondered if he had been too hasty in dealing with Toka and the other two, but quickly shook it off. Toka and Jetmir had disrespected him, and he'd reached his position by being ruthless and by never allowing any breach of besa to go unpunished. The cop was just in the wrong place at the wrong time.

'T'hangert dreqi,' he hissed under his breath, his mind whirling with options. Hoxhaj never swore, but the Albanian curse 'may the devil eat you' seemed appropriate.

He couldn't be arrested, not now. He couldn't be sure that there wouldn't be microscopic evidence somewhere on his body; it was too soon since he'd shot three people and he knew all about firearms residue, DNA and fibres. He was as sure as he could be that they'd find nothing, and even if they did, his DNA wasn't on any databases.

He picked up his phone from the coffee table and dialled.

'Yes, boss,' said Enver after just one ring.

'Come and get me now. We need to get to the safe house.'

'On my way. Anything I need to bring?'

'No, everything I need is in the safe house, but we may have a cop in the building.'

'I saw an old guy getting a pizza at the door when I left. He was staying in the studio. He looked too old to be a cop.'

'Who's in the other apartment?'

'Young family, definitely not cops.'

'Must be him then, the dog. Come and get me, but not in the Range Rover. Use the safe car.'

'On my way. Just a few minutes.'

Hoxhaj stood in the massive, open-plan space, his feet cosseted in the deep pile of the carpet. He knew the cops couldn't get him. They'd always planned for this, hence the safe house and a clean car always ready to be used. He could disappear easily, but he felt the familiar rage begin to surge.

He went to the large picture window and looked out over Glasgow, the lights sparkling in the distance at the city centre. He had enjoyed living here, but he needed to move on, which didn't bother him. He was always ready to go at a moment's notice, but it was inconvenient. He snarled, and his face flushed red as his anger boiled at the thought of scum cops spying on him. He thought of a man sitting in the studio, just a few metres below him, watching the cameras, intruding in his home.

Hoxhaj walked across the room and into the huge bedroom, with its super-king-sized bed, floor-to-ceiling cupboards, deep carpets and wide-screen TV on the wall. His anger rose even more at the thought of leaving this comfortable place behind for the much smaller, more basic safe house he'd now have to spend weeks in whilst the dust settled. The fury was rising faster now, his body almost quaking, as if electricity were penetrating his muscles.

He went to the far cupboard, opened it and pulled out a small Burberry holdall. Delving into it, he ignored the thick roll of cash, wallet full of untraceable bank cards and three mobile phones, instead closing his hands around the cold polymer handgrip of a Glock 19 handgun. He racked the slide of the firearm and looked at it, his face darkening as he felt a sense of power creeping up his hand, his arm and into his chest.

He'd show them.

52

BARNEY FROWNED AS he looked at the data stream on his laptop, trying to make sense of what he was seeing. He'd set up a filtration system with keywords that he'd use on the packet data. He knew how bad guys communicated, often on secure messaging apps, like Telegram or Wickr, but this didn't look like that.

Hoxhaj had been accessing some kind of Albanian message board or community forum. Barney noted with interest that he'd used it regularly over the past few months. He opened a browser page and copied and pasted the web address into the search engine. A web page entitled *Komuniteti shqiptar në Glasgow* appeared on his screen. He ran the title through a translation page in Google and 'Albanian community in Glasgow' flashed up instantly.

Why would an Albanian gangster suspected of a brutal triple murder just a few hours ago be on a community notice board?

His mind flared with the memory of a small group of Islamic fundamentalists who had used message boards and forums to communicate. They'd used a custom car webpage forum to send each other direct messages, or they'd create threads in forums in basic code to direct operatives across the world. It was a simple and effective method of sending messages when secure apps couldn't be used, or when they wanted to keep messages off phones, on the basis that a seized phone would give up all their secrets.

Barney extended his search parameters, looking for usernames and passwords connected to the forum. It would be something familiar to Hoxhaj, he figured, and if he was as narcissistic as many gangsters it would almost certainly be something macho. Barney studied the profile that Norma had sent him earlier that day, taking in the photo of Alban Hoxhaj. He observed the slicked-back hair, shining with oil; the gold tooth; the dark, unfathomable eyes.

He put 'The Surgeon' in with a margin for error. Nothing found.

He tapped the keys again. 'Kirugu', again with an allowance for error or misspelling.

There were numerous results, all on the forum page, all with the username Kiru. Barney smiled and sat back. He reached into his shirt pocket, brought out his tobacco pouch and rolled a thin cigarette. He stood up and cracked the window open, and applied a flame from a battered Zippo to the roll-up. He took a long pull and exhaled with deep pleasure, as the nicotine seeped into his bloodstream.

He went to the forum login page, and entered the username and password that was visible on the packet data dump.

He smiled as the page refreshed. He was in. He looked at the top of the page where there was an envelope icon with the words 'mesazhe direkte'. Direct messages. He clicked and a new page opened. There was just one message on it, from someone called Sceptre.

Barney wasn't one to panic; he'd been in the game too long and realised that panicking in his line of work was what got you killed.

He picked up his phone and dialled.

Ross's phone went straight to voicemail.

He dialled again, whilst maximising the CCTV feed, staring at it intently, with just a trace of butterflies beginning to make their presence felt in his stomach.

53

MAX WAS SITTING on the sofa, Nutmeg snoring lightly, her head on his lap.

'Tea?' said Katie, standing up and yawning.

'Aye, why not? I'm ready for my bed, so maybe something herbal?'

'Rooibos?' she said, rubbing her eyes.

'Go on then, spoil me.' Max smiled at his wife, who looked as beautiful as ever in her slouchy pyjama pants and one of Max's old, worn hooded sweatshirts.

Nutmeg opened her eyes and lifted her head from Max's lap, before deciding that nothing much was happening, so she lowered her head again and stretched luxuriously. Max tickled her ears absent-mindedly as he turned over the day's events in his mind. They were close, so close to bringing this case to a resolution, and the temptation to keep on pushing was strong. Ross had his faults, but he always knew when his people needed a bit of a break, and Max was forced to agree.

'Here you go, babe,' said Katie, handing over a steaming mug.

'Thanks,' said Max, accepting the hot drink.

'You look tired.'

'Aye, busy few days.'

'How's Affi?'

'Still not engaging, and claiming that she just went away for a bit. No one's buying it for a moment. She didn't think I saw, but I know she got a message on her iPad that shook her up. I don't want to keep on nagging her, or she'll just retreat further into her shell.'

'How about I have a word with her? We always got on really well when I was doing her forms and during all our appointments.'

Max paused and considered this. Katie was a paralegal at an immigration law firm and was well regarded for her efficiency, but more than that. Katie cared. She really cared about other people. 'You know, that's not a half bad idea. Tomorrow will be really busy, but after that maybe that's a solution. You have her trust, so if anyone will persuade her to tell us what's going on, you will. Maybe in a couple of days we can shoot up there and spend an hour with her. Particularly once we bring this to a conclusion, which could be any time, now.'

'I don't mind, and I know Douglas won't mind,' she said, referring to her boss. Douglas was nudging late middle-age and was somewhat curmudgeonly, but he had a good heart and was very fond of Katie.

Max's phone buzzed on the arm of the sofa, making Nutmeg jump, her head up, ears askew. He looked at the display before answering. 'Barney, everything okay?'

'I can't get hold of Ross, and I may have a situation,' he said, with no trace of panic in his broad Yorkshire-accented voice.

'He has patchy signal. What's up?'

'I've managed to hack into Hoxhaj's Wi-Fi, and I've just seen a concerning message. I'm screenshotting and sending to you now.'

A buzz in Max's ear indicated that the message had arrived. He looked at the screen and read it with a rising dread.

'Shit, you need to get out of there,' said Max.

'Aye, I reckon, but I'd rather someone was on their way nearby, just in case, you know. Looks like some bastard is telling tales, eh?'

'I'd say that's a fair assessment, but shit, who knows about you being there? I thought it was just going to be us and the chief.'

'Ross said he was going to see the boss for authorities, but I don't know if anyone else was there. Don't think the chief is bent, do you?'

Max paused for just a moment, then shook his head. 'No, not a chance. Look, I'll get on my bike, and be there as soon as I can. Try and get hold of Ross again; he's closer than me. If the wheel really comes off, dial 999, but if you can, get the hell out of there. I'm leaving now.'

There was a long pause on the line before Barney spoke. 'Bugger.'

'What's going on?'

'Hoxhaj's gorilla of a minder is back. I hacked the CCTV and he's just come through the door – not sure where he came from, the Range Rover didn't pull up in its parking space.'

'What's he doing?'

'Just stood in't lobby looking at my front door.'

'Can you get out?'

'It's okay. He's heading up the stairs to Hoxhaj's place. I'm cool, nowt to worry about. I'll give it a minute, then I'll pack up and piss off, but we need to get together. Some bastard is tittle-tattling.'

'On my way.' Max hung up.

Katie frowned. 'That didn't sound good. What's up?'

Max didn't reply but quickly forwarded the screenshot to both Ross and Janie via their WhatsApp group. He then dialled again.

'I've literally just got home, Max. What's up?' said Ross.

'Something's happening with Barney. Check out the screenshot I've just sent you,' said Max, standing up.

There was a brief pause before Ross spoke again. 'Shit.'

'Yeah, I'm on my way on the bike, but he sounds relaxed enough and is leaving imminently.'

'Barney would sound relaxed if his van was on fire whilst he was in it. Do we call for the uniforms to back him up?'

'Not yet. We don't know who's listening, and Barney's an old campaigner. He'll have a plan, but someone is close to us and is reporting everything they hear to Hoxhaj, the bastard.'

'Okay, I'm on my way. I'm twenty minutes off. Mrs F is going to be scunnered with me, though.'

'See you there. I've texted Janie – maybe give her a bell on the way.'

'On it.' Ross hung up.

Max turned to Katie. 'It's nothing, babe, but I need to pop out for a bit.'

'Max?' she said, concern on her face.

He forced a smile that he was sure didn't look genuine. 'All fine. Barney just needs something. I'll take the bike, and I'll be back later. Maybe you hit the sack, yeah?' Max kissed the top of her head and went to the cupboard in the hallway. He quickly dragged out his bike jacket and boots and went back to the living room.

'Max, I know when you're not telling me something, so I won't ask anything else, but please be careful,' she said, trying to force a smile that didn't reach her eyes.

'It's nothing, babe,' he said, zipping up his boots and pulling the heavy jacket on. He kissed her again, tickled Nutmeg's ears and left the house heading up to the garage. He pulled the up-and-over door open, climbed on his big 1300cc KTM motorcycle and fired it up, the engine a low burble as he eased it out of the garage. He took the helmet from the tank, slipped it on and fastened it securely under his chin, and then roared off, his stomach feeling as though it were full of lead.

54

MAX RODE FAST. He rode as fast as the roads allowed on the hugely powerful KTM. He wasn't the best driver of cars, hence the reason Janie almost always drove when they were on four wheels, but Max could ride well.

So, by smashing all speed limits, he was able to pull up outside the central Glasgow townhouse within twenty-five minutes. He switched off the engine and removed his helmet, reaching immediately for his phone and dialling Barney.

There was no reply and the phone diverted to voicemail. 'Shit,' said Max, dialling again.

'Where are you?' said Ross.

'Outside the place. No reply from Barney.'

'I know, just rings out to voicemail. I'm a minute away,' said Ross.

'Have you heard from Janie?'

'Aye, she should be here imminently. I'm coming up now.' Ross rang off.

A minute later Max saw the lumbering form of his boss coming around the corner, still dressed in the suit he'd been wearing earlier.

'What's the daft bugger got himself into?' said Ross.

'We should have been closer, Ross. He shouldn't have been there on his own with no backup.'

'Is what it is, Max. Come on, let's get in there.' They looked up at the sound of a car pulling up and saw Janie's Volvo park by Max's bike. She stepped out of the car and joined them on the path, her face flushed in the harsh yellow sodium lights.

'Any news?'

'Barney's not answering the phone,' said Max.

'I know, I tried him. Straight to voicemail.'

'Come on, let's go,' said Max and they all went down the path to the main door, which was locked tight.

'How do we get past this?' said Ross.

'Hold on. I've a drop key,' said Janie, reaching into her pocket and pulling out an L-shaped key which she slotted into the fire access slot at the top of the intercom panel. A quick twist and they were in. Janie reached into her jacket and produced her telescopic baton, which she racked open.

'This is why I have you on my team, Calder. Preparation, unlike Max here,' said Ross in a whispered voice as the entered the lobby.

Max pointed to the right of the space where there was an alcove and a simple brass plate that read 'Studio' in black letters. He held his fingers to his lips.

Max approached the alcove, stepped to one side and peeped around the corner at the heavy glossy black door, the silver door furniture stark against the sleek surface. He froze, his insides turning cold.

The door was half open, the lock broken, the wood by the handle splintered. The inside of the studio was pitch dark and as foreboding as a graveyard.

55

MAX SIGNALLED TO Ross and Janie, his face registering the alarm that was coursing through his veins.

'Door's been boshed. Shit, shit, shit.'

'Let's go,' said Ross, his face grim. He didn't hesitate, he didn't rush, he didn't panic, he just squared his shoulders and marched into the flat, shoving the door open with a crash and charging in.

Max and Janie followed close by into the pitch-dark studio, every synapse firing with dread as to what they were going to find in that small space.

It was empty. Janie flicked a switch and harsh light from LED spots flooded the room.

Totally empty, beyond an open pizza box with three slices untouched, and a beer can on the bedside table. A worn and scratched leather pouch was next to the can.

'Fuck, this is really bad. He's left his 'baccy pouch,' said Ross.

Max picked out his phone and dialled again, a buzzing noise, like an angry wasp, was audible from the other side of the bed. Janie stooped down, found the vibrating phone on the carpet by the bed and cancelled the call.

'Shit, what have they done with the daft old bastard? We'd better call this in,' said Ross.

Max was just about to dial when his phone rang. He looked at the screen, seeing a landline number with a Glasgow area code.

'Hello?' he said, his voice laced with suspicion.

'Ayup, Max. I've just watched your assault on the studio on CCTV. Very impressive. Have you got my 'baccy pouch? It must have fell out of me pocket when I legged it, along with my phone, and I'm desperate for a puff,' said Barney, cheerily.

'Where the hell are you?' said Max.

'Upstairs in Hoxhaj's flat. It's a reet grand place this. Come on up. They've pissed off and won't be back.'

56

-KOMUNITETI SHQIPTAR NË Glasgow-

Sceptre: Did you get away?
Kiru: Yes. Call me.
Sceptre: Number?
Kiru: Same as last one.

57

'**WHAT THE BLOODY** hell happened, then?' said Ross as he sat down on the plush leather sofa in Hoxhaj's duplex.

'Well, after our call, two masked buggers turned up in the lobby from the back garden, one of them was packing heat. I nearly shite meself, I'll tell you.' He paused to take a deep draw on his roll-up, Ross screwing up his face as the acrid blue smoke billowed.

'Who the hell were they?'

'Hoxhaj and his gorilla. They had balaclavas on, but how many people that big are there in Glasgow at this particular moment? Added to that is the fact that they aren't in here now, and didn't appear on camera coming down the stairs, is pretty damning. I suspect they came down the fire escape, just to give them some deniability on the CCTV. Well, I grabbed me bag of kit and picked the window lock and managed to get out just before the door came bashing in. Too bloody close. I was lucky that the window lock was a piece of garbage. I couldn't have opened it any quicker if I'd had the bloody key.'

'Did they follow?'

'Nay, lad. Don't think they knew what I'd done, and their lock-picking skills are clearly not as good as mine. They came into the garden by the back door and searched it, but by then I'd gone up the fire escape and picked my way in here. Fire door, piece of piss to get in.'

'Jesus Christ, you've got bollocks the size of Balnakyle, Barney.

They were ready to put a bullet in you,' said Ross, shaking his head in admiration.

'Nay point panicking, is there? It turned out okay. They're on their toes now, but we have an advantage. Hoxhaj is using this forum to communicate securely with his bent cop, but he can't know we know about it, can he?'

'How? They seem to know everything else, including the fact that you were in the studio, which I thought was only known to us, the chief and maybe someone at the surveillance commissioner's office,' said Max.

'Aye, that's a concern, which we can address later, but I'd say they don't know that we've compromised their system.'

'How?'

Barney just nodded at his laptop. They all looked at the screen, which showed a message board.

Sceptre: *Did you get away?*

Kiru: *Yes. Call me.*

Sceptre: *Number?*

Kiru: *Same as last one.*

'Bastards. We need that phone number. There must be a way,' said Ross.

'There will be and this gives us an advantage, but before we avail ourselves of it, we need to plug the leak and put the buggers in the dark. When can we speak to the chief?'

'He'll be in at six.'

'Okay, it can wait until then.'

'What can?' said Ross.

'You buggers always take the piss out of my advancing years, but they do give me an advantage. I've been there and done it, and I have a suspicion where they're getting their intel from. I'll take my van back to Tulliallan and grab a couple of hours' sleep there. I suggest you all find yourselves somewhere to get your heads down. We all know it'll be a long day tomorrow.'

'Who made you the boss, Barney?' said Ross, without anger.

'You have any better ideas?'

'Good point, well made. Okay, all back in the office at six, ready to go.'

'One thing, Ross.'

'What now, you geriatric old goat?'

'Not the office straight away. Meet by my van in the car park. I'll have t' kettle on.'

58

THE SAFE HOUSE was adequate. Just adequate, thought Hoxhaj as he sat in the small, but comfortable lounge. It was, however, a long way from the palatial duplex that he'd just left a couple of hours ago, when Enver had collected him in the anonymous Vauxhall that had been kept for a moment like this, the Range Rover being far too hot to be in right now.

He really didn't want to leave the UK, having been his home for some time now. He had influence and a strong network, so he was hoping that just keeping his head low for a short while might allow him to resurface once they'd exhausted all the leads. He was certain that there was nothing else to link him to the case. It was only he and Enver who knew what had happened in that tenement, apart from the asset, and there was no way he would be informing on him, not with the hold that Hoxhaj had over him. Not only was the asset overtly corrupt, and therefore unable to inform without self-implication, but Hoxhaj knew everything about the asset's home life, family and children.

There was no firm evidence linking Hoxhaj to Toka and Jetmir, and he'd never even met the cop. All in all, he needed time, to bathe repeatedly, scrub and cut his nails and just wait. The asset was watching the investigation, and he would have warning should his name be mentioned and more importantly whether they had any evidence. Allied to that, false reports were being put in of sightings of suspicious individuals at the scene at the time of the incident, as well as numerous intelligence reports being given to Crimestoppers alleging that another gang was responsible for the murders. All in all, he was in the clear. Hoxhaj smiled widely.

Enver entered the room, nodding at Hoxhaj as he did.

'All done?'

'Yes, the Vauxhall's been deposited at Macca's yard. He'll dispose of it, and I've secured another vehicle.'

'Good work. I think we're in the clear, Enver. I always tell you about the importance of care. There's now nothing to link us to Toka, or her brothel, is there?'

Enver paused, his brow furrowing just a little.

'Enver?' said Hoxhaj, recognising the sign of disquiet in the face of his old friend and minder.

'The girl.'

'Which girl?'

'The kid, Afrodita. She saw me at Toka's place a few days ago when I went to collect taxes for West End places.'

'How did she get to see you?'

'She was in a room with Jetmir. Toka was scolding him for something, but she definitely saw me.'

'That's not good, Enver. If she talks to the police and describes you, that is a possible link to me.'

'It's unlikely, no?'

'A risk. I don't like risks and you're very distinctive.'

'What do you want me to do?'

'Nothing for now. I'll speak to the asset. If the girl is speaking, it could be a problem we'll have to consider. Now food. I'm hungry, go and find something for me.'

Enver nodded gravely and left the room.

Hoxhaj picked up his iPad, navigated to the forum and composed a message.

Kiru: *We need to speak.*

The reply came back immediately.

Sceptre: *Same number?*

Kiru: *Yes*.

The phone buzzed immediately. 'What about the girl Afrodita?' was Hoxhaj's opening gambit.

'She's at home with her foster family.'

'Is she cooperating?'

'Last I heard, no. Clammed up tight.'

'You know her address?'

'Sorry, what? Why would you need that?'

'That doesn't concern you. Address?'

'I don't know it. It's locked down tight.'

'Find out.'

'I'm not sure I can.'

'I don't want to hear this. It's your job to do as I say. Have you forgotten who I am, and what I can do?' His voice was dark and molten and he felt his cheeks burn as the simmering rage he'd been trying to keep down began to rise again.

'I . . . I'll try and find out. I have someone who can find out,' the asset stuttered.

'Can you trust them?'

'Yes, they have as much to lose as I do.'

Hoxhaj hung up. He stood and walked to the window, looking across at the long terraces of identical houses in a suburb of Glasgow. He had a sudden urge for a drink, even though the sun was only just beginning to emerge. He picked up a bottle of good malt whisky from the sideboard and poured two fingers into a chipped and worn glass. He downed it in one gulp, relishing the burn as the fiery, peaty liquid carved a trail down his throat.

A grim smile stretched across his face as the alcohol immediately leached into his bloodstream, calming him.

He was going to win again. He always did.

He was unstoppable.

59

THE ASSET STARED at his phone, his guts churning as the fear gripped like a vice. Hoxhaj was a bastard, and he hated that he'd got into this situation, but what choice did he have. He'd have to make the call.

He dialled. 'Yes?' a voice full of suspicion answered.

'It's me.'

'What?' The voice was hesitant and nervous with a slight tremor.

'I need an address for the girl who went missing.'

'What?'

'You heard me. Hoxhaj is insisting, and you're the only person I know who has access to it.'

'You can look at bloody police computers easily enough.'

'I can't; they leave a great big audit trail. You have it accessible, don't you?'

'Yes, but fucking hell, this isn't what I signed up for.'

'Look, just get me the fucking address, okay? Call me on this number when you have it, or would you rather I gave your name to Hoxhaj as being the person who won't cooperate? I take it you heard what happened at the brothel in Glasgow?'

The voice sighed deeply. 'I'll get it to you as soon as I can.'

'See that you do.' The asset hung up and jammed the phone in his pocket, his mind reeling at what he'd become.

60

THE KETTLE BEGAN to whistle as the water bubbled away on the small gas cooker that was set into a shelf of the VW California, which was parked right outside the main entrance of Tulliallan Castle.

'How the hell did security let you park this old shed here?' said Ross.

'Yorkshire charm. Studies show that the Yorkshire accent is the most trustworthy in the UK. And I resent you calling Mavis a shed,' said Barney. He was still dressed in his pyjamas, under a checked dressing gown, with tweedy-looking carpet slippers on his feet.

'Mavis?'

'Aye, Mavis.'

'You're a bloody mental case, and this is fucking typical. We had to park bloody miles away on the parade square, with my dodgy feet, as well. I guess you get an OAP parking badge or something,' said Ross.

There were tired chuckles in the van from Max and Janie, and Barney just grinned. 'Nay, blue badge, look.' He picked up a disabled badge from the dash and held it up.

'How the hell do you have one of those, you cheating git? You're not disabled, you're just old,' said Ross.

'I resent that remark. It's discriminatory against the disabled or summat,' said Barney.

'You're not disabled, you freeloading bugger.'

'Aye, I am. False leg.' Barney rapped against his lower left leg with a teaspoon. There was a metallic rat-a-tat as he did.

A silence descended in the van. 'Hold up, so you genuinely have a prosthetic leg?' said Janie, open-mouthed.

'Aye, look, I got a new one recently. It's a beaut, right?' Barney pulled up his pyjama leg a little, displaying the sleek black weave of a carbon-fibre prosthesis.

'What the actual fuck?' blurted Ross.

'Barney, why have you never mentioned this before?' said Max, his eyes wide.

Barney just shrugged. 'You never asked.'

'But how, and when?'

'Iraq, 1991.'

'What were you doing there?'

'Sneaky shit, and I got a bullet in the leg.'

'And we're just hearing about this now?' Ross said.

'Don't like to make a fuss. Tea?'

No one spoke. They just all looked at each other as Barney whistled along with the boiling kettle. He dropped teabags into four cups that were on a small, collapsible table in the centre of the space between the front and rear seats. The front seats had been swung 180 degrees so they were facing the rear, and Barney was sitting on the driver's seat. He poured hot water into each and added a drop of milk.

'Put bags in the pot there when it's strong enough,' he said to Max, Janie and Ross, all sitting on the remaining three car seats.

'I cannot bloody believe we are just learning now that you're bloody Long John Silver. You could have told me. I have to do bloody risk assessments and it'd been nice to know one of my people is a peg leg,' said Ross.

'Give over. It don't matter. Drink your bloody brew.'

'Where's Norma?' said Max, shaking his head.

'On her way, but she needs her computer, so she's going straight to the office. How do you live like this, Barney?' said Ross, looking distinctly uncomfortable in the confined space.

'Just have to be organised. I like it.'

Max, Janie and Ross had returned home for a few hours before they all gathered at Barney's van at six at Tulliallan car park. The building was coming alive with the arriving staff and a small group of tired and irritable-looking recruits jogged past the front of the castle.

Everyone appeared shattered, with pale faces, eye bags and rumpled hair, even Janie didn't look her immaculate self.

'So, what's next?' said Max.

'We have this brew, then we'll head into the office, but I just wanted to extend my hospitality to you all first.'

'What, so I left my warm house, warm wife and lovable dog, just to come and sit in the back of a van that stinks of Old Holborn parked in the car park at Tulliallan? I could have had a proper coffee at home,' said Max, stifling a yawn.

'I smoke Golden Virginia. Holborn is rancid, lad.'

'Aye, and I left my house with Mrs F in a somewhat irascible mood, so what's the point of this?'

'You'll see. Anyone want toast?'

'No, I bloody don't,' said Ross, sipping his tea. 'And you put too much milk in. It's fucking honking,' he added, with a grimace.

'Hoxhaj was in contact with his tame cop a while ago.'

'What did they say?'

'Just said they needed to talk. Same number.'

'So, nothing to take us farther forward?' said Janie.

'Not exactly. It means lines of communication are open. May give us a chance,' said Max.

'I agree. Hoxhaj sends his message, and Bent Bobby replies immediately. That opens all sorts of possibilities. I'd say he's on the back foot, which we can exploit. We find him, you lot can lean on him until he gives up Hoxhaj and all the others in this nasty little group.'

'It's kind of like dominoes. We just need to knock over the first one,' said Max, brightening.

Ross looked at his phone, which had just buzzed on the table in front of him. 'It's the chief. He's in the office and wants us in there, now.'

'I'm coming,' said Barney.

'Not in your PJs, you're not,' said Ross.

'Then give me a minute,' he said.

*

Ten minutes later, Ross, Max, Janie and Barney were walking into the chief's office. He was dressed casually in jeans and a polo shirt, and was busying himself at a large drip-coffee machine.

'Coffee?' he said as they all filed in.

'Aye, be nice to take the taste away of Barney's bogging tea,' said Ross.

'You still drank it,' said Barney.

'I was being polite.'

'You said it was fucking honking.'

Macdonald chuckled at the banter. 'Okay, people, what do we know?'

Barney put his fingers to his lips and held up a piece of A4 paper, which read, *Don't talk about the case* in scrawled writing.

There were furrowed brows and pointed looks at Barney as he pulled out what looked like a chunky walkie-talkie and switched it on. He began to sweep it around the room, focusing on the desk, computer and lamp.

'Well, Ross, have you been given an update on the reactive murder by DCI Leslie?' said Macdonald.

'Not yet, sir.'

'Well, she has a full team on it. Scene is still being processed, house to house is fully underway and CCTV parameters have been extended.'

'Any leads?' said Ross, watching Barney with interest as he continued to sweep the device around the room, his lips pursed in concentration as he looked at the unit with its blinking and dancing lights.

'As I understand it, nothing concrete yet, but it's early days,' said Macdonald, his eyes wide as Barney swept closer to the desk, his forehead creased in concentration.

The LED lights danced on the unit, and Barney drew a line across his throat, the clear inference being 'say nothing compromising', and he held his piece of A4 up again and turned it around so the other side was facing outwards. *KEEP TALKING.*

'Okay, anything from the PM?' said Ross, his eyes narrow as he watched Barney.

'One down, two to go. All as you'd expect,' said Macdonald, his forehead creased and brow heavily furrowed with confusion.

Barney pointed at the underside of the desk at a three-gang plug socket unit and quickly scrawled on another piece of paper. *Bug in the plug socket.*

Macdonald's mouth gaped open with shock.

'So, cause of death is bullet to the head. Were the mutilations post- or antemortem?' said Max.

'Postmortem, very clean wounds, probably caused by a scalpel or similar. What can you tell me about your progression so far, Ross?' Macdonald's face had turned pale.

'Interesting is the best I can probably say, so far,' said Ross.

'How so?'

'Maybe best I show you. Norma has prepared an i2 chart thing in our office, and you know that they confuse me, boss, so maybe it's best if she explains it, or I'm bound to fuck it up. She has it all plotted on the big screen, and she's terribly excited about it.'

'Okay, I have to drop in and see the finance manager who wants an early word, then I'll call by yours. I also have a meeting at Holyrood with the First Minister, so I really need to prepare for that. Shall we say your office in an hour?'

'Perfect,' said Ross.

They all stood, and Ross, Max, Janie and Barney left the office, walking past the empty desk normally occupied by the staff officer and out into the corridor.

'You cussed old git. Why didn't you tell me you were going to do that?' Ross pointed at Barney, his finger almost quivering with tension.

'I wanted to see the look on your face,' said Barney, chuckling.

'I'm gonna pay you back for that.'

'I just didn't know. I wanted to be sure before I raised it, and if we'd pre-empted it, it would have been less natural. That sounded perfect to anyone listening. If I'd have warned you, the meeting would have been somewhere else, and as it was already planned, it needed to go ahead.'

'We need to get rid of the bloody thing,' said Ross.

'Actually, that's the last thing we need to do,' said Max.

'What the fuck are you talking about, Max? It's a fucking bug in the fucking Chief Constable of Police Scotland's office. He talks to the First Minister from that very office, and you think it's okay for a bastard bug to be in there?'

'It's an opportunity,' said Max.

'What?'

'You know it is. The bent cop knows it's there, but he doesn't know we know. It's perfect.'

'Shit, you're right. I'm too bloody tired for this.'

Macdonald burst out of his office. 'What the hell's going on?' he said, eyes wide.

'A bug, boss. Definitely, and it's in the extension gang plug. They're commercially available off the shelf from Amazon – any mug can buy one, so we're not talking about a pro, here. I could take it out, but I don't think that's a good idea. Just get back in and work as normal,' said Barney.

'Shit, but in my office. Who the hell has access to it?'

'Half of Tulliallan, I'd say. It's not like it's locked, is it? That's your motto, right? "My door is always open"?' said Ross, shrugging.

'I need you on this, Ross. Look, I have to run, but we need answers and a plan of action, okay?'

'Crystal, come and see us in an hour, and we'll have some options for you.'

'See that you do. This stops now. Like today, am I clear?'

'Boss, this is a cast-iron opportunity. If we suddenly pull the bug out, whoever it is will be on their guard, and we'll never find them. We need to use this to our advantage, and we need to do it now. Time is running out,' said Max.

'Ross?'

'Much as it pains me to agree with DS Craigie, I agree with DS Craigie, boss.'

Macdonald stared at his polished shoes, his jaw set tight, his eyes hard. He looked up, and caught every eye of the team.

'Right. We do this, you go to your office. Barney can sweep it to make sure there's no more bugs and let's get this job done. I'm sick of playing catch up. Let's take the fight to them.'

61

-KOMUNITETI SHQIPTAR NË Glasgow-

Sceptre: I have the information.
Kiru: Good.
Sceptre: New SIM this time. We must be careful, and make sure
    to delete messages from this.
Kiru: +35-71120909099.
Sceptre: ?
Kiru: Albanian. Impossible to trace. Call me in 1 hour.

*******************Message deleted**************

62

THE OFFICE WAS buzzing with activity when the chief arrived, now wearing his uniform of black trousers, a white shirt with the sleeves rolled up and a black tie. His epaulettes bore the rank insignia of crossed tipstaves in a laurel wreath below a crown.

Everyone stood as he entered, apart from Barney, who was looking wistfully at a roll-up. He was tired and really wanted a smoke, and couldn't see what he'd now bring to this party. Barney hated meetings, with everyone thinking they had to contribute, somehow. Barney generally spoke only if he felt it necessary; the rest was all bullshit.

'Okay, so where are we now?' said the chief.

'I've an update, hot off the press,' said Norma, a hint of excitement in her voice.

'Norma?' said Macdonald.

'The little black book you guys photographed at the brothel, it's interesting to say the least.'

'Black book?' said Macdonald.

Ross's face flushed, just a touch, and he glared at Norma. 'I was going to mention that, boss. Looks like Toka Kurti was assiduous in record keeping. She kept a list of names and numbers, figures and things like that in a wee leather black book, like The Fonz always did.' He tried to laugh, but it came out as a semi-embarrassed cough.

'Who the fuck is The Fonz?' said Norma, her brow furrowed.

'I did hear about this, Ross. Marina was a little perturbed, but I'm all for initiative. The Fonz was a 1970s American hero who had a "little black book", Norma. Awful analogy, which ages Ross terribly. Go on,' said Macdonald.

'Well, I've sent all the numbers through the usual databases including open source and it's thrown up some very curious results. It's raw data at the moment and will need to be parallel proved to attribute to the owners, but we have some interesting individuals that seem to have been associated with our recently departed brothel keeper.'

'Such as?' said Macdonald.

'Have you heard of Mr Justice Colm O'Neill?'

'Should we have?'

'Well, it took a little digging, but one of the phone numbers is attributed to him by an email he used on an adult services website. He's a senior immigration and asylum tribunal judge.'

'What the actual fuck?' said Ross, his mouth open in shock, before he turned to Macdonald. 'Sorry, boss, I forgot you were here,' he added, sheepishly.

'I agree with your first statement, Ross. Jesus, this is bad, and perhaps explains the concerning statistics on trafficking victims. Norma, I'm guessing he's not the only concerning name?'

'Well, I've plenty still to do, and I'm going to need help sweeping this up, but no. I'm fairly sure I have a senior member of social services in Highland region, at least one other junior cop, and at least one Immigration officer, probably from Glasgow. The reality is, this wee black book is going to be dynamite once it's been fully investigated. And added to that, if the numbers I'm looking at are accurate, then the amounts of money are eye watering.'

A silence descended in the room as the enormity of what they were dealing with began to land.

'Anything else?' said Ross, quietly.

'Possibly someone from Holyrood, but I can't be sure about that.'

'Oh, so just a minor thing like someone bent at the heart of the Scottish Government, brilliant,' said Ross, brimming with sarcasm.

Macdonald closed his eyes briefly, then opened them and looked at Norma. 'Before I say anything else, is that finally it, Norma?'

'No, a number for Hoxhaj, listed as "Kiru". It looks like he's ditched it, however. Also, did I hear that there had been a camera bell on the door that then disappeared?'

'Aye. I saw it when I did the walk-by the other night, but it had gone when we boshed the door,' said Max.

'Well, there was a username for a cloud-based server in Toka's black book, which may relate to it, but there's no password. Maybe Barney can help me out with that?'

'Aye, love. I'll give you a hand. Send it my way,' said Barney.

'That could be seriously useful if we can access the footage from the door. If they removed the camera, it means there was something significant to hide, right?' said Max.

'Make that a priority, yeah?' said Ross.

There was another pause, punctuated only by the ticking of the central heating from the ancient, thickly painted radiator.

'Okay, I get that this is all pretty earth-shattering, but does it change what we do, right here and right now?' said Max.

'No. We still are where we are. We have a bent cop at Tulliallan feeding a murdering bastard of an Albanian gangster. We can't do anything on the other stuff until we bring them down. We can sweep the rest up after that, with a load of extra manpower,' said Macdonald, his face firm.

'Well, we still have a hack on the Albanian community web page that Barney is keeping watch on. Any updates, Barney?' said Ross.

'Dunno, it's in my van.'

'What?'

'I forgot it when we went to the boss's office. I was so focused on a bug sweep I left it. I'll run and get it now,' he said, seizing the opportunity for a smoke.

'Excuse Barney, boss. He's old and forgetful, and we've just learned he has a missing leg,' said Ross.

'Sorry, what?' said Macdonald, his eyebrow suddenly shooting up.

'That's what we all said.'

Macdonald stared at Barney, an incredulous look on his face, before he shook his head slightly. 'No worries, everyone's been full on. If you can monitor that, Barney, that'd be great,' said Macdonald with a genuine smile.

Barney nodded and left the office. He walked along the dusty corridors until he emerged blinking in the spring sun, yawning as he crossed the car park towards his van. He unlocked it and got inside, opening the laptop after he did. He jammed his roll-up between his lips and applied a flame, sucking on the smoke with relish. He looked at the screen, still with the web page up, which he refreshed with a click on the trackpad.

Another message. More contact, but they were clearly getting careful by using a foreign SIM, which would make tracing the calls more difficult. Whilst not impossible, the bureaucracy surrounding the applications would take time. Time that they didn't have. Barney sighed and took another draw on his cigarette, closing the sliding door against the early-spring chill. He looked at the kettle.

'Bugger it, they can wait,' he muttered to himself as he sparked up the gas burner and slid the kettle onto the flame. Another brew and another fag would set him up for the rest of the day, which was bound to be busy. He wondered if he really was getting too old for this game, never at home, always on the move. He lived alone, having been divorced for many years, and he was mostly happy, but maybe it was time to relax a little and do a bit of fishing. The kettle's shrill whistle dragged him away from his daydreams of fly-fishing in the Lakes, as he poured boiling water into a mug and added a teabag.

His roll-up was getting perilously low, so he cracked the window open and tossed it outside.

As his eyes followed the path of the roll-up onto the tarmac outside, they were drawn to a tall man facing the building and wearing a long, shapeless dark-grey coat and what appeared to be a flat cap. Barney's years skulking about in the shadows behind terrorists and agitators had made him an expert in body language, and although he couldn't see the face of the man, he could tell that he wasn't happy. The staccato gestures of his free hand whilst his other hand was clamped to his ear suggested a difficult phone call. Not uncommon anywhere that there were lots of cops working such irregular hours. The man began to massage his temple with his spare hand, as he raised his face to the bright sky. *Poor bugger*, thought Barney, clearly having a domestic. That was the one thing he didn't miss about being married was the arguments that he and his ex-wife had always had, predominantly because of his long absences from home doing secret stuff for MI5. He did miss his wife though, he thought for a moment, remembering her smiling, kind face with a sudden tug. He liked his freedom, but he missed the company and sense of sharing that his solitary life had imposed upon him.

Barney sighed as he stirred his tea, pulling the bag out and dropping it in the small ceramic pot on the table that was half full of spent teabags. He added milk and sipped at the scalding brew. He looked at the message, which had been sent about an hour ago.

He looked at the man again; he had clearly finished his call but remained rooted to the spot, his shoulders hunched and head down. Suddenly he started to walk off back towards the building, fiddling with his phone. As he crossed to the footpath by the building the sun glinted on something as it fell to the ground. Barney frowned; something about the whole thing looked off, although he couldn't entirely work out what it was. Barney had spent his whole life judging people from a distance, through camera lenses, binoculars, covert recording devices and even satellite imagery, and his instinct told him that something was wrong with what he'd just witnessed.

He took a sip of his tea and quickly rolled another cigarette, which he lit straight away. He gathered up his laptop and slipped it in his kit bag, opened the door and stepped out into the sunshine, taking a long drag as he did. He set off back towards the building, retracing the man's footsteps. As he approached the footpath, he saw the grate of a drain where he'd seen the item fall from the man's hands. He paused, just momentarily, and peered through the grate down to the water a couple of feet below. The water's surface was dotted with litter floating on the stagnant surface. Barney stopped, something telling him that he needed to look harder.

There was a flash of gold as a shaft of low sun hit the water's surface.

A SIM card was glinting, sitting right on top of an empty crisp packet like a shipwrecked survivor on a small desert island.

63

THE OFFICE WAS a hive of activity when Barney walked back in, already wanting another roll-up as he dumped his bag on his desk.

'You took your time. The chief buggered off he was so bloody bored. You stink of smoke, so I know you've been lazing about,' said Ross.

'What's he doing about the bug?'

'Ignoring it for the moment. He has a meeting at Holyrood this morning, so it allows us some time to assess what we do next.'

'Well, I may have something to throw into the mix after what I've just seen in the car park whilst having a sneaky brew and yon fag that you've just been moaning about.' Barney told them what he'd just seen and held out his hand clutching the crisp packet, with the SIM card nestled in the centre of it.

'Jesus, so our intercepted message suggests that Hoxhaj wants to be called on an Albanian number in an hour, and then an hour later we see someone making a call in the car park and then ditching this SIM down the drain?' said Max.

'That's about the size of it.'

'What's the Albanian phone number?' piped up Norma from behind her screens.

Barney told her.

'I'm on it, but I have to tell you, getting data from a foreign number can be a real ball ache, not that I'd know about ball aches,' she said, peering over the top of her screen.

'Well, he's our mannie, then. What did he look like?' said Ross.

'No idea. Tall fella, long coat and a cap. I never got within a hundred yards of him, and he wasn't facing me,' said Barney.

'Well, that's less useful. Any CCTV around that bit of the building?'

'No. It's why I park there as I like my privacy when I'm sleeping in't van. It's out of sight of security guards, and presumably why he made his call from that point.'

'Ach, bawbags,' said Ross, rubbing his eyes.

'Well, he looked reet dodgy. Does anyone have a friendly CSI that can dust this for prints, quick time?' said Barney.

'I play hockey with a CSI. She teaches crime scene management,' said Janie.

'I didn't know you played hockey,' said Ross.

'A typical Janie idea of fun, running around with a stick smashing people in the shins. Will your pal do us a favour?' said Max.

'Let me give her a call,' said Janie, picking up her phone and dialling.

'What can you do with it, Barney?' said Ross.

'Hold up.' Barney rummaged in his bag and came out with a pair of blue gloves and what looked like a small thumb drive. He opened his laptop and snapped the gloves into place. He carefully picked up the SIM card from the crisp packet and slotted it into the drive, which he then inserted into a USB port on the side of his computer. He clicked and swiped on the trackpad for a few moments before ejecting the flash drive and pulling out the SIM. 'I've extracted all the data on the SIM, so you're clear to fingerprint.'

'She'll do it now and use it as an exercise with her class. Give it here and I'll package it,' said Janie, holding out a gloved hand.

'Shall I leave it in the envelope?' said Barney.

Janie nodded.

Barney passed it to Janie, who tucked it into the corner of an envelope which she folded tight and then slotted into a self-seal bag.

'I take it you're staying off the radar, Barney?' said Janie as she filled in the productions label on the bag.

'You know what us ex-spooks are like. I'm a little shy of appearing at court.'

'Fine, I'll give it my initials for a productions number, and we can tidy it all up at the end.'

'It's because no one would understand your unintelligible Yorkshire blether in the witness box, Barney,' said Ross, chuckling.

'God's own country, mate,' Barney said, grinning widely before busying himself at his laptop.

'Right, I'm off. She'll process it now, shouldn't take too long. Is there going to be any point searching it on the IDENT1?' said Janie, referring to the national fingerprint database.

'Maybe, maybe not, but that's not the priority. We need to tie him to that SIM, and we need the handset that's presumably in his pocket. We get that and we've got him,' said Max.

'Aye, we need the handset, right enough,' said Barney.

'Why?'

'Sod all on the SIM beyond the number that's attached to it, and the fact that it confirms that it made a phone call to the Albanian number. It's good, but it's not enough.'

'Guys,' said Norma quietly from behind her screen.

Everyone looked up at the analyst who had a perplexed look on her face. There was a long pause as Norma seemed to be gathering her thoughts.

'Spit it out, woman,' said Ross.

'If he's got a spot he'll use to go and make a surreptitious phone call, why doesn't Barney just send him a direct message on the Albanian forum saying he needs to speak urgently? If he deletes it as soon as it's been received, I take it that it wouldn't appear as a notification on Hoxhaj's DMs, as the page would think that he'd sent it, so it wouldn't be necessary. It seems that they delete messages as soon as they're sent, most of the time anyway, right?'

There was silence as they all digested Norma's suggestion.

'Bugger me, we all need some bastard sleep. That's been staring us in the face and we're all too tired to see it. So, for once your work-shy attitude has been a bonus to the team,' said Ross, grinning.

'Ross?' said Norma.

'Aye?'

'Get fucked.' Norma followed this with a sarcasm-laden smile.

'Potty mouth. How about the bug in the chief's office?' said Ross, standing up and walking over to Norma, where he handed over a box of Tunnock's teacakes. She scowled at him but took one of them and put it down on her desk, replacing the scowl with a wide smile.

'He can't be listening to it live. Not if he's working here, it would be just too obvious. I bet he just speeds through it periodically after we've been in with the boss. I've a suggestion,' said Max.

'Go on?'

'When the chief comes back, we give our bent cop a double whammy. Make it so he simply must make a call, and then . . .' Max paused to sip at his tea, screwing up his face with distaste.

'And then?' said Ross.

'We nick the bastard.'

'Er, Ross,' said Barney.

'What?'

'One minor thing. I was thinking about who had the opportunity to bug the office, so I ran a few names. You know, just to get a feeling for who it could be.'

'You're talking in fucking riddles, man. Spit it out.'

'Well, obviously the chief had the opportunity.'

'What, to bug his own bastard office?'

'Well, maybe, maybe not, but were you convinced about his performance in there when I found the bug? I'm not sure he seemed as surprised as I thought he may have done, and I wanted to see his face and how he reacted, as let's face it, bad shit seems to happen around him.'

'Fuck's sake, man. He's the fucking boss. It's not him, okay?'

Barney shrugged. 'Well, then other than him, the folk with easy access is Barry, the slimy dickhead, but he's clean as a whistle. Not a thing on him on any database I could access, which is a shitload more than you lot can get into, and he's far too much of a wimp, I'd say.'

'Barney, any bugger could get access to the boss's office. Cleaners, building services, all sorts of folk,' said Max.

'How about his PA?'

'Sofia? What about her? She's a sweetheart,' said Ross.

'Aye, seems lovely and that, but I poked about, as her accent was familiar.'

'And?'

'Sofia McLennan is her married name. She was born Sofia Lucaj in 1970 in a place called Berat.' Barney looked at them all in turn, his face half-amused.

'What?' said Ross, his expression incredulous.

'Aye, that's right. Sofia McLennan is Albanian.'

'But we know our man is, in fact, a man. Unless she's really good at dressing up,' said Ross.

'There is another explanation,' said Barney.

'What?' snapped Ross.

'There's more than one of the buggers.'

64

THE ASSET'S HEART jumped at the sight that met him in the lobby at Tulliallan as the Chief Constable crossed the floor accompanied by DI Ross Fraser. They appeared to be in deep conversation, both looking very serious. His phone buzzed in his hand, and the message he received wasn't comforting. Things were getting heavy. Far too heavy. He deleted the message as soon as he'd read it.

It felt like a lead weight was sitting in his gut as he looked at their grim faces, and the chief seemed particularly angry. As a normally avuncular and jolly man, this meant one thing only. Bad things were happening.

He felt for the burner phone in the deep pocket of his long wool coat, his hands touching the smooth metal and glass of the cheap smartphone he had used for some time now. It felt cold and inert to his touch, but he resisted the urge to pull it out of his pocket. He kept his distance from the pair as they crossed into one of the corridors that he knew headed towards the chief's office.

A meeting between a DI and the Chief Constable was a bad sign, and he felt his face begin to flush at the thought of the major investigations that were underway, including the multiple homicide case at Gartcosh. He also knew for a fact that DCI Leslie was a bloody attack dog when she had the bit between her teeth. This was all getting too close, and with Ross Fraser's connection to anticorruption, he realised that he needed to know what was going on. Seeing the toilet sign, he made a sudden decision. He strode off and pushed the door to the gents' toilets. Checking that each of the three cubicles were empty, he went in one, shutting the door behind him. He pulled out his burner phone and was thankful to see a blank screen. No new messages.

He pulled a pair of wired earbuds out of his pocket and slotted one in his ear whilst navigating to a nondescript app on the home screen. He pressed on the 'play live' button on the app.

Silence. Total silence.

The asset cursed under his breath, opened his browser and navigated to the Albanian app. Looking at the message page he saw that it was blank with no trace of any of the messages that he had sent or received to or from Hoxhaj. He sighed with relief. The last thing he needed were incriminating messages being left on a phone in his possession. He didn't trust Hoxhaj one little bit to be careful, as he always needed reminding to change SIM cards before and after messages were sent, or calls were made. The asset was no expert on phone intelligence, most of his service being as a uniform cop, but he knew enough to realise that phones could be your best friend, or your worst enemy.

A crackle and bang in his ear erupted, making him jump from his position sitting on the closed toilet lid. He recognised the voice of DI Ross Fraser.

'We're getting closer to the bent bastard, sir. We'll have him soon.'

'We need to, Ross. This has gone way too far, and the press will have a bloody field day when they realise we have a cop in league with an Albanian gangster. When do you anticipate arresting Hoxhaj?'

'Soon. We're closing in on him now. Just waiting for the latest update from the team on the ground. Tactical firearms commander has the strategy set, and we have a whole team ready to take him out as soon as it's appropriate.'

'Okay, thanks, Ross. Keep me informed. The press strategy will *be crucial on this one, and the First Minister was not impressed when I briefed her.'*

'I bet. Look, I have to run.'

'As soon as you know anything, Ross.'

'Understood.'

The unmistakable sound of a door slamming almost made the asset jump.

A cold, naked fear gripped him as he looked at the screen of the phone, hearing only a slight hiss in his ear. He had to warn Hoxhaj, now. If he got arrested, it was all over. They'd been careful, but he wondered if they'd been careful enough.

'You *have a conference call with the Crown office soon, sir,'* came the light, accented voice of Sofia.

'Of course. Thank you, Sofia.'

The asset smiled. They still had nothing on him, and hearing Sofia's dulcet tones was reassuring as he sensed an opportunity.

The phone buzzed in his hand, and a notification flashed up on the screen. It was a message on the forum.

Kiru: *Call me urgently.*

His fingers flashed on the keypad. *Number?* The reply was instantaneous.

Kiru: *Same. Albanian.*

He typed again. *5 mins.*

Sweat began to prickle his back and his blood felt like it was curdling in his veins. Bastard Hoxhaj wasn't changing SIM cards, which was slapdash, but he had no choice. He had to call him.

He ejected the SIM card from the smartphone, and standing up, he lifted the toilet lid and dropped it into the water and flushed, watching the gold card glitter as it circled before it disappeared down the U bend. He delved into his pocket and brought out a fresh SIM, which he slotted into the phone. He navigated to the call history and was relieved to see that the Albanian number was still there in the phone's memory. He didn't want to ask Hoxhaj for it again, or he'd have raged at him when he answered the phone. Tucking the phone into his pocket, he opened the cubicle door and left the gents'. He picked up his pace as he crossed the lobby heading for the crisp, early-spring day outside, the butterflies in his stomach beginning to flutter at the prospect of speaking to that animal Hoxhaj once again.

65

BARNEY SAT IN the back of his van, the kettle beginning to bubble as he took a long and pleasurable pull on his roll-up. He looked out of the window but saw nothing too much between him and the grey stone of Tulliallan Castle. He'd somehow managed to bag the best parking space, and for some reason none of the security guards seemed to have noticed he was there, and not where he should have been, on the parade square on the other side of the castle. His stump ached a little after the days of activity, but for once, he was thankful for the freedom that his blue badge gave him. He was parked alongside a small line of other cars, most of which seemed to belong to senior cops, including a chauffeur-driven Range Rover that he was led to believe was used by the chief.

His phone buzzed on the table top.

'Ayup,' he said.

'Ready?'

'Aye. Message was sent, Albanian number as before. Says five minutes.'

'What are we looking for?'

Barney opened his mouth to answer, then closed it again. His eyes were drawn to a tall man leaving the castle's main entrance, his long coat's collar up. He wasn't wearing a hat, but his bearing and stride pattern were the same. Barney lifted his camera and zoomed in tight, taking in the thick, greying hair and sallow face.

He didn't recognise him, but that meant nothing. He knew hardly anyone in Police Scotland, being as off the radar as he was, but he was sure that this was the same man that he'd seen earlier. Barney snapped away at the pale, bespectacled face. Stress shone from every pore as he stared at a phone held in his hand. With his other hand, he vigorously scratched his scalp.

'I think our man's here. He came out of the door, turned right and is along the building line towards the trees. Long coat, glasses, no hat this time.'

'I see him. He's facing away from us, but we're too far away to get a face. Are you getting this on camera?' said Max, who was parked at the far end of the car park.

'Filming now. He's looking at his phone, and he's dialling,' said Barney.

'See if you can focus in on his face. I could get Auntie Elspeth to lip read it,' said Max, referring to his aunt who had assisted them in the past with forensic lip reading.

'No chance, not full face. I can barely see his mouth even on max zoom. Are you going in now?'

'Not yet. Let him finish the call. We don't want Hoxhaj knowing we've intercepted.'

'Fair enough. Okay, still on the phone now. Body language is not that of a happy man.' Barney observed the same staccato movements and hand gestures that told of one thing. Whoever this person was, he was under the most severe stress.

'Still on?' said Max.

Barney zoomed in as close as he could, but the man had half turned, his face was away from the camera. Suddenly his hand dropped to his side, and he ran his other hand through his thick thatch of hair.

'He's off the phone.'

'Okay, is he moving?'

'Not yet,' said Barney, zooming out slightly. The man held the phone with two hands, staring intently at the screen. 'He's texting. Give him a second.'

'Okay, I'm getting out now. I'm meeting Janie back at the entrance, and we'll get him there. Stay on the line,' said Max.

'Roger that. He's still just stood, staring at the screen, like he's trying to decide what to do next. Must be a senior officer, with that level of indecision,' said Barney with a chuckle.

Suddenly the man began to fiddle with the phone again, before turning on his heel and striding off back towards the entrance, determination replacing his dithering. His hand flicked to one side, tossing something into the treeline.

'He's on the move, over to you two. I'm gonna check to see if he's been littering again.'

66

MAX AND JANIE stood just inside the door waiting, one either side of the entrance, leaning against the stone walls. Max had his phone to his ear listening to Barney giving commentary.

'Twenty yards,' said Barney.

'We're here. Long grey coat and glasses, you say?' said Max.

'Aye, and thick greying hair with a pissed-off expression on his face.'

'About to get more pissed off, I suspect. Okay, see you in a minute, Barney.' Max hung up and nodded at Janie.

They both looked at the large double-doored entrance, arms folded and ready.

Five seconds later the bespectacled Detective Chief Superintendent Barry Carlisle, staff officer to the Chief Constable of Police Scotland, rounded the corner wearing a long, grey coat. He stopped, his face quizzical.

'What's going on?' he said, the stern tone in his voice quickly giving way to one of uncertainty, and then to fear.

Barney rounded the corner, a self-seal evidence bag in his hand, a small gold-coloured SIM card in the bottom corner, a broad grin on his face. 'Ayup,' he said, holding the bag aloft. ''Appen you dropped your SIM card, pal.'

Carlisle's face fell, the colour draining from it almost cartoonishly.

'Who were you on the phone to, sir?' said Max, his voice light, a smile playing at his mouth.

'I've no idea what you're playing at, Craigie, but I don't answer to you. I was making a private phone call, so it's none of your bloody business. Now get out of my bloody way. The Chief Constable is expecting me,' Carlisle said, bravado quickly returning. He strode forward towards where Max and Janie still stood, unmoving, their faces impassive. 'Did you hear what I said? Get out of my bloody way.'

Max and Janie didn't move.

'This is ridiculous. May I remind you that I'm a chief superintendent?'

Ross Fraser appeared from behind him, a pair of handcuffs in his fist.

'Aye, you are, Barry, but not for fucking long, and as my cockney pals would say, "You're fucking nicked, my old son."'

Carlisle opened his mouth to speak but then closed it again. Ross moved up and, within a second, had the handcuffs applied behind his back. Ross reached into Carlisle's coat pocket and pulled out a smartphone, which he handed to Barney.

Barney touched the home key. 'Locked,' he said.

'What's the unlock code, Barry?' said Ross.

'I've nothing to say,' said Carlisle.

'You're aware that part three of RIPA applies in Scotland, eh? Possibly two years in jail if you fail to disclose it?' said Max.

Carlisle said nothing, just stood there looking at his shoes, his face as pale as alabaster.

'What's Hoxhaj going to do?' said Max.

Carlisle stayed silent. Didn't react, didn't flinch, just stared at the ground but began to sway, as if drunk.

'Get him out of here. They're expecting him at Dunfermline nick.'

67

CARLISLE REMAINED SILENT throughout the twenty-minute journey to Dunfermline Police Station, just sat in the rear of the Volvo, his face fixed on the back of the seat, his hands secured in front of him by rigid handcuffs.

The custody suite was totally silent, with only a lone custody sergeant and a custody support officer present, the place having been cleared and prisoners dispersed to other nearby stations. A police officer of this seniority being arrested was serious enough and they didn't need a busy station which would always lead to wagging tongues.

He spoke only to deal with the custody reception procedure, answering the custody officer's questions monosyllabically, never looking directly at anyone as he trembled throughout the process. He appeared utterly broken as he was led away to a cell to await a solicitor that had been chosen from the duty list. Once he had gone, Ross, Max and Janie found an empty office to regroup.

'Has he given up the PIN code for the phone, yet?' asked Barney, who had just arrived, clutching the phone in an unsealed bag.

'No, he's saying nothing at all. Not a bloody word,' said Max.

'Shit. I can't get into the bugger. My software can sometimes bypass, but it's not working this time. Even though it's a basic smartphone, it's new, and they're bastards to get into without a code. I don't think he's enabled fingerprint, and it doesn't have facial recognition, so we can't force the sod's thumbprint on it, or hold it up to his face. It's just a six-digit code, and it will lock for a period if I enter it wrong more than five times.'

'How many possible combinations are there?' said Ross.

'A million.'

'What, a metaphorical million, or an actual million?'

'Nope, an actual million. We're buggered unless we come up with something else,' said Barney.

'No other software out there that can bypass it?' said Max.

'A deep-dive forensic extraction at a specialist company may be able to, but how long will that take? How quickly and how badly do we need to get into that phone?'

'Very quickly and very badly. We may not have enough unless we know what he's sent, and what was sent to him. If we can get into it, what can you extract?'

'Everything. Whatever he's done on that phone I can get to, even if he thinks he's deleted it. All the calls, messages, photos, web searches, GPS data. The chuffin' lot, but only if I get past the PIN code.'

'We need to get in there. We don't know where Hoxhaj is, or what he's planning, and we need to get him. He killed and mutilated three people on our fucking watch, people,' said Ross.

'With that phone unlocked, the case is strong; without it, it's weak?' said Janie.

'Certainly not strong, and difficult to put to a jury. With the phone, we have a simple fact. We watched him make that call, and we took the phone from his pocket. That same phone will sink him and Hoxhaj, once we get hold of him. There's something else,' said Max.

'What?' said Ross.

'Afrodita. She's still not spoken a word, yet. Unless she does, we don't even have a kidnap, and the whole thing is a struggle. We can maybe prove that Carlisle is snidey, but what else do we have? Without the kidnap, how do we sell this to the Fiscal as a full-on conspiracy?'

'What do you suggest? We can't force her to tell us, can we? And the fact that Toka and Jetmir are now dead may not help,' said Ross.

'Affi and Katie got on really well, so if we both get up there as soon as possible, we may be able to get her to talk. If she does, I can take a witness statement from her, and then we're golden. We have the evidence to give to the Fiscal which brings the whole job together, especially if Barney can get into that phone.'

'I'm going back to the van to carry on with it. All my kit's in there, along with me kettle and me 'baccy,' said Barney, standing up, a frustrated look on his lean face. The prospect of an electronic device defeating him was clearly bothering him.

'Will Katie be okay with a road trip? You're a shite driver,' said Ross.

'I'm sure. I'll give her a call now, and then I'll get going. Can I get the keys, Janie?'

Janie tossed them over. 'Don't crash it, and make sure it comes back clean, Craigie,' she said, her face showing a trace of concern. No one liked a clean car more than Janie.

'Are you guys okay to interview Barry?' said Max.

'I'm sure we'll manage without you, pal. I've seen you interview people, and I'll be honest, I've seen better, so bugger off.'

68

NORMA WAS SITTING in the office at Tulliallan staring at the screen, which was open to a web page, the address of which had been copied from Toka's little black book. A smart-looking website which declared, 'Secure hosting for all your cloud-based security camera products'. Her username was simple enough – just a Gmail address, TokaK@gmail.com – but there was no password. Norma bet that Toka had one email address that she had used for everything.

There had been no obvious candidate for a password, leastways not one that she could decipher or clearly attribute for the web page. She picked up her phone and dialled.

'Ayup, Norma.'

'Barney. I'm trying to get into this cloud storage server that I found in Toka's book. Any ideas on what we can do next?'

'Nowt in the book?'

'Nothing.'

'What's the web address and what's her username?'

Norma told him.

'Okay, give me a minute. I'm gonna call a pal who is a bit of a ninja at this kind of thing. I'll give him your number and he'll call you. I'm reet busy with Barry's phone at the moment. Is this on books, or off books?'

'On books. It's been authorised for a deep-dive hack and password crack by the surveillance commissioner.'

'Ace, he'll send us an invoice, but he'll have it sorted in a minute or two.'

'Thanks, Barney. What's his name?'

'Clive.'

'Clive?' said Norma, a touch of humour in her voice.

'Aye, are you suggesting that's a geek's name?'

'Well, my name's Norma, so who am I to say?'

'Norma's a grand name, lass. Now I need to get on,' said Barney with a chuckle.

'Cool, good luck with the handset.'

'Aye, I'll need it.' Barney rang off.

Norma continued staring at the intricate and complex spreadsheet that dominated her central screen. She yawned, feeling the creeping exhaustion begin to nip at her. The last couple of days had been brutal in their intensity, and made even more so with the knowledge of what they were dealing with. It was always like this; everything was always big, important, vital and urgent. Her phone buzzed on the desk. It was a message from Andy, her husband, who had sent a picture of their twin boys, Jacob and Lewis, both with tongues poking out at the camera. She smiled and felt her heart lurch at the sight of them. She had a sudden longing to be home with them, snuggled up on the sofa, watching a movie. Her finger hovered over the call button, desperate to speak to them, but she hesitated, her eyes being dragged back to her chart. This was important. There was a highly placed person in law enforcement feeding a vicious and murderous Albanian gangster. They had to find the link between Barry and Hoxhaj, and any other bent buggers, and she was sure that it was contained within the contents of Toka's black book. They needed evidence. Not intelligence, not rumour, not supposition. They needed castiron, solid admissible evidence.

Her phone buzzed again, this time with a message from an unknown number.

It simply said: *Username TokaK@gmail.com, Password is Toka_Ohid. I'll send invoice to Barney. Clive.*

Norma quickly brought the web page back up and entered the username and password.

A huge smile spread across her face as the loading page showed three thumbnails of live feeds marked 'West End, Southside, Gallowgate'. Each had an image of a front door on it, apart from the Southside one, which was simply blank, unsurprising as she'd been told the cameras appeared to have been removed.

Norma clicked on the West End thumbnail and a split screen filled her monitor. There was a live feed of a front door, and three others of what looked like bedrooms, all made up in a similar style. There was a time-and-date readout at the bottom of the screen, and checking the time on her monitor, it seemed accurate. She maximised one of them to full screen and took in the bed, covered with a throw; the mirrored wall; the fairy lights; a large box of tissues; and what she was sure was a box of condoms.

'Ew,' she said, wrinkling her nose at the impossibly seedy room. 'Brothel,' she whispered under her breath, feeling her excitement rise.

She exited the full screen and found a folder marked 'saved clips' on the website. She clicked into this and there were dozens of sub-folders within it, each with a name underneath. She scanned the names looking for something familiar, and stopped when she came across one marked 'SV'. Inside were three video files. She opened one and watched, knowing what she was going to find. The image appeared, pin sharp and lurid as she maximised it, and she wasn't surprised to see a naked couple writhing in one of the bedrooms, a tangle of limbs as they gyrated on the towel-covered bed. It was a scene of utter seediness. The date and time at the bottom of the screen showed that this was over six months ago. She was about to stop the video and move on when something made her look closer. The young girl, who was slim, dark-haired, shifted off the man below her, exposing his face for the first time as she stared upwards, in apparent ecstasy.

It was Steve Vipond, the Immigration service intelligence analyst who'd been in the office just a few hours ago.

69

MAX WALKED DOWN to the yard where Barney was sitting in his van, the sliding door open, his face creased with concentration as he stared at his computer screen, his tongue protruding out of the corner of his mouth.

'Any luck?' said Max.

'Nay, lad. I'm researching it heavily, but it's a right bastard. I just can't seem to bypass. It's becoming more and more of a bugger to do, as manufacturers put more and more security on these bloody things. I'd hope there's a backdoor into them, you know what I mean?'

'What, like a shortcut into it that bypasses the security?'

'Aye, that kind of thing. They do exist, but no one I know has one, and they tend to be very specific to individual brands and models. You off with your lass up north?'

'Yeah, going now. Katie's sure she can get Affi to cooperate. We'd best hope so, anyway. Just a quick thing, do you have the IMEI number for the handset?'

'Aye, of course, it's here, why?'

'Just in case I need it. It may come up in billing data when we get it.'

Barney scribbled on a piece of paper which he handed to Max; his eyes narrowed suspiciously. 'What're you up to, you snidey bugger?'

'Nothing. You just never know, it may come up.'

'Bullshit. Drive carefully,' said Barney, turning back to his screen, shaking his head.

Max smiled as he walked back to the Volvo and got in, settling into the leather and adjusting the seat. Before he started the engine, he got his phone out and dialled a number stored in the memory marked 'BF'.

It rang, with the international tone, as opposed to the usual UK one, and was answered after about thirty seconds.

'DS Craigie, long time no speak. How are you?' said Bruce Ferguson in his soft Caithness accent.

Bruce was a mysterious character Max had encountered during a recent case. An ex–Special Forces senior NCO and a current head of security for a Russian oligarch who owned several major telecommunications companies, he was uniquely resourceful and more importantly, felt that he owed Max a favour.

'I'm good, Bruce, but wondering if I can pick your brain on something?'

'What, something that my employer may have some insight on, I imagine?'

'Kind of. We have a bent cop working for an Albanian gangster who's killed multiple times in the last few days. We have the bent cop nicked and are trying to get into his phone, but can't bypass the security PIN. Any suggestions?'

'A smartphone?'

'Aye.'

'Do you have the handset number?'

'I do.'

'Okay, I know you wouldn't ask if it wasn't important, but if I do manage to help, you know you'll have to keep my name well out of it. You'll need to come up with a cover story as to how you broke the code, yeah?'

'Goes without saying, pal.'

344

'Well, I still owe you, Max, so . . . text me the number and I'll see what I can do, yeah?'

'I'll do that. Thanks, Bruce.'

'Nae bother.' The phone went dead.

Max took out the slip of paper and photographed it, attached it to a text message and sent it to Bruce. The familiar tone whooshed as it sent the photo to wherever Bruce was in the world.

70

IT WAS FORTUNATE that Max and Katie's home was just fifteen minutes from Tulliallan, and they initially made good time on the journey north to the Highlands, but the sun was beginning to lower in the sky as they passed Inverness after almost three hours without a stop. Max yawned extravagantly, a sudden wave of fatigue washing over him.

'Do you need to stop?' said Katie.

'I'm just a bit jaded, been a couple of tough days,' he said, yawning again.

'You've got me going now,' she replied, yawning in sympathy with her husband. 'Maybe a coffee somewhere before we get to Valerie and Reg's? I've been there myself and I know the standard of their coffee.'

'Good idea. There's a machine in the garage just two minutes away, and we could do with fuel, anyway, to save getting it on the way back.' Max turned at the roundabout just before the Kessock Bridge and pulled into a large garage forecourt. He refuelled the car, grabbed the agency card from the log book and went into the shop, his legs feeling leaden as he wearily walked.

Just as he was filling the first cup from the Costa machine, his phone buzzed in his pocket. He looked at the screen, which just said 'no number'. Max smiled.

'Hello?'

'Max, it's me,' said Bruce.

'Hi, Bruce.'

'Able to speak? Sounds like you're in a shop.'

'Aye, just filling up on coffee. Go on.'

'Right. You ask me no questions and I'll tell you no lies, but I'm about to send you a code. It'll be a mix of numbers and stars and hashes, which will all be accessible from the lock screen. Basically, the phone needs to be woken, and then select the emergency call function, and then key in the sequence exactly as you see it, okay?'

'Understood.'

'Repeat it.'

Max looked around him, but there was just the cashier, behind his screen watching a small TV. 'Wake the screen, select emergency call function and input the sequence of numbers and symbols exactly as they appear.'

'You got it. Right, we never had this conversation, okay? That's a backdoor into the handset. Once in, you can disable PIN protection and you'll have unrestricted access to it.'

'You're a star, Bruce. I owe you one.'

'No, you don't,' said Bruce, with an amused throaty rasp.

Three beeps in his ear told Max that he'd gone. The phone immediately buzzed indicating that a text message had been received. There was no recognisable phone number attributed to it, just a sequence of numbers and symbols. The message field was blank. Max frowned. Where was the code?

Then he looked at the number it had come from, noting a long sequence of digits, hash symbols and stars. He smiled to himself and shook his head with admiration. This wouldn't mean anything to anyone who looked at the handset.

Max pulled out the first paper cup and applied the lid before slotting the next one into place and pressing the button for a large Americano. He dialled Barney's number.

'Max? I hope you're going to tell me something useful, because this phone is a reet bastard. I've locked myself out twice.'

'Okay, ask no questions to what I'm about to tell you. Just claim all the credit for breaking the code by some clever computer jiggery pokery, okay?'

'What you up to, you beggar?'

'I'm going to forward you a message. It's just a sequence of digits and symbols. Wake the handset and select emergency call function, then input the sequence exactly as it appears on the screen, okay?'

'Understood, but—'

'No questions, Barney, remember?'

'Aye, I remember.'

Max hung up, smiling to himself. He fixed the lid onto the second cup and went to the counter and paid for the drinks.

Climbing back into the car he handed the scalding coffee over to Katie. 'Ooh, that smells lush. You look pleased with yourself,' she said.

'Aye, let's get this show on the road. We need Affi to talk.'

'Well, let's get on with it then. I quite like working with you.' Katie returned his smile, leaned over and kissed him on the cheek.

Max started the engine, engaged the gears and headed off into the darkening Inverness streets.

Game on, he thought.

71

CHIEF SUPERINTENDENT CARLISLE looked broken. Utterly broken, as he sat in the corner of the interview room, his hair dishevelled, eyes red-rimmed and face as pale as bread dough. He stared at the desk as Janie opened the interview with the familiar procedure. He said nothing. Absolutely nothing in response to Janie's request that he identify himself and whether he understood the caution. He was sitting next to a well-dressed, slim young woman, with an open laptop in front of her. They had privately consulted for almost two hours before she announced that they were ready to begin.

'Kate Lyons, duty solicitor acting for Mr Carlisle. I can confirm that I have received brief disclosure of the evidence against my client and must inform you that my client has elected not to answer any questions during this interview. However, he will make a brief statement that I will read out now.' She picked up a piece of A4 paper. 'I, Chief Superintendent Barry Carlisle, deny all the allegations which have been made against me. I have been concerned about a leak from the Chief Constable's office for some time for a number of reasons and was therefore reluctant to report it officially, as I didn't know who I could trust. I had developed a covert source of intelligence, which will explain my movements in the car park at Tulliallan earlier. The allegation was made to me that the Chief Constable's PA Sofia McLennan has been supplying intelligence to the Albanian Mafia. She is in fact Sofia Lucaj and was born in Albania. There have been a number of incidents which aroused my suspicion including when I witnessed her underneath the chief's desk, interfering with the cabling to his computer. I thought nothing of it at the time, but I believe it possible that she was planting some kind of device to monitor communications. This is all I will say at this time.' She nodded and turned back to her screen, her well-manicured fingers tapping at the keys.

'Thank you. Mr Carlisle, please tell us what your relationship is with Alban Hoxhaj?' said Janie, who had a paper file on the desk in front of her.

Carlisle didn't look up from the table. 'No comment.'

'What was your relationship with the now deceased Toka Kurti?' Janie leafed through the file, before glancing up at Carlisle.

'No comment.' A single tear carved a trail down his pale cheek.

'What was your relationship with the now deceased Police Constable Luigi Ricci?'

'No comment.'

Janie paused and turned to Ross, who just shrugged, his face impassive. 'Did you plant the listening device in Chief Constable Macdonald's office?'

'No comment.'

'Do you know who did?'

'No comment.'

'Who else had access to the office?'

'No comment.'

From under the desk, Janie produced two bags that contained SIM cards. 'You were observed to drop these cards at separate times after making calls. Who were you calling?'

'No comment.'

'One of the calls was to an Albanian SIM. Who was that call to, Mr Carlisle?'

'No comment.'

'Was it to Alban Hoxhaj?'

'No comment.'

'Where is Alban Hoxhaj now?'

'No comment,' said Carlisle, who flinched at the repeated mention of the gangster's name.

'Tell us, Barry. Tell us about him, and we can protect you,' said Ross in a surprisingly low and gentle voice.

There was a long, agonising pause, and Carlisle looked up at Ross, his eyes full of tears.

The sudden knock at the interview room door made Carlisle flinch, and gasp softly. A uniformed custody support officer poked his head around the door. 'Can I have a moment? Something has come up,' he said, his face flushed.

Janie shifted her gaze to Ross, whose eyes narrowed with suspicion. There was something in the face of the officer that told him they needed to hear what he had to say. Interrupting an interview isn't common, and it normally indicates that something requires urgent attention. Ross nodded at Janie.

'Okay, interview suspended whilst we confer.' Janie pressed the button on the interview recorder. 'I'm going to leave the discs in whilst we have a quick chat, okay?'

The solicitor nodded, her eyes full of scepticism. Carlisle didn't move a muscle; he just continued staring at the desk top.

Barney was standing in the corridor outside the interview room, his face pale. He held an iPad in one hand and an evidence bag in the other.

'Barney?' said Ross.

'In here.' He nodded at an empty interview room.

They all filed in and closed the door behind them with a soft thunk.

'What's up?' said Ross.

Barney held up the smartphone secured in the evidence bag. 'I got into it.'

'Mate, I take back all I've ever said about you being an elderly incompetent who smells of pish. That's brilliant. What's on there?' said Ross, his face split with a wide grin.

'Lots. Like shitloads that he's tried to delete, but I've extracted anyway. There's evidence on here to link him to the whole bloody shebang. He knew about the murders. There's an app for listening to the bug in the chief's office and loads more. That's not why I burst into the interview room, though. Look at this last sent text. The one I watched him send outside the castle. He tried to delete it, but I managed to recover it. I've downloaded it all. Look here on the spreadsheet of deleted messages.' He held the iPad up, his finger pointing to a line of data in a spreadsheet.

'What am I looking at?' said Ross.

'Last messages in and out, number sent from, number sent to, IMEI number, time and date. Look at the content of the message. He received the address from another number just before, then he forwarded it on to Hoxhaj.' Barney's eyes were wide, and his face was pale. As an ex-spy who'd worked under the noses of the enemy, he knew this was a bad sign.

Janie's face suddenly drained as she looked at it. 'Oh no. Oh, for fuck's sake.'

'What? It says Scotia Cottage, Evanton, IV16. And?' Ross's face was blank.

'That's Afrodita's home address. Carlisle sent it to Hoxhaj just a few hours ago.'

'Shit, Max and Katie are on their way up there now.' Janie looked at her watch. 'In fact, they may be up there already. We need to get hold of them.'

'Right, make the call, then we need to get back into that fuck-head Carlisle. I'm gonna tear him a new fucking arsehole if he doesn't cooperate, I can promise you that, and I want to know which bastard sent him that address. We have another mole out there, somewhere,' Ross said, his face dark.

'There's something else on his phone, as well. Look,' said Barney, holding up the screen. A photograph of a set of computer monitors also showed a detailed i2 chart.

'That's Norma's fucking chart. That photo was taken in our bastard office; some fucker sent that to Carlisle. Who the fuck took it?' said Ross, his face darkening as he lifted his phone to his ear. 'Norma?' said Ross, before moving away to speak.

Janie picked out her phone and dialled. 'Max's phone went straight to voicemail,' she said, dialling again. 'Still the same. Voicemail. I'll try Katie.' She dialled again, her face pale.

Ross stared at her as he listened to Norma, his face impassive but full of suppressed fury. 'Okay, lock down the office. No one in or out, Norma, and get hold of Miles Wakefield. We need a team to pick Dougie Vipond up, urgently. This is gonna leak soon and we don't want him ditching his phone.'

'What's going on?' said Janie.

'That intel officer, Vipond from the Immigration service, took that photo of Norma's chart when he visited her earlier. She's just broken into Toka's camera feed and he's on there clear as day shagging one of her prostitutes. Norma's calling Miles Wakefield for a response. We need the bastard nicking urgently. Have you got hold of Max?'

'Voicemail,' said Janie.

'How can they both be on voicemail?' said Barney.

'Signal,' blurted Janie. 'There's no signal there at all. They use the landline or Wi-Fi for calling on mobiles.'

'Have you got their numbers?' said Ross.

'Hold on. They'll be in the report which I have here.' Janie pulled out a sheet of paper from the file in her hand. She ran her finger down an A4 printout and dialled again.

'Landline is engaged. Dialling mobiles now.' Janie's fingers flashed on the keypad of her phone. 'That's Valerie's voicemail.'

She dialled again. 'Shit, that's Reg's voicemail. Let me try the landline again.' There was a pause whilst she dialled again, before shaking her head.

'Okay, get onto the local cops. I want a car running to that address.'

'I'm on it,' said Janie.

'Barney, we need your help with getting live traces up and running on all phones, including the last known one for Hoxhaj.'

'On it.'

Ross's phone chimed again. He looked at it and performed the biggest of double-takes. 'Oh, dear oh dear. Look what we have here. Norma's a fucking genius,' said Ross, a tight smile on his face.

'What?' said Barney.

Rather than speak, Ross held up his phone screen, which was showing a video clip in lurid, graphic clarity. Detective Chief Superintendent Barry Carlisle was naked, half bent over a young woman, a rolled-up banknote in his hand, and he was snorting a line of powder that was on her flat, taut belly.

'Janie, we're going back into that interview room, and if that fucker doesn't tell us the truth, I'm gonna pull off his arm and beat him to death with the wet end.'

72

'MAX, KATIE, COME in, come in. It's cold out now the sun's gone down. It's so wonderful to see you both,' said Valerie, throwing the door open. Her smile was wide and genuine, but her eyes were still sad.

'Hi, Valerie, thanks for letting us come, but we've had a development that we didn't want to speak about on the phone. Is Reg with you?' said Max.

'He's been out after the pigeons for one of the farmers whose spring barley has been getting decimated. He'll be back soon, I hope. Tea?'

'Tea would be lovely, thanks. I take it Affi's here?'

'Aye, she's upstairs with wee Jock in her room. I'll run and get her.'

'Has her story changed at all?' said Katie.

'No, love. Basically, refusing to talk about it.'

'Before you do, I think it's wise that I give you a heads-up. Did you hear about some murders in Glasgow on the news?'

A shadow fell over Valerie's face, and her eyes widened. 'I did?' she said, framing the statement as a question.

'Well, look, we need to be honest here, and it may come as a shock to you, but we need to let you all know, as it's really important right now that Affi is honest with us,' said Max.

'What are you getting at?'

'The three people killed are, we think, those that are connected to Affi's abduction.'

'What?' said Valerie incredulously.

'It's early days yet, and there's a lot of work to be done, but of the three killed one was the man called Jetmir, who trafficked Affi to the UK; the other was a madam of a brothel in Glasgow; the other, and this may come as a shock, is the local cop PC Ricci.'

Valerie reached her hand out to steady herself against the banister rail, swaying a little as the colour drained from her face.

'Let's go into the lounge and sit down.'

A sudden gasp at the top of the stairs made Max stop and look. Affi stood on the landing, her hand clamped over her mouth as she hugged Jock in the other arm.

'Jetmir is dead?' she said, her voice hoarse and eyes wide with shock at what she'd just heard.

'Yes, Affi. They're all dead. There's no one who can hurt you now,' said Katie, holding out her arms.

Affi let the now struggling Jock down and almost fell down the carpeted stairs and into Katie's arms, her head buried in her coat, the sobs coming from her in a high-pitched wail. The little dog followed her, barking excitedly.

*

It took a good fifteen minutes for Affi to calm enough to be able to speak. She sat on the sofa, her face buried in Katie's shoulder as she sobbed. Katie stroked Affi's long hair and whispered to her that things were going to be okay.

Then as suddenly as she'd starting crying, she stopped and sat upright, her face firm, wiping her eyes and taking the mug of hot chocolate that Valerie had handed to her.

'Is Melodi safe? They threatened to hurt Melodi in Albania, which is why I said nothing to you. They told me they'd put my little sister into the Tirana brothels. They sent me a picture of her to my Insta with a gang man behind her. Is she safe?'

'Affi, Toka and Jetmir are gone. We're not sure why, but we're working on the theory that taking you was dangerous to their organisation. Now we really need to know what happened, and how you were taken,' said Max.

Affi straightened herself up and wiped her tears away with the large handkerchief that Valerie had handed to her. Then she told them. She told them everything. How she was taken in the car park, how she was kept in a derelict house, and how they took her to a brothel. She told them about Jetmir, Toka and the huge, dangerous-looking man who she'd seen with Toka. Finally, she told them about how they had let her go, dropping her at the station with enough money for a ticket to Inverness.

'I only lied to you because of Melodi. Am I in trouble?' she said.

Katie was the first to answer. 'Affi, I know I'm married to Max, and that Max is a cop, but I work for you. You're my client and I can assure you that you are in no trouble. You did what you had to do to keep yourself and your sister safe. Affi, you're the bravest girl I know,' said Katie, hugging her again.

'Now, Affi,' said Max. 'I need to write this down, just a brief account for now as we have someone in custody who helped Toka and Jetmir. This is hard to explain, but he's a cop. He's a corrupt cop.'

'What, like in *Line of Duty*?' she said, her face brightening.

'Exactly like *Line of Duty*,' said Max.

'Cool. I love *Line of Duty*.'

Everyone laughed and the tension in the room was distinctly dialled down a notch.

'I need to make a call and let my boss know about this,' said Max, picking out his phone and starting to dial.

'You'll not get a signal here, Max. Use the landline in the hall,' said Valerie.

Max looked at his phone and saw that he had no signal whatsoever. 'So I see, a real dead spot. Typical Highlands, eh?'

'Ach, it's a pain, and yet they want the same money per month, which is a cheek. We use Wi-Fi for most calls and Skype with Melodi, but you use the landline,' said Valerie.

'Thanks,' said Max, walking out into the hall and seeing an aubergine-coloured old-fashioned phone with a dial, and a handset attached by a curly wire. He smiled at the antique and wondered if it had been in that same spot in the hall for as long as Valerie and Reg had been living at the house. He lifted the handset and began to dial, having to dig deep into his muscle memory on how to perform the simple task. He dialled Ross's mobile, feeling the long-forgotten frustration of a pulse-dialling phone. When he'd dialled the number, he raised the phone to his ear.

Nothing. It was dead, inert and silent. He clicked down on the cradle several times, but there was no sound. He frowned, his synapses suddenly firing and the hairs on the back of his neck beginning to tingle.

73

STEVE VIPOND SAT at his desk at Gartcosh and felt his insides turning to ice as he hung up the phone from one of his pals at Tulliallan. He'd called out of the blue, all excited about the fact that a senior police officer, believed to be from the Chief Constable's office, had been dramatically arrested outside the front entrance of the castle. The rumour mill in law enforcement could be unreliable, at best, but this had a serious ring of truth about it. He scratched at an itch, his hands trembling as he did, and felt his breathing quicken.

One thing was sure. If Barry Carlisle had been arrested, then they'd possibly be looking for him, as well. Barry was a weasel, and would soon start grassing if he thought it could save his own skin.

Vipond's mind raced as he tried to organise his thoughts and think about where his vulnerabilities lay. Obviously, Barry was the main risk, but then would he grass? The Albanians would skin him alive if he did, so maybe he'd keep quiet, but could he rely on that?

'Shit, shit, shit,' he muttered to himself, as he stared blankly at his laptop screen on the desk.

'What's up, Steve?' said Charlie, his colleague who was sitting opposite, his face quizzical.

'Nothing,' said Vipond, shaking his head and gripping the edge of the desk to hide his shaking hands.

'Look like you've seen a bloody ghost, man. You sure you're okay?'

'Feeling a bit queasy, that's all.'

'Well, dinnae pull a whitey in here, pal. Get to the bog if you're gonna hurl,' said Charlie with no trace of concern.

Vipond ignored the attempted humour from his colleague as he tried to think. Where was he vulnerable? His brain felt like it was being scrambled with a mixer and his mind was just a rush of static. He cursed how vulnerable his sexual proclivities had left him. All because of a stupid hooker that Barry had introduced him to. He sat back in his chair, his fingers clasped on the armrests. Then it hit him.

His burner phone currently in his car in the car park. That was dirty as hell, and even though he'd changed SIMs and wiped the messages, he knew that a forensic download would reveal the messages and calls he'd sent, including the photo of the chart he'd snapped at the analyst's office. If they found that, he was done for. He had to get rid of it, and fast.

'Aye, I'm feeling rotten, Charlie. I'm gonna get some air,' he said, standing up and rushing to the door.

Within a minute he was passing through the huge lobby and into the car park heading towards his scruffy, ancient Micra, key in hand. He slotted the old key into the door and flung it open. He reached under the seat to where the phone was hidden, secured with a loose webbing strap.

It wasn't there. The strap was still loose and slack, but there was no phone.

'Looking for something?' came a well-spoken female voice from outside the car. Vipond felt himself almost shrink inside his clothes. He turned and saw a small, petite woman in a smart business suit, stood next to an equally smartly dressed, tough-looking man. Both had half-smiles on their faces and wore Police Scotland lanyards around their necks. The woman held up a phone between a well-manicured finger and thumb. The polish was a deep, blood red.

'DCI Leslie from the Major Incident Teams. Not a bad hiding place, Stevie, but DS Hanrahan here is an expert at searching cars, and he found it in just a minute.'

Vipond didn't answer; he just slumped his head on the filthy, dank-smelling carpet and felt the tears begin to flow. It was over.

74

MAX STOOD THERE, receiver in hand, senses alive. 'Guys, we need to be care—'

Suddenly, the door exploded inwards with a crashing of glass and splintering of wood, and a gargantuan man appeared in the doorway before smashing into Max and sending him sprawling in a heap on the floor. Stars exploded in his head as it thumped against the carpeted floor. The giant stomped towards Max, his booted foot drawing back and aiming a kick at him. Instinctively, Max moved his head to the side, feeling the disturbed air an inch away from his face; he quickly rolled onto his side as the massive intruder almost lost his balance with the missed kick. Max leapt to his feet, his head spinning, hands out in front of him, ready to fight.

The brute smiled, showing broken and stained teeth in his bull-like face. 'Think you can fight me, little man?' he snarled, his accent heavy and thick.

Max said nothing, just held the stare of the intruder, his hands still raised in front of him ready for what came next. Max was a good boxer, but he wasn't the most offensive. His skill was counterpunching. Let the bigger man make the first move, and then strike. Max stood evenly, feet placed firmly on the carpet, his breathing under control.

'Come on then, big-man. Give me your best shot,' said Max, feeling a smile stretch across his face.

The man reached for his waistband and moved his jacket to one side, showing the black stock of a handgun, but instead of pulling it out, he let his jacket fall back, concealing it again.

The bigger man matched Max's smile and shifted his weight on his back foot. Max saw the wind-up in preparation for the inevitable punch: he saw the elbow flex, the shoulder move back, and the fist – as big as Christmas ham – curl as it drew back. Then it sailed forward fast, but not so fast that Max couldn't track it. He let it come flying towards him, gathering momentum as it gained force. If it had connected with Max's head, it would have been game over.

But it didn't. Max moved his head to the side, and felt more disturbed air as the mammoth fist whizzed past his ear and crashed into the newel post at the end of the staircase. There was a smash and a crack of splintering wood, followed by a howl of pain as the dense, old wood shattered the bones in the big brute's hand. He let out another agonising bellow and cradled his ruined fist in his other hand, his face contorted in agony. Max followed this up with a fast and snappy punch into the side of the man's head, which felt like punching a hard sandbag; it had almost no effect and didn't even move the man's stare from his broken hand.

A sudden silence descended on the hall.

A deep, dark and unpleasant voice came from directly behind Max.

'Impressive, DS Craigie, but I suggest you stop now, or I put a bullet into the back of your head.'

Max turned and looked at the man standing by the kitchen door, a rising dread clutching at his chest. He took in the cruel, black eyes, slicked-back hair and the gold tooth in the middle of a smile that was totally without mirth.

'Alban Hoxhaj, I presume?'

'I see you're as well informed as I am, DS Craigie. It's perhaps fortunate for me that Highlanders feel so safe that they leave their doors unlocked. In Glasgow, not so much.'

'Yeah, really fortunate,' said Max, flatly.

'Now if you don't mind, you can join the others in the living room.' He followed this with a short blast of Albanian at Enver, who glared at Max, his eyes full of loathing, but he pulled out his pistol with his good hand and strode into the living room. There were sudden screams, including from Katie, and it took all of Max's resolve not to spring into action again, but he knew it was futile. He had to wait, to comply, and to be alive and ready to act. His stomach gripped almost painfully as he heard Katie's voice. 'Please, no,' he heard her say, her beautiful, warm voice shot through with terror. He breathed in, held it for a beat, and then exhaled, forcing the fear down. He had to be ready to act.

'I really wouldn't. I promise you I won't miss, not at this distance. Now join them in the living room.' Hoxhaj smiled, and even snickered with laughter, his eyes sparkling.

Max walked into the room, feeling rather than hearing Hoxhaj following close, but not too close behind.

Katie, Affi and Valerie were all huddled together on the sofa, dread on their faces as they looked at the hulking form of Enver. He was brandishing his pistol at them with his left hand, his right fist hanging limply down by his side, blood dripping from a gash on the knuckle, his face pale and riven with unmitigated fury. Affi's head was buried against her foster mother's shoulder, and the thought flashed through Max's mind about what the poor girl had been through.

'Sit on the chair,' barked Hoxhaj.

Max turned and looked at Hoxhaj, who had a pistol trained on his torso from the doorway. His heart sank as he realised that he had no chance whatsoever. Enver had the others covered, even if it was with his weak hand, but even if he could try something, Hoxhaj would shoot him before he even moved. He sat down on the high-backed armchair, not taking his eyes off the gangster, whose own eyes flicked around the room with interest. Max remained tensed, his feet firmly planted on the floor as close to the base of the chair as he could, his hands gripping the armrests, ready to explode out of the chair should the opportunity arise.

Hoxhaj's expression gave nothing away. There was no fear, no excitement, no shaking, no accelerated breathing. Just calm interest, and possibly a little anticipation.

There was also something else. It was in how he carried himself, the set of his jaw, the absence of even the slightest trace of emotion in those dark eyes. Max had encountered psychopaths before, and he knew now that Hoxhaj intended to kill each of them right here, right now.

'Let them go, Hoxhaj,' said Max, his voice low and even, his eyes never leaving him.

'Oh, DS Craigie, this isn't personal, but the young girl here saw Enver at stupid Toka's brothel. He's well known to work for me, so the association would have been too strong for the police to miss. It's regrettable, and I take no pleasure in this, but business is business.'

Max said nothing. There was nothing to say. Anything he could have said about the evidence they had would only have hastened their demise. The only thing to say was nothing. So, Max kept his mouth shut, and his eyes fixed on Hoxhaj. The sounds of sobbing from Katie, Affi and Valerie was heartbreaking, but he didn't flinch and he didn't move a muscle. He just kept staring straight at Hoxhaj. He wanted to be seen as the threat, not the others.

A tiny, almost imperceptible noise came from the hallway. A chink of a piece of glass, a waft of wind moving the shattered door? Hoxhaj froze, his eyes swivelling, but he didn't shift his position. He nodded at Enver and uttered a word in Albanian.

Max tensed his muscles again, readying himself, every sinew in his body preparing to explode into action. He moved his eyes momentarily and took in Katie, Valerie and Affi, all clutched together, limbs entwined in an attempt to block out the horror that they were experiencing. Katie briefly opened her eyes and they locked on Max's. They were full of panic, and Max felt loathing begin to replace fear in his chest.

Enver nodded and moved towards the hallway, his pistol extended awkwardly in front of him, and Max became even more sure that Enver was right-handed as he looked totally uncomfortable with the pistol's weight. Enver peeped around the doorframe and into the hall.

He looked back at Hoxhaj, shook his head and shrugged.

Hoxhaj barked again in Albanian, clearly telling Enver to check properly.

The big man went to the hall, pistol still extended, and slowly eased towards the front door until he was out of Max's view.

'Don't do anything stupid. You try and I put a bullet in the bitch,' he said, levelling the pistol at Katie.

Max still said nothing. There was nothing he could say that would help, so he sat there, tense and ready, his eyes burning with a hatred that was so visceral he could almost taste it.

The explosion that came from the hall was deafening and overwhelming. Hoxhaj turned to the source of the blast only to see Enver propelled backwards by some unseen and terrible force, his chest and stomach a sea of red. He landed with a thump on the carpet. Hoxhaj was swivelling at the hips to bring the gun to bear on the door, and whoever had just shot Enver. Max exploded out of the chair, every muscle fibre in his legs and arms propelling him forward with one aim. To smash Hoxhaj into total and complete oblivion. He let out a roar as he collided hard with the Albanian, his shoulder connecting with the exposed side of his rib cage as Max drove him into the hallway where they tripped over the stricken and dying Enver, collapsed in a heap on the floor. The pistol flew out of Hoxhaj's grasp, hitting the wall and coming to rest on the carpet just inches away from his outstretched hand.

Max looked towards the door and saw Reg, dressed in tweed and a Barbour jacket, his face pale and his mouth agape. He clutched a smoking double-barrelled shotgun in his hands, pointed towards both.

'Reg, get in the living room, get them out and call for help,' yelled Max.

Reg stood there, transfixed.

'Reg, move!' Max bellowed, trying to restrain the bucking and thrashing Hoxhaj.

Hoxhaj reached forward, stretching for the pistol. He suddenly bucked, loosening Max's grip on his torso, and his hand grabbed at the pistol; he raised it wildly towards Reg. Max's arms were encircling and trapped underneath his opponent's body, so he let a headbutt go, smashing into the side of Hoxhaj's head with terrible force. That loosened Hoxhaj's grip on the pistol, which jerked, the report deafening in the confined space of the hall as a bullet smacked into the wall. Max roared with aggression, managing to free an arm from under the man, and he grabbed at the Albanian's neck and headbutted again, right on his ear, again and again and again. Max felt wet blood on his face as he pounded his forehead into the gangster's head, around the ear and jawbone. He felt the distinct crack as bone met bone.

A shadow fell across them, and Max saw Reg spurred into action. He rushed forward and kicked the pistol away from Hoxhaj's limp hand and it flew safely out of reach.

'Reg, living room, now. Make sure the girls are okay,' yelled Max.

Hoxhaj relaxed, semi-conscious and defeated, and Max shifted his position, encircling the man's big neck with his forearm and dug his wrist into his windpipe, his hand clutching his forearm in a classic rear naked choke. A game changer, the fight was now over.

Max squeezed. He squeezed tightly, and Hoxhaj struggled as the blood from his carotid arteries was suddenly interrupted. Max squeezed some more, until Hoxhaj slumped. Sirens became audible in the distance, growing louder every second.

'Max?' Katie appeared in the doorway, her face full of horror.

'It's over.' He squeezed tighter, feeling Hoxhaj's breathing begin to fail at the pressure on his windpipe. Max eased the pressure; much as Hoxhaj deserved to die, that wasn't how today would end. He'd end up spending the rest of his life in jail.

Max looked up to see the tough, stocky form of Reg above him, his face flushed red.

'Bastard,' spat Reg, his voice tight and shot through with fury, the shotgun held tightly in his hands, the barrel pressed against the side of the unconscious Albanian's bloody head.

'Reg?' said Max.

'He shouldn't be allowed to live, Max.'

'No, Reg. Not like this. Shooting him was righteous.' Max nodded at the mangled body of Enver. 'But shoot him, and that's an execution. Not here, Reg. Not like this. You need to be here for your family, not in jail.' Max's voice was low and even.

'Reg, please?' Valerie's tone was soft and full of sorrow. 'Not here, in our home. It's over, Reg.'

Reg's eyes flicked away from Hoxhaj, and he looked at his wife. He relaxed and lowered the gun with a sigh.

Max looked at his beautiful wife standing next to Valerie, eyes wide with shock and her face pale. As blue strobing lights appeared outside the house, Max knew.

He knew that no one else would die tonight.

It was over.

75

IT WAS ALMOST forty-eight hours before they could interview Alban Hoxhaj, such was the damage that Max had inflicted on the big Albanian with his repeated headbutts to the jaw.

He just sat there glowering at Janie and DS Chick Tattum, his dark eyes blazing with loathing. DS Tattum was DCI Leslie's interview specialist, so Max had been ordered back home to look after Katie, and to recover from the mild concussion he was still feeling the effects of after the confrontation with Hoxhaj.

DS Tattum was a well-fleshed officer in his early forties and was immaculately dressed in a grey suit with a neat, plain blue tie. He smiled disarmingly as he went through the interview introduction procedure, whilst Hoxhaj stared at him unrelentingly, a bored expression on his face.

There was no solicitor next to Hoxhaj, so he was there alone, sitting on the chair, with his bloodstained legs crossed, defiantly. A trace of a smile played on his bruised lips, and there was still a significant swelling where his jawbone met his ear. He radiated the same menace that he had displayed in the house in Evanton, only a little more dishevelled. His hair was awry, his clothing stained, and buttons had been ripped from his shirt. He also smelled powerfully of body odour, and his face was pale and lined with fatigue. But the eyes still sparkled, dark and unfathomable with malice.

'Mr Hoxhaj, the doctor says that you're fit to be interviewed, despite your injuries. Do you feel well enough for this interview to go ahead?' said DS Tattum.

'I'm fine.'

'Sure you don't want a solicitor?'

'I don't need a solicitor,' he said in a low growl, clearly meant to project maximum intensity.

'Are you sure? We can pause to get one. These are very serious allegations, Mr Hoxhaj,' said DS Tattum, his lightly accented voice serious.

'Where's DS Craigie?' he said, his teeth still clamped together.

'He's at home, looking after his wife, Mr Hoxhaj. You just get us today,' said DS Tattum.

'Is he a coward?' His teeth remained fixed tight.

'No, just sick of the sight of you, and we thought you may feel the same way. So, are you okay to be interviewed, or would you like more time?' said Janie.

Hoxhaj moved his gaze to Janie and smoothed his thick hair, pulling his lips back in something approximating a smile. Wire glinted in his teeth alongside the flash of gold from the capped incisor.

'No. You make a mistake. I try to stop Enver doing what he did, but he forced me with gun. He's a very violent man, and then when he was killed by the old man, DS Craigie attacked me and broke my jaw. Look, it wired together now,' he said with a trace of amusement as he pointed his stubby finger at his teeth.

'Oh, we don't want to talk about that yet, Mr Hoxhaj. We want to talk about Toka Kurti, PC Luigi Ricci and Jetmir Xhilaj. What can you tell me about them?'

'I hear they're all dead. It was on the news. I wasn't anywhere near them, and I can prove it. Lots of alibi, and my phone will prove it.'

'Are you sure about that?' said DS Tattum.

Hoxhaj paused, his brow furrowed and his face darkened.

'You call me a liar?' he growled.

'I don't think I said that. I just asked you if you're sure you know nothing about the death and subsequent mutilation of Toka Kurti, Luigi Ricci and Jetmir Xhilaj.'

'And I said, Mr Tattum, I know nothing about who killed them, or who cut ears and eyes out,' he said, sitting up straighter and squaring his shoulders. He laced his fingers and cracked his knuckles to emphasise the point.

DS Tattum looked at Janie and smiled. 'Did he say something about ears and eyes?'

'I think he did,' said Janie.

Hoxhaj looked at both officers in turn, his eyes narrowed.

'Thing is, Alban, old son. It's not been released to the press that the mutilations were ears, eyes and mouth. No one's said that at all, so how did you know?'

Hoxhaj paused for a full half minute. 'I hear cops talking in custody and at hospital.' His smile widening with a suggestion of triumph. 'Is this all you have? You have nothing at all, my friend, maybe I get problem with what happen in Evanton, but how much? Only my friend die, and I get beaten badly by a brutal cop. I get a couple of years, and that's it. This murder I know nothing about. I've never even been to the property on Southside. I never go to Southside. It's a shithole.' He sat back and began to chuckle, a dark, wet sound.

'Okay, just so I'm clear. You never went to Toka Kurti's brothel in Southside, at or around the time of the murder?'

'Not at any time. Not even once. I have witnesses as to where I was, and you can check my phone. That will prove where I was. You have nothing. Nothing at all.' He smiled and folded his arms.

DS Tattum returned Hoxhaj's smile and nodded at Janie, who reached under the desk and pulled out a laptop computer and opened it up. Hoxhaj's expression changed to one of confusion as Janie tapped at the keys.

'What's this?' said Hoxhaj.

'You'll see, just hold up a moment.'

Janie swivelled the laptop around so that the screen was facing Hoxhaj and clicked the play icon.

'For the benefit of the recording, we're showing Mr Hoxhaj an extract from production number JC/12, which is a digital capture from an online digital recording hosting. Did you know that there were recording devices at the premises where Toka, Luigi and Jetmir were murdered?'

Hoxhaj said nothing. He just stared at the screen as it flickered, showing the doorway of the brothel, the reflection of the image visible in his dark irises.

'Now, we know that prior to the incident, when PC Ricci was seen to go into the premises there was a camera-enabled doorbell present, because DS Craigie saw it. When they returned the following morning, it had gone. Do you know what happened to that doorbell, Mr Hoxhaj?'

'No comment,' Hoxhaj said through his clamped teeth, still fixated on the screen.

'Well, we don't have images from within the premises, as the internal cameras hadn't been installed at that point it seems, but the doorbell was active and was connected to the server that was used by Toka Kurti. Well, we've found that server, which confirms that the IP number attributed to that property was used to transmit the images to the server. So, just so you're clear, we've proof that this image on the screen here came from Toka Kurti's brothel in Southside, Mr Hoxhaj. Oh, and in case you're wondering, the internet was connected under the name Toka Kurti and paid for with her bank account, am I clear?'

'No comment.'

'No problem. So, we know that this imagery comes from the right place, that you say you've never ever been to. Are you sticking by that?'

'No comment.'

'No problem. Just keep watching, and keep your eyes on the timestamp, eh?' said DS Tattum.

Hoxhaj's stare didn't waver as he watched the picture spring to life showing a clear image of Enver at the door. He stood there for a few moments, until he was illuminated by the light from within the building as the door was opened, and then he disappeared into the property, closely followed by Alban Hoxhaj, smiling with the light glinting from his gold tooth.

'Is that you, Mr Hoxhaj?'

Hoxhaj's mouth may have gaped open in surprise were it not wired closed, but he let out a strangled rattle from his throat and his eyes bulged almost out of his head.

'Get my fucking solicitor here, now.'

76

Six months later

ROSS, MAX AND Janie stood along with the rest of the packed public gallery at the High Court of Justiciary in Glasgow as the Judge entered the room in his full regalia. He nodded at counsel on the benches in front of him and sat down, his face dark, just to the side of the royal crest. The rest of the court's occupants took their seats as the general hubbub of murmurs, coughs and shuffling stopped until there was complete silence.

'Fuck me, His Honour looks fuckin' ragin' to me. I reckon he's gonna throw away the bastarding key,' said Ross in a hoarse whisper that could have been heard three rows away. There were a couple of muffled titters in the rows close by.

'Shh,' said Janie.

'I want to see the look on the fucker's face,' muttered Ross.

Janie glared at him. 'Shh, you're gonna get us thrown out of here.'

DCI Marina Leslie, who was sitting behind prosecuting counsel, looked back at Ross, grinning widely.

His Honour Judge Hugo Carmichael settled his spectacles on his nose and picked up the sheets of paper in front of him. He looked at the man in the dock before him.

'Will the defendant please stand,' said the Clerk of the Court.

Alban Hoxhaj got to his feet, dressed in an immaculately tailored suit, his face full of the arrogance that never wavered throughout his six-week trial. He stared at the Judge, his eyes blazing with hatred.

'Alban Hoxhaj, you have been unanimously found guilty by the jury on the clearest of evidence, of the most serious offences that I have had before me in all my time on this bench.

'Throughout the trial you have conducted yourself in the most arrogant of fashion, with disdain for the solemnity and seriousness of the process. You sat atop a cruel and wicked organisation that was trafficking vulnerable women from the poor regions of Albania and beyond to be exploited in the most unimaginably terrible way. When your activities began to unravel, you then went to barbaric lengths in order to protect your operation. Only you, and you alone, can know exactly what happened at that property in Glasgow. The cameras at the property make it very clear of your presence at the scene, and your pre-existing knowledge of the level of mutilation that was not in the public domain sealed your fate. The jury is rightfully satisfied to the highest of standards of proof that you and your henchman were guilty of these barbaric murders and mutilations of Toka Kurti, Jetmir Xhilaj and Police Constable Luigi Ricci. I also have no doubt that without the bravery and fortitude of a small group of officers from Police Scotland that the death toll would have been significantly higher. My commendations for the actions of those officers are on file, and I will be writing personally to the Chief Constable of Police Scotland to express my gratitude.

'I also extend my respect and indeed, my admiration to Mr Reginald Smith for his brave actions that terrible night, and I will be recommending that he be considered for the highest award available. I am in no doubt that his actions that night saved four lives, and it was only right that the Procurator Fiscal speedily decided that his actions that resulted in the death of your bodyguard Enver Dervishi were entirely justifiable in order to preserve his own life, and those of the others in that property, on that fateful evening.

'It now falls to me to sentence you for these matters. It is of record and of note that a number of other individuals have already pleaded guilty to serious offences and have been sentenced to significant terms of imprisonment. These are former Chief Superintendent Barry Carlisle, former Intelligence officer Steven Vipond and shamefully Colm O'Neill, formerly an Immigration judge. I have no doubt that these individuals were corrupted by you in the furtherance of your criminal enterprises and it is clear to me that you used your relationship with Toka Kurti to obtain compromising material of the egregious behaviour of these individuals.

'It is of further record that a multitude of trafficking victims passed through your organisation's hands, and the international law-enforcement community continues to trace these throughout Europe. The accounts of their appalling treatment continue to emerge and make for distressing reading. I must commend the competence of the trafficking lead at Interpol for her team's continued efforts to trace and ensure the safety of those victims. A shameful set of circumstances that I take as an aggravating feature of your crimes.

'I must make it abundantly clear that the sentence I will now pass is for the matters for which the jury have found you guilty, and those offences only.

'I find no circumstances that will mitigate the terrible acts you undertook which were carried out simply out of your desire for power, money, and ill-conceived and ill-perceived respect. You have refused to engage with any pre-sentence reporting or psychiatric evaluation, so no account can be taken of that. Indeed I view your intransigence to reflect on your crimes as an aggravating factor.

'For the murder of Toka Kurti, the only sentence available to me is that of life imprisonment.

'For the murder of Jetmir Xhilaj, I sentence you to life imprisonment

'For the murder of Luigi Ricci, I sentence you to life imprisonment.

'All other matters in the furtherance of these offences I direct be left to lie on file. Therefore, it is a matter of agreement between the Procurator Fiscal and those which represent you that you only be sentenced for the murder convictions.

'I am now obliged to issue a recommended length of time which must elapse before you can be considered for release. Having given consideration to all the facts in this terrible case, your disdain for the sanctity of life and for the sheer cold-blooded brutality of these murders, I find that there is only one option available to me. In these whole circumstances therefore, I now impose upon you on all charges of this indictment a sentence of life imprisonment and fix the punishment part of that life sentence at a period of thirty-eight years' imprisonment. It is perhaps fortunate for you and unfortunate for the general public that the option of a whole life tariff is, as yet, unavailable to me.'

The Judge looked up at Hoxhaj over his spectacles, his vivid blue eyes penetrating. 'Take him down.'

Hoxhaj remained rooted to the spot as the security guard moved towards him, handcuffs in his hands. He stared straight at the Judge and spoke in a clear and indefatigable voice. 'T'a hangert dreqi shpirtin,' he almost spat as he was led away, through the door and out of sight.

The Judge rose, bowed at counsel and left the court with the usher.

'What did Hoxhaj say?' said Max.

'No idea, but it sounded unpleasant,' said Janie.

'Aye, insults in foreign languages always sound a fuck-ton worse than in English.'

'I dunno, Ross. You make a fair go of it,' said Max as they all stood and began to head towards the exit.

'May the devil eat your soul,' said a smartly dressed young woman who was in the row behind them. Her accent was light, but unmistakably Albanian.

'Pardon?' said Janie.

'That's what he said. "May the devil eat your soul." Albanian insult,' the woman said, with a smile. 'Nice work, officers. Hoxhaj bring so much misery to many young girl, so we glad he's in jail. Albanian community wanted him gone.'

'Glad to be of service,' said Janie as they filed out of the court-room and into the marble-floored area outside.

'Fuck me, a bastard of a sentence, eh?' said Ross.

'Indeed, a bastard of a sentence, in fact the longest ever in Scotland,' said DCI Leslie, who had appeared behind them, smiling broadly.

'Really?' said Ross.

'Aye, by a year. James McDonald got minimum thirty-five for a gangland hit in 2006. I think Judge Carmichael was sending a message that he viewed this as a worse crime. You guys coming for a drink? The team's going around the corner. It's been a hell of a job, this one.'

'Aye, I'm game,' said Ross.

'Me too,' said Janie.

DCI Leslie looked at Max and raised her eyebrows, questioningly.

'Not me. I've somewhere I need to be,' said Max.

'You sure, Max? We'd all love to buy you a pint. Without you doing what you did, then that bastard would no doubt still be out.'

'Well, the way I see it is that the credit goes to Reg Smith. Without him, we'd all have been killed, so I think I'll duck out, guvnor. Enjoy yourselves, everyone.' Max nodded, and left. He pulled his phone out of his pocket and dialled.

'Hey, babe, are you done?' said Katie.

'Aye, I'll meet you in five minutes out the front of the court.'

'How long did he get?'

'Thirty-eight years. Biggest sentence in Scottish history.'

'Jesus, and fully deserved. See you in five. I want to get up there. The meet's at four, and we promised we'd be there.'

'I'm coming now.'

77

THE ATHLETIC STADIUM at the Inverness leisure centre was alive and buzzing with the biggest crowd they'd seen at the venue for some time. The locals knew something big was happening when Affi began to accelerate on the final lap of the 5,000 metres, her face flat and expressionless as her long, slim legs pounded the tartan track, her ponytail whipping side to side.

'Come on, Affi!' yelled Katie, bursting with excitement as she stood up from her bleacher seat.

'She's gonna do it,' shouted Max as Affi's stride increased and she powered past the girl in the lead, who was starting to look tired. The expression on Affi's face didn't shift; she accelerated again, her arms pumping as she flew down the final 100 metres towards the tape, all the other racers in her wake.

'Affi, Affi, go, Affi,' shouted a young girl, aged about thirteen, who was sitting between Katie and Valerie, who was also leaping up and down, shouting deliriously as Affi unbelievably increased her speed for the final few metres until she hit the finish tape, the clear winner by a solid thirty metres.

'She did it, she bloody did it,' shouted Reg, his normal quiet and controlled demeanour completely forgotten now as he jumped up and down then hugged his wife, both with tears streaming down their faces.

'I can go? I want hug her,' said the young girl, her slim face beaming with a wide, delighted smile. Even there, in those bleachers in Inverness, you could tell.

'Ach, yes, off you go, pet,' said Valerie, ruffling the girl's hair.

Melodi Dushku ran from the bleachers and leapt the barrier with the same graceful athleticism as her sister, shouting, 'Affi, Affi.'

Affi turned to the source of the noise, her face breaking out into a huge smile as her little sister flew into her arms and they hugged.

'How's Melodi doing?' Katie asked Valerie as she wiped tears from her eyes. She squeezed Max's hand.

'She's doing grand, pet. Absolutely grand. It's just so lovely to have them together, where they belong. I owe you so much, Katie, for getting her here. She's with us now. A proper family, that's what we are.'

'Ah, you know. It was nothing. The arrests and court case helped speed things up, maybe.'

'We'll never be able to thank the both of you enough. You know that right? Max, you risked everything for us.'

Max just shrugged and smiled.

'Now we must go and see Affi. We'll see you in a bit, yeah?' said Valerie.

'Of course, we're going nowhere for a while,' said Katie.

They filed past Katie and Max towards the aisle, both bubbling with happiness as they made their way to their daughters. As he passed, Reg stopped and looked at Max; he nodded and held out his hand, which Max took in a firm grip. Their eyes met, but they didn't speak. There was no need.

Katie and Max watched as the Smith family stood together, arms around one another, the perfect family.

'They look good, right?' said Katie.

'They look like a real family,' said Max, smiling.

'Maybe we should get ourselves one of them, Craigie?' Katie turned to Max, a mischievous look on her face, her eyes sparkling as she slipped her arm around his waist.

Max returned her smile, leaned forward and kissed his wife on the mouth. 'Maybe we should.'

Acknowledgements

I'm forever thankful to a whole raft of people who have helped me turn this pile of words into something approximating a book that people may actually choose to part with a sum of money to read. Without all of you, it would be nothing, so with that in mind, here we go.

My agent, Robbie Guillory, for all your sage advice, belief and astute understanding of the business. I'm glad we're on this journey together.

Lots of people at HQ work tirelessly to make sure these books go out in the best possible shape, and then are visible to the public so they can buy them. Many of you I haven't met, but I want to thank you all for all the efforts that go into producing these books. So, all you guys in sales, distribution, analytics, marketing, design and all the other areas of the business, a big, hearty thank you.

Specific thanks go to:

My editor at HQ, Belinda Toor. You've really helped me shape this book to be the best it can possibly be, and to keep the series going in the right direction. I adored writing this book, and your influence has helped move DS Craigie and the team onwards and upwards.

Audrey Linton, Belinda's right-hand woman, who grafts hard on making these books do all the good stuff.

Sian Baldwin, publicity ninja who keeps the books out there so that the public know that they (and me) exist.

Jo Kite. Marketing guru, who makes everything look beautiful and make them stand out from the gazillion others on the shelves.

All my writer pals, for all the advice, laughs, encouragement and piss-taking (Tony Kent, I'm looking at you, here).

Colin Scott, for doing what you do!

My big, mad and crazy family for all the love and encouragement.

My boys. Alec, Richard and Ollie. You guys rock.

If you loved *Blood Runs Cold*, don't miss this exclusive sneak peek from book 5 in the Max Craigie series…

THE DEVIL YOU KNOW

A CASE GONE COLD

Six years ago, Beata Dabrowski arranged to meet her lover in Glasgow and was never seen again. There were no leads. . . until now.

AN UNRELIABLE WITNESS

Imprisoned gang boss Davie Hardie wants to talk in exchange for his freedom. He knows exactly where Beata is buried, and he's prepared to take the police to her grave.

A KILLER DESPERATE TO ESCAPE

But when the mission to locate Beata's body is hijacked, DS Max Craigie is drafted on to the case. Someone is selling secrets.

Max will stop at nothing to expose police corruption and uncover Beata's murderer. . . **but can you ever really trust a killer to catch a killer?**

Prologue

Six years ago, Glasgow

BEATA DABROWSKI SWIPED at the tears that were streaming down her face, feeling the flush of heat on her cheeks as she hurried out of the grimy town centre. It was a balmy summer evening, but she didn't really notice as she swallowed a sob – the door was held open for her by a smiling young woman.

She halted suddenly on the pavement, looking at, but not really seeing, the pulsating traffic in central Glasgow. She ignored the drunken shouts of the revellers pouring out of the pubs, all heading for the late bars and clubs. She just stood, stock still as young men and women, dressed in their Friday-night finery, swept all around her, like an inrushing tide washing around a half-buried rock.

She was alone, completely isolated in this sea of humanity, whereas ten minutes ago, she genuinely thought that her new life was about to begin.

She felt a flush rise from her stomach. Nausea gripped as his words, spoken just a few minutes ago, returned to her.

'I'm sorry, darling. I just can't. I just can't leave her and the kids. It'd break them, and it'd finish my career forever. I'm so sorry, as much as I love you, it's over.' His voice was simpering, and sympathetic, but she could see it. She could see it in his eyes, the same deep, dark blue that had first captivated her.

He didn't care. He didn't give a shit. He'd had his fun, but now he was going to discard her like he'd discarded many over the years.

She felt the sorrow begin to mutate as she stood there, tense and quivering like the string of an archer's bow before an arrow is released. She'd screamed abuse at him, as he sat on the rumpled bed, the musk of sex still redolent in the seedy hotel room. His face registered surprise at first, which soon relaxed into mild amusement, only to be replaced by scorn and disdain, demonstrated by the sneer she'd seen many times in the past. Although it had normally been reserved for his opponents, or those who displeased him, rather than her.

'Go on, fuck off out of here then, you Polish slag. You were only an easy shag, and not a great one at that.' His face wore a contemptuous, shit-eating grin as he stood, the sheets falling away from him revealing his pudgy middle-aged form.

'You'll be sorry. You'll be very fucking sorry, you think I don't know what you do, eh? You think I don't know that you wash money for big criminals? You think I'm always asleep, but I hear your phone calls. I know who you work for,' she'd hissed, her face contorted with suffused rage, trying desperately to hold back the tears that were threatening to overwhelm her.

'Oh, I doubt it very much, old girl, you're not the first I've dealt with. Remember who's been paying the rent on your scummy little apartment and keeping you in stupid handbags. Maybe start looking for somewhere new to live, eh?'

Beata felt her cheeks begin to burn; how could she be so stupid? Her apartment, her whole life was paid for by the bastard. She had few friends, and all her family were back in Poland. She was suddenly disgusted with herself that she'd been so foolish as to put all of herself into this man.

'Bastard,' she spat, tears running down her face.

'Don't be silly, Beata. It had to end one day, we've had our fun, and now it's time for you to run along, there's a good girl.' He paused, a vulpine smile spreading across his thin lips.

'Fuck you,' she'd said, her voice cracking, before she turned and stormed out of the hotel room, slamming the door behind her.

'I'll fucking show you,' she growled to herself, her voice loud enough to cause a young reveller wearing an inflatable sumo wrestler suit to stop and stare.

'Talking to me, hen?' he slurred, his eyebrows raised in surprise and an amused lop-sided grin on his bright red face.

'Sorry, no,' she stuttered, as she began to walk away from the hotel, head down, her pace increasing as she joined the throng of pedestrians in the warm Glasgow evening. Her steps became quicker as she rounded the corner towards the dimly lit side street where she'd parked her car. It was always this way. The same low-key hotel, where he seemed to know the manager, it had no on-site car park, and no CCTV. He was careful, as a man in his position would be expected to be, and there never seemed to be a bill to pay. 'Never you mind that, my dear, all taken care of with no paper trail,' was as close as she ever got to an explanation. As a final insult, he always insisted that they arrive and leave the hotel separately. It made her feel dirty and cheap.

As she approached her car, a little Renault, she was rummaging in her bag for the keys when she heard a vehicle pull up. She turned to see an old, battered white transit van alongside her, the window down and a man looking at her, his smile revealing white, even teeth.

'Are ye moving, hen? Nae parking spaces around here,' he said in a heavy Glaswegian accent.

'Yes, I'm going now,' she said, blipping the car open.

'Stoatin, I'll just back up,' he said, grinning widely.

She turned back to her car and in the gloom, felt for the handle, opening the door wide and throwing her bag inside.

Suddenly, and with terrible force, she felt an impossibly big and strong arm encircle her neck and she was jerked back from her car so hard that her feet left the damp cobbles. She heard the van door slide open and she was dragged inside with horrifying speed, the backs of her stocking-clad legs bashing painfully against the edge of the door frame. She was dumped onto the flat sheet-metal floor of the van in an undignified heap. She opened her mouth to scream, but the arm just tightened, and no sound came out. Her head swam as the blood supply was interrupted – the arteries on her neck constricted. Her vision failed, and then everything went black.

She could have been unconscious for just a few seconds, or possibly an hour, but when she blinked, a harsh overhead light in the windowless van was blindingly bright. She was sat on the cold floor of the van, her wrists secured with plastic ties, and a man was looking at her with deep, sad eyes. His face was huge, jowly and covered in hard stubble. His eyes were hooded with heavy lids that gave him a sorrowful expression, but the dark pools glittered with something sinister.

He let out a long, sad sigh before he spoke, his Glasgow accent strong. 'Ye cannae do this, ye ken, missie. Ye cannae threaten the boss,' he said in a dark, nasty growl. He had a phone in his hand which he was fiddling with.

'I'm sorry, I'm sorry . . .' she began to blurt out, but the sad-looking man just raised his hand laconically.

'Dinnae want to hear it, lassie. He's no' happy, so what do we do, eh?' he said without looking up.

'I'll say nothing, I promise, I promise I'll say nothing,' she said, the terror descending on her like an icy blanket.

Sad-face just sighed deeply and raised a massive fist which he used to rap on the screen that separated the load bay of the transit with the driver's compartment. The engine barked into life and the van moved off.

'Where . . . where are you taking me?' she said, her voice trailing off to barely more than a whisper.

He said nothing, just stared at her for a full ten seconds before raising the phone and pointing it towards her. He nodded, almost imperceptibly over her left shoulder. She became aware of another looming presence behind her and she turned to look, a sick feeling rising in her churning stomach.

There was a sudden crackle and a rustle and then she felt a plastic bag being pulled over her face and cinched tight. She tried to scream, but as she inhaled, the plastic was sucked into her mouth and she retched, vomit exploding from her. With nowhere to go the thick mucus went up her nose as she breathed in, the panic rising. She tried to cough, but the thick plastic allowed nothing to escape, and she felt the vomit in her lungs, just as her vision began to cloud again.

The final thing she saw, through the clear plastic bag, were those sad eyes, a phone to his ear as he surveyed her with little interest. She stopped struggling, defeated.

'It's done, she'll no' be found,' were the last words she heard, as the blackness swept over her like a warm, enveloping blanket.

Dead Man's Grave

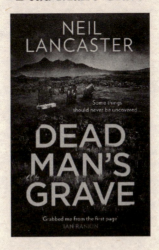

This grave can never be opened.
The head of Scotland's most powerful crime
family is brutally murdered, his body dumped
inside an ancient grave in a remote cemetery.

This murder can never be forgotten.
Detectives Max Craigie and Janie Calder arrive at the scene,
a small town where everyone has secrets to hide. They soon
realise this murder is part of a blood feud between two Scottish
families that stretches back to the 1800s. One thing's for
certain: it might be the latest killing, but it won't be the last...

This killer can never be caught.
As the body count rises, the investigation uncovers large-scale
corruption at the heart of the Scottish Police Service. Now Max
and Janie must turn against their closest colleagues – to solve
a case that could cost them far more than just their lives...

The Blood Tide

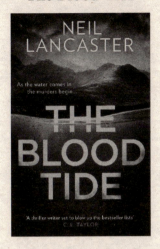

You get away with murder.
In a remote sea loch on the west coast of Scotland, a fisher-
man vanishes without trace. His remains are never found.

You make people disappear.
A young man jumps from a bridge in Glasgow and
falls to his death in the water below. DS Max Craigie
uncovers evidence that links both victims. But if he
can't find out what cost them their lives, it won't be
long before more bodies turn up at the morgue…

You come back for revenge.
Soon cracks start to appear in the investigation, and Max's
past hurtles back to haunt him. When his loved ones are
threatened, he faces a terrifying choice: let the only man he
ever feared walk free, or watch his closest friend die…

The Night Watch

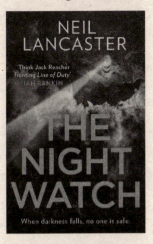

He'll watch you.

A lawyer is found dead at sunrise on a lonely clifftop at Dunnet
Head on the northernmost tip of Scotland. It was supposed to
be his honeymoon, but now his wife will never see him again.

He'll hunt you.

The case is linked to several mysterious deaths, including the murder of the lawyer's last client – Scotland's
most notorious criminal… who had just walked free. DS
Max Craigie knows this can only mean one thing:
they have a vigilante serial killer on their hands.

He'll leave you to die.

But this time the killer isn't on the run; he's on
the investigation team. And the rules are different when the murderer is this close to home.
He knows their weaknesses, knows how to stay
hidden, and he thinks he's above the law…

Dear Reader,

We hope you enjoyed reading this book. If you did, we'd be so appreciative if you left a review. It really helps us and the author to bring more books like this to you.

Here at HQ Digital we are dedicated to publishing fiction that will keep you turning the pages into the early hours. Don't want to miss a thing? To find out more about our books, promotions, discover exclusive content and enter competitions you can keep in touch in the following ways:

JOIN OUR COMMUNITY:
Sign up to our new email newsletter:
http://smarturl.it/SignUpHQ
Read our new blog www.hqstories.co.uk
https://twitter.com/HQStories
www.facebook.com/HQStories

BUDDING WRITER?
We're also looking for authors to join the HQ
Digital family! Find out more here:
https://www.hqstories.co.uk/want-to-write-for-us/

Thanks for reading, from the HQ Digital team